HORN OF STRANGERS

N. R. Phillips

*To Bill & Jenny
with best wishes

Ray*

HALSGROVE

First published in Great Britain in 1996 by Halsgrove

ISBN 1 874448 15 9

British Library Cataloguing in Publication Data

A CIP record for this title is available from the British Library

HALSGROVE
Publishing, Media and Distribution
Halsgrove House
Lower Moor Way
Tiverton
Devon EX16 6SS
Tel: 01884 243242
Fax: 01884 243325

Cover illustration by Rob Stockdale.
Author's photograph by Tom Tregenza

Printed in Great Britain by BPC Wheatons Ltd, Exeter.

CONTENTS

Dhe gemmys, yn termyn ys passyas,
lemmyn, hag a'n termyn a-dhe,
neb a'glapp Kernewek.

To those, past, present and future,
who gabble Cornish.

CHAPTER ONE.

Yn termyn ys passyas... wrote the poet in the old and mystic language... *Yth esa den.* In times gone by... there was a man...

His hand paused in contemplation as the morning sun rose over the distant hill. It would be a fine day, he thought, with no wind, and a calm sea for Boy Steve.

...In times gone by, there was a man... and there was a woman!

Now, there were other men and there were other women; such as Boy Steve, Ezekiel the Man and Maid Katie, but this particular man lived alone in a far country with a backbone of granite. The country was named, by the ancestors of those who still venture among its aborigines, *Cornu Weahlas,* The Horn Of Strangers, for the land tapers like a Cornucopia towards the golden sunsets in the western sea, and the language of the inhabitants was unintelligible to the interlopers.

Yn termyn ys passyas, he continued writing in the ancient way, with a smile about his eyes, *owen o an den omma...* In times gone by, happy was this man here. He knew who he was, what he was doing, where he came from and where he was going. His name was Wheaten Bread.

Hag an Barth a wruk scryfa... and the Poet did write...

The man had but one weakness: the love of women, which everyone knew about. He also had one fear, which he kept to himself. During his solitary life he had been led into many temptations and delivered from many evils, and now lived the quiet life born of experience. His contented life-style might be considered boring and circumspect by some but, at various times in the past, he had succumbed to all the vices, briefly indulged himself and survived unscathed. He had burned his fingers, true, quite literally on one indelible occasion, but they had healed, as had his heart, which he protected from further combustion by keeping well away from female fire. He attributed his resilience to his upbringing, to being loved by his mother and permitted by his father to attempt anything, to learn for himself the dangers of foolish action...

The poet frowned, and laid down his pen, overwhelmed by fatigue...

The man had believed the woman when she said that she would always need him, that she would love him for ever. What a fool he had been. Yet, still he loved her. What, as his contemporaries said, a bleddy tuss he was.

The sun was already streaming through the window, and the dark hours of the man's anguish were being driven into memory by its warming rays. He went to the door of his cottage and watched the morning spread down from the high moors, the shortening shadows of the carns and hedges, the glint on the distant sea. It was to be a brilliant day, and the memories of those other dreaded days filled his mind like a turbulent stream through which he waded to their source... to where it all began.

He stared around him as if waking from a dream at his neglected garden, last year's crops gone to seed, the ground sprouting with weeds, the grass of the little lawn grown rank, and the dead leaves piled at the threshold by the wind, whereas, in times gone by.... *Yn termyn ys passyas!*

'God damn her!' he said aloud. God Damn her for what she had done to him. *An gysty crefny sawsnek!*

He gazed about him with incredulity, appalled at the neglect he saw, recalling the garden as it was before she came, with its shelter-beds of clipped escallonia around the vegetables, and the flower-beds bordering the path. There was the camellia, showing the first pink tip of an emerging flower. He suddenly saw some daffodils, nodding the tight folds of their yellow petals above the long blades of grass in the overgrown lawn. Tomorrow, he would cut it, run the mower around and begin turning the soil in preparation for another year's seeds, but now he returned to his pen, thoughtfully closing the door, for there was so much to record, so little time, and he knew not where to begin.

Of the end he was sure, for the end was the woman, and she had been the death of him. They had all died, in one way or another, during the events of her sojourn here: Steve Trevorrow, the Old Man, Uncle Joe, and even Anne and Beth were no longer as alive as they were before her arrival.

The beginning of them all, as of their identity and culture, was so distant now that reaching back to it was like retracing the course of a ship by returning along its wake, a futile journey. But the man was once a boy, he thought, and the woman a girl, for we are all the offspring of our childhood.

'Ah,' said the poet, 'childhood. There is the beginning and the end, for childhood's shadow is our constant companion.'

Was that the day when Barny's troubles began, the day he drove into town to see Father Steve about his cottage. The day when he thought of those distant days of childhood as he passed the school where they had all peed in the rain together against the tarred wall of the outside loos?

The school, the poet wrote, was halfway up the Stennack, on the outskirts of the town when it was built, and was the most prominent piece of architecture in the place, apart from the parish church and the umpteen chapels. Over the entrance porch, leading into the long corridor where the children hung their wet clothes on rows of pegs, was a tall spire which housed the school bell. At the time when hoops and marbles were still the favourite toys, you could have heard the bell ringing from all over the town. Do...ong. Slowly, Do...ong. Do...ong, as if stretching the minutes, to give the pupils time to eat their eggs and porridge before grabbing hats and coats and rushing through the cottage doors. Yes! That was a fine bell, a good, deep-toned bell, although no one ever saw it, up there in the tall spire. They saw only the rope, hanging down through a hole in the wood-panelled ceiling by the great iron-studded door, by means of which generations of children were to enter and be prepared for life. During the day, the rope, with the intricately woven Turk's-head at the end, was hung out of reach of impetuous young hands on a hook by the granite-mullioned window. To have tolled that bell, he thought, what a joy it would have been. To send one... just one... sonorous, reverberating Do...ong, over the slate roofs, over the Wesleyan Chapel, past the parish church and out beyond the harbour to the Breton fishermen in the bay until muffled in the mists of the Eastern shore. Oh, what a thing for a child to have done. But even Tim Penberthy and Joe Curnow didn't have the nerve to do it before all bells were silenced for the duration of the war, and the school bell was never more rung to call the boys and girls, and nothing was ever the same again.

However, the poet continued, Barny was a happy and contented man that day when he drove into town to see Steve. It was cold, and there was ice along the verges. Thin triangles of hailstones lay in the corners of the fields and among the boulders on the hillsides, retreating before the rising sun which whitened the billows of the sparse, grey clouds. The hail had fallen in the night but he had not heard it, for when he slept the house could have fallen about his ears unheeded.

No matter how often Barny traversed this road, he never became complacent about the scenery, and at this time of year it was more colourful than in summer, when the tall fronds of bracken blanketed the slopes in dull green uniformity. Today, the clouds over the sea trailed dark

7

shadows which slithered toward the cliffs, undulating with the waves and slipping over the rocks like an opaque film between the splashes of light, so that he was now in the warmth of brilliant spring sunshine and then driving through the last cold spells of winter.

The long descent into town, with the bay and coastline stretching into the distance towards the lighthouse standing white on the island, always induced doubts as to whether he should have left and gone to live those few miles out in the country. There was no doubt that he was slowly losing contact with his oldest friends, and he missed them. He missed all the gossip and jokes about times past, but, whenever he went to visit, to see his father and look at the harbour, he saw familiar faces with growing infrequency. He wondered where all the locals hid themselves.

After parking among the houses of the higher part of the town, he walked down through the terraces of guest houses, small hotels and empty shops. There were several of Tim Penberthy's boards stuck on spikes in the small gardens or hanging precariously from drain-pipes and railings. For Sale. Some of the shops were boarded up, their thresholds grimy, growing moss, with the north-east wind blowing litter in tight circles among the dog shit in the entrances.

On that day, after calling at Steve Trevorrow's house and then his loft, Barny found him down in the harbour, working about his boat, where he should have looked in the first place.

'Well,' Steve said, 'what's the mad poet doing in town?'

Of all his friends, Barny thought, it was Steve who should have been the poet. Perhaps he was, for sometimes he revealed a certain curious capacity for observation. 'You never see no young barnacles, do 'ee?' Indicating, with that wry smile he had never lost, that he was thinking in terms of metaphor known only to himself.

'Come to see you!'

'Come to see me?' He was nearly bald, though not so grey as Barny, who was a few years younger, but he still had all his teeth and his beard was still dark, as were the brows over his intelligent brown eyes. 'You must want something.'

'I do,' Barny said. 'You're not so good looking that I've came all this way just to gaze into your eyes.'

Steve looked at him, allowing Barny to do just that, gaze into his eyes.

'Where is everybody?' Barny said. 'I feel like a stranger in my own town. Never see anybody I know.'

8

'You are a stranger,' Steve said 'Gone away down there out of it. Gone down west with all the other cranks. It's like a Christmas stocking here...'

'Yeh yeh, I know, all the nuts go to the bottom.'

'I's true, boy, There's more nutters per square mile down here than anywhere else in the world.'

'cept California.'

'Oh, well. California. Ask Joe about California.'

'Never see 'n,' Barny said. 'I never see anybody. I see you've got your new boat.'

'Thought you'd never notice. But she edn mine. She d' belong to the boy.' He could not keep the pride from his eyes. 'You know what happened last time I had a new boat. Well,' he added, 'we do have a share in her, Mary and me.'

I'll bet! Barny thought. Steve's son could not find enough money of his own to buy and fit out a boat like this. Steve was talking about over fifty thousand pounds lying there. 'There must be brea money in fishing,' he said.

'I hope so, Barny. We've put everything into her.'

'Go on. You're all right. Rolling in it.'

Steve laughed. 'Some hopes.'

Rolling in it he was not, and he had gone into debt for the first time in his life to buy a boat for his son, at his age, when he should be thinking of retiring, if he had any sense. 'Sold the damn guest house,' he said. 'And bought the house next door to where we lived before. The boy didn' want' nawthen to do with taking in lodgers when he came back home, and Mary had had enough of it. We gave it ten years, or she did. I didn' want anything to do with taking in damned lodgers either, but I gave in to her after... you knaw... '

Over twenty summers and damp winters which no one remembered had come and gone since then. And that artist party had come and gone too, like so many others, gone and forgotten, and the year of her presence had become one of those fine summers of the past, always sunny and warm, but a year with no date. It would be the year when so-and-so happened, remember? A year of isolation, occurring in no sequence of chronology. That was one of the years when Barny had been out abroad and he remembered it as events related, not experienced, as if the course of his life had been split into two paths, only one of which he could follow, like a railway train shunted onto a loop line, or a car diverted on to a byway for a mile or two. The memories of that exile were as those of a dream now, and the events related here were of more significance to him than those he had experienced in his own life at the time.

Steve would never forget that year, although he too may never have lived it as far as his conversation was concerned, and his friends were careful in referring to it in only the most guarded terms. Mary alone, now and then, would remind him, by implication, that the year had been the most decisive in her life too, and this by omission in her conversation rather than statement. Steve needed no reminding. He remembered the warm days, conversations, how much mackerel he had caught, kisses, how much money Mary had made from the damn lodgers, their holiday in Spain, those blue eyes, the birth of Sarah's child; he remembered it all and said nothing. It was a past life.

Sometimes, however, as now, one of his closest friends might ask a pertinent question...

'Ever hear anything of Shimshai, do 'ee?' They both knew what Barny was implying.

For once, Steve made direct reference to her. 'She's still with 'n,' he said, remembering what had happened the last time he bought a new boat.

Barny had been in Nigeria when all that happened, for which he was very grateful. 'What about Joe?' he asked. 'Haven't seen him for ages either. He's still around, I suppose.'

'Joe idn' going anywhere. He did all the travelling he wanted to do years ago. He's working with me and the boy, fishin', with a bit of labourin' when I'm working ashore. Joe's all right.'

'How didn' he ever get married 'en, Steve? He always had plenty of women.'

'Never had the need, I s'pose. He said to me, once, that he liked women too much ever to marry one of them. He said he was too rough and ready.' Steve looked at his friend. 'You're a fine one to ask questions about Joe staying single. What about you?'

''es,' Barny said. 'Well, I'm different. I'm too refined.'

'Yeah. I've noticed.'

Joe had travelled more than Barny in his youth. Every now and then he had been up and off somewhere, out abroad, doing whatever came along, and suddenly he had settled down. People said it was when he had made enough money to buy his house, a little cottage, down'long, but that wasn't the whole story, people knew that, too.

'He still can't read,' Steve said with a smile. 'The stupid bugger.'

They knew that Uncle Joe was anything but stupid. He was as sharp as a razor but there was no such thing as dyslexia when he was a boy, just dunces, made to stand in a corner by the likes of Miss Taylor, who could not understand his accent, and Willy Jory, who could, being one of them, a Janner.

The English teacher may have been Good Old Willy Jory to his contemporaries but was Holy Terror to Class One of the big boys, who were seven years old. He had an evil squint which practically closed one eye, while the other glared maliciously at the class of fools as he walked between the rows of long wooden desks, jingling a fistful of coins in his trouser pocket. His mouth was distorted by an evil sneer to match his eye, and both may have been caused by some misfortune in the past. The children didn't know - or care - for that matter. They were terrified of the man.

Willy Jory: 'A noun is the name of a person, place or thing.'

Chorus: 'A noun is the name of a person, place or thing.

Willy Jory: 'Write that down.'

Heads bent over exercise books, pens scratched on paper, while minds concentrated on the proximity of the jingling tanners, bobs, thre'penny bits and farthings in the pocket, and the malicious eye peering over their shoulders. Willy Jory had a reputation among his colleagues for maintaining one hundred per cent discipline.

'Come on! Make haste!'

They made haste.

Willy Jory: 'A concrete noun is something real.'

Chorus: 'A concrete noun is something real.'

'Write that down.'

They wrote that down, while Willy waited impatiently. 'Now,' he said at last, 'what's an example of a concrete noun? Something real?' He glared at them, with the coins jingling in his pocket. 'And for pity's sake, think before you shove up your hands. I said something real.'

Something real. Uncle Joe's hand rose confidently among the few others who dared risk the wrath of Willy Jory. Something real... it was easy. Uncle Joe found writing difficult, but here was an opportunity to earn a red star at last, if only Mr Jory chose him to answer. He was sure of it.

'You, boy!'

'Jesus, sir.' There was a dreadful silence as Willy Jory paused in his pacing and jingling. He scowled at Joe and shook the coins in a violent spasm.

'Idiot!' Willy Jory said.

So, there you are, Jesus was not real and Young Uncle Joe was an idiot. There was no doubt about it, for Mr. Jory was a learned man, and there was little future for an idiot in a godless world. So Joe looked forward to Saturdays, when he could go and play in the harbour or out to Porthmeor and tack across the sand in a *cok an baban*, a tin boat made from a flattened can opened up and shaped with stone tools into a double-ender like the English kids made from paper, only without that damn silly bit stuck up in the air amidships like Carn Brea minus the lighthouse. A good one would ride the waves like the proper thing, dipping the bow and shipping seas, far better than a boughten one, from a shop. Or the boys could make *cok an babans* from cork net-floats washed ashore on the beaches, with slate keels and tall sails made from the feathers of moulting gulls. They could take them out to the Back of the Island and sail them in Crock o' Dumplin's, the deep pool with rounded boulders lying in the depths like puddens in a pan. Only his young contemporaries had accepted Uncle Joe as being among the brightest, Steve, Barny, Mary, Sarah, Shimshai...

'He's coming home,' Steve said.

'Who?'

'Why, Shimshai.'

'Is he, now?' Barny said. 'Looking for material for another book, I suppose. Nothing ever happens up London.' He wondered how the two of them could have remained friends, after all that.

'Wonder you don't write a book,' Steve said. 'You're another one of these here intellectuals.'

'A book of poems?' Barny said. 'P'rhaps I will, one day.'

Steve laughed. 'You'll be wasting your time,' he said, 'nobody reads poetry any more, 'cept their own. We're all poets in our heads. Some write it down, and some don't.'

Such a statement from Steve, Barny thought, would have been impossible before all that business. He realised his friend had neatly diverted the conversation from Shimshai, and he let it slide.

It was by such brief exchanges that they came to know each other, to grow together towards a maturity which was always in the perpetual future and, in this latest, they had each declared his ambition: Steve's yearning for the contentment of what he saw as the traditional way of life for himself and his son, and Barny's dream of expressing himself in words which would outlive him, this most presumptuous desire of living beyond our allotted span.

'Some sand coming in,' Barny said, looking toward the quay.

'The harbour is nearly blocked. He'll get worse before he gets better. It's a nuisance.'

Nuisance, Barny thought, is an understatement if ever there was one. It was getting downright dangerous when there was a sea running.

'Worse over Penavon Bar,' Steve said. 'They've stopped sluicing the river.'

'That's hardly surprising. Nobody d' use n.'

'We do. Now and then we have to. When we lay up for refits, and sometimes we have to run over the bar in bad weather. This harbour is getting impossible in northerly gales.'

'Penavon is going to rack and ruin. The port is obsolete. Quays falling down, channels silting up. It would cost millions to revitalise the place. You fishermen wouldn't bring in enough revenue to pay for sluicing, much less repairs.'

'We don't bring in enough revenue to pay for fuel some trips.'

'Poor old chap. My heart bleeds for 'ee.'

They laughed, and let the matter drop. Penavon was not the only place going to rack and ruin. Half the property here was for sale, too. Every hotel seemed to be on the market. There was nothing they could do about it.

'Some cold, down here, idn a?' Barny said. 'You must be perished. Everything is frozen up, down west, but at least it's sheltered from this east'ly wind.'

Steve appeared unaffected by the chill breeze coming across the bay. He snapped the padlock shut on the wheel-house door. 'Got to lock everything, these days,' he said. 'It idn like i' was.' He jumped down on to the sand, his wet hand remaining on the rubbing strake. 'She's a fine craft,' he said, 'but she's going to take some payin' for.'

They walked up to the slipway, leaping over the rills and pools of water left by the ebbing tide, for both wore shoes, not boots, for this brief visit to Steve's boy's new boat. Once or twice, Steve turned round to look back at her, as if to reassure himself that she, this fine craft, was not an illusion or a day-dream. She was what he had always wanted, but could never afford. If it had not been for the boy, working up country and out abroad, and Mary's work in taking in damned lodgers, they would not have afforded her now. He would never forget that. They went past the pub.

'I don't go in there much now,' Steve said. 'All damned strangers.'

They went up through the narrow streets towards Steve's loft and, as they rounded the corner by Back Road West, they saw two women approaching, the elder in a warm coat, the younger in anorak and jeans. Sarah Stevens and her maid, Katie, who was away to college.

'Hullo, Sarah.'

'Hullo, Katie.'

'I didn' know you were home, Katie.' Barny said, as Steve mumbled a greeting and was obliged to stop and wait. 'How are you?'

'I'm fine, thank you,' Katie said. 'I only came home yesterday.'

Sarah listened and watched quietly as they discussed Katie's progress at university, glancing occasionally at Steve, who avoided her eye. Katie was progressing well in her research, she said, and had made some important new discoveries. 'I have to do some fieldwork and this is as good a place as any to do it, so I hope to be home all this summer.' I was intending to phone you. I want to see you about the mine shafts and adits in the area.'

'Of course. Just give me a ring, and we'll fix something up.'

The two were so alike, Barny thought. Katie was so like Sarah in her youth that there could be no doubt that they were mother and daughter. Katie's brown hair and eyes, her trim figure, were exactly as Sarah's had been, and she shared the same frank expression, a little shy, yet not self-effacing, quietly confident. Only Sarah knew who Katie's father was, and he wondered if she had ever told anyone else. Probably not.

'She'll be Doctor Stevens soon,' Barny said to Sarah. 'You must be proud of her.'

'I am,' Sarah said.

While talking to Katie, Barny was aware that Steve and Sarah avoided each other's eyes after the polite greetings, looking at him and the girl, anywhere but at each other. Well, what can 'ee expect? he thought.

'Come out and see me, Katie,' he said. 'I'll get my mining records out. We can go through them together. And I can show you some of the adits, if you like, where I've been underground myself.'

They agreed to meet, and the men left the women, to continue on the way to Steve's loft. If he doesn't mention Sarah, Barny thought, then I'm damned if I'm going to. It was far too sensitive a subject. She had aged well, considering. To have a child at thirty-nine, an illegitimate child at that, with her background of strict religious upbringing, and bring her up alone to become a girl like Katie, with no help from anybody, while retaining her pride and her faith, was something of an achievement, and

Barny had always admired her for it. His thoughts were interrupted by a voice, overtaking them from the rear.

It was the voice of Ezekiel, who was a short, broad-shouldered man some ten years younger than Barny, wearing a long overcoat and a trilby hat. He bought his clothes from the charity shops and was more concerned with getting a bargain than with style or fit. 'Must have cost a bleddy fortune when it was new,' he'd say. 'They don't make clothes like this today, boy.'

'Hullo,' Ezekiel said. 'What 'ee about? Two good men got together here.'

Only his feet, clad in a pair of ex-service boots, 'ammunition, O.R.'s for the use of', showed beneath the voluminous coat.

'Hullo, Zeke. What's the news?'

'News? Why, you'll hear the news soon enough. Ha! bleddy rogue. Tha's all he is.'

'Who?'

'You'll find out.'

And Zeke was gone; off up the road muttering to himself.' Damn rogues. Comin' down here.'

The two friends smiled at each other. Poor old Zeke. He was three score short of a gurry, people said, and called him 'The Prophet', because of his pronouncements on the future of the world. 'You'll see. Just you wait, it's all foretold.' Always something to obsess him. 'What's up with him now?' they said as they made their way through the narrow streets to Steve's loft. 'Somebody's upset him.'

The loft was dark, full of ropes, nets, tools, buoys, anchors and engine spares. Across the small windows there were festoons of cobwebs holding the desiccated corpses of flies and a dusty red admiral. Steve dragged out a couple of threadbare old chairs, and they sat down for a serious yarn.

'There's hardly any lofts left now,' Steve said. 'They've all been converted into flats, and the boys keep their gear in their garages on the housing estates while their cars are eaten up by rust in the salt air. What a thing we've come to!'

He produced cigarettes and offered one to Barny, who declined, saying, 'I thought you'd given up.'

'I have,' Steve said, 'when I'm home,' and he blew a squall of smoke to tremble the cobwebs.

A thin spider darted from its tunnel of grey silk, and paused, assessing the tension in the net as the two men caught up with each other's news.

'Where's the boy?' Barny said.

'Gone to a meetin'. About fish quotas. He'll be here dreckly.'

'Still not married ?'

'Don't seem to be interested. He ab'm settled down since he came home from abroad, not really. Anyway, he got too much on his mind, at the moment, to worry about women.'

Barny caught a trace of self-deception in Steve's voice. It was he who had too much on his mind, thousands of pounds of debt, when he should be thinking of retiring.

'You've laid a lot of money out between 'ee.'

'Ess, but i' edn that. The trouble is we shan't know from one day to the next whether we're allowed to go to sea. We were encouraged to go into debt by the Government and now there's all this talk of cutting the quotas and restricting the number of days at sea. Bad enough havin' fish quotas, and now we've got time quotas lined up too. Tie up, they call it. We sh'll have to stay ashore while foreign boats are out there catchin' what they like. Tie-up be damned, more like strangulation to me, *and* we have the fault for wiping out the dolphins. And now there's bird-watchers spying on us all the time for accidentally catching a few kiddas. Make 'ee feel guilty for doing what we be'n doing for generations.'

'Well, you know what happens when there's a free-for-all. The fish get wiped out. It's happened before.'

Steve looked at his old friend with a long-suffering sigh. One generation ashore, he thought, and they d' forget everything.

'The men are takin' chances,' he explained patiently. 'Goin' to sea when they shouldn', just to get a livin' and pay off the debts they were encouraged to incur by the ministry.'

He wasn't sure if Barny understood. 'Takin' chances,' he insisted. 'In bad weather. Riskin' their lives.'

Barny looked at the gear around Steve's loft. There was a time when the nets piled around the floor would have been of black twine, smelling of tanning, the floats made from cork, and the dahns from the inflated bladders of pigs. But now, although the smells in here were still of ages past, of industry and memories, it was all plastic; the floats red and orange, and the nets the colour of shallow sea on those sunny, windless days when the rippled sand beneath the surface reflects blue light like the scales of herring. Barny lifted a few meshes from the floor, a piece cut out in repair. The single-stranded plastic filament was so fine as to be almost invisible in the dim, deep water of the sea. It would ensnare every living thing that swam into its meshes, dolphins, seals, birds, and if lost would lie unrotting in the depths, entangling everything that came in contact with it, until eventually it was cast ashore to add to the debris on the beaches. It hung like a delicate malignancy in his hand. He tossed it aside, and looked at his friend.

'Don't start on that,' Steve said. 'What am I supposed to do, stay in the past and starve?'

'Never said a word.'

'You don't dammee have to. I can see what you're thinkin'.'

Barny shrugged. As he saw it, the net was symptomatic of the way in which man's limited intelligence was leading him to disaster. Eventually, he thought, we would all be entangled in the deadly meshes of our own ingenuity. We are like the individuals in a vast shoal of fish, aware that the vanguard is leading them to the ominous wall of annihilation, but afraid to leave the shoal and face the prospect of life alone, in a deep and dangerous ocean.

'Well,' Steve said eventually, 'I ab'm got time to sit here all day. What do you want to see me for, anyway?'

It had taken only an hour to come to the point, Barny noticed, almost a record. 'It's about my house,' he said.

Only up-country people called these little dwellings 'cottages', he thought, but some of them called their five-bed, double bath, double garage in five acres their 'cottage'. Depends where you start from. His own place was old, built as a home for a miner when the country was scarred with tips and dotted with smoking engine houses. It had withstood the damp and gales of a hundred and fifty years, with only a lick of paint, now and then, to preserve the woodwork.

'What's the matter with your house, apart from being in the wrong town?'

Barny had become used to the remarks about going down there to live, so he ignored this one. 'The roof is going, the window sills are rotten and the door d' fit where it d' touch. I want 'ee to have a look at 'n. Tell me how much it would cost to do 'n up. It's like we,' he said, 'new too soon.'

' It will cost more 'n you can afford,' Steve said. 'Bleddy down-and-out poet.'

Barny looked at him, said nothing. Waited for Steve to continue.

'I was hoping to concentrate on fishing with the boy. With the new boat we should have been able to make a good living, but it's a very uncertain future all of a sudden.'

Steve doubted if Barny realised how expensive building work was, these days. And on top of it he would have to add the expense of travelling all the way out there every day. It was a bit remote. It would cost a lot, but a few jobs from reliable customers, like this renovation for Barny, would be invaluable between seasons.

Barny remained silent.

'The last time I was down that way,' Steve said as he watched the spider jerk its way back into the hole, hungry as ever, 'they were still roofing with turves and plastering the walls with cow-shit.'

'Tuss!' Barny said.

Steve wondered how long the spider would live, with no flies. Sometime, he would have to clean the windows and wipe off months of work. 'The old skills are dying out, don't 'ee knaw.'

'Tha's why I want you to do it. I want a good job done.'

'I'll drop in and have a look, next time I'm passing.'

'No hurry,' Barny said, refusing again to react to Steve's apparent procrastination. It might be a long time before Steve passed Barny's door.

They were silent for a while, sitting in the gloom of the loft, watching the spider's quick movements in the funnel of its net. Soon it would die, and the web continue to trap flies to no purpose in the gathering dust.

'You're still writin' en?' Steve said, eventually, when he thought perhaps the silence had gone on for long enough.

'Oh yes.' Barny said.

'What about ?'

'Us.'

'Us? What do 'ee mean, us? '

Steve had always looked his most handsome when he raised his eyebrow in that inquisitive expression while trying to conceal his amusement. His question had been unexpected, his comment upon the answer a frivolity to hide his genuine interest, and he had offered Barny an opportunity to avoid the subject, should he wish to do so. Playing with words was all part of their games.

Barny threw the piece of net onto a heap of rubbish in the corner. 'You know what I mean. Us! We party.'

'Not another one!' Steve said.

Barny watched his old friend lean back in his wobbly chair and take a breath.

'What do 'ee want to write about we for?' Steve said. 'You're as bad as Shimshai.' He laughed at some recollection. 'It's all over, boy. All gone.

You're too late. What's left is in a tourist attraction just down the road from where you live. I read about it in the paper. "The Total Experience", they call it. Tin miners, fishermen, ships ashore, wreckers, pirates, the lot. I'll take 'ee down there sometime. You might be inspired.'

His laugh was internal, a few wheezy 'hee hees' of scorn at the way in which his heritage was being commercialised.

'How can it be "Total"', Barny said, 'if we're not there?'

'Well, it won't be long before we are. They'll have us in glass cases, like bleddy dodos, stuffed and mounted.'

'Or just holding hands,' Barny said. And he wondered which of them was indeed the poet, the commentator upon the human predicament, as they laughed away the fate of tribes throughout the world.

'I'll walk up'long with 'ee,' Steve said. 'I want to call in to the boat house.'

So they walked together, through Fore Street to avoid the east wind cutting in across the harbour from the bay, bound for the lifeboat house at the top of the west pier.

'Still learning the language?' Steve asked.

'Oh yes.'

'Waste of bleddy time. Livin' in the past.'

Barny smiled to himself. He had seen the name on the stern of Steve's boat, a name which Steve's son had translated.

His friend saw the smile, and grinned. 'Well, that was the boy. Thought I'd better let him have his way, to keep his interest.'

'Sure.' Barny said. 'He's getting quite fluent. *Morwennol*, Sea Swallow, Tern, I like it.'

'You would.'

A few specks of stinging rain struck their cheeks. 'North-east wind and rain,' Steve said. 'Very good weather.' And the wind drew tears from their eyes as they turned down the hill to the harbour again. A few steps and they were at the back door of the lifeboat house. 'They want,' Steve said, 'another man, in the crew.'

'You're too old.'

'I know.' Steve paused, with his hand on the doorknob and furrows across his brow.

Inside the door the blue-and-white hull, high on its carriage, gleamed with polish. They walked along the starboard side and climbed the steps up to the gantry. Everything about the boat was in perfect condition. She was ready, as always, for instant service should the crack of the maroons echo over the rooftops of the town.

'You wouldn't catch me,' Barny said, 'going aboard there.'

Steve suppressed a smile, which Barny saw. "es, well,' Barny said, 'you knaw what I mean.'

'Somebody has to do it,' Steve reminded him. 'They d' want somebody who d' knaw their way about. There idn many of us left.'

But Steve's boy, Barny thought, was one of them. He had learned from his father, who had learned from the old men, long dead, who had learned from older men; fathers and grandfathers who had only the wind in their sails and the muscles in their arms for power. Men who could row fifteen miles to Pendeen and back to draw bait before setting sail for the long-lining grounds, or sail a lugger to Australia in search of an escape from poverty. The young ones were experts in technology, the use of electronic devices to look at the weather, tell them where they were, detect fish and wipe them out, or even say good night to their wives, tucked up in bed fifty miles away. Not many of them knew the ins and outs of the coastline, the behaviour of the tides and the lie of the rocks close to shore where ships still ran aground and it was all a matter of experience and familiarity. There were some, but not many, and even fewer who could, or would, go aboard here.

'Well, I'll leave 'ee to it.' Barny said. Barny wanted nothing to do with this, he had seen enough of it. Some of his earliest memories were of the predecessors of this boat: of the dreaded bang when the maroons went off, the expression in his mother's eyes when his own father had gone rushing off in answer to the summons, and her silence while waiting for the boat's return. His friend had not replied. He was casting his eye over the immaculately maintained equipment. Somebody had to do it, and there was never a shortage of volunteers, but not Steve, he was too old and a damn good job too.

'They've asked the boy,' Steve said.

Barny felt his throat dry up, he heard men shouting in the sea, the splintering of wood on rock. 'Well,' he said, keeping his absurd premonition to himself, 'I'm off, to see the old man.'

'Ask he to come aboard,' Steve said. 'He's a good man.'

But Barny's father had been aboard long enough. Surely Steve had not forgotten that. He said so little, Steve, that one never knew what he had forgotten or what was in his mind. There were reasons for that, so Barny left Steve in the lifeboat house, thinking he knew not what thoughts at the prospect of his son joining the crew, and trudged up the steep hill to where his father lived, in one of the terraces with a view across the harbour and bay to the eastern shore.

His father was out in the shed in the back court, a warm, weather-tight workshop where he spent most of his time.

'Where is he?' his mother used to reply, 'Wheer es a'? Why, out in the damn 'ut. Weer else would a be?' Or, 'Why, down the damn harbour, wheer else would a be?' Or she might say, when particularly aggrieved at the lack of his company, 'Why, down the damn lodge, wheer else would a be? You'd think he never 'ad no home.'

Barny's father was, as Steve had said, a good man. One who had always looked to the future, unaware that the future was to be so distant from the past. His vision had been forward, for the backward glances invariably reviewed hardship and struggle, long hours of hard work with little reward, and his lot had improved steadily over the passing years. His own father had been a tinner he never knew, for the mine had killed him before the birth of his child. His mother's father had brought him up, for *that* old man had made much money out of fish. He had provided a home and income for his daughter and her baby and they lived well until the fish were wiped out, all the herring and millions of pilchards, which people thought were impossible to deplete. This was Barny's great-grandfather, but he might as well have been his father or his brother, so familiar was he to Barny from his father's anecdotes about the bearded figure whose portrait in faded sepia gazed down from the wall of Barny's family kitchen.

'Drowned!' Barny's father complained. 'When I was fourteen, now, leaving school, here, with no boat to go fishin' in. Should never have gone out, eighty-odd, a man that age, wouldn't give it up.'

His father was always vague about the details, even when prompted by Barny, who had been a precociously curious child, for the truth of the incident had never been proven.

'Was it rough?'

'Fine weather. Fog.'

He had learned from others that his great-grandfather's lugger had been run down in thick fog by a steamer which did not stop, even to look for survivors, for she was trying to catch the tide in Avonmouth.

This unsatisfied curiosity had led Barny into an inordinate desire to probe the past, although he had been obliged to seek sources other than his father's memory and the teaching of history by Miss Taylor. The old man could not comprehend that the twenty-five years before Barny's birth were as ancient history to the boy, chronicles of another world, for to him it was all part of the present time, the one span of life which was his. He had never been interested in the past and, suddenly, it was too far back to remember or bother with, all irrelevant, and the future gone too, all used up, expended on the present, so he stayed in the now, where he belonged, while it lasted.

He was working at his bench, upon which was a home-made contraption for steaming wood. It comprised a length of four-inch iron pipe, sealed at one end, with a clamp shutting off the other. It was perched precariously on a home-made iron frame over a roaring blowlamp. Clouds of steam were escaping from a doubtful safety valve soldered into the pipe, and Barny was afraid that one day the whole thing would blow the shed sky high, and the old man with it.

His father was a laconic man, not given to argument or reiteration, a statement, once made, was enough for anybody with any sense. 'Don't touch that!' he said once as he left his young son in the shed that he used as a workshop even then. Young Barny could see no reason for not touching it. The blowlamp did not look dangerous for it was not lit. There was no smoke or flame, no sharp edges to harm him, and had his father not placed it there with his bare hands? It was, he decided, one of those occasions when adults seek to exclude children from their world with orders and directions for the sake of them. Hold my hand. Don't run. Put your coat on. It was quite obvious that his father was forbidding him from playing with the thing and possibly breaking it. His father had never lied to him, but the boy reached up to the dull black burner, hoping perhaps to prove some failing in his father which might match his own.

The skin of his fingertips was immediately cauterised into hard, white leather, and an acrid smeech invaded his nose. Neither spit nor frantic flinking would alleviate the pain. He hugged his fingers in his armpit, doubled up in agony and rage, hopping about the workshop in the grim determination to deny himself the indulgence of tears. He could tell no one, and hid the wounds in a clenched fist until the pink skin reformed over the stigma of his disobedience and, which was a greater sin in his father's eyes, foolishness.

In a like manner, Barny had overcome his weaknesses for women - by becoming aware of them, by learning from his own pain and the experience of others. He had been cured of his weakness by involuntary aversion therapy. Whenever he ventured to reach for the heat of passion, the flames had seared him to the heart and vaporised the liquid flow of love. He knew of very few who had not smarted from touching the hot iron of desire. He had been conditioned into obeying the orders of reason. Don't touch that! You'll burn your bleddy fingers.

So most of his love had never left him. He let it out sparingly in small, controlled emissions, as of a fine spray of perfume, to envelop those who were close to him. No woman had possessed the whole of him since his first love, a tragedy of which he rarely spoke and could never write. Yet, there were some of whom he was very fond and, as he drove his little old car along the coastal road on that day which seemed so long ago, when he went to see Steve, and his father, he was thinking of one of them, hoping she might be at home when he left the old man.

"'loh Da'," he shouted above the roar of his father's blowlamp. 'What 'ee doin'?'

'Doin,? Why you can see what I'm doin', makin' a dish of tay.'

It was always like that. Ask a silly question and you got a silly answer, or else a straightforward sensible answer which made you feel a bleddy fool and wish you hadn't asked. The old man jerked his head towards a partly constructed model boat at the other end of the bench. Barny examined the model, stooping to inspect the details. She was was about two feet long, a skeleton of ribs, planked almost to the bilges. When complete, she would be an exact model of one of the old mackerel drivers, like his great-grandfather's, some of the finest sea-boats ever built. They were just under fifty feet in length, carried some fifteen hundred feet of sail when fully rigged and were among the fastest sailing craft afloat. Their hulls were full for taking the bottom in this treacherous harbour of ground swells, yet sleek at the waterline for speed. They took the crews to Scotland, the North Sea, or anywhere else where there was fish to be caught. The boats reached the ultimate in refinement in the 1880's, but, by the turn of the century, had been ousted by steam and fishing became too efficient, and men too greedy. In 1846, Barny knew, one such boat, the *Mystery*, sailed to Australia, taking six desperate and adventurous men from the poverty which overtook the community when the mines closed down and they had caught all the fish in the sea.

He had to be a bit careful here. His father was a touchy old cuss when he had a mind to be. He looked inside the model to see the tiny copper fastenings holding the planks to the ribs. 'She's coming on,' he said'

'Had a brea job with the garboards,' the old man muttered. 'Could have done with a bit of a hand.'

Now, as Barny knew full well, the last thing his father wanted was help with his model. This was merely his way of remonstrating with his son for not visiting him more often, for all his models were fashioned only by his own two hands and if anyone else made the slightest contribution his accomplishment would be diminished. 'Gone down there to live,' he grumbled. 'There's no sense in it.'

'I'm on the phone,' Barny said. 'The number's in the book.' As if his father did not know it. As if it were not written on the pad by the phone in case of emergency. 'I can be here in ten minutes.'

The last time he had seen this model she had been but the keel and a few ribs. The detail, in craftsmanship and design, were in absolute contrast to the chaos in the shed. Nothing was ever put away, it seemed. His mother remarked, on one of the few occasions when she dared set foot inside this sanctuary, that there was a place for everything and nothing in its place. There were tools and bits and pieces all over the shop, littering the bench, hanging from nails or jammed in racks against the walls. The floor was inches deep in sawdust and shavings.

'One of these days,' Barny assured him once when the blowlamp was roaring away among the litter on the bench, 'you'll burn the place down.'

'What would I want to do a damn silly thing like that for?'

The only time he conceded that there might be some merit in keeping the shed tidy was when he dropped some small item, some tool or a special screw, and it fell among the shavings at his feet when, if he thought no one was within hearing, he would say, 'Shit! Shit-shit-shit.' and begin the laborious task of searching through the debris. On one occasion, when his wife was still alive, he dropped a tiny winch barrel, made from a piece of six inch nail. Barny had found a length of electric cable leading from the house to a table lamp his father had stolen from the front room. He had untwined the flex and wound a single strand around an iron bar.

'Don't come in here!' he cried as Barny appeared. He swept the home-made electro-magnet over the top of the shavings until there was a 'ping' as the winch barrel shot up from the litter and stuck to the end of the bar.

'Hee, hee,' he said. 'Don't tell she I pinched the lamp. Put 'n back before she d' notice.'

From time to time he was forced to clean the place up but said it was a bad sign, meaning that if the shed was tidy, he was between projects, there was no work being done and he was wasting his time.

'Who is she?' Barny asked, running his hand along the even curve of the bilge, for she was not merely the model of a type but of a particular boat, one which would have been familiar to all the town in the days when a boat meant everything, livelihood, status and life, and when complete she would be accurate in every detail.

24

'Who is she?' his da' said. 'Why, you can see who she is.'

To him, there was already some detail in the construction which should preclude confusion with any other craft, some swelling of the bilge, or rake of stem or stern. In the old days, the boats were built by individual craftsmen around the harbours and were to the exact requirements of the owners. A bit more sheer, as they examined the prototype, a bit more beam to carry the load of fish, not too much mind, or she'll lose speed. No two were alike, although they looked so to the unpractised eye.

'Looks like the *Barnabas*,' Barny said, thinking his father might be building a model of his son's namesake.

'The *Barnabas!*' the old man spat in exasperation. 'How can she be the '*Barnabas?*'

He had always been like this, Barny thought. Those aspects of life which were common knowledge, such basic facts, needed no tuition, except to a fool. Everybody knew the *Barnabas* and to indicate her salient features would be an insult to another of his father's generation, like pointing out the difference between skillivan and balshe or a cart and its horse. His skills had been insulted by his son's misidentification, as if he were building a bleddy punt, or a *cok an baban.*

'Steve Trevorrow's son is going aboard the lifeboat,' Barny said, to change the subject and to observe his father's reaction to this intelligence.

'What as?'

'One of the crew.'

'That's what I thought,' the old man said. 'What else would a go aboard as? A bleddy plank?' Sometimes he wondered how he could have reared a boy to fifty years and more of age who could be so bleddy stupid. 'What as?' he demanded. 'Bowman? Cox'n? Mechanic? There's six men aboard.'

'Oh, I don't know. Steve didn' say.'

The old chap opened the end of his steaming contraption to remove one of the now-flexible lengths of wood which he had been steaming. It was to be shaped into a plank and fastened along the ribs of his model. He burnt his fingers on the hot iron.

'T' hell.' he said, spitting on the pain. 'He'll be all right. Be a good man.'

Barny watched him shape the plank and fasten it to the ribs. When it was finished there was not a hair's breadth between it and its neighbour. 'Like a thing grawed there,' he said.

The old man leaned forward and, with a squinted eye, looked along the line of her.

'She's the *Ebenezer*', he said. 'Built in 1869 for John Stevens by William Paynter, a cousin to Bessie Grose that was.' He straightened his back. 'You wouldn't know them.'

He hadn't really said what he thought about Boy Steve joining the lifeboat crew and Barny had not said what had occurred to him about the old man's work. Models, he thought to himself. What have we come to? There was no boat-builder here now. The old workshop was a gift shop and a Chinese take-away, but you can't stop progress.

He went in to tea with his father, who fed him on a home-made pasty and chloresterol-saturated cream and butter, saying 'It'll keep the cowld out.'

Barny watched him bustling about the kitchen, where everything was clean and tidy, all ship-shape and Bristol fashion, with the paint-work shining and the brass of the old black-leaded slab and the ornaments on the shelves all brightly polished. It was one of the last old ranges still intact and working.

'Baystly owld thing,' Da' said. 'D' smoke like the devil.' As he lifted the cast-iron rings to feed in another shovel-full of coal taken from the brass bound box he used as a scuttle. 'I would have heaved 'n out years ago if I had my way. But she wouldn't have it. Said 'lectric don't taste the same. Too late now,' he grumbled.

On the dresser were a few of his mother's treasures, bits of china, a brass plate and a piece of ore, gleaming iron pyrites, which his father's father had brought out of Wheal Dowr before he had been killed in the disaster. Barny picked it up and it nestled in his palm, heavy, like lead, but gleaming gold. It was beautiful, and worthless to anyone except his father, Barny thought as he returned it to its accustomed position on the shelf. It belonged next to a photograph, which Barny had taken, of his parents sitting on a wall down by the harbour, his father in shirt sleeves and his mother in a cotton frock. They were both laughing, somewhat embarrassed by this vanity, Da's bald head glistening with a slight perspiration, and Ma demure, like a young girl caught doing something mildly improper. She was small and plump and had slipped her hand through her husband's arm for courage. It was the last picture they had of her, for her illness had been long and painful, not conducive to happy snapshots. On looking at the photograph, Barny thought of all the things he had omitted to tell her, the irredeemable opportunities for expressing endearments and gratitude. His father poured tea from a huge brown pot into fine china cups. 'Might's well use them,' he said, but Barny knew that he drank from an old mug when alone, with the cups kept safely in the sideboard. He tried to do things the way his wife had done, and would not alter the position of a single thing in the house where every room, every artefact, was of her taste, choice and initiation. He was not seen to cry when she died, had even avoided being alone with Barny for a while, and had spent more time down the lodge with his old friends. 'Just yarnin',' he said.

Barny felt a sudden compulsion to reach out and touch his father, to take his hand and say 'You're a good man, Da',' tell him he loved him. Such a show of affection would be impossible. His father would be obliged to utter some rebuff to hide his embarrassment. 'Be a good man stuffed.'

The man Barny could no more tell his father that he loved him than the boy Barny could have wept on his shoulder and pleaded for enlightenment, asked for a cuddle and an explanation of it all. 'What's it all about, Da'? Why am I still so terrified by these awful dreads?'

'Now hark!' his father had said once, some time after he lost her. 'Now, hark to me. I don't want to be kept afloat. You knaw... when the time d' come. I want to be shoved ashore. I want to be put going... '

Barny remembered his mother's pain, her dear face, drawn and haggard from suffering.

'...and I d' want to be burnt.'

His father had been speaking of euthanasia and cremation, and Barny had suppressed a desire to hold the old man in his arms, kiss his bald head.

'If that's what you want, Father.'

'Tha's what I d' want.'

Barny left him watching the telly, crowds of Germans standing outside a burning hostel for Auslanders, and went to see his old flame.

Barny was still very fond of his old flame, although the heat of their passion had exhausted itself during periods when neither of them was free to feed its fire. She was forty odd, and had been a voluptuous, beautiful girl before embarking on a disastrous marriage which had left her remarkably well preserved except for the lines of fatigue around her eyes. There were no secrets between them. She always welcomed him, and made him cups of tea, unless there was wine in the house, and, as he sat at her table and she stood at the sink, he would feel her up, sliding his hand up her leg beneath the skirt, syaing, 'Your thighs are a silky as ever,' until she slapped his face with her hand or a wet dish cloth. It was a game they played, a pretence at desire which neither felt any longer. He would get hard when she allowed him to do it long enough for her knickers to dampen, bu they didn't go any further, there was no point. They had done it all before and did not wish to spoil there friendship.

She was standing at her ironing board, a broad-shouldered woman, firm and lean, with dumpling breasts, strong legs and shoulder-length fairish hair.

"Hello, Anne.' he said. And she answered 'Come in,' although he was already through the house to her kitchen. 'Like a cup of tea?'

He declined and sat at the table, watching her work, her strong arms rippling as she pressed the hot metal across a skirt.

'How's your father?' she asked, looking at him with a glance away from the steaming iron.

'All right. Right as rain, really, considering his age. He's never idle. He's down there steaming wood to make planks for a model mackerel driver.'

'It's a good thing he keeps himself busy,' Anne said. 'It'll keep him young.'

'Yes, but he ought to slow down a bit. I came in town to see Steve, to tell the truth, about renovating my house. He's bought a new boat.'

'I know. She's beautiful.'

How like her, he thought, to see only the beauty. 'I don't think much of the gear he's using. His loft is full of monofilament nets. Terrible things, they're killing everything in the sea. I didn't say anything though.'

'Why not?

'Well, what can 'ee say? If one uses them, they all have to use them, competing against each other in destroying their own livelihood, same as they did with the herring and pilchards.'

He watched the muscles of her thigh flexing against her skirt. She had a fine pair of legs, he thought.

'They'll be banned, sooner or later, depends how soon they wipe out the stocks. It's crazy! Steve must know what's happening, he's not daft.'

'You should write a poem about them. Send it off to *Fishing News*.' She laughed at the idea, throwing her head back as she saw him become annoyed.

She said it in such a trite manner, as if it were the easiest thing in the world to sit down and write a poem, that he sighed in exasperation as she continued,' or you can file it away, with all the other stuff you never let anyone see.'

He was well used to her making fun of his poetry. All his friends did it. Barny the Bard. The mad poet. You're a versatile sort of bloke. He'd heard it all, but shrugged it off, keeping his comments to himself.

With Anne, he made a joke of it too. 'I've had a few things published,' he said now. 'One day I'll be rich and famous. You wait.' He often said to Anne, 'That's all I've ever wanted, to be rich and famous. It's not a lot to ask.' Said with a wry smile, as if acknowledging that such an aspiration was beyond all possibility.

'What needs doing on your house?' She was not to be drawn into boosting his ego this evening.

'Nothing urgent. It would go on for years as it is, but I thought I'd see how much it would cost for a new roof, new windows and a new door. I can do the rest myself.'

'You can't afford all that,' Anne said. 'You haven't any money.' She laughed, tossing her hair like a girl thirty years her junior. 'You'll have to get a job.'

'Thanks. I knew I could rely on you to cheer me up. I have a job.'

'I mean,' she said, 'a proper job, with work and wages. Or are you too old?'

Barny grabbed her backside, intending to smack her, but she flicked him across the cheek with a damp shirt and a button stung his cheek.

'Hey!' he cried. 'That hurt. God, you're a vicious bitch.'

He rubbed the pain, and examined a finger, looking for blood. There wasn't any, and he was disappointed that there was no visible injury with which to reproach her.

'Come here,' Anne said. 'Let me kiss it better, you g'eat baby.'

She attempted to kiss him on his wounded cheek, but he brushed her away with a grimace of intolerance. 'Leave me alone. You might poison me. You have more venom than a dammee adder.'

'A daaaameee aaadder!' she said, mocking the long vowels of his accent. But as she turned away he smacked her behind with a stinging swipe which made her jump with pain, and she rounded on him with clenched fists. He grabbed her wrists and they struggled together, with Barny laughing and Anne pretending fury until they parted in a breathless truce, for which he would pay later.

There had been more than one occasion in recent years, after playing with her thus, when he had wondered if the old fire could be rekindled.

He had sat here in her kitchen and considered life in her company. She was what his mother had called a 'comfortable woman', easygoing, good natured, homely and kind-hearted. That she was also passionate his mother might have guessed, and he knew from their past, illicit tussles. She would have made a good wife for any man, except the one she married, of course. But there are lots like that.

They had spoken about the prospects of living together in the past, when it had been an impossibility. Their prevarication and doubt had switched from one to the other according to who was free, and their freedoms had not coincided until it was too late, when the habits of independence had become too strong. But now, with a house each to sell, or share, they could have been well off from the point of view from which they both regarded wealth. Money, to both of them, was a tiresome necessity which had taken too much of their lives in its acquisition. They could neither of them understand why it was that people with most were always after more. It seemed that the more you had, the less valuable it became and required constant augmentation, like egos or sex. We share the same sense of values, he thought, the same sense of humour, and the same fear of commitment that comes with scarred emotions.

'Love' was never mentioned after the time when she said. 'I gave my love to my husband, all of it.' With a quaver in her voice. 'And he squandered it with my money, in the pubs and other women's bedrooms.'

Barny was not sure what love was any more and would not have revealed it if he did, except in his poems, where nothing was concealed, which was one of the reasons why he never showed them to any one.

Now, however, after the physical contact of their tussle, there flashed between them one of those sparks of attraction which made them, if nothing else, such close friends. They put their arms around each other.

'Come to bed with me,' Barny said.

'No. I don't go to bed with anyone.'

'What a waste!'

He did not want to either, and would not have suggested it had there been any probability of her acceptance. He sat at the table again. She would, of course, if he had really wanted her, just as he would if she were to entice him, as they both knew. But the initiative would have to come from him at present and then he would be obliged to her, which he did not want.

He looked around her kitchen, and saw all the little jobs that needed doing, of which she was unaware: the rotted skirting board, the dangerous electrical wiring with the old-fashioned, round-pinned plugs overloaded with adaptors, the draughty gap around the door. There was so much he could do for her but, as his thoughts turned full circle, what was in it for him. Sex? They had done all that, and would do so now if they wanted to. Love? They loved each other now, in their own ways, and in any case there was Beth. He had two of them to bestow affection upon him, and upon whom he bestowed his. Why complicate matters? They had both decided what they wanted from life, and what they had to offer. Anne told him why she preferred to live alone, and her reasons were all practical, so Barny had never told her what she could give him, apart from superficialities, and never would, for he had made tentative attempts to broach the subject and knew, from her response, that she, like so many others, could not begin to understand, for without personal experience of the thing it was beyond comprehension.

Ah. The thing, his fear, The Dreads. To share that would require a woman of such understanding as he had never met.

The thing had plagued him all his life. Had, he thought, made him write poetry, love life and the planet that supported it. This terrible thing of his own imagination which tormented him in the still nights, and crept like a stealthy serpent into his innocuous daytime thoughts, was the secret of his life which he would gladly have shared with someone, but the burden would have been too great for them, so he kept it to himself.

He thought about it now as he contemplated the solid common sense of her, the practical advice she offered for the most impractical problems, and for this one: 'I don't know what you mean. If things upset you, don't think about them. It's *your* mind.' And this from her who wore the lines of worry around her eyes. So he must endure it alone, if he could not go to a woman for help and comfort in the times when he most desperately needed them. If he could survive those awful moments alone, then he could survive life alone. The rest was easy peasy.

As always when his thoughts drifted in this direction, he steered them back on course, thinking to himself, keep the helm amidships, boy. Steady as she goes. He smiled to himself. He had learned that philosophy from Steve.

'Steve's boy is joining the lifeboat crew,' he said.

Anne paused in her work and looked at him with an expressionless stare, avoiding that which had also been in Barny's mind, his father's mind, Steve's mind, and now in her own.

31

'On standby, I expect,' Barny said. 'Probably never have to go. There's always plenty of volunteers.'

'What did Mary say?

'I didn't ask.'

Anne pursed her lips and finished her ironing. She folded the clothes and piled them in a heap on the table. They smelt fresh and warm.

'Did you hear about Simon Sweeting?' she said.

'No. What about him?'

'He's bought Penavon.'

Barny looked at her incredulously. So this was what Zeke was upset about. 'Never!' he said.

'It's in the local paper.' She tossed it across to him. 'Front page.'

He read in silence. 'He's bought the lot,' he said eventually. 'All the Harbour. Half the town. Two miles of coast. All the old mine workings. Great news. Prosperity for all. Or at least that's what it says here.'

'You sound cynical, as always. Don't you want to see the place revitalised?'

'Depends how. The harbour will never be used for ships again, and the sand bar is treacherous for small craft. The Quays are falling down. The old mine has been closed since the disaster and, although there's still plenty of minerals down there, it's just not economic to work them. It would cost millions to open the mine up.'

'You'll be able to get a job.'

'I have a job. How many times do I have to tell you?' he said. 'I'm a poet.'

CHAPTER TWO

Ha lemmyn, An Venen. And now, The Woman.

And the woman thinks... I know what I am doing. This is my will. I write no note, for the message is here about me, the pills, the alcohol, the locked door of this cheap hotel, my assumed name. This time, I have succeeded. They don't know where I am and there is no one to deter me, either by coercion or force. They may interpret my action as they wish, and there is no doubt that they will be as mistaken in this as they have been regarding everything else about me. No one understood me in life, so why should they in death? This is my own life I am taking. They will not understand that I am at last in command of my own destiny with no influence from others, not even Barny.

Barny. Oh, Barny! But I will cry no more for him. Now, they all can cry for me.

The final sleep is overwhelming me. This dingy room has evanesced into an amalgam of my past environs, through which I may wander to relive my life at will. I can go to the sea, the moors, visit the Stones, hand in hand with Barny, see my childhood and my various desks in the several company stores to whom I sold my soul, and I am finally free from the loving care of the psychiatric ward. I told them too much and there is nothing left of me to call my own except my life. Death is my desire.

The doors of the ward were kept locked. The patients were not allowed to use knives, scissors, mirrors, glass tumblers, or any medicines unless under supervision. They sat around in brooding silence, avoiding each other's eyes, for they were all mad except for Loopy Lou.

She was alone in a room with little furniture, just a bed, a built-in wardrobe, a bedside cabinet and a wash basin with a blocked drain that took ages to empty and left a smear of grime around the white porcelain. She spent the day doing nothing but sleep, lying facing the window, with the curtains closed, or gazing at the walls, which she never saw, only the terrifying images in the pattern of the wallpaper. Outside, the weather was cold, with a persistent drizzle and she could hear traffic somewhere, roaring continually, day and night. The nurses came in from time to time to talk and one was a black man from Mauritius who was handsome and strong. He rocked her like a baby to soothe her, did her more good than a hundredweight of pills, and almost convinced her that her life was worth living. The pills, antidepressants and sleeping draughts, made her permanently thirsty, and she could not speak properly, which added to her misery. Gradually, she began to get up and walk about. She went down to the day area, which was full of other patients, cigarette smoke and the noise of the television, which was on all day long.

There was one with bandaged wrists, one with two broken legs; there was a living skeleton who was taken out at intervals to be forcibly fed, another with a dislocated neck and rope burns concealed by a high surgical collar. A woman of twenty-nine, with the eyes of a septuagenarian, gazed listlessly through the common-room window at the changing sky over the chimneys while chain-smoking endless cigarettes. She was the only one who had spoken to Loopy.

'Want a fag?'

'No thank you. I don't smoke.'

They were mostly middle-aged, only a married couple were of the same age as Loopy, and they didn't speak. They were there to dry out after being on a bottle of vodka each a day and spent their time lying about in bed. Another woman had also been living on alcohol, gin, and was drying out under duress. She was only five feet tall and less than six stone in weight. Sometimes, she tried to eat, but couldn't. She was in the room next to Loopy, and she could hear them begging, cajoling her to eat before they used the tube. Why, Loopy demanded of herself, couldn't they just let her die, if that was what she wanted? Several times, the woman packed her things and attempted to leave, but gently they led her back, and her protestations on these occasions were not too vehement. At visiting times her husband brought their two pretty little girls.

Loopy was not like these people. She was thirty-seven, black-haired, tall, with intelligent green eyes. She was heavily sedated to reduce the strain of those hysterical bouts of wailing despair. She was well aware of this and was determined to do it as soon as she could escape. This was the one act she could perform in which she could be totally in control of herself, her repulsive body and impetuous mind. It was the ultimate way of proving that she was the master of her own destiny and dependent on no one.

She had tried several ways to beat them. She tore the sash from her bath-robe but there was nothing to hang it from. She slashed her wrists with a pair of tweezers they had overlooked when searching her on admission, but they were too blunt and she merely succeeded in badly scratching herself, which hurt a lot.... She tried to get the glass out of her powder compact and failed. Both tweezers and compact were confiscated. She lay in her room, terrified of the multicolored shapes and fearful images, faces and grotesque animals lurking in the splodgy undergrowth among the patterns on the curtains.

She had also tried to run away, with just a few pounds in her purse. The nurses were busy feeding the old people at meal times, so she waited until they were preoccupied, and went. She wanted to walk into the town centre, buy all the aspirin she could; get some alcohol, and find somewhere quiet to sit and do it. She had not gone three yards before they collared her. First they asked her to go back. She cried, and said she had to go to the shops, moved forward. Three of them grabbed her and there was a brief struggle in which they all tumbled down the steps and one of the nurses lost her watch which fell to the ground and was crushed underfoot. Loopy was taken back to her room feeling very angry and frustrated.

'The dietitian doesn't even know that vegetarians don't eat fish,' she wailed to the Mauritian nurse.

Hag an barth a scryfyas. And the poet wrote...

Barny had three sets of neighbours in the hamlet where he lived, which was two miles from the village and ten from town. There was Denzil Trethewy, the old retired farmer who lived with a wife they never saw, a couple from up-country who had bought and converted one of his barns and, on the other side of the twisting road which divides the hamlet in two, Sam and Beth.

Denzil lived in an 'agricultural dwelling', an ugly bungalow, built in an Area of Outstanding Natural Beauty on condition that it was used and occupied only by a farm worker on Denzil's farm. Denzil had moved in himself and sold the lovely old farmhouse to Sam and Beth, for there were no restrictions on the use of the original buildings. His wife had always wanted a bungalow, so she was happy, and Denzil had beaten the system, which made him happy too. He had made a crafty move in selling the barns at the peak of the insane property boom, could retire in comfort from the proceeds and still retain the land, which he let to a neighbouring farmer for grazing. With high interest from his investment, and rent from the grazing, he was better off than when he had been working. 'You caint ab'm better than that,' he said.

The newcomers also thought they had a bargain, considering the price of property where they came from, and were spending thousands more on converting the place, with the intention of doing bed and breakfast for the passing tourists in the summer and going off to the sunshine in the winter. 'We came here to escape the rat-race,' they said while waiting for the first potential guests to knock on their door. 'You have no idea how stressful life can be, back there.'

Barny's cottage was a little way off from the main cluster of buildings, and had been built for a miner when the land was as productive below ground as it was above. He had a couple of bedrooms, a minute bathroom, a living room full of books and a 'compact' kitchen from which a door led to a utility room and toilet under a corrugated iron roof. He had bought it as a retreat, away from the holiday crowds, where he could write, grow things and be near his friends.

Seen from the top of the carn, which rises steeply beyond the fields to the west, the hamlet appears to be tightly clustered together, with the barns and haylofts backing their windowless walls towards the prevailing westerlies like horses in the rain. The small, stone-walled fields creep up the lower slopes of the carn and become even smaller, poorer, stonier as the incline steepens. They have been used and abandoned many times over the centuries, depending on the vagaries of climate, blockade, economic expediency and government grants. Now, when Denzil looked from his picture window, he could see the invading bracken sweeping down to envelop them all. He observed the deterioration, but his tenant was not prepared to spend money on them and neither was he. The little fields up there were not worth it when there were grants to be had for breaking in the moorland at the top, and now there was money for letting them lie idle again. On the flat stretches between the slopes and the sea the fields are larger, their patchwork of a richer material, dark brown on the plough, golden in the autumn with barley and oats and bright green on the nitrate-saturated pasture. It is a harsh, treeless view when the cold sweeps in with sleet off the ocean, and there are times when globules of foam are blown from the cliffs by storms and strike the windows, hanging there, yellow and throbbing, or slither

36

upwards, defying gravity before the fury of the wind. Yet in summer, or on those brilliantly sunny days in winter when the bracken glows like burnished copper, the colours dazzle the eye and the beholder is overwhelmed with joy at the sight of the ancient vistas stretching away into the distance.

Beyond the fields are the cliffs and the sea. The sea is always there, murmuring, roaring, inviting, threatening, fickle as a maiden in her moods.

Along the coast, eastwards, are the other farms and hamlets, strung out along the footpath, with lanes branching towards them from the road, and over in the distance is the bay, with the white tower of the lighthouse standing on its rock at the edge of the reef. Denzil Trethewy had never been on, or in, the sea in his life and had no intention of ever doing so. That was for fishermen; a neary bleddy lot, in his opinion.

Westwards, on the headland in the distance, stands another lighthouse, and beside it the foghorn, bellowing in the muggy autumns, damp winters and in the fine white mists which roll on to the land when the weather becomes too hot in summer. The sound rumbles over the stone walls, through doors and windows, out over the cliff to the horizon which almost encircles this peninsula of granite and blue elvan, and is heard by the lifeboat men going about their business in the harbour.

The road to town winds among the fields in a continual meandering, like the track of a truffling pig, and jerks convulsively through the hamlet with a couple of right-angled bends around the barns and houses. Sam and Beth's house stands a little aloof from the others when seen from among the conglomeration. It has its own cluster of cow-sheds and barns, all stone and slate, and is set back off the road, behind a hedge of tormented escallonia. The house is large and there is an open yard between the low stone wall of the garden and the barns. Chicken, geese, guinea fowl and ducks are restricted from the road by a white gate, with wire netting stapled along the bars. Some obstinate fowls persist in flying over, or sneak out when visitors leave the gate open, believing that the pickings are richer on the forbidden ground across the road. They are usually in the pot the following day, provided they are not squashed flat by the cars that kill them.

One was killed by a brand-new expensive estate car the day they received the letter from Louise. The damned thing flew up to the top bar of the gate and, thinking itself capable of sustained flight like the buzzards and ravens which soared overhead, attempted to flap across the road to the fields. The car came speeding around the corner and the gleeny, having no time to *go-backee go-backee*, hit the windscreen, broke its neck and ruptured a blood vessel somewhere in its innards. The driver braked and the car went into a skid as the gleeny's claws became entangled in the ventilation grid on the bonnet. The car hit Denzil Trethewy's barn wall (three feet thick), and the driver's passenger thrust her hands forward to save herself from injury, switching on the lights, while the driver's hand slipped from the steering wheel and inadvertently flicked the control switch of the windscreen wiper.

When Sam and Beth came out to see what had happened, after hearing the crash, the driver was already out of the vehicle inspecting the damage, closely watched by Denzil. Only the headlamps, the bumpers and radiator grill. He could drive away. His woman was sitting in the car looking dazed and white, with her head wobbling as she watched the wiper sweeping back and forth, striking the head of the dead bird on every sweep as the glass became smeared with its blood. She fainted and slumped forward in the seat, hanging over her safety belt.

'She all right?' Denzil asked as he peered in at her.

'Look at this,' the man said. 'Hundreds of pounds worth of damage. A new car.'

'She d' look a bit queer to me,' Denzil said. 'Switch your lights off, fehther. You're runnin' the battery down.'

Sam took the speckled bird off the bonnet. Beth offered to take the woman into the house.

'Somebody will have to pay for this,' the man said, glaring at them accusingly.

'Tha's right,' Denzil said before Sam could protest. 'So I should think.' He prodded the bent metal with the toe of his boot. 'There's a lot of damage there.'

'We could have been killed,' the man insisted.

'Tha's right,' Denzil agreed, while looking at the woman who was recovering under Beth's administerings. 'You ought to be more careful, driving around these roads.'

The man's temper got the better of him. 'What the hell do you mean?' he said. 'That damned bird caused it and someone is going to pay. I hope your animals are insured.'

'Edn mine,' Denzil said.

The man turned to Sam, who was holding the dangling corpse by its legs.

'It's a wild one,' Denzil said before Sam could open his mouth. 'Don't b'long to nobody.'

The man stared at him, seething with anger. Beth asked the woman if she would like to come inside for a cup of tea.

'And how much would that cost us?' the man said.

Beth closed the car door and went back into her house without another word. Sam was about to say something, but Denzil Trethewy stopped him with a barely perceptible shake of the head. 'You'd better get back on the road,' he told the man. 'You've parked in a very dangerous place. Might cause an accident.'

As they drove away the man put his head through the window. 'You'll be hearing more about this.'

They did too, a letter from his solicitors, from which they learned that the man was called Langley. They hung it up for their friends to laugh at, and Beth told Louise when she answered her letter. 'The gleeny was an old one,' she said, 'so we had it in a casserole.'

'She doesn't seem very happy,' Sam said that night after re-reading her letter. 'I suppose she can come down here for a break, if that's what she wants.'

'Don't see why not,' Beth said , 'it will be nice to see her again.'

'It's been a long time,' Sam said. 'I wonder if she's changed.'

Beth smiled an exaggerated smile. Those days, when they had been at that northern university, did seem a long time ago. More than ten years. She had met Sam there, together with Louise and her future husband and a whole host of friends, most of whom were still in touch. Louise's husband had not really been one of their circle. 'I can't remember his name,' Sam said.

'George. The children are called William and Tina,' Beth reminded him as she sat at their massive kitchen table, easing her pregnant belly under the edge. 'She can have the small room, with the view of the carn.'

Sam pulled on the long wispy strands of his thin blond beard, a gesture that Beth had come to recognise as a sign of doubt or nervousness. 'She might not like it here,' he said.

'Too bad.' She knows what we're like.' Beth giggled, remembering aspects of Louise's character that Sam, as a man, might have forgotten. Loopy Lou, they called her, a term of endearment for her artlessness which had charmed them all, at first.

They drove into town to pick her up on a day when a brisk south-easter was driving spray over the harbour wall. She came down the platform carrying a large grip and holding the hood of her waxed jacket tight against her cheek for protection from the wind. She was taller and much thinner than they remembered her,' and older, with tired eyes and pale skin. She threw the hood back and embraced them in turn.

'You've grown your hair,' Beth said. It's lovely.' Beth had a way of expressing delight with a quick smile and a slight toss of the head, accompanied by a giggling laugh.

'It's not as nice as yours,' Louise said. But hers was still jet black, while Beth's was already streaked with grey.

As they drove over the moors in Sam's old car with the torn upholstery and rusty, mud-spattered bodywork, they expected to be chatting with exchanges of news, but Louise had little to say. She stared through the window at the passing hedges and fields with listless eyes. She's tired, they thought, and did not press her into conversation. Sam hummed softly to himself, a little self-consciously, one of his own tunes, until they began the descent from the moorland towards the coast. He pulled in to the side of the hedgeless lane and stopped. Beyond the tiny, stone-walled fields, spotted with cows, the black headland was stark against the green sea, with white-headed waves rolling onshore from the distant horizon. There was a vast space of sea and sky before them.

Sam said, 'Well, there it is. The large house with the white walls.'

'It's beautiful,' Louise said. 'You are lucky living here,'

'I suppose so,' Sam said. 'But I belong here. This is my home. I was born here. '

'And me,' Beth said, smiling.

'I don't have a home,' Louise sighed.

The rain from the previous night had left the fields glistening, and the lane ran with water, trickling off into the ditches. In their yard, by the house, there were pools of mud, and as they entered by the back door Louise wiped her heavy men's brogues on the threadbare mat. Inside, were heaps of rubber boots, old socks and a sack of coal. Coats and waterproofs hung in a bulging mass behind the door.

'There's mud on my shoes,' Louise said.

'Never mind,' Beth said, and led the way in through the passage to the huge kitchen.

But Louise turned her shoe on edge, trying to remove a smear of mud from the welt. 'I'll take them off.'

'Don't worry about it,' Sam said.

She followed them, in her stockinged feet, into the kitchen, where Beth took a massive saucepan from the Rayburn and poured the partly heated water into an electric kettle to boil up for tea.

'Where's Susy?' Louise asked, and she clasped her feet together under her chair, to protect them from the cold stone floor.

'Over with Barny.'

'Who's Barny?'

'Our neighbour,' Sam said. 'He's a poet.'

They showed her up to her bedroom, where she unpacked her things and placed them neatly in the wardrobe and drawers, refolding those items which had become crumpled in transport. While Beth prepared the meal, Sam went over for Susy and was gone for more than an hour.

'Where is he?' Louise asked when she came down to rejoin Beth. 'Do you think they are all right?'

'Probably chatting about music. Barny is writing some lyrics for Sam and Goldie, a fellow who sings with the band.'

Louise was standing against the kitchen table, her hands thrust deep into the front pockets of her fisherman's smock, watching everything that Beth was doing. She was evidently tense, wanting to talk, a look of anxiety on her face, and her shoulders were hunched up, as if she were trying to withdraw into herself. Beth asked her about mutual acquaintances at college, learning that she had no news of any of them, having lost touch with nearly everyone since her marriage, but she avoided the most obvious questions, which were why was she here and what was so evidently troubling her.

'I don't know anyone famous,' Louise said, 'like poets and people like that, even though my father is an actor.' There was a trace of envy in her voice, as if she had been somehow deprived, like someone who had arrived at a destination after taking a wrong turning and missing all the best scenery.

'Barny's not famous,' Beth said. 'He's not had much published, just a few things locally by the poetry group, I think. I don't know what. I've never seen any of it.' She offered one of her little grimaces, a wry smile and a slight nod. 'He's just a nice man. A bit lonely, I think, although he doesn't know it.'

Beth remembered how Louise had been at college; the total unworld-liness, the sudden moods of exuberance, the withdrawal into herself and the inability to be at ease with others, the panic over exams, the fearful reserve which was occasionally broken by excessive behaviour and coarse language as a show of sophistication, to be followed by remorse. 'Did I offend you? I'm not really like that.' The behaviour of a teenager. She seemed not to have changed.

41

Sam came back with Susy, who was filthy with earth and mud, and they sat down to eat. Throughout the meal, Louise watched little Susy, talking to her in gurgling expressions like, 'Aren't you lubly. Who got a dirty face den?' Speaking to the child in cooing baby talk, in contrast to Beth, who addressed her little daughter as if she were a fully receptive individual, and the child stared unblinkingly and without expression at Louise as Beth tipped spoonfuls of food into the smeary mouth.

'How old are yours?' Sam asked.

'Tina's seven, William's four.' Her eyes suddenly filled with tears, which she absorbed on a tissue, saying, 'I do miss them. I hope they are all right.'

'Course they are,' Sam said. 'George is with them.'

'No. They're with his parents.' She rose from the table and began taking dishes to the sink, looking for something to do, unable to relax. Sam and Beth exchanged glances of exasperation.

'Come out and see the animals,' Beth said. 'Leave all that stuff until the water is hot.'

They went out in the yard and Beth led the way through a wide gate which opened onto a grassed field. The cackle of geese greeted them, and a white gander came hissing towards them, with its neck stretched out and its beak open to reveal a row of sharply serrated teeth.

'Don't worry,' Beth said. 'It's only his greeting ceremony. He's quite good. We had to get rid of his father. Attacked everybody who came through the yard.'

Louise cowered behind Beth, pretending not to be frightened of the bird, and they went out to where two goats were browsing beside the wire fence. The animals ran to greet them, almost knocking Beth over as they rubbed against her thighs. The larger of the two animals reared up on its hind legs and brought its head down to within inches of Louise, crashing its forelegs to the ground in an audible thump.

'Oh!' Louise said, backing away in alarm.

'She's only saying hello,' Beth said. She sat on her haunches on the ground, and the two animals competed for her affection, pushing against her until she fell over.

Louise stood watching timidly. 'They're lovely,' she said, 'but mind they don't kick your belly. Be careful of the baby.'

'Goats don't kick. Don't worry.'

Louise kept well out of the way of the animals until Beth led them into the stalls in one of the barns. They locked up the geese and chickens. The guinea fowls flew to the top of a sycamore tree in the yard. 'The foxes will get them, stupid birds,' Beth said. 'But they won't go in.'

'You have a good life, here, Beth. I envy you'

'It's all right,' Beth said, 'Suits me.'

They had a quick look at the large, enclosed vegetable garden before dark and returned to the house. Sam had cleared up the kitchen and was playing with Susy on the floor. Beth took the child up to bed, leaving Sam to entertain their guest. He was at a loss as to what to say to her. She was a bundle of nerves, refusing to sit down and relax at the table.

'Well,' Sam said, pulling his thin beard. 'Well, well. So here you are.'

Next morning, Louise was awake early. She had not slept well, for the pictures troubled her. They came upon her and disturbed her slumbers with all the terrifying shapeless forms which never materialised into tangible entities from the chaos of lurid colour swirling in a three-dimensional vortex somewhere between her eyes and her mind. She could not see what they were but knew they were evil, her bogey men. If only she could see them and recognise their horrible faces she could either face them or run away, but they would not come out in front of her eyes, always lurking in the dark, back out of sight, forever threatening.

She washed and dressed, made the bed and tidied the room before descending the wide old stairs to the confusion of the kitchen. Her intention was to sit there drinking tea until the others came down and then go out, but Beth was already there, quietly laying the table.

'I think I'll go for a walk before breakfast,' Louise said. 'Just along the lane.'

'All right, if that's what you want.'

But Louise stayed there because it was raining. Through the big window of the sitting room she could see the dark clouds looming over the carn. She did not know what to do with herself, and began to wish she had not come here, for the reunion was not proceeding as anticipated. She felt utterly superfluous and alone.

'It's only a few showers,'Beth said. 'We can go for a walk this afternoon and call in to see Barny.'

Her first impression upon entering Barny's cottage was of a wonderland of books. There were scores, hundreds of them. One entire wall was of shelves filled with an untidy disarray of lines and stacks of books, some old with cracked and faded spines, rows of paperbacks and others in new and colourful jackets. Among the chaos were magazines and papers folded between volumes on Greek mythology, geology, atlases, birds, plants, all the major poets, many with pieces of paper protruding as markers from between the pages. On his desk was a new electronic typewriter, somehow incongruous in its statement of modern technology among the dog-eared dictionaries, bits of scribbled paper, jars of pens, splashes of white correction fluid and a coverless thesaurus, yellow with age and the accumulated stains of spilled coffee. A further concession to modern technology was an expensive-looking set of hi-fi equipment, with rows of compact discs, built-in among the shelves.

A fire burned in the rough granite fireplace, warming the room, which was carpeted in an oatmeal berber, and flicked a warm glow from the white, evening-washed walls. There were two small armchairs, a sagging sofa draped in an old candlewick bedspread, and two chairs at a wooden table, upon which more books were piled beside a vase of bursting pussy willows and daffodils. Before the sofa was a long low double-shelved coffee table of unpolished elm, which held a piece of driftwood, sculpted by the sea and bleached by salt and age.

'Is it all right,' Louise said, 'to come in?'

'Yes, of course. Barny won't mind. People are always coming in. I'll put the kettle on. He shouldn't be long.'

Beth went into the kitchen, which was remarkably tidy after the sitting room, and Louise followed her, nervously, unwilling to be discovered alone, as an intruder, should the owner return. 'Doesn't he lock the door?'

'No. Not unless he goes away, when we have the key. He never locks it when he's here, in case someone comes to see him.' She knew which drawer to open, which cupboard to reach into for tea and mugs, as if the kitchen was as familiar as her own.

'Are you sure he won't mind?' Louise kept asking. 'I wouldn't want anyone searching through my house.'

Such familiarity in someone else's home was something she had never encountered before and she thought Beth was being forward in presuming that Barny would not object to them abusing his hospitality. She stood in the little kitchen, moving aside each time Beth went to and fro, a worried look on her face.

'I'll go into town,' Louise said. 'And find bed and breakfast or something. You have enough to do.'

Beth led the way into the sitting room and put the mugs on the low table. 'Why? You don't have to do that. We told you, you can stay with us

44

as long as you like. There's plenty of room, and you can give me some help about the place. There's always plenty to do.'

Before she sat down, Louise suddenly hugged her close, trembling slightly with emotion.

'Don't worry,' Beth said. 'We'll take care of you.'

'Oh, Beth,' Louise sobbed. 'You're so good. I do love you.'

'Don't be silly.' Beth said, as she pulled away and sat down on the sofa, a little embarrassed at this emotional outburst,

'I just don't know what to do,' Louise said, collapsing into one of the chairs. 'I just don't know.'

She was near to tears, and fought them back, fearful that the man should come in and find her thus. She dreaded meeting him. She wanted to meet no one, and wished she had not agreed to come to this house, although it was to such a house that she had dreamed of escaping. The books, the cosy firelight in the darkening evening, the comfortable chairs and the soft, untidy sofa, were all that she had yearned for in that absurd regimentation she had left behind. She looked at Beth's round belly, and thought of her own children, of the decisions to be made. 'You are good for me, Beth. I do love you.'

In the silence that followed, she stared unseeingly at an inscription carved into a piece of polished driftwood over the fire. It was in a foreign language.

An laver coth, yu lavar gwyr –
Byth dorn re ver dhe'n tavas re hyr
Mes den hep tavas a-gollas y dyr.

Barny came in half an hour later, when the two women were sitting quietly staring into the fire, Beth with her two hands folded over her belly, feeling the movements of her child, Louise with her mind a merciful blank, the dusk filling the room with shadows around the firelight.

He was greying, his beard streaked and the hair, tangling from underneath his peaked cap, silver and soft. He was wearing a pair of faded blue cords and a navy guernsey which fitted tightly over his shoulders and slim waist. His arms were holding a large flower pot, containing a bushy camellia, which he put down at the door. The cap was removed and thrown on to the table as he entered, revealing a thinning scalp. Louise avoided a direct gaze as he hugged Beth, with one arm around her shoulders, and remained seated, still uncertain of his reaction to finding them here.

'This is Louise,' Beth said, and Louise stood up, holding out her hand. He was shorter than she, came up to her eyes, yet, as they took each other's hands, Louise felt that he was looking down at her. He had the most expressive eyes she had ever looked into. They were dark brown, almost black, quite narrow and deep set, with a trace of wrinkle at the corner when he smiled. He looked at her, she thought, as one might gaze upon a dove with a broken wing or a petal bruised by rain. She was disconcerted by his gaze, yet could not withdraw her own, for he held her as if in an embrace, holding her close to him in intimate contact. Despite his kindly expression, however, he was searching her, looking for something deep inside her, and she blushed at what he might discover, turning away, but was compelled to return again and submit to the scrutiny. He smiled, as if he had found some secret hoard of treasure, known only to himself.

'Hello Louise,' he said in a deep, soft but confident voice. 'Sit down. Make yourself at home.' There was a strong accent, much stronger than Beth's or Sam's, and as he spoke to Beth, Louise returned to her chair, utterly perplexed, blushing, pretending interest in the books in order to hide her face.

This was what she wanted: the ageing hippy of her foolish, speculative day-dreams, a man of words and creativity, someone to whom she could relate. She realised immediately that she had nothing to offer him, however. Such a man would seek beauty and intellectual stimulus, and her own body was repulsive, her mind confused. He would not give her a second look. She found herself shrinking from him and sat in silence or answered in monotones when they attempted to draw her into the conversation, and was astonished when he said, as they were leaving to walk across to Beth's house in the darkness and silence of the drizzly dusk, 'How about coming over to the pub this evening? See what you think of the aborigines?'

'OK,' she said.

The pub in the village was set back from the road, in a cluster of houses forming three sides of an open square. There was one large room inside, the saloon bar, public bars having long since been done away with, he told her. There was a huddle of figures at the bar, others sat at tables and two young men were playing pool. Some women, laughing loudly at coarse banter with the men and evidently spilled over from some meeting in the

46

village, were sitting around a couple of tables pulled together near the curtained window. Barny led Louise to a quiet corner near the pool players, where he took off his hat and coat and went to the bar.

Louise looked around, somewhat surreptitiously, at all the men in the place. They seemed terribly rough and uncouth, unshaven, wearing dirty, working clothes. Barny seemed to know most of them, acknowledging their crude greetings or brief nods of recognition. She could not understand half of what they were saying. Some of the men eyed her up, which she found disconcerting. She dreaded the possibility of their unwashed bodies coming anywhere near, and hoped that Barny had no intention of inviting any of them over to meet her. There was one particular individual who put his arms around Barny's neck and spoke earnestly into his ear as he waited to be served. He was evidently drunk and his face contorted with effort as he tried to form coherent sentences, with his eyes glazing over in a cynical smile. Barny placed a drink in front of him, patting him on the back before returning to Louise with an indulgent smile on his lips.

The man smiled at her when she glanced over at him, and she hastily averted her eyes.

'Who is that man?' She asked. 'Did you buy him a drink? He seems already drunk, to me.'

Barny looked over his beer towards the bar. 'I don't know who he is,' he said. 'One of the oddballs who come here to live for a while before moving on. The place is full of them. I did buy him a drink. Yes.'

'Do you think it wise to buy drinks for drunken strangers?' she said. 'Will you be able to get rid of him if he comes over? Do you think he might become violent?'

Barny turned his eyes to hers. 'You'll have to ask me one question at a time,' he said. 'My old brain gets confused with two or three answers to sort out at once. Firstly, he is not a stranger. Secondly, he never gets violent. He gets randy, but no one will oblige, except Pissy Lilly, the local tart, and she's gone away for dehydration. That's why he's drunk tonight, drowning his sorrows, of which he has many.'

'I don't understand, I'm sorry. First you said you didn't know him, and...'

'No, I didn't. I said I didn't know who he was. Not quite the same thing.' He looked at her over his drink, grinning.

'I don't understand,' she said.

'Well... .'

He put down his glass, and leaned over the table towards her and said, in low confiding tones, 'He sez... .' He glanced around in a theatrically furtive manner. 'He sez, he's called Nathaniel, Nat, but I know for a fact that when he first came down here, he was called Matt. So, as I said, I don't know who the hell he is. You will find scores like him down here, the place is full of them. I know *what* he is. He's an author... another bloody crank.'

'You're making fun of me,' she said.

'He dismissed the subject of Nat/Matt with a shrug. 'Have it your own way. I hope it's fine tomorrow. I want to get my runner beans in.'

Her curiosity got the better of her. The place seemed full of characters, writers, painters, poets; she had never encountered so many before in her life. They intrigued her. 'What's he writing?'

Barny grinned, and she added, 'Well, he does look like everybody's idea of a tormented poet. Oh, sorry.'

'That's quite all right. We get used to it. But you are right about Nathaniel. He certainly looks the part, with his wide brimmed hat, wild grey locks and flowing beard. He's not often drunk, to tell the truth, and I only discovered he is a writer because a little while back he got too drunk to walk and I took him home, for which he is eternally grateful when he's pissed. When he's sober he doesn't remember me. Strange.'

'I can't believe that.' Louise said. 'He's probably too embarrassed to speak to you.'

'Usually, he won't speak to anyone, just a mumbled greeting, if you can call it that, but that night he insisted on me coming in and finishing a bottle of wine with him. That's when he told me about himself.'

'He looks very intense.' Louise said. 'What does he write?'

'Nothing! Well, just letters.'

Louise said, 'Nothing? What do you mean, nothing? How can he be an author if he doesn't write?'

'Oh. There's plenty of them around here. Half the cottages in the parish are populated by writers who don't write, painters who don't paint, sculptors who don't sculpt, dyers, weavers and spinners looking for colour and texture in their lives. That's what they come here for, to be creative.'

'I wish you wouldn't make fun of me.' she said. 'You don't have to lie to me.'

Oh Lord, Barny thought, hasn't the woman any sense of humour at all? 'Ask him,' he challenged, 'If you don't believe me.'

Of course she could not do that. 'Well,' she said, 'if he is a writer, he must write something. What happened when you took him home? What did he tell you?'

Ah, Barny thought, A spark of life. 'You are quite sure you want me to tell you? Yes? Right then, he writes letters to himself.'

He looked at her blankly, a look which she returned. An irrepressible smile curled the corners of his lips and, by the smile on her own lips she let it be known that she knew he was kidding her. Barny made sure no one was within earshot.

'He used to write books.' he said, 'novels, and although they were all turned down by publishers and agents he kept on trying. Five, I think he said, all epics on a continuing theme, the power struggle in a bee hive. It has fifty thousand characters and a sting in the tail. The sterile workers want a taste of royal jelly so they can all develop into queens and have a crack at screwing the drones. It's an allegory on feminism. There are not enough drones to go round; one flying fuck and they are dead, after all. The workers all become lesbian queens and the colony dies out.'

Barny took another sip of his beer. 'Makes *Watership Down* and *The Badger Book* look like Enid Blyton.'

Louise burst out laughing and all the men in the pub turned to look at her.

'You don't believe me, do you?' Barny said.

She was utterly transformed by laughter. Her eyes lit up and her body relaxed as the tension left her. She showed her teeth and ignored the glances of the men, unaware of their curiosity.

'Of course I don't believe you.'

'I think he's a genius.'

He had not laughed with her, but watched with incredulity as the sullen girl became a vivacious woman, ready to challenge him with confidence. He felt a certain smug self-satisfaction in the knowledge that the men would be envious of his ability to stimulate her. The long black hair fell over her shoulders as she folded her arms on the table and leaned towards him, looking into his eyes. It was a public intimacy and he half expected her to reach for his hand, and he didn't want that. Not here, not now. Nathaniel raised his glass to him in a gesture of thanks and Barny returned it, with a nod and a sip.

'Every week,' Barny said, 'he reads the literary pages of the so-called quality press, to see what was being published and acclaimed, and he told me, that night, that the reviews were more concerned with the biographies and correspondence of the authors than with their work, most of which is soon forgotten or never read. What's the point of creating literature, he said, when the public is more interested in the scandalous sex life of the writer.'

'Are you talking about yourself. ?'

That was a bit too astute an observation, he thought. My sex life is far from scandalous. It is dead boring. 'Yeah, well, Nathaniel decided to reverse the process and become famous for his letters first. He has reams of correspondence, acres of it, all carefully annotated and filed away. He showed it to me. He writes to everybody who's famous, telling them all sorts of intimate details of his life, most of which are completely fictitious but he says this applies to most published accounts of writers lives, so what's the difference?'

'You're still kidding,' Louise said. 'You needn't look so serious.'

'It's all true, I tell you. He refers to his books as if they were established classics, and it's surprising how many famous people reply to him. They're afraid to admit they have never heard of him, that they are not well read, you see. Some of them even say how much they enjoyed the books, going on about the intellectual and allegorical aspects of the work just as they do on those pretentious arts programmes on Radio Three. You must have heard them. Most of them, Nat said, are simply restating his own comments, but in more obtuse language. He loves it. Sooner or later, he says, they will have to publish his novels, even if he is dead, and they can all claim their letters were written about 'Work in Progress'. He might be right,'

Louise shook her head at his apparent ingenuity with words. 'You silly fool. You're making it all up.' And then, after a pause, 'You are a lovely man, Barny.'

'Ask Shimshai, if you don't believe me. He received a letter from Nat, or Matt, whoever he is, about his own book. I'll get him to show it to you. He reads it when he's depressed, to cheer himself up.'

'Shimshai ? He's in the Bible.'

'Yes, Shimshai the scribe. Funny thing is that Nat, when he was Matt, without the gloss, I suppose, originally came down here, he said, to grow organic vegetables. He gave it up after a while, said all this natural manure is just a load of old bullshit.'

When he drove her back to his cottage, she was more relaxed than he had seen her before, although it was evident that she thought he had been telling her lies, attempting to make fun of her gullibility and ignorance of the people in the area, and was congratulating herself in having the courage to retaliate. Barny could not tell her that all the anecdotes about Nat and the other characters in the pub were true. Well, yes, he had done, but she would not believe him, so he let it lie.

'Have some coffee before you go across,' he said.

'I'd better not, thanks.'

'OK. As you wish.'

He guided her across the road to Sam and Beth's with his electric torch, and she said, 'That's a powerful light you have there.'

He switched it off, and they were in total blackness, and she was scared of the dark. 'Switch it on,' she said, and he took her to the door.

'A good torch is essential out here, especially when there is a power cut.'

'I have enjoyed this evening,' she said.

Yes, he thought, and so have I. It's been a bit of a strain, but I enjoyed it.

'I'm going into town tomorrow, if you'd like to come. See a bit more of the place, a few more eccentrics.'

Beth was still up, and Louise insisted on helping with the washing-up before going to her room with a hot-water bottle. She tried to read, shivering under the duvet, and eventually slept in a thick pullover, dreaming at first of Barny, until the bogey men woke her and she cried into the pillow.

CHAPTER THREE

Yn Pow Sawsen yma hy. In the land of the Saxons is she.

'I'm all alone. Nobody cares about me. I *want* to die.' The haggard woman stubbed out the butt end of a cigarette from which she had just lit another. 'It ain't easy,' she said. 'I've tried three times.'

'I tried to get out,' Loopy Lou told her, 'when they left the door open, but they caught me in the foyer. They injected me.'

The woman was not listening. 'Gas,' she said, 'razor blades, pills. He found me every time. When they send me home, he'll beat me up.' Her voice was resigned, her gaze vacant, like one dreaming aloud. 'I've got four kids by him. He ain't never given me no money.'

Louise listened to her rambling on, the tales of misery, beatings, perversion. She must be weak to put up with it, she thought, stupid woman, and she reassured herself that she had made the right decision in escaping from domesticity. The poor woman was a born loser and, if she would only admit it, simply crying for help. Such people had neither the will nor the determination of Louise, to do it irrevocably, of her own free will. Three times! To fail three times was absurd.

'Three times,' she wept to the doctor, 'I was raped three times.'

Droklam war'n mor. An accident at sea.

Boy Steve was so like his father in looks that everybody said it, 'Why, zackly like his fehther,' assuming he would be like him in nature too, but in this they were mistaken. Boy Steve was as impetuous as Father Steve was cautious, and known for a quick temper, which could change as rapidly to laughter. He was as dark in compexion as in temperament, clean shaven but, as like as not, with a stubble on his chin. His dark eyes were quick to laughter, yet regarded strangers with suspicion. He was not working, for the tides were all wrong, and he told his parents he was off for a ja'nt.

With these nor' westerlies, you can be under blue skies one minute and in a heavy shower the next, that's why he was taking his wellies and waterproof gear, he told Steve and Mary, but he didn't tell them about the torch or that he was going down the mine. They would object now as when he was an adventurous boy. He parked his car just off the road, and walked down the track to the cove. You can't go anywhere these days, he observed, without finding somebody parked in your space. The adit was only a mile or so west of the town, but it was quicker to drive out and walk down the lane and there was also less likelihood of anyone seeing him making off along the cliffs. He could never understand it, but he always felt uneasy if people saw him going out there alone. Silly! It was a long time, Boy Steve remembered, since he had been down the bal, but there was no harm in having a look. He hitched the canvas bag higher on his shoulder and stepped out, towards the cliff. The sea was rising under the strengthening wind, so just as well the tides were wrong, he thought; it will be rough enough 'safnoon. He followed the coastal footpath for a while and then made his way along the narrow ledge, hewed out by miners, halfway down the cliff. Fair old drop here, he remembered, wouldn't have much chance if you fell overboard.

The opening into the cliff was some five feet high and between two and three feet wide at the entrance, becoming narrower as it went in, so the adit was a big one, and must have been used as an entrance as well as for drainage. Barny-the-Bard would know about these things. Boy Steve unslung his pack and slipped the waterproofs on, for the roof was dripping a heavy curtain of water into a stream which ran out and trickled down the cliff. He looked back at the sea below him and the racing clouds above, realised that he had forgotten how nervous he had felt about going down here as a boy, pulled his hood up and tried the torch before slipping it up his sleeve with a sigh of determination.

The sides of the adit were red with stains from the water, here and there bright green with copper oxides or trailing iron from a rusty spike driven into the rock and abandoned. How anyone could be a miner he could not imagine. Fancy spending your life down here. The place was creepy, all echoes and drips. Thousands of tons of rock hanging over your head. Boy Steve decided he would not go very far in. The drips eased when he reached the solid granite. Just a bit further, he thought. When he had penetrated far enough to lose the drips entirely, and there was a damp mixture of spoil and soil at his feet, he saw other footprints, wellie prints, and only one set, going in, so whoever had made them was still in here, or had come out by an entrance he didn't know of. They, somebody, had beaten him to it. 'There wudn no other way out when I was a boy,' he said to himself, and proceeded quietly forward into the pitch darkness, showing as little light as possible. The adit was an oval tube cut into the bedrock of granite for the purpose of draining the mines high on the moors. There had been no metal at the entrance, no lodes to follow in but, as he penetrated further, he reached the workings, and the adit opened out into a chamber the size of a Wesleyan chapel, the little one by the road out of town say, and this was as far as he had dared venture as a boy. It was from here that he saw the other light.

He switched off his torch. Someone was sitting beside an old iron wheel, writing in a note book, with a torch wedged in the rusty spokes above their head. He saw the person pick up what Boy Steve first thought was a calculator, turn a dial on it, and listen. A bleddy geiger counter, he thought. I might have known it. He could hear the clicking as it read the level of radioactivity, and he shone his own torch full at the man.

The noise she made wasn't exactly a scream, but it was certainly a cry of alarm, and when Boy Steve approached her he was full of apologies.

'Katie Stevens!' he cried. 'It's you! I'm sorry. I didn't mean to startle 'ee.'

'Steve Trevorrow!' she said in relief. 'What ever are you doing in here?'

'Oh, just out for a bit of a walk. Makes a change from the promenade.' And he paused, refusing to ask the obvious.

'Well,' Katie said. 'I wish you'd knock, next time.'

He laughed, and his voice echoed around the chamber, reverberating into the tunnels leading off under the farms and moors high above them. 'It's a bit creepy in here, isn't it?' he said.

And now the girl laughed. 'I'm used to it. And there's nothing to worry about. There aren't any *buccas* left.'

'I'm not so sure. Are you a geologist, then?'

'No. A biologist.'

He knew she had been away to university, but not what she had read there. Her family, he had learned, was never mentioned in his family's house. He knew little about her, only that she was the illegitimate daughter of Sarah Stevens, a quiet little woman who only spoke to his father when his mother was not present. 'Hello, Steven,' she would say, in a quiet little voice from a mouth that would not melt butter. She must have been hot enough at least once in her life, Boy Steve thought, to produce a girl like Katie.

'Biologist?' he queried, obviously intrigued at what life she expected to find here, deep in the darkness of the mine.

'Bats,' she said. 'I'm studying bats.'

'Oh.' He was not convinced. 'Then why the geiger counter ?' he asked, unable to keep the suspicion from his voice.

She had a completely uninhibited laugh, there are not many who have, and her teeth showed white in the torchlight as she handed him her instrument.

'It's a bat detector,' she said. 'The clicking is the amplified sound of their sonar system. Listen.'

She increased the volume of the device by means of a dial, and the clickings echoed briefly around them before she quickly turned it down. 'They are very susceptible to disturbance at this time of year,' she said.

'Where are they.' he asked.

'Up there. In crevices in the roof. They're just waking up from hibernation, but there doesn't seem to be as many as I thought, though they may be further in. I was expecting to find two or three hundred. Perhaps more.'

'Really? I've seen them flying about the cliffs in summer, and thought they flew off south for the winter, like birds.'

'No, they stay here, hibernating in the mines,' Katie said. 'They're getting agitated. I think we ought to go. Well, I'm going. You can stay, but they won't like it.'

'No, no.' I'll come out with you.' He shone his torch up to the top of the stope. 'What kind are they?' he asked as he thought, if there are crevices for bats to hide in up there, the whole rock might be unstable.

'Greater Horseshoes,' she said. 'Come on then, let's leave them alone.'

Getting out from the adits is always easier than going in, for the light gradually increases from the utter, unimaginable blackness of total darkness to the gloom and then the glare as daylight approaches. There was a shower falling when they reached the cliff, so they stayed in the entrance of the adit for a while, reluctant to go back to their cars, although both were equipped to cope with any rain. It was a short shower and, when it passed, they came out on to the narrow ledge in the cliff and climbed up to the path.

'No one would know the adit was there,' Boy Steve said.

'No.'

They removed their waterproofs, and Katie looked out over the sea, brushing her brown hair from her eyes.

'Look at that,' she said, and indicated a large yacht cruising up the coast, just offshore.

'Oh Yes. Look at that, all right' Boy Steve said. 'There's some money's worth there, eh? Ten times more than our fishing boat. For a toy, look. She must be going for shelter in the bay. The wind is rising.'

'She has lovely lines,' Katie said.

And so have you, he thought. And nice eyes too. He had not been able to see her properly in the gloom of the adit, but now he took a long look at her, and found her doing the same to him. They both laughed, and he looked back to the sea.

'You can't earn that kind of money by hard work,' he said. 'Wonder who she belongs to?'

Katie rummaged in her pack and produced a small pair of binoculars. She sat down and steadied her elbows against her knees, with the lenses to her eyes. 'She's called *Adventuress*,' she said. 'That name seems familiar.'

'Yes. She's Simon Sweeting's yacht,' he said. 'Or one of them. He has a couple of racers too. This one is his second home and office. A tax- deductible expense, I expect. Not bad, eh? To tell you the truth, it's because of him I came down here. If he's bought Penavon, and all that goes with it, then he would be acquiring the old mines too, and all the minerals in them. According to Barny-the-Bard there are still rich lodes to be worked if ever the price was right. It could bring a lot of work to the area.'

Katie handed him the glasses and he looked at the yacht in silence. Sarah Stevens' maid, he thought. She's like her mother, small and dainty, with that same air of self-assurance. A woman his mother could never abide, for some reason.

'Yes, I can read the name, *Adventuress. Anethyores*... . Sounds better in the old language.'

'Can you speak it?'

'No, not really, I just pick up a few words from Barny-the-Bard. Do you know him?

'Of course I do. He's a friend of Mam's.'

'That's part of the language.'

'What is?'

'Mam, Mother. *Mamyeth*, mother tongue. *Mamvro*, motherland.'

'Is there a word for bats?'

'I don't know. I 'spect so.'

Katie looked at him. He had not dropped the binoculars from his eyes, but now he did and caught her looking at him. 'You're like your father,' she said.

'He doesn't think so. We quarrel all the time. Nothing serious; it'll be better when I get my own place. Everything's gone into the boat.'

'You are still living at home, then?'

'Yeah. Same as you. You spend a lot of time in old mines, do you?' he asked. 'Looking for bats?'

'Mines and caves. Trees, houses, depends what species I'm studying.'

'I thought you might be someone working for Simon Sweeting when I first saw you,' Boy Steve told her. 'Looking for uranium.'

'Not likely. I think he's bad news.'

'Why ? He could do a lot of good for the area.'

'We'll see.' Katie said.

He thought about that, not wishing to disagree with her over someone he knew very little about, said nothing for once. Yes, she was very like her mother, he thought. Quiet, yet with a certain self-confidence. 'We'll see.' with that modest smile.

So they went back through the wet grass, up the the lane to the coastal road, and when they reached the cars, he said, 'You shouldn't go down these adits on your own.'

'I'm used to it. I told you.'

'That's not the point. Anything might happen down there. A slight slip, or a dropped torch, a twisted ankle, minor things in the open, and you're in serious trouble.'

'I've got my work to do. I have asked one or two to come down with me, but they're all too busy, or too scared.'

'Well, p'rhaps, provided you go down on days when I'm ashore, I could come with you. I might learn something.'

'All right then,' Katie said. 'Give me a ring.'

'At home ?'

'Of course. Where else?'

Barny stood over the newly planted camellia. He had put it beside the path, near the door, where it would be sheltered from the worst of the westerly gales. Pink, semi-double, he thought, late blooming to miss the frosts, and self-shedding so that the bush would not be full of faded blossoms. He would have to wait a while to see that.

Oh, my life, he thought, talk about faded blossoms, I forgot all about Louise. He shoved the blade of his shovel into the ground with his boot and hurried in to wash and change out of his old gardening clothes. Time I threw them away, he thought.

Louise had been waiting for him, although pretending to be engrossed in helping Beth about the kitchen and garden. He apologised for being late, and as a compensation drove the long way in, over the moors, to show her the scenery. As they climbed the hill the sky cleared to a deep blue from which the sun warmed the interior of the car. He was very quiet, and she thought she was boring him. They passed a circle of granite rocks, tall, encrusted in lichen. Louise looked at them as the car passed by and asked what they were.

'Stones,' Barny said. 'Keep away from them. They're dangerous.'

'What do you mean? Unstable?'

He turned to her suddenly, suspecting she had been reading his mind.

'They're unpredictable,' he said. 'Magic.' And Louise looked back at the stones without comment.

In the streets of the town he met numerous acquaintances who greeted him cheerfully or stopped to exchange news and enquiries. 'Hi, Zeke. 'afnoon, Nat. Yow! Hello, Sarah.'

'You seem to know everyone.'

'It's a small town,' he said. ' 'llo, Ste' Tell 'n not to forget my roof.'

'I'll tell 'n,' Boy Steve said. *'Dew genes.'*

Barny laughed. *'Dew genes,'* he said as they left him. *'Da dha weles omma.'*

'What was all that about?' Louise said.

'Oh. Just greetings. God be with you. Good to see you here. He's picking up quite a bit.'

Boy Steve turned to look at Barny. *'Us benen noweth dhys?'* he wondered. Is there a woman new, to you?

Barny showed Louise the town, where his father lived, where his grandparents had lived, where his friends lived, where they had played as children, and they sat for a while on an old wall by the harbour, watching the people passing by. The tide was going out and long sweeps of ground swell entered the harbour. Some fishermen were landing fish on the quay.

'I'm surprised they've been out in this,' Barny said.

'It looks calm enough.'

'It is in here. Let's go out and have a look outside,' he said.

He led her through the narrow streets to a small beach on the northern side of the town, where they felt the force of the wind in their faces. There was a large white yacht at anchor in the bay and they saw the coastguard in the lookout on the headland watching it through binoculars. In the lee of the headland the sea was fairly smooth, but over the exposed reaches of the bay white-capped waves spilled plumes of flying spray. The light was now intense from the sun behind them, and it shone off the white bellies of flights of birds they could see struggling against the wind. There were gannets, kittiwakes, a few gulls and parties of auks, skimming over the crests. There were two small fishing boats offshore, each with a couple of men aboard, wearing yellow plastic leggings and smocks.

'I remember,' Barny said, 'when their waterproofs were made of heavy cotton, soaked in linseed oil. They were called 'barwells.' I don't know where the word originated. They used to stink.'

'What are they catching?' Louise asked, as if she had not been listening to him.

'Fish.'

Her reaction was to say, quite seriously. 'What kind of fish?' Evidently not appreciating his ironic comment.

'I don't know. I don't know anything about fishing. Bass, I expect. Something expensive, to be out in this.'

'Are they your friends?'

'No. I don't know them,' he said. And then, 'Yes. They're after bass. I can see the net floats. Mackerel are caught with hand lines in this close. They shouldn't be out in this weather, if you ask me. I think I'll nip back to the car for my binoculars.' And he ran off, leaving her to watch the scene alone.

The flights of birds were whirring past the boats and many of them had come to rest on the surface. The two men in the nearest boat began hauling their nets, pulling them aboard by hand. They were wearing rubber gloves, red against the yellow of their waterproofs and the deep blue sea.

'Here,' Barny said, when he returned. 'Have a look.'

The first floats came over the gunwale, then the pale green of the monofilament nets. She could see the silver scales of fish, gleaming in the sunlight, and smaller, black and white, limp, irregular shapes tangled among them.

'Oh,' she said. 'What a lot of fish. What are the black and white ones?'

Barny took the binoculars, and looked at the activity on the sea, all in bright colours, with the white-crested waves in the distance. Both crews were now hauling, shaking the fish loose as they came over the gunwale.

'Birds,' he said. 'Razorbills and Guillemots.'

The men were disentangling the dead bodies of birds and throwing them over the stern. Soon, a line of black and white corpses, with their heads hanging below the surface, were drifting away from the boats, strung out on the line of current among the close-packed flocks of other birds which ignored them and continued diving, seeking the same shoals of sprat which had brought the bass so close inshore. Barny counted the corpses.

'That's sixty-eight,' he said. From only two boats on one haul. They must be killing hundreds... thousands.'

'Can't you stop them?' Louise said. 'It's so cruel.'

To the birds, he wondered, or to the fish? Whether it was more agonising to drown in the sea, or to expire slowly, gasping for water in fresh air. Her question and statement were from the urban consciousness, isolated from that which provided it with sustenance. He put the binoculars to his eyes and watched the men clearing the nets. One of them saw him looking, and called to the other crew, raising his voice above the noise of the wind and the throbbing engine. All four looked to shore, with the boats pitching alarmingly into the rising swell as the flying spray showered over them, luminous with rainbows, then they shrugged and resumed their work.

'At least,' Barny said. 'They're not trying to hide what they're doing. I've seen them off the coast putting the bodies into plastic bags weighted with stones before chucking them overboard. I've seen the harbour littered with corpses when bad weather has forced them to clear the nets on the moorings.' He dropped the binoculars and handed them to her. 'These monofilament nets catch everything - birds, seals, dolphins, turtles... it's happening all over the world, but what can I do about it? The men have to make a living.'

'They know the birds are there,' Louise said. 'Why can't they fish somewhere else?'

No idea, he thought. Not a clue. Would she go to a grocer for books, or to an empty well for water? The men hauled the nets and cleared the catch. They'll go back to harbour now, he thought; it's getting too rough and the tide is going out. But they took the boats outside the shelter of the head into even rougher water, and began casting them again. They separated, to allow each a clear run, and the furthest boat was often lost to view in the troughs, when the men appeared to be standing waist deep in the rolling swell. The little boats were shipping showers of spray over the starboard side as they came slowly ahead, with the line of floats curving away astern.

'It's getting rougher,' Louise said. 'Isn't it ?'

'Yeah. The tide's going away against the wind. They must be mad, to fish in this. Or else strangers. They're the only ones out. All the locals will be aground on their moorings in the harbour.'

The birds on the water dived or flew off into the wind as the boats came close to the resting flocks. 'I think the tide is taking the nets,' Barny said. He glanced up to the coast-guard's look-out and saw the occupant, also looking at the boats through a pair of binoculars mounted on a stand. They heard voices, and turned to see Steve and Joe approaching.

'Ioh, Barny.'

'Ioh, Steve. Hullo, Joe! I thought you'd gone up country to live.'

Joe was stubble-chinned, tanned of face and deeply lined, with a cloth cap over his wiry hair, from under the peak of which his blue eyes viewed the scene with disdain. 'We aren't all like you,' he said.

'Bit choppy out there, edn 'a ?' Barny said, as they watched the tossing boats.

'Rough enough,' Joe said.

Joe was looking at Louise with a bland stare, and he turned to Barny, who was obliged to say, 'This is Louise, a friend from up country,' as Joe tried to suppress a grin. 'This is Joe, and Steve, you've heard me mention them.'

They nodded to her, and turned to the boats. 'Too rough for we,' Steve said.

They watched as the boats shot their nets and returned to the lee of the head, circling to hold their position in the shelter. The crackle of voices on their radio receivers reached the shore above the noise of wind, waves and engines.

'There's a swell risin' on the cock bank,' Joe said. 'He's ben and shifted.'

Barny explained to Louise about the sandbank at the mouth of the harbour. 'Can be a bit tricky,' he said. 'The waves break over it as the tide goes out. Are these two all right?' he asked Steve.

His two friends would not have come out here to watch these boats without good reason. They had seen a lot of boats.

'They're all right,' Joe said before Steve could answer. 'So long as they're all right.'

Yes. That's right, if they succeed they are brave. If they fail they are foolhardy. Barny looked at Joe, who obliged him only with a grimace, and they watched the sea in silence, until Barny said. 'Have 'ee signed on?"

'I'm too old. They've took the boy.'

'Well,' Barny said. 'He'll be a good man.'

'He's a good man now,' Joe said. 'Like his fehther.'

Steve tossed his head. 'Huh.' And Louise looked at Barny, who told her, 'In the lifeboat. Steve's son is one of the crew. Just signed on.' He turned back to his friends. 'Who are these party 'en?'

'Don't know. Strangers. Come from round Land.' The men all grinned, but at what, Louise could not imagine.

'They're going to haul,' Joe said. 'They've had enough.'

The crews were making signs to each other, waving their arms towards the harbour, although the nets had been barely cast.

'They're draggin" Joe said. 'Be a brea coddle here dreckly.'

The coastguard, who had emerged from the shelter of the look-out, was standing behind the stone parapet surrounding his hut, with a smaller pair of binoculars trained on the boats in the brilliant sunshine.

The boat closest to the head went to the buoy marking the nearest end of the net and Joe said, 'Tah!' with his tongue rasping his teeth.

'I wouldn't haul with the tide,' Steve said. 'Not now.'

Louise glanced at him and saw the worried look in his eye. 'It's getting rougher,' she said, 'by the minute.'

'It's the tide,' Steve said, without looking at her. 'I wouldn't haul with the tide where they are.' He looked up at the coastguard. The man was going inside. They saw him pick up a microphone.

The nets were full of fish, heavy with them, and the men were struggling to get them aboard. 'Shut right in the middle of them,' Joe said. They brought them in without attempting to clear the fish or dead birds and, as they went further out into the turbulence, the bows began dipping into the swell. The outer boat managed to get the nets in but the other was having difficulty, for they were in the roughest water, where the race was strongest, and the men were straining against the rising waves and weight of fish and birds. Then, when about three-quarters of the floats were in, the boat rose on a swell and then the bow was dragged down in a plunge by the weight of the net, just as another violent sea rose and broke right into her.

'Cut the nets!' they heard Steve shout. But the current took the boat on a surge, and she overran the net as another sea struck her and came inboard, knocking one of the men to the boards. The net fouled the propeller, and the engine stopped, letting the boat broach broadside to the weather. The second man tried to get to his companion, who was lifting himself up, and as he came past the engine box he was thrown off balance as another violent breaker struck them. He fell overboard with hardly a splash. The shapeless bundle of yellow, trailing two black rubber boots, toppled over the gunwale, slipped beneath the surface, and was gone. They waited, but the figure did not reappear.

'Oh, My Christ,' Steve said, and began unbuttoning his heavy coat.

Uncle Joe took him by the shoulder. 'Stay where you are, brother,' he said, and Steve looked at him in indecision. 'Stay where you are.' Joe said again, quietly. 'We caint do nawthen.'

Louise was staring at the boats with her hand up to her mouth, eyes wide open in horror at the brilliant scene before her, unable to believe what she was seeing. The man still in the boat rose to his feet and stretched overboard to below the surface and just managed to reach the head of his companion. He grabbed him by the hair and then the collar of his yellow plastic waterproof, leaning over with his armpits on the gunwale, straining to keep his grip against the rise and dip of the sea.

'His legs are tangled,' Joe said, 'in the nets, under water. He waint get 'n aboard on his own.'

The other boat was coming up at full speed and they let off a flare, unaware that the coastguard had already called for help and was back out on the parapet.

'Get a line aboard, brother,' Joe said. 'Pass them a line.'

'He won't be able to take it,' Steve said, 'without letting go of him. They'll have to get a man aboard.'

The second boat came in and circled under the other boat's stern. The helmsman brought her up close, the two boats now pitching violently, and eased her closer. The two boats were thrown violently together and the watchers on the shore could hear the crack of timber and fibreglass.

'We shall have two overboard, if we're not careful,' Steve said. But the man in the bow held on to the other boat and fell inboard as they surged together, taking the line with him. He seemed to have injured his leg but he made the line fast to a stanchion in the bow, and then went aft to help the one holding on to the man in the sea.

'They've got damage,' Barny said. 'They've smashed the rubbing strakes.'

'Tha's nawthen,' Steve said, 'as long as they can hold on.'

The towing boat brought them slowly into smoother water and the two held on to the man in the sea, waiting for help.

Barny said, 'they'll be all right if they can hang on. So long as they don't try to make harbour.' He looked at Louise. 'Ten minutes,' he said.

'But the boat is sinking,' she cried. 'Why doesn't the other boat help?'

'Because,' Barny said patiently, 'if he came alongside they would probably get their propeller tangled in the net too, and crush the man in the sea. They have to wait.'

'They'll send the I.R.B,' Steve said.

Barny turned to Louise. 'Inshore Rescue Boat.'

They heard the throb of the engine as the towing boat tried to go astern and keep the second boat free from the nets, but it became evident that they were being taken by the tide toward the black, looming rocks of the headland and all became silent as they waited.

'They are all going to be drowned!' Louise cried at last. 'Why doesn't somebody send for a helicopter or something?'

'I expect they have,' Barny said, and even as he spoke they saw the fast inflatable throbbing over the waves from the direction of the harbour. It came in a shower of spray and went alongside the boats. Then two of the crew grabbed hold of the man in the sea and dragged him over the low rubber bow, cutting the submerged net to free his legs as they went rapidly astern to avoid fouling the propeller. They went back to the harbour even faster than they came, running with the weather like a surfboard, and the rescue was all over in minutes.

'He'll be all right now,' Joe told Louise, 'if he idn dead already, but they won't get they two boats over the bank. They'll have to beach them here.'

'They'll want a bit of a hand.' Steve said.

He and Joe went down to join the cluster of men gathering on the little sheltered beach beneath the headland, and they waved to the three men still out in the boats, calling them in.

'Was the man drowned?' Louise said, when they left her and Barny on the path.

Barny turned to her, realising she was in a state of shock, her shoulders hunched and shivering. 'No. I don't think so. I expect he'll be OK.'

They watched the men bringing the boats in, one towing the sinking other, and the people on the shore, now in a small crowd attracted by the spreading news, waiting to haul them clear of the tide.

'I must go down and lend a hand,' he said, and squeezed her arm before scrambling down to the beach where the boats were being hauled out of the surf by men up to their knees in water and soaked to the skin.

'No need for you to get drowned,' Steve said. 'We've got plenty of hands.'

He was right. The boats were almost clear, so Barny stayed on the sand and helped to haul the boats above high-water mark, where men began clearing the fish. There was nothing more he could do, so he turned to rejoin Louise, standing alone above the beach, and saw Anne, running towards him across the sand.

'What's happened?' she gasped. 'They said someone has been drowned.'

'No, not quite.'

He told her what had happened and moved aside to allow a pick-up truck, laden with fish boxes, to come across the beach. 'They've had a good catch,' he said. 'They'll need it, to pay for the damage.'

'Your feet are wet,' Anne said,' You'd better come home and dry out.'

'No. It's only my shoes. I didn't go in the sea. Thanks for the offer.... ' Barny floundered, aware that Louise was looking at them from the path.

'But you must.' The idea of his refusal astonished her. 'You'll catch your death.'

She saw him glance up to the path above the beach, and she too saw that tall figure standing with her hands deep in her pockets as protection from the cold wind. They looked back at each other and Barny felt irrationally guilty for being with another woman, and was annoyed with Anne for making him so. What he did with his life was his own business, he told himself. He had no commitment to Anne, no obligation, so why did he feel disconcerted by her presence when the other was waiting for him up there, like a tall waif, alone and anxious?

Anne was obviously piqued, yet a little amused at his embarrassment. 'Who is she?' she asked. 'Aren't you going to introduce us? Call her down.'

'A friend of Sam and Beth, my neighbours,' he said, 'I hardly know her.'

He waved to her, wishing he had not brought her here to see this incident, for she was shocked, having never experienced anything like it before. He was anxious to go back and comfort her, but he did not want to be churlish to Anne, despite her mocking tone.

'I'll have to go up to her,' he said, pleadingly, 'she's quite shocked, I think.'

'Well, go on then! I don't care!'

'Oh, Annie !' he said, 'don't be ridiculous.'

She suddenly laughed at his predicament and threw her arms around his neck, kissing him on the lips, something she would never normally do in public.

'Get off!' he cried. 'Leave me alone, you bitch,' as he disentangled himself from her grasp.

Anne laughed, showing her teeth and tossing her head, as she stepped back from him with her long skirt blowing around her legs, and she watched him stalk off in the direction of the girl up on the path. When he began climbing the rocks she sang out, 'Bye, darling,' so that Louise could hear above the wind.

Despite his rage, Barny found himself laughing when he reached Louise. Anne never, ever, called him darling.

He looked back and saw Joe and Steve standing beside her. Joe's shoulders were shaking with mirth as they all three enjoyed some joke at Barny's expense. The small crowd was dispersing, going home to change their clothes, fill their shoes with sawdust. One crew member of the two boats had been carted off to hospital with a sprained ankle to be attended to. The two remaining crewmen, with the help of some local fishermen, were clearing the nets from the beached boats, bass to the boxes and bodies of birds to the beach as the cold sunshine threw lengthening shadows towards the sea. Joe put his arm around Anne's shoulder, and all three turned towards the steps on the far side of the beach. Barny watched them for a minute. They formed an elemental group in the complete picture, part of the cove, with the black headland, the bright, white-flecked sea, the cluster of helpers beside the boats, and the lighthouse on the rock across the bay. They were also, he thought, part of the communal spirit, part of that essential unity which brought them together in times of adversity, and for a moment he felt isolated, as if rejected by his friends in retaliation for his deserting them in favour of Louise. It was such a little doubt that he dismissed it.

Anne turned to wave as she reached the steps with Steve and Joe. Barny responded with a brief raising of his hand. 'Darlin',' he said to himself. 'I'll give 'ee darlin', next time I see 'ee.'

He led Louise away and, as they walked around the cove toward the harbour, she held him by the arm for comfort.

'Is the man dead?' she insisted. 'Was he drowned?'

Barny felt uncomfortable with her arm through his as they approached the town, for the disparity in their height was emphasised and it might appear as if she were guiding him, like an ageing relative. The thought irritated him, and he disengaged his arm on the pretext of reaching into his pocket for a handkerchief to blow his nose, 'I expect he has a drop of water in his lungs,' he said. 'But he'll be all right.'

She was not going to make any comment about Anne. Ah well, it was up to her. 'He'll be in hospital getting pumped out.'

'It was all so quick,' she said. 'I couldn't believe what was happening. And it's such a lovely day, with all the sunshine and the colours.'

They came upon the harbour, with the boats left by the receding tide all lying athwart their moorings, and there was a heavy surf breaking over the sandbank, trailing plumes of white spray. Here in the harbour, where they were completely sheltered from the wind, it was still warm in the sunshine and people had come out to sit on the benches and low walls to enjoy the scene and a bit of gossip.

'Never should have been out there,' he heard one say, 'In this weather.'

'Why, gone dammee mad.'

Barny smiled to himself in appreciation of their assessment of the incident, the bad weather of this lovely day, and nodded to them as he passed. He knew them 'by sight', the names of one or two, and was aware that they all knew him, had known him from childhood, and soon there would be a space on the wall for him and Steve and Uncle Joe, Mary, Sarah Stevens, all of them.

'Were they your friends?' Louise asked.

'No. My father's friends,' he said. 'Or his enemies. Depends what mood he's in.'

'I mean the two on the beach, Steve and Joe.'

'Oh, yes. Known them all my life. They're very close, those two, always have been.'

What storms they had weathered, those two, he thought, how they had matured together in propinquity.

'They're a most unlikely pair, really. Joe is a bit, well, rough and ready, as we say, used to be a hard case in his youth, a heavy drinker. Both of them were, for a while. He's very straightforward, says what he thinks.' Too damned straightforward at times, Barny thought. 'Whereas Steve is more reticent. You have to drag it out of him, what he's thinking.'

How much should he tell this girl about his friends? 'Steve is religious.' he said, and despised himself for the irony in his voice.

'Is he ?' Louise said. 'One wouldn't think so.'

'Why not?' he retaliated in defence of his friend.

'I don't know. He looks too... I don't know... tough.'

'He is tough. Tough as hell. You have to be tough to be a Christian these days. Some years ago, he... '

All that was none of her business. Barny's brow creased in consternation. 'He's a Born Again Christian.' He decided to tell her nothing more.

'He was converted,' he said, smiling, 'by a parson or parsons unknown.'

He stopped, and leaned over the railing. Louise stopped beside him and they looked down at the slipway where the inflatable Inshore Rescue Boat was being hauled up on a trailer. It would be towed back to the boat house in a corner of the car park and immediately made ready for another launch. There were half a dozen young men there, wearing the orange life jackets of the RNLI, together with a wizened coastguard with a grey beard, and a young policeman.

'That's Steve's son,' Barny said. 'The young man who spoke to me in our old language. The one talking to the girl. And the policeman is Sam-the-taxi-Man's boy. They went to school together. So did their fathers.'

And so did their mothers, he thought. Steve Trevorrow's boy with Sarah Stevens' maid? No, he can't be.

'Surprised to see those two together,' he said, 'Steve's son and that girl, Katie Stevens.'

'She's very attractive. Why are you suprised to see them together?'
'Well...'

He had obliged himself to offer an explanation. What could he say? '...the families don't get on. Her mother, Sarah Stevens, went out with his father for a while when we were young, and was heart-broken, people said - I was away at the time - when he married someone else, Mary Trenowden, the boy's mother. Sarah was never seen with anyone else. Years afterwards there was a bit of a scandal when Steve had a brief affair with an artist, and just after that Sarah had an illegitimate child, Katie.'

'Was Steve the father, then?' Louise asked. 'Did he go back to her?'

Barny looked directly at her. She was the first one he had ever heard to voice that question. But then, she was an outsider, while he was close to them all. Should he tell her that the answer to that question had also never been spoken? No, it was none of her business, a damned stranger. 'Sarah has never told anyone,' he said, 'who the father was.'

Boy Steve left the girl, Katie, and went down to help the men attending the boat. They were taking their time, laughing among themselves, greeting passers by, easy and relaxed about their business.

'He's very good-looking, too,' Louise said. 'He has his father's eyes.'

So you think Steve is good looking, Barny thought. I suppose he is, and he felt a shiver run down his spine and a certain apprehension pass through his mind. He tried to ascertain what had caused it, but could not. He had been reminded, he thought, of something which was too far back in memory, or too deep in the subconscious, to comprehend.

'What's his name?' he heard Louise ask, and he had difficulty in remembering their conversation, although mere seconds had elapsed while these thoughts were in his mind. He felt as if he had been granted a glimpse into the secret archives of his destiny where there was no distinction between past and future. An obscure phrase occurred to him, and repeated itself as he strove to find some answer to Louise's question: *Nyns us whethlow yn brys yn an rew, and no sequence to events remembered*

'Are you all right ?' Louise asked.

'Yeah, sure,' he said doubtfully. 'Why do you ask? He's called Steven, or Boy Steve, to distinguish him from his father. And soon he will be "Steve" and his father "Old Steve" and the boy's son, if he ever marries and has one, "Boy Steve" in turn. And so it goes on... .'

Why was half of it in the old language, he wondered, for he was not yet so fluent that he thought in it.'

'Are you sure you are all right, Barny?' You look strange.'

'Quite sure,' he said, hesitantly. 'No! I'm not. I've just had a what-'ee - call-it, *déjà vu*. Premonition.'

'What about?"

'I don't know! Something to do with Boy Steve.' He had lowered his voice. 'Life, death... . I don't know.'

He laughed, an arid, cold laugh of consternation. 'I'm always getting the damned things.'

'Was it anything to do with the fishing boat?' Louise asked, with a deep frown furrowing her brow like, Barny thought, the ripples left in sand by receding tides.

'No. Well, yes. I think so. There was a boat, an idea of a boat, but I couldn't see it.'

'Was it in fog, a sea mist?'

'My God, I hope not.' Now he laughed aloud. 'What tricks our minds d' play on us.'

The crew of the I.R.B. had secured the craft onto the trailer and they pushed it away from the slipway, up to the car park, laughing as they gained speed and ran up the slope of the short hill.

'You wouldn't think,' Louise said, 'that they had just saved somebody's life.'

'No,' he said, not following her reasoning. 'There was a phrase in my head just now. I don't understand it, but somehow accepted that it was profoundly significant. It was in both languages... *There is no chronology to the narratives of the mind, and no sequence to events remembered.* It seemed like something I must do, or a book I will write.'

He shook his head, and looked around at the bright harbour. 'A poem, perhaps.'

'We'll see,' Louise said, and he realised he had dismissed her own observation on the casual way the rescuers were behaving, in favour of his own discourse, forgetting that she was still somewhat shocked by events which, to locals, were all too familiar.

'Come on,' he said. 'I'll take you for a drink and a bite to eat. Worse things than that happen at sea, believe me.'

And worse things, he thought, than Boy Steve in the company of Katie Stevens. Oh dear yes. But what would their parents have to say about it?

CHAPTER FOUR.

Benen demethys o hy. A woman married, was she.

Tell me about your marriage, Ms. Fern.

I met the man who was to become my husband when he was a serious young law student. He was big, thick-boned and broad-shouldered, fair and good looking, but not handsome. I see now that his eyes were dead. There was no fire in them. He concealed himself. He had been a train-spotter as a boy and was still obsessed with railways as a hobby. He knew the network of every main and branch line in the country, remembering time-tables and connections as other people remembered plots and characters in fiction. I found it intriguing that an undergraduate could still collect train numbers. He claimed an interest in pop music and bought dozens of albums, but couldn't dance. Neither could I.

Our courtship, if it was that, was a protracted affair of brief visits to each other's lodgings when I was working as a research assistant in the Archaeological department of the university. I had begun a career in retail management but hated it and left, I told him, for something more intellectual.

Like me, he came from a working class background and was hard up as a student. On one of his visits, a few months before his finals, he told me he had signed on for a short-service commission in the armed forces. I was horrified. I hated violence and thought he should have told me of his intention. If we were to be married, this should have been a joint decision. He said it was merely a ploy to continue his studies on an officer's pay and, after serving three years, return to civilian life and a career in a highly paid profession.

He had given me no inkling of his intention. He wanted to surprise me, he said, to show me that he was ambitious for us both, and he was so pleased with himself that I kept my misgivings to myself. That was a mistake. I should have finished the relationship right then. I mean, I was in Greenpeace and Friends of the Earth and a pacifist. How was I to reconcile all that with the regimentation of being a military wife?

'You won't have to,' he said, 'I'll be out soon after we are married.'

This was his proposal to me, a bland assumption that I would meekly acquiesce to his wishes, and I decided immediately that I had no intention of marrying him. I didn't know him, and he certainly didn't know me. I made sure of that, for he was the jealous, macho type and could not have coped with the knowledge of my previous lovers. Just before his next visit was due I phoned to say I was working all weekend and there was no point in wasting the train fare. I did the same the following week, but after that I relented, unable to cope with the loneliness.

After that weekend with Sam and Beth, I left on the early morning train. I looked out of the window, with the familiar tensions already constricting my breathing, thinking of Barny. The east wind blowing across the bay was still whipping the spray, but the rising sun illuminated the coastline in the clear, crisp air as the trawler fleet left the harbour, one after another, for the fishing grounds; and the train pulled out of the station in a silent, barely perceptible acceleration, as if abducting the passengers by stealth before we changed our minds about leaving.

On Beth's advice, I had booked a seat facing the engine, despite my father's oft repeated warning that 'back to the engine' was the safest seat in an emergency. 'You're not going to crash!' Beth said. 'And if you have your back to the engine the sun will be in your eyes all the way to London at this time of year.' But her precaution was superfluous. The rising sun was soon obscured by a darkening sky and grey showers of rain smeared the windows and obliterated the view as the train travelled rapidly eastwards. The rain became sleet, then snow as night fell, and I gazed through the windows at the reflected light from towns and stations on the other side of the train, sliding away into the distance, like my life.

I thought of Beth's happy existence and the misery to which I was returning, becoming more despondent as anticipation became increasingly nearer reality. The landscape too became more depressing, it seemed, as the train approached the most prosperous area of the country and slowed down to travel through the dreary backyards of the capital. The journey to London depressed me to such an extent that I arrived back more mentally exhausted than when I left for the break.

After crossing London on the tube and then spending another hour in the local train, I arrived at my destination tired and hungry.

He was waiting at the station with the children in the car. 'You're late,' he said. 'It's time these kids were in bed.'

'I'm sorry,' I said, too tired to argue that the train was exactly on time.

Both children were fractious and clamouring for my attention in the car, but my husband drove back to the house in silence and retired to his 'den' as soon as we entered, saying he had some important case-work to prepare for the following morning.

No meal had been provided, so I was obliged to cook for them all, and prepare the children for bed. When I had tucked them up and was about to flop into bed myself, I found there were no clean clothes for the morning and a heap of dirty washing on the airing-cupboard floor. That this was intended to prick my conscience, a deliberate ploy to induce guilt for abandoning them for the weekend, I had no doubt, but I stifled tears of anger and fatigue and, two hours later, I climbed into bed with all the benefits of my first short break away alone utterly negated.

My husband eventually switched off the light in his study and came into our darkened bedroom and lay close to me, his arm across my ribs as I stared at the ceiling, too tired, my mind too full, for sleep. I waited in dread for his sexual advances, his hope for loveless carnal gratification, and turned my back to him, feigning sleep.

'I don't know what's the matter with you,' he said. 'Why are you so cold?'

The silent tears wet her pillow, but she could not sob, nor turn to him for comfort, because, as she knew from many nights of memory, he would interpret her embrace as an invitation to physical arousal. Soon he turned away from her and they lay back to back, as they had done for the past two years, in frustration and despair. Her husband was asleep before she, and there was anger in his breathing and unrelaxed body.

As sleep enveloped Louise, she thought, or dreamed, of her friends, Sam and Beth, and of Barny the poet and his tender eyes. All that she saw as an alternative to this miserable existence was there among the hills, the moors and the coves, where people appreciated the true values of life, while her own was slipping away unused, wasted in the daily boredom of domesticity and the nightly frustration of loveless, silent indifference. There had to be more to it than this!

And what, exactly, were you feeling then?

As the waves of fatigue swirled me in and out of the caverns of sleep, the thoughts, memories and anticipatory dreams became a single confused emotion which dragged my mind away from reason. I saw myself as a decapitated head, being swung round and round by the hair, with blood dripping from the severed neck, and then thrown by some unseen hand, some force, over a high cliff, like a macabre shot from a sling, with the turmoil in my mind turning with the screaming head as it fell, with my hair streaming, to the rocks along the shore of the flaming sea. I woke in the certainty that I was going mad, or about to die, horrified at the inevitability of my eventual descent into the fires of Hell and eternal punishment.

With an involuntary gasp of fear, Louise turned to her sleeping husband, croaking in a voice she could not recognise as her own, 'Hold me. Hold me.'

'What?' he said, waking in alarm. 'What's the matter?'

'I'm afraid,' she whispered.

'Afraid?' he said, turning over to face her. 'What are you afraid of, for God's sake? I'd just gone off to sleep.'

She turned away, and buried her face in the pillow, unable to suppress the choking sobs that convulsed her body, and let the tears release themselves in wailing despair. 'I'm afraid.'

'Don't wake the children,' he said in exasperation. 'You get more hysterical every day. Control yourself.'

Her tears soaked into the pillow, leaving a crusty salt around her eyes as she lay exhausted beside her husband, yearning for the comfort and kindness she had perceived in a man old enough to be her father. The young man beside her, sleeping like a walrus with his fair military moustache and heavy shoulders, would never, not now or in the future, revitalise the dead emotions they once had shared. The excesses of the past, all the pain, had been the stimulation to sexual gratification which should have been induced by love. She sat up and looked at him, her head resting wearily against the bed head. He was good-looking, but his eyes, now closed and indifferent to her presence, were expressionless. Even in anger his wrath was evident only in his twisted mouth. She remembered the bright, darting eyes of Barny. I love him, she thought. She had never loved the man beside her, and he had never loved her. He had wanted her, no more than that. She remembered the doubts, the realisation that she was making a ghastly mistake when the arrangements for the wedding were all complete and she had told him, 'I can't go through with it. I'm not ready.' And his insistence that they could not let everyone down at this stage. She had lost control, submitted herself to the will of others and had never been her own mistress since. She had married for the sake of other people. 'It's only nerves,' he had said, and she had been unable to tell him anything about herself, all the others, and the guilt was unbearable alone.

'Control yourself!'

As if her emotions, like his own, were to be manipulated like disciplined soldiers.

She sank down into the bed, disturbing the warm air trapped between the sheets - even the smell of him was repugnant to her, and turned away from his fleshy body, craving sleep and oblivion.

This, she told herself on the following morning, could not continue. Her life was not her own. As her husband had said, she had no control over herself, and she made the decision to rectify this weakness forthwith.

That evening, when she had fed him after his return from duties, she said to him, 'I'm going away.'

'You've just been away.'

'I'm leaving you.'

'Don't be bloody daft,' he said dismissively, and turned on the television.

She came again in April, for a long weekend. Barny saw her walking along the road, and gave her a lift back to the hamlet. She was just out for a stroll, she said, but he saw it as wandering aimlessly about, for her eyes had been downcast when he saw her in the distance. When he had parked the car he said, 'Come in,' and led on through his garden. 'The camellia seems to have taken,' he said, pausing at the door.

'Which is that?' she said.

'The shrub with the shiny green leaves. It's not been planted long, and there are some new shoots growing already.'

'She followed him in and he said, 'What shall we eat?'

'Am I invited to dinner?'

'Yes. Why not?'

'I'll have to go over and tell Beth.'

When she returned he was putting a dish in the oven. 'Only a casserole,' he said. 'But I've a bottle of good wine to go with it. Made it myself.'

'I'm sure it will be fine.' she said.

'We have time for a stroll while it's cooking,' he said. 'Just down the coast. Not very far, but I need to stretch my legs after sitting down all day. If you'd like to, I mean.'

It was a short walk to the part of the cliff to which he took her. They left the road and followed a cart track that led to the remains of a mine engine-house on the slope above the sea. The sun was still warm on their backs as they left the track and followed the coastal path to the east towards Wheal Dowr, in the direction of the town.

There were clusters of blossoms bordering the path. Scurvy grass was flowering, some early thrift, sea campion, and celandines still shone beside their feet. Patches of yellow gorse hung among the outcrops of rock above the lichen-encrusted cliffs where fulmars wheeled on the rising air.

She asked him what the flowers were. 'Which ones?' But she knew none of them, and he told her their names as she stooped and touched their petals with her slender fingers.

'The celandines are sweet,' she said.

They sat beside the gaping hole of a mineshaft, out of the breeze, to enjoy the view, and the smell of gorse came to them like the waft of almonds, or coconut, on the warm air. Across the cove, they could see the nest of a green-glossed shag on a ledge already plastered white with guano, and they watched a raven carrying food to its young in a nest somewhere along the coast, a beakful of raw, red flesh. Below the cliffs, the sea was a brilliant turquoise, glistening with motion from the breeze, yet not provoked to anger, and the black shadows of clouds were few; dark streaks among the pale reflections in the distance. A tall yacht, black-hulled, three-masted, schooner rigged, with topsails and foresails set, ploughed steadily westwards near the horizon, from whence long low rollers arose and welled over the shore, fringing the rocks in surging foam.

'That,' Barny said, 'is some boat. She rides the swells like a scuthen.' He laughed, 'Like a shearwater, a sea-bird.'

By the time they left the cliff, the sun was setting, and although dark clouds, low over the horizon, obscured the final glory of the day and foretold of rain in the night, the evening was warm, buzzing with insects. The black sweep of the headland thrust seawards like a stranded whale, and the sky was ripped apart by the jagged outcrop of the carn, rising to the south.

'The celandines,' she cried when they had walked a little way and she looked along the edge of the path,'They've all closed up.'

'They do, at night.'

'They've all gone to sleep.'

As they walked up the darkening track, they were inspected by flittering bats which swooped round them in silent, swerving flight, skimming low over the path and diverting in erratic deviations to catch insects in the dusk. Barny threw little bits of gravel up in the air and the bats swept nearer, chasing them, before flying off undeceived in their sonic scrutiny. Louise asked him if he knew what species they were, but he did not, only that they came from somewhere deep in the mineshafts. 'Not pipistrelles,' he said. 'The're too big.'

'Oh, I do love it here Barny.' she said, suddenly. 'I feel this is where I belong. I've never felt I belonged anywhere before but I know I want to spend my life somewhere like this, put roots down, become part of it,'

She slipped her arm through his, and they dawdled back to the farm, stopping now and then to see the changing light as the night descended over the sea.

'Yes. This is what I have always wanted. To live somewhere like this. Away from the crowds and the noise and dirt. I know I could be happy here.'

He had heard that before. He wondered if anyone was happy on the other side of the river. They all seemed so anxious to get away. What had they done to the bleddy place? 'There's a lot to be said for it,' he said. 'Doesn't suit everybody, mind.' What else could he say? It was not up to him to influence her decisions, yet he remembered her face as she looked at the celandines, 'gone to sleep', like a child in her wonderment. There would be much to delight her here. 'I must tell Katie about the bats,' he said. 'The young friend of mine we saw in town, remember?'

As they approached the road, the moon rose over the hills, full and red, and its light fell upon them and reached far out to illuminate the gathering clouds approaching from the west.

Her moods were as sudden as summer showers, and, when they arrived back at the cottage, her gaiety left her, squashed by some thought or recollection which had troubled her. It was almost, Barny thought, as if being within the confines of his home imposed some restriction upon her and she withdrew from him, back into her melancholy, hardly speaking, and then only to offer help with the cutlery.

He put two plates on the table, produced a bottle of wine, and served out the casserole. They sat opposite each other in the living room. Barny was famished and ate the meal with relish, enjoying his food as part of his happy life, while Louise picked delicately at her plate, saying that she was not really hungry.

'Eat up, my 'ansome,' he said. 'One swallow does not a banquet make.'

She was not to be persuaded, although she drank all her wine, and when the meal was over he cleared the table and refilled the glasses, placing them on the low table before the sofa. He replenished the fire and they sat in silence, watching the flames, while Barny resisted all impulses to initiate conversation, allowing the silence to linger until, against his better judgement, he said, 'Why don't you tell me all about it?'

At the end of her story, she was in his arms, her eyes streaming tears which he kissed away, taking them from her cheek with his lips.

Louise felt safe with him as he comforted her, stroking her hair, gently kissing her temple, and she wanted more of him. She felt a rising desire for him which she had been attempting to conceal since entering his house. She wanted him to hold her, to love her, to drive them away, the bogey men, drive them away and hold her and love her. She wanted it. She wanted his sex and passion to fight them with, and was ashamed.

'Perhaps,' he said, 'I ought to take you over to Beth's. Put you to bed.'

Why not here? she thought. Beside the fire. It was another of her dreams. The warm glow on their skin. In the dim light he would not see her ugly body with the fat on her thighs, she could hide it and love him in the dark.

He kissed her, holding her head in his hands. 'Come on,' he said, and drew her up from the sofa.

In bed, she thought, in that little bed, under the duvet.

They spoke with Sam and Beth for a while, and Barny mentioned the bats they had seen, wondering if they had come from the mine.

'There's talk,' Sam said, 'of Simon Sweeting's company using the mines to dump nuclear waste.'

'Never!' Barny said. 'They'll never get permission.'

'I hope not,' Beth said, patting her belly.

Louise was silent, and her face fell at the possibility of such an eventuality. There was no escape, she was thinking, from the horrors, no matter where you went. She didn't want to hear about it. 'I think I must go to bed,' she said. 'I'm tired.'

'I'll be up,' Barny said. 'To kiss you good night.'

Louise avoided his eyes and looked at Beth, who smiled knowingly.

Louise went up to the bedroom, loosened her hair, washed, cleaned her teeth and prepared the bed. After such a long period of dormancy in her unhappy marriage, her desire was overwhelming and she felt herself alive with it. She could see it in her own eyes as she looked in the mirror. Two years. How could she have endured the frustration? Barny had roused her without even being aware of it and he was twenty-five years her senior. Twenty-five years, she thought, and he had stirred emotions which her husband never knew existed. Barny might not prove to be passionate in his lovemaking but she had suffered enough from sadistic lust. That was not what she wanted, she told herself, she needed tenderness and understanding, a gentle arousal, which, judging from his eyes, Barny would not deny her. She switched off the centre light and waited in the dim glow of the bedside lamp, which she placed on the floor, throwing the room into shadow. Under the duvet she became warm, glowing with excitement as she lay in her long night-dress, anticipating his penetration. She felt herself trembling with desire at the very thought of him climbing in beside her, stroking her. She was as roused as she had ever been in her life, and he had not even touched her.

She heard the occasional laughter from below, and the distant clink of crockery, then silence. She was sure he had gone, back to his cottage, until the door opened and he came into her room. He knelt beside the bed, looking into her eyes with his arms folded beside her on the duvet. An irrational fear came over her, for his eyes told her nothing, there was no desire in them. She drew the cover up to her neck, looking at him in trepidation.

A faint smile brushed across his lips. 'I won't hurt you,' he said, and she relaxed, returning his smile.

He reached for the duvet and drew it down over her body to her waist, and she placed one arm along her breasts, ashamed of those little lumps beneath her night-dress, afraid that he would reject her. She lay still as his hand passed down over her body and slid around her waist, but as he leaned forward, she turned, accepting a soft kiss on the mouth. 'Oh, Barny,' she said as the tremors convulsed her, and she put her arms around him, drawing him towards her. He found the hem of her night-dress, and she eased her hips from the bed as he drew it up, past her waist and then over her head as she raised her arms. He slid the duvet down and knelt beside the bed, looking at her naked body with the long hair covering her breasts in a curtain of black. He ran his hand down from the neck, brushing the curtain aside, and looked at her, caressing her body with his eyes.

'Don't you want me,' she gasped. 'Am I ugly? Is my body ugly? Am I fat?'

Barny slowly shook his head, and kissed her again, with a hand below her breast. 'You are beautiful,' he said. 'Beautiful.' And she looked at him wistfully, as if he were lying.

He leaned over her and kissed her upon the mouth, pushing her head back on to the pillow, with his hand behind her neck, passionately, lusting after her, and drew away, breathless.

'I think I'd better be going,' he said

'You can't go,' she said desperately. 'Not now! You can't leave me like this.'

'Oh God.' he said. 'You are so vulnerable.'

'Please, Barny... .'

So he held her close to him, with a soft laugh in her ear, and ran his hand down, over her stomach to the bush of black curls, then between her legs, and she groaned with pleasure, looking into his eyes with open lust. 'Yes.' she said. 'Yes. Yes.' And he caressed her, as gently as she would allow as she drew his hand more firmly on to her until she came to a gasping climax, almost against her will, in a surge of release, and he fell against her neck, holding her as she recovered her breath.

He embraced her affectionately, holding her close, and kissed her with soft brushes of his lips against her hair and she said, 'I'm sorry. What must you think of me?' Hiding her face in the pillow.

He touched his lips along her body and kissed her, his cheek nuzzling against the dark, damp curls. 'Good night.' he said, and covered her up. 'You'll sleep now.' Tucking her up, pressing the duvet into her neck. 'I must go.'

He paused, his smile gone. 'You are very beautiful,' he said. 'And very, very vulnerable. Please, be careful.'

There was nothing she could say to him, and she watched him close the door. 'Good night,' he said. 'Good night, Louise.'

Louise curled up in the little bed, feeling warm and satisfied, her lusts assuaged by a man such as she had never before experienced. Previously, while often using men to satisfy her own hunger, she had felt used and disgusted by them. This had been so generous and tender that she recalled it as if waking from a dream. It was as if he had transmuted her base lust into a golden surge of emotional release, and this by the touch of his hand in a situation where many men would have abused her with their pricks.

But why? He had told her she was beautiful, and he had obviously been aroused, so why had he not taken her and loved her with his body? It was obvious. She was not desirable, and she knew it, for she had been told so in the past. Her body had repulsed him, regardless of what he had said, and yet she had been unable to control her desire for him. Her beastly desire for sex, which had dominated her life for as long as she could remember, had got the better of her again. But she loved him.

She loved him, she loved him. And she slept a deep untroubled sleep in which she dreamt of spending years at his side.

Barny, meanwhile, sat at his table with his pencil in his hand until the early hours of the morning, attempting to evoke in words the infinite sadness he saw within her, and the conflicts she aroused in him. When the floor was littered with discarded scrawls he gathered them up and threw them into the fire. Forget it! he thought. Keep out of her life, and keep her out of yours.

Louise did not see him again that weekend, for next morning he had gone into town before she was up. She spent the day helping Sam and Beth, trying to compensate them for having her to stay for a while yet again. What must Barny think of her? She had allowed her basest instincts to overwhelm her and was deeply ashamed but could not mention a word of it for embarrassment. Despite herself, however, she continually looked to the gate or listened to the door, hoping he would come across to see them. They would not know what had happened last night for he had been in her bedroom such a short time, just long enough for a good-night kiss and a little chat, so in the afternoon, she could resist it no longer and asked, as casually as she could. 'Where is Barny today?'

Everything seemed so serene here, the people she met so uncomplicated, their lives so orderly and calm. There was none of the frenetic striving of the cities, none of the competition for promotion and the social distinctions of the army. That was a life she could not bear. It was driving her mad, for she was being forced to live a life of deceit and lies in which she could never be herself. She didn't know who she was any more. Were it not for the children, she would have abandoned it years ago, she told herself, and gone in search of a man like Barny. She could not stop thinking about him.

'He's gone into town,' Beth said. 'To see his father. And he has a girl-friend there, I think.'

So that was it. The woman on the beach. Louise could mean nothing to Barny. She didn't even know his full name.

CHAPTER FIVE

An dedhyow a'y flogholeth. The days of her childhood.

And how did you get on with your family?

My mother is Italian. Her name is Valeria. She was brought to England as a child before the war. Her memories of her Italian childhood were always vague, but she retained a slight accent, of which she was unaware until reminded by my sister Heather making fun of her. She was a very proud woman with an abiding fear of grime and poverty. As infants we were kept scrupulously clean, and she was invariably horrified at any dirt on our clothes or skin, warning us about germs and what people would think if they saw us in such a state, dirty or untidy. She ensured that no matter how poor we were, and at times we were extremely so, we were always neat and tidy when we left the house to go to school or church. My father's name is Bruce. He is an actor.

We went to a convent school. The nuns at the school were conscientious in their tuition, and also regarded themselves as the guardians of our morals and innocence. I was very impressed by their holiness and self-discipline which gave them such self-assurance in their daily tasks. They were in extreme contrast to my mother's indecision and frequent panics, and I envied their serenity. Their pink, devout faces welcomed us in the mornings with a warm formality which was remote and reassuring in the knowledge that my virtues would be justly rewarded, as my sins would be punished in the eternal fires of Hell. My sins were always of the flesh.

They attended a convent school because Valeria had been brought up as strict Catholic and wished to have the morals of the church reinforced in her children. She rarely attended Mass herself, except on Christmas Eve, when she prayed fervently for forgiveness of past transgressions and promised to attend regularly in the future. Her job and weekend housework prevented the fulfilment of such promises, however, and she feared that her eventual punishment would be justifiably severe. Bruce's liberal upbringing, in New York, where his parents had lived during his youth, had been almost to the exclusion of matters spiritual and, secretly, when finding the courage to do so, he regarded himself as an atheist. On Sunday mornings the girls were sent off, neat and tidy, to Sunday School, during which time, in the early years, Bruce and Valeria returned to bed for the only time they had the flat to themselves, in an attempt to relieve the frustration of their growing dissatisfaction with life and each other.

Only my father was close to me. He always wanted me to do well. He is an actor. Did I tell you? My sister was jealous and didn't like me. She was younger, and more attractive and used to try to belittle me because I was more intelligent. She used to seduce my boyfriends as soon as I got to know them. She would do anything to humiliate me. She said I was a lesbian and tried to make me have sex with her. This was after my father left. She was only fifteen and I was two years older. It was horrible. And one of her boyfriends raped me when I was still a virgin.

Anne was not at home, though her front door was unlocked, as usual. He went in, and wrote a short note on the back of an envelope he found among the chaos on her kitchen table. *Gone to visit the Old Man, see you later.*

His father was out too, so Barny went down'long again, to look around the harbour where the flowing tide was smooth and sparkling in the warm sunshine. His father was not to be found and the fishing boats were out, so he would not see Steve and Joe either.

Among all the people, leaning over the railings, sitting on benches or strolling along the wharf, each looking to the others to provide some entertainment for the day, there was hardly a soul he knew. He went down to the quay, past the piles of green plastic nets, to the lighthouse at the end, where he stood looking out to sea.

The old-style fishing boats, all the old gigs and double-enders, the drifters and mackerel drivers, of which his father was making a model, had all been sold, scrapped, burned or lost at sea, and the old crews had been scrapped with them, buried, burned or lost at sea too, and everything was new, now. The boats were fast, driven by powerful engines, and their crews watched dials and listened to pings and bleeps emitted from microchips. All but a few of the old crews scrapped stayed at home watching television and no longer came to the fishermen's lodge to spin yarns, for their place in the succession of story-tellers had been usurped by this box of images. No one wanted to listen to them, for everybody had heard it, done it, been there, seen it, on the telly, which was where life was lived these days. People know more about whales and dolphins in the Pacific Ocean, Barny thought, than they do about porpoises and sea-birds caught in nets under their own noses, for these have never been on the screen in their living rooms and therefore do not exist.

The small handliners were all fishing in the same area, off the head, where the man had fallen overboard, while the larger boats had gone off to the West, where their electronic pulses probed the secrets of deep waters and the movements of declining shoals (they call them 'stocks' these days) of fish. Soon there would be none left, for fishing methods are so efficient that the boats are capable of catching the last sprat and diatom of plankton, and might well do so, even when they are to be used for fertiliser on surplus crops which would be left to rot in the ground. Barny could see a small dory, with two men aboard, shooting nets in the inshore shallows, over the sandbank, after sand eels to be sold as bait to anglers.

He turned away from the sea. He did not belong out there. He belonged neither to the sea nor the land, and was as much a mere spectator as Louise, or these people idling about the harbour on holiday. As an observer, and not a partaker, as a poet, he had removed himself from his community. He went back towards his father's house, forgetting his note to Anne, feeling alien among his own.

The picture of the other came repeatedly into his mind. Louise, with her frail body and petulant mind. The smell of her. And he was not sure if he was remembering or inventing the incidents of her visit. She was like a dream, a recurring dream, of which he could remember nothing, only that he had dreamt it.

He saw Boy Steve, walking up'long, and wondered why he was not at sea with his father and Uncle Joe.

'Hullo, Steve.'

'Hullo, Barny,' as they passed.

He saw Sarah Stevens, and her daughter, Katie, come out of the chemist's, Ledra's that was.

'Morning, Sarah,' Barny said. 'Hullo, Katie. I've found the mine records. Come out and go through them whenever you like.' Sarah was still a very attractive woman, Barny thought. Just do me, if I was looking for somebody. Ha! Some hopes.

'Goodbye, Katie. Goodbye, Sarah.'

84

Boy Steve had seen Katie and Sarah walking up Fore Street too, and slowed his pace so as not to overtake them, but now they stopped, and Sarah walked back towards him while Katie stood still, watching them converge. Sarah smiled at him, and Boy Steve smiled in return as they passed. Katie was so like her, he thought, the same small frame, brown hair, brown eyes, dark skin, the same genial expression on their faces. God knows who her father was, but he had not decreed that the paternal likeness should be perpetuated in the illegitimate daughter, it seemed. Boy Steve stopped when Katie smiled and said, 'We forgot the soap. Mother has gone back for some.'

'How are the bats ?' he said.

'I haven't been back. I decided you were right, it would be foolish to go down there on my own. Barny has agreed to go down with me. He knows the mine. Somebody else promised to come with me, but seems to have changed his mind.'

Her eyes were smiling at him, her mouth slightly open, relaxed, an uninhibited, candid expression of self-confidence.

'Yes. Well. I really haven't had a minute for weeks. In fact that's why I'm ashore today. Decided to give myself a break.'

'I don't believe that.'

Boy Steve laughed; there was no way you could fool this one. 'No,' he said, and held out his left arm. The hand was bandaged, with the thumb immobilised. 'Got a hook in it. Nearly better now though.'

'Oh,' she said. 'How did that happen?'

Yes. She knew it all, the maid Katie did. You don't get hooks in your hand, or your eye, if you're careful.

'I slipped,' he said, 'as we were shuttin' the lines.'

Which meant that the three-inch hook would have been pulled into his hand by all the force of the lines trailing astern against the forward motion of the boat. It would rip through the flesh like a... . She shivered at the thought.

'Joe cut the horsel, so it wasn't too bad.'

That must have been a quick reaction, she thought, imagining Old Joe grabbing the line, whipping out his knife and cutting the hook free before the flesh began to tear. 'Your attention must have been distracted,' she said.

'I was thinking of something else.'

'Thought so.'

'You.'

85

'Oh.'

Her mother came out from the chemist's. She was shoving things into the shopping bag, her head down.

'All the time.'

'Why didn't you phone?'

'Problems.'

Sarah was approaching, she looked up and saw them talking. Her face was momentarily clouded before she dropped her head and adjusted some item among the shopping.

'Look,' Boy Steve said, I'll see you tomorrow morning. By the Bible Christian Chapel, ten o'clock. Hullo, Mrs Stevens.'

'Hullo, Steven.' She watched him walk away. And the cold hand clutched her heart again. 'Here,' she said to her daughter, 'carry this, will 'ee. It's too heavy for me,' as Katie took the weight of the basket.

They still lived in the same house that had been Sarah's parents' home, the house where they both had died and Sarah and her daughter were born. These houses in the granite terraces were built to last, would suffice for generation upon generation if they cared to live in them, and Sarah had not considered joining many of her neighbours who had moved to the outskirts of town for the sake of somewhere to put the car. For one thing she didn't have a car and, even if she did, she couldn't drive one. Katie had a car, and, when they dumped the heavy shopping on the table, said, 'If we lived up'long, we could drive to the new supermarket and not have to carry all this stuff.'

'What new supermarket ?'

'The one Simon Sweeting is proposing to build over Penavon.'

'First I've heard of it,' Sarah said. 'And, in any case, I don't want to go traipsing all the way over there every time I want a packet of tay.'

'Tea,' Katie said.

'What was Boy Steve Trevorrow saying to you? I didn't know you were getting so friendly with him.'

'He's going down the adit with me, out Wheal Dowr, to check the bats.'

'Bats,' Sarah laughed. 'Some bats.'

'You don't approve.'

'I didn't say that.'

'You don't have to. It's obvious. What's wrong with him? He seems very nice to me.'

'Well,' Sarah said. 'For one thing, he's too old. And for another thing, he's he's a bit of a mad-brain, been a bit wild.'

And the other thing? Katie said to herself. There's more to it than that.

On the following morning, Boy Steve had equipped himself with a powerful electric torch, spare batteries, waterproofs, a length of fine nylon rope, a ball of string, a thick canvas hat, boots, and a whistle.

Katie laughed at the amount of gear he was bringing, but she was also well-equipped for the descent and, as well as protective clothing, torch and hard hat, she was carrying her electronic bat detector in a waterproof bag.

'That's more like it,' he said, causing her to smile, as if he were the expert in the matter of descending into disused mines. There was no one else on the cliff when they entered the adit, and the dripping water had diminished since their last visit in the spring, yet Steve found that there were again fresh footprints in the soil at the bottom of the tunnel.

'Look,' he said. 'Somebody wearing heavy rubber boots. You can see the treads.'

'Perhaps the rumours are right,' Katie said, 'and they are sending geologists down to investigate the possibility of reopening the mine.'

'I haven't heard that.'

'There was something in the paper. Simon Sweeting is saying there'll be hundreds of jobs if they do.'

'And you don't believe it?'

'No. Do you ?'

'Why not? The price of tin is going up.'

'We'll see,' she said.

They soon reached the place where they had stopped before, and Katie switched on her detector. They could hear rapid clicks. 'Greater horseshoes,' she said.

'You can tell by their sounds ?'

'Oh yes. Quite distinctly.'

They sat on the old iron wheel. Apart from the sound of the bats, there was only the faint drip of water falling somewhere deeper in the mine. Their whispered voices echoed faintly as Steve shone his torch around the walls of rock.' Can't say that I like it in here,' he said. 'I'd rather be out at sea in a gale.'

'There's nothing to worry about. These adits were cut in solid granite. The old miners would rather be down here than out at sea.'

'Not so sure of that,' he said. 'How many bats are there, you reckon?'

'Not so many. I wonder if they've been disturbed. They're very sensitive to disturbance, you know. Even a slight change of temperature or humidity will put them off.'

'Perhaps they've gone further in.'

'That's what I was thinking.'

'Come on then, if we must.'

They found that there were two adits leading off from the chamber where they had been sitting. Steve tied the end of his string to the wheel. 'Five hundred yards,' he said. 'And that's as far as I go. At least for this time.'

'Are you claustrophobic ?'

'Not until now. This place gives me the creeps.'

'Well, come on then, before you change your mind.' She stopped to look at him, their faces lit and shadowed by the torches. 'I'll understand if you do.'

'No. It's all right. Go on, I'll follow.'

He had passed a small dowel through the ball of string, so it unwound as fast as they walked. They were soon obliged to slow down, for the chamber became a mere man-sized tunnel, a drainage pipe for the mine workings much further in. Then they were bending low to avoid knocking their heads, and they had to remove their packs and carry them in their arms, for they were scraping against the roof and walls. After two hundred yards the tunnel opened up again and they were in the workings proper. There was the remains of a tram line and two rusting rails leading off into the gloom at the other end of their torch beams. The roof of the stope was high above them. Steve shone his torch about the walls and underfoot.

'This is as far as they came,' he said.

'No. Over there,' Katie said. 'They've had a look, and changed their minds.' The footprints ended in a mass of overlapping scuffs, where someone had sat or stood for a long time. She switched on the detector, more interested in the bats than in who else might have preceded them into the mine. There was nothing to be heard. 'Pr'aps we're too far in.'

'Right,' Boy Steve said, eagerly.

'Let's see where the tram lines lead.'

'If you say so.'

They led into a chamber quite big enough for them to walk along side-by-side, which they did until the string ran out.

'We can't get lost,' Katie said, 'if there is only one tunnel.'

'A bit further, then.'

Fifty yards on, they came across a working which had been abandoned as it stood. There were heaps of rotten timbers, tools, a work-bench and ropes disintegrated into coils of mould. There was a trolley full of ore on the tram line, with hammers and shovels lying on the top, their handles crumbled to dust.

'Something must have happened,' Boy Steve said. 'Look!'

There was a gaping hole just in front of them. Wooden props were sagging under the weight of rock which had fallen from the roof. There were the remains of a rickety ladder leading down into the abyss.

'It could be where the miners were killed. Barny's grandfather. I must have a look.'

'No you mustn't,' Steve said.

She inched forward and shone her torch down the shaft. 'It's not very deep,' she said. 'I can see the bottom.'

He joined her at the edge, and shone his torch too, illuminating the pile of rock and rubble at the bottom. It was some fifty feet down, a jumble of stone and rotten timber. 'There must have been a fall,' he said, and kicked a loose stone over. It landed with a crack like a gunshot. 'All that lot down there is probably unstable, just wedged there, ready to fall hundreds of feet to the bottom of the mine.'

'I wonder if this is where the disaster occurred,' Katie said. 'I remember Mam saying something about it. I'll ask Barny.'

'Who'd be a miner?' he said. 'There might be men buried under that lot. Come on, let's get out of here. This place gives me the creeps.'

And as she turned, she slipped. One minute she was with him, the next, her light was gone and she was slithering over the edge and, before he could grab her, she was down the shaft, with a shower of stones and the rotten ladder accompanying her fall and continuing with her torch to the bottom of the pit. The noise seemed deafening as it reverberated along the chambers.

'Katie,' he called.

Boy Steve lay flat on his stomach, leaned over as far as he dared, and shone his torch on her. He could see only her legs, twenty feet down, where she was wedged on a piece of rotten timber jammed in the side of the shaft.

'Katie!'

'I'm all right.' she said. 'I'm all right.'

'Don't move,' he said.

He took the rope from his shoulder and made a big double bowline on the end and passed it round the axle of the heavily laden trolley while calling, 'Don't move! For God's sake, don't move.'

'Don't move!' he heard his voice echoing. 'Can you hear me ?'

'Yes. I'm all right.'

He lowered the bowline down to her, and watched her legs as she carefully slipped it over her shoulders, while showers of stones accompanied her every movement.

'Right,' he called. 'I'll haul in as you try to climb up. Can you do that?'

'Yes. I think so.'

He stood on the edge, looking back at her as he took the weight of her on the rope around his shoulder. She was a good climber, but on the steepest section, just before the top, he was almost pulling her up. She would gain a bit of ground while he took in the slack around the axle and then hold on to her as she struggled a little further. It was slow, but safe, the bowline would hold her if he should be obliged to leave her and fetch help. The possibility of being left in the utter blackness of that hole filled him with horror and he found the strength to pull her to the rim, where she lay exhausted.

He sat beside her and they both recovered their breath. 'Sorry,' Katie said. 'I was careless.'

'I'm just glad it was you, and not me, who went over.'

'I said I'm sorry.'

'You wouldn't have been able to pull me out. You would have had to go for help, with the torch. The thought of being left in here in total blackness and silence terrifies me.'

Katie put her grimy hand on his equally grimy bandage. 'How's your hand?'

'Hm. I'd forgotten all about that. Can you walk? I have to get out of here.'

They stood up, and Boy Steve kicked a stone into the shaft, it was as big as a net float, a football, and it fell onto the jam of timber and rock with a sharp, reverberating crack, granite on granite. As they turned away there was a rumble from underground, the sound of splintering wood, and the mass of rubble, timber and iron fell ten fathoms into the black depths of the bal.

'Don't run,' Katie said as a cloud of dust rose from the depths, 'Just follow me out.'

The sky, and the sea, were bluer than Boy Steve had ever seen them. He and Katie lay in the sunshine watching the light surf surging at the base of the cliff, the gulls wheeling overhead. They were both filthy, still slightly trembling, but the sun was warming them up. Katie removed her anorak.

'Good Lord,' she said. 'I've got rocks in my pockets.'

She took out a handful of earth surrounding a stone, saying, 'I didn't even feel it there,' and was about to throw it over the cliff but Steve said, 'Hang on! Let's have a look at that.'

He rubbed it clean with his finger, revealing a bright nugget which glistened in the sun.

'Thought so,' he said. 'Fool's gold. Iron pyrites. There used to be lots of it found in the ore, but that's a very nice piece. It's almost solid.'

'It's very heavy.'

'You can keep it as a souvenir of our first date.'

They smiled at each other. 'Will there be others ?' Katie said.

'I hope so. As long as we stay above grass.'

When they had sat in silence for some time, watching the sea, he said, 'There's fehther.'

'Your father?'

'That's what I said.'

'You said, "fehther".'

'Fehther. Father! Wus the difference? *Yma ow tass yn y cok.* There is my father in his boat.

'You said you couldn't speak the language.'

'I can't. Just a few more words I've picked up from Barny-the-Bard.'

'What did you mean by "problems" this morning?

The directness of her question took him off guard. 'What problems?'

'You know perfectly well what I mean.'

"es, well.' He floundered. 'They, well, mawther really, objects to me seeing you.'

'You haven't been seeing me.'

'Well, no. But after the last time we went down the bal, I told them I'd been with you. Mawther was full of the devil, said some pretty awful things.'

'That I'm a bastard?'

Boy Steve felt the hot blush flood his cheeks like a red tide. 'No. Not exactly. But more than that.'

'Like what?'

'I don't know. They wouldn't say.'

'Oh. That's not much help.'

'No.'

They stared silently at the sea, where the *Morwhennol* was motoring homeward around the head.

'My mother's not too keen, either.'

Boy Steve bristled with indignation. 'Why not?'

The very idea, he thought, that the mother of a bastard should object to anyone from his family seeing her daughter. 'Wu's wrong with me?'

'She didn't say. She didn't say anything. She didn't have to, there was just something in her reaction when I told her I was coming here with you today.'

'What the hell is the matter with people in this town,' he said, 'My mother has never liked your family. I don't know why.'

'There are only two of us in my family.' Katie let him consider that. Then, 'What are we going to do about it ?"

'Go home and get cleaned up,' he said, 'and I'll take 'ee out for a posh dinner tonight.'

Katie found a few bruises when she lay in the bath. There were several on her back and thighs and one on her forearm which Sarah saw as she was combing her hair.

'I fell,' Katie said. 'Down the shaft in the adit. Steve pulled me out. He had a rope.'

Sarah visibly blanched. 'Oh my dear,' she said. 'Will 'ee be careful. You're all I've got.'

'I'm sorry, Ma. I was careless. Never again.'

'Are 'ee seeing him again tonight?'

'We're going out to dinner.'

Sarah watched the brown waves glistening through the comb. Not long now, she thought, before she'll be gone. I hope so. I don't want her to know the loneliness that I have endured. But I shall miss her and be obliged to love her from afar, as her father has done. But not Boy Steve, she thought. That wouldn't do.

'I don't want 'ee to be careless in other respects either,' she said. 'Think about what you are doing with your life.'

Katie sensed the apprehension in her mother's thoughts, together with all the love she had for her. Was this the time? Katie thought, shall I ask her now. She followed her mother into the sitting room, where the bay window afforded a view across the bay, and sat in her chair. Sarah sat in hers. My mother, Katie thought, looks like the last person to have an illegitimate daughter. She always looked so prim and proper, so demure, yet she's brought me up so broad-minded and worldly that I can talk to her about anything and everything - except that! She looked at her, pouring tea, grey haired, trim figured, well read, enigmatic with her fleeting smiles.

'Mam,' she said. 'When are you going to tell me?'

Sarah was well prepared for this. She had kept herself prepared for it over the past twenty years, yet she nevertheless had difficulty in speaking for a moment. She placed the teapot on the tray and slumped back into her ancient chair. 'My cheeld,' she said. 'My dear cheeld.'

Katie came forward and knelt before her mother, with her head on her lap, 'I'm sorry, Mam.'

'I don't regret what I did,' Sarah said. 'And neither must you. I had lost both my parents, your Granda and Granma, and was an old maid at thirty-eight, with nothing to look forward to but my own company for the rest of my life. He was the only one who understood what I went through, that year.'

Her hands were fondling the brown hair on her lap. Katie raised herself to her knees and looked at Sarah, who was staring into space across the the bay before focusing on her daughter's eyes.

'Was he nice?'

'Yes, in his way. He's very kind.'

'But he wouldn't marry you?'

'No. That wasn't possible. Besides, I didn't want that.'

'And you can't tell me?'

'No. He would lose the respect of the town, don't 'ee see? Getting Sarah Stevens pregnant. My dear life.'

'Can't you trust me? Not to tell anyone?'

'No. It wouldn't do. Besides, you'll know one day.' Sarah was bringing the discussion to a close.

'You mean, 'Katie said, 'when you die.'

'Yes. Or when he does. There's a sealed letter in that drawer. I thought it only right.'

'Oh,' Katie said, dropping her head to her mother's knees again. 'I do love you, Ma.'

'Well, that's all that matters.'

Katie let the subject of Boy Steve Trevorrow lapse. Problems, he had said. Problems about seeing her.

'Caggled,' Mary said, 'Why, dammee caggled. All his clothes - why, even the very head ob'm.'

Boy Steve shrugged at his father, who grinned at Mary's remarks. Steve had learned to ignore his wife's comments on dirty clothes. They got dirty, and had to be washed, and that was that.

'And now he don't want no tay.'

'Can't help getting dirty,' Steve said, wishing his son would learn to tolerate his mother's remarks for what they were, 'when you're working.'

'You abn't asked 'n where he been,' Mary said triumphantly. 'There's no work in it. Ask 'n where he's been.'

Steve turned to his son with a wry smile. Watched him drink tea from a large mug. They were missing him aboard the *Morwhennol*, for he had turned out to be a better man at sea than ever Steve could have hoped. He had to admit that he depended on him. Couldn't his mother ever see that the boy was in command now, a grown man, and stop treating him like a child?

'Where did 'ee go, boy?'

'Down Wheal Dowr. Down the adit.'

'Gone mad,' Mary said.

'They are saying,' Steve said, 'that Simon Sweeting and they are going to use the mine for dumping nuclear waste.'

'But I heard they were thinking of working the mine for tin,' Boy Steve said. 'Thought I'd go in and have a look. I haven't been in there since I was a boy.'

'Nor me.'

'Gone mad,' Mary said. 'Why, dammee stupid! Going down there by yourself.'

'I was with Katie. She wanted to check on the bats in there and I wanted to see what Sweeting was up to, so we went together.'

'Katie Stevens!' Mary cried, and turned to her husband. 'Now, there you are. What did I tell 'ee.'

Boy Steve waited for his father's comments, to hear what they had against the Stevenses, but Steve was silent, watching his wife from under those half-closed eyelids, with a look that Boy Steve had learned to interpret as meaning: hold your tongue, before I lose my temper.

'Well,' the son said. 'I have to get ready. I'm going out tonight.'

'Going out with she I suppose.'

'What's wrong with her, for God's sake?'

'Wrong with her? Why, she's like her mother, that's what's wrong with her. Like all the other damn Stevenses. Her mother was man mad and she's the same. Of all the nice maidens in this town, you have to go out with the likes of Sarah Stevenses.... Why, Sarah Stevenses...' She faltered in frustration, reluctant to say it.

'Sarah Stevens' Bastard. Is that what you mean?'

'Now that's enough, boy,' Steve said, with quiet authority. 'Say no more.'

Boy Steve left them sitting opposite each other at the kitchen table. They said not a word until he had gone out.

The restaurant was the converted count house of a tin mine down west. In winter it was cold, for the proprietors had removed all the insulating plaster in order to expose the granite walls. They had then built a huge fireplace at one end, which drew all the warmth from the other and sucked it up the chimney. Diners near the fire had half their faces, one arm and a leg scorched by the heat of the flames, while the others were cold from the draught. Then, an additional fire had been built at the other end, which meant that the smoke from one or the other fireplace was drawn down among the diners according to the direction of the wind, and the few locals who could afford to eat here had called it the Kipper House. In summer, however, it was cool and light, with a view over the engine houses and cliffs to the sunsets in the sea, and well worth the drive out from town for the excellent, though over-priced food and, Katie thought, it's not very likely we'll meet anyone we know in here.

'He told me once,' Boy Steve said under his breath, 'that he's aiming up-market, and doesn't want the fish and chip brigade as customers.'

'Did he ?' Katie said, as she studied the menu.

'Yeah. He didn' know I was a fisherman.'

Katie laughed. 'It seems to me,' she said, 'that his scampi and french fries are the most expensive fish and chips you can buy. What are you having?'

'I always have steak, when I eat out. Mother can't cook it. What about you?'

She would pay for her own, she decided, but he need not know that yet. He was not what her mother had described... a bit wild. He was a bit shy, if anything. He caught her looking at him.

'Sorry about the plaster,' he said, waggling his thumb.

'You should see my bruises.'

He smiled at that. Yes, she thought, I can see what she means. He has a wild look in his eye, sometimes. A bit of a temper, perhaps.

'I'm going to shock them and order fish and chips,' she said. 'I fancy the trout. Is that all right?' '

Of course. Have what you like.'

'We can pay with gold,' she said, and reached into her pocket. 'Look. I've cleaned it up.'

She placed the mineral on the white table-cloth, where it caught the light from the window. Steve picked it up.

'That's one of the finest pieces I've ever seen,' he said. 'Barny would like to see that.'

There was a car pulling in to the car park outside, a Mercedes; it swerved in next to Steve's Escort and stopped too close to his offside door.

'Yes,' Katie said. 'I'll give him a ring.'

'We could call in and see him on the way back.'

'That's David Langley,' she said. 'Sweeting's agent.'

'What? Who is?'

'Out there. With Tim Penberthy. Getting out of the Merc.'

There were three men by the car, all laughing and talking loudly, their voices penetrating the quiet evening. They slammed the doors and strode towards the entrance of the restaurant.

'Only place I've found to get some decent food,' they heard Langley say as they came in. 'It would cost three times as much up in Town.'

They were shown to a table at the other end of the room, passing Steve and Katie on the way. Langley swerved along the carpet and ran his hand along the tables. 'I'm starving,' he said, 'and dying for a drink.'

'Looks drunk, to me,' Katie said.

Steve had his back to them, and turned around, briefly, to have a look. 'Who's the other one ?'

'I don't know.'

He was the only sober one, for it was evident that Tim Penberthy was also the worse for drink, a state that neither of them had ever seen him in before.

The waiter eventually brought Steve and Katie's food, and they did their best to ignore the voices of the men at the other table, until they too were served and began eating and drinking.

'Barny,' Katie said, 'will probably be at home tonight.'

'I heard he has a new girlfriend. Or so Joe says.'

'Oh, Joe,' she laughed. ' You can't take any notice of Joe.'

'Joe's all right.'

'Well, you know what I mean.'

He wasn't sure that he did. Joe was one of the most intelligent, reliable men he knew. He was as intelligent as his father, or Barny, in his own way. 'I've never been to Barny's house,' he said.

'I'm sure you'd be welcome.' She was looking beyond him and then back at him. 'Langley keeps looking at me,' she said. 'It's very disconcerting.'

Steve turned around. Langley dropped his eyes and turned to Tim, smiling broadly. 'It will be the best thing this area has seen for a hundred years,' he said, and drank deeply of a brandy glass. 'The people here deserve a break,' he continued, 'after the hardships they have suffered in the past.'

He was slenderly built, tall, pale-faced, looked as if he might have been athletic in his youth, with a runner's hips, but was no longer fit. There were the beginnings of folds of skin under his eyes. His clothes were expensive and well cut. A man who had done all right for himself, Boy Steve thought, and who could do well for Tim Penberthy too, if he played his cards right.

'How is the trout?' he said, turning back to Katie. 'I've never tasted fresh-water fish.'

The conversation of the men became subdued, as they smoked cigarettes over coffee. Steve and Katie were about to leave when Tim Penberthy came wavering past them, on the way to the gents. They heard doors slamming with hard resonance after he disappeared.

'Ready ?' Steve said, about to stand up and lead her out.

Katie waved him down with a little finger. 'Shh.'

'Wake the bloody place up,' they heard Langley saying. 'Drag the the bloody natives, kicking and screaming, into the next century. They won't know what's hit them, when we've finished with them.'

Boy Steve glanced around. Langley's companion was trying to subdue him but was brushed aside.

'Give them something to do around here apart from fishing and fucking their own daughters,' Langley said. 'Not that any of them are worth fucking.'

'Come on,' Steve said, standing up 'Let's go. Before there's any trouble. I think he's looking for a punch in the guts.'

'He can hardly stand up,' Katie said, as she stood beside Steve, 'He's really drunk.'

Langley rose and lurched toward them. 'Ah,' he said as he approached Katie, 'You look like a nice little fuck. I expect you think you're worth it, eh darling, ten quid? Twenty?'

Boy Steve turned and stood between them, his hand grabbed Langley's collar and tie as Tim Penberthy returned and the waiter came out from the kitchen with the proprietor. Langley threw a punch which Boy Steve avoided, lifting Langley almost off the ground with his left hand and punching him with a short jab to the ribs before throwing him back to his unidentified companion.

'Come on,' the waiter said, 'outside! You've finished your meal.'

The proprietor, wishing to assert himself, but impressed by Boy Steve's strength, said, nervously, 'Now then, young man, we don't want any violence.'

'If he don't control his tongue,' Steve said as he watched Langley struggling to catch his breath, 'I'll murder the Sod.'

Barny answered their knock and was astonished and delighted to see them, saying, 'No, no, it's not too late. Come on in.'

He made them coffee as he listened to their story. 'The other one will be Thorpe. He's a geologist. I've been checking up on him. A very competent man. Sweeting wouldn't employ any other, of course. Langley is a mystery. No one knows anything about him, except that he was out in Nigeria at the same time as Sweeting. But then, so was I.'

'We know someone else has been down Wheal Dowr,' Boy Steve said. 'We saw footprints when we went in looking for Katie's bats.'

'I know that Zeke has been down there,' Barny said. 'Testing for energy fields under ley lines.'

'He's a beauty,' Boy Steve said as they burst into laughter, 'Zeke is.'

'There'll be hundreds going down there soon. Either for the copper and tin, as Sweeting says, or to dump nuclear waste, which is what everybody else is saying. They'll have to conduct a proper survey, whatever they intend doing, so the bats are sure to be disturbed.'

'That's not allowed, ' Katie said. 'Bats are protected. We might be able to stop them.'

Boy Steve protested. 'You can't stop the prosperity of a whole area for the sake of a few bats.'

'We found this,' Katie said.

'Oh.' Barny said. 'That's a nice piece.' Holding it in his hand. 'Iron pyrites. Even better than my father's. My grandfather brought it up, just before he was killed in the Wheal Dowr disaster. The shaft you fell into was the one that collapsed on the miners, killing fifteen young men. There had been no maintenance, the mine was losing money, so they closed it down and no one has been down there since.' He held the glinting mineral against the light. 'Some of the old miners were quite expert at identifying minerals, you know. Some of them had wonderful collections of quartz and ore samples but officially they weren't allowed to take them. They might have sold them for a farthing or two.'

'I suppose,' Boy Steve said, 'It's called Wheal Dowr because of all the water dripping from the roof.'

'Yes, could be, but it's an unusual grammatical structure, Water Mine in English, or Mine Water, in *An Yeth*, where the adjective follows the noun. Wheal Glyp would seem more appropriate - Wet Mine.'

'It's not that wet,' Katie said.

'Wet enough for me. I'd rather be out in a squall of rain,' Steve said. 'The mine gives me the creeps.'

'You don't have any miners in your ancestry,' Barny said. 'All your family were fishermen. I have both.'

'I doubt if Langley has either,' Boy Steve said. 'The supercilious sod. I could murder him.'

The frost which had killed a few tender plants in the gardens had crumbled the turned furrows and brought the soil into a fine tilth. There had been no snow. The cold winds which had chilled the marrow of Loopy Lou were of short duration and no wished winnards had perished from starvation while sheltering in the lee of frozen clods. The ravens, which in late January had been seen carrying sticks to their nest site on the cliff or rolling upon their backs in triple-croaking flight, had fledged the young they were feeding when Louise saw them on the cliff with Barny. By the end of February Beth's garden had been tilled and Barny helped her plant the potatoes when his own early seeds were sown. She had insisted that the swelling of her belly should not prevent her from doing the heavy work in her garden, saying that her muscles were strong, the exercise would do her good.

March had remained cold, for the wind had prevailed from the east, but there had been a welcome shift to the south in April, with a warm drizzle which had germinated the seeds before dying out at the end of the moon. By May month, everything was sprouting. The spring of the year invariably invigorated Barny and he had worked with enthusiasm, erecting poles for the runner beans, hoeing the neat rows of vegetables and, with a sackful of leaf mould stolen from the woods around one of the big houses, carefully mulched his camellia.

Louise found him leaning on a long-handled shovel as he examined the rows of growing vegetables, and when he saw her at the gate he sliced the shovel into the ground with his boot, leaving it standing there, and went to greet her.

'Hello,' she said diffidently, 'Beth sent these over,' handing him a cardboard box of plants.

He was surprised at her appearance in his garden, for no one had mentioned her for weeks. 'What are you doing here?' he asked. His surprise more evident than his pleasure at seeing her.

After relinquishing the box, she did not know what to do with her hands. Briefly she clasped them behind her back, then thrust them deep into the pocket of her smock. The ephemeral smile of her initial greeting resolved itself into a stare of apprehension, as if she was unsure of his reception of her. She was afraid he might dismiss her, send her away as an unwelcome intrusion into his garden, his work, his life.

'I can go away if you're busy,.' she said.

He smiled at her timid eyes, which she withdrew from his gaze as she said, 'Beth asked me to bring the plants over.'

'Didn't you want to see me, then?' he teased her.

She found his direct question and steady gaze disconcerting. There was that element of something in his look which probed into her, searching for that which she revealed to no one. She could see that he was remembering that night, and the things she had told him when she wept in his arms, secret things, which she regretted disclosing. She feared he might despise her for being so weak, and glanced at him, briefly meeting those direct, questioning eyes. He seemed so self-assured, in a quiet, unassuming way, a man of total self-awareness. His gaze was that of an animal, primitive and open, unconcerned with what he might reveal of himself, entirely receptive and therefore revealing nothing but an intense curiosity. She sensed an innate power in him, a sensuality which frightened her.

'If you're busy,' she said, 'I can see you some other time.'

'Old men are never too busy to talk to pretty girls,' he said, as if there had never been those moments of intimacy between them, as if he did not know her.

'Am I pretty?' she asked, feeling that he would tell her the truth.

He did not answer her. He merely looked at her, wondering why she could ask such an adolescent question in response to his frivolous remark.

'My husband doesn't think so,' she said, justifying herself.

Barny placed the box on the low stone wall that surrounded his cultivated plot, turning away from her. My husband doesn't think so. The usual intimation of dissatisfied women. My husband doesn't appreciate me, but if you do, you can have me. He had heard it before.

'Did he tell you that?' he asked, turning back to her. 'Did he tell you that you are not pretty?'

'Yes.'

'Then he's a bloody fool.' he said.

What kind of man could say such a thing? he asked himself. Or what had she done to induce him to utter such a disparaging comment?

'But I'm not, am I? I know I'm not.'

She was actually inviting another depreciation, to justify her rejection. Barny refused her. 'Not at the moment,' he said. 'You look miserable and unhappy. A smile would transform your looks, if you want the truth.'

She's like a yard of pump-water, he thought, a Penavon Bar lancie sure enough. There wasn't enough meat on her to flavour a pasty. Her shoulders were slightly stooped, in the posture of tall women who are self-conscious about their height. The long black hair was hanging loose, draping her shoulders and falling in a thick cascade down her back. It was the first time he had seen it unrestrained by the tight plaiting and he noticed the sheen on it, reflected from the the light filtering through the expanding leaves of his sycamore tree. She was like a timid kitten, curious, but ready to flee at the slightest sign of danger. Yet he saw, as he looked directly at her, that her eyes were languid, their movements slow as she turned her attention from one thing to another, almost as if she was reluctant to relinquish the subjects of her gaze as being inadequately observed, or understood. No. She was not 'pretty'. Her mouth was too big, and her nose too pinched. Yet there was a classical beauty in her: the high forehead, the deep-set eyes with their broad, unplucked brows and the sensual curl to her lips. She was good-looking, too classic ever to be described as 'pretty'. Her beauty required searching for. It was in her expressions and her intelligent green eyes.

'I don't have much to smile about,' she said after a pause in which he had almost forgotten what he had said, and she turned away from him, that he might not see the welling tears.

He left that statement unqueried, as being just too much of an invitation. 'Come inside,' he said, leaving her standing as he went to the cottage door, where he kicked off his boots and waited for her. The flood of tears had not burst, so she followed him through the kitchen to the tiny living room, where he sat at the table and she on the tattered sofa.

'I didn't know you were coming down this weekend. Beth didn't say anything.'

'I didn't either. I've been trying to get away for weeks. My mother-in-law agreed to have the children at the last minute. She didn't want me to come.'

'How are they, the children?'

'Oh, all right.' She dismissed them, as if they were unimportant, and he waited for an explanation. She offered none.

'It's still bad, is it? You haven't been able to sort things out? Your marriage, I mean.'

'I don't love him,' she said, flatly. It was evident that she did not want to discuss her problem now. She had changed her mind, not wishing to burden him. 'What have you been doing?' she asked brightly.

Sometimes it seemed to Barney that no one ever said anything to any-one which was of the slightest importance. They changed the subject, avoided the truth, kept themselves secret, and, as he looked at her, he decided that she was best left within hereslf, that he would respect her reticence and ask no questions. 'Been pruning the garden.' he said. 'Helping Beth and Sam, reading, listening to music, writing, avoiding the world.'

'Have you seen this?' she said suddenly. 'I got it from the library.' Handing him a folded leaflet.

It was publicity for a forthcoming literary prize, to be awarded for poetry from a regional author. He skimmed through it to please her, but with little interest. There are many poetry competitions, all attracting thousands of submissions, each with a substantial entry fee. No thanks! But this one was a bit different. There was no entry fee for a start, and it was being promoted by the Regional Arts Association and sponsored by a national financial institution. There was a five hundred pound prize and publication in the form of a small paperback.

'Huh,' he said, 'there'll be thousands going in for this,' and, as he turned the leaflet over, saw that the closing date for entries was three months away and they wanted poetry on the theme of heritage.

'It's just what you are doing,' Louise said. 'Why don't you go for it?'

'Yes,' he said, absently re-reading the leaflet. 'Yes, perhaps I will. Thanks for thinking of me.'

Louise looked around his room. By the standards she was used to, it was shabby, and there was a thin layer of dust on the low table before her. The light from the window was showing it up as a dull film where he had not placed a book or a coffee mug to disturb it. She saw him following her gaze and turned her attention to his books, reading the titles.

'I do the housework once a month,' he said, 'or whenever people who call when I'm out write their names in the dust as a hint.'

She looked back at his smiling, self-deprecating eyes. 'You know,' she said, 'how to live, don't you?'

'Do I?' He considered her question. 'I do try to live my own life. So many people live the lives that others impose upon them, living to other people's standards, other people's ideals, aspiring to someone else's idea of achievement. I've given that up. Done it. Been there.'

'The Jones' syndrome,' she said. 'Takes a strong will to overcome it.'

He shrugged that off. 'Takes a strong will to learn to play the piano.'

'I'd better go,' she said, suddenly standing up. 'I'm interrupting your work. I thought I'd go down and look at the sea.'

She was avoiding his eyes, frightened of him, he could tell, and he wondered what there was in his demeanour which made her so, for he felt only pity for her. 'You are welcome to stay,' he said. 'I'm not doing much. Have some tea or something.' He heard his own voice, unconvincing and insincere as he also stood up, to see her out, through the garden.

'Your soil looks very fertile,' she said, looking along the neat rows. 'It must be very rewarding, to be self-sufficient.'

'I'm not that. I don't think anyone is.' Was she speaking in metaphors? 'It is rewarding to try, but frustrating too, at times.'

They looked directly at each other, trying to read more into what had been said.

'That row of stems,' he indicated a line of white stalks, 'were cabbage plants yesterday. Now look at them.'

'Slugs ?' she asked. 'Were they eaten by slugs ?'

'Doves. They go for the tender stuff. Always the tender stuff. It's the doves that do most damage.'

He resisted an impulse to accompany her. He knew the therapy in watching the motions of the waves, and they could have sat together, but she was seeking a confidant upon whom to unburden herself, and he wished to encourage no dependency.

'Another nut!' he said as he watched her walking away. 'Dropped to the bottom of the stocking.'

And how did you feel about the other man?

103

I followed the footpath that led down through the fields to the massive bulk of the headland. In seeing him again I had confirmed that the attraction I felt for him was more than physical desire. I loved him. I loved his voice, soft and deep, the sensitivity of his eyes and the way he moved his body, confident and strong. And he had dismissed me, for there was no reason for him to do otherwise. His life was full and there was no point in him becoming involved with me and my problems. I was a liability and I knew it. Had been told so more than once.

I climbed high among the rocks on the headland and watched the sea rising in dark smooth waves which made no progress towards the shore. Only the sea was moving, in a swift current as the tide swirled past the promontory over some unseen reef beneath the surface. There was a rock offshore, trailing a white smear of foam along the tide. The current of the ebb flowed west, planing over the undulations of the motionless waves and slipped along the coast in a silent race to the ocean. I saw some item in the water, a long way off, drifting slowly towards me. It was a box, made of cardboard or plywood, almost submerged and coming nearer. It gathered speed when it eventually reached the waves, swirled over them, rolling and turning in the glassy-smooth turbulence, and was lost to sight beneath the surface, never to reappear.

I felt the fear of the sea in me, saw the awesome power of it, and watched a fishing boat come motoring up from the west. It surged through the current, plunging into the black troughs, parting the waves in white curls along the bow. I could see letters and a number, painted on the side, and thought they were too close to the rocks. There were three men on board, one inside and two on deck working on the equipment, totally indifferent to the motion under their feet. As they came nearer I could read the name on the bow, *Morwennol*. They cannot see, I thought, the evil in the black, melancholy swell beneath them.

There was no sign of the box. It was gone, sucked under and disintegrated by the drag of the tide. I shuddered in a sudden chill, although the sun was warm upon my back. Not in the sea, I decided. Never in the sea.

Barny returned to his work in the garden after watching Louise go off toward the cliff. I suppose, he thought, she'll be all right, for there had been that look of desperation in her eyes. The woman was trouble. All his instincts and experience told him so, and he told himself again that he should discourage her, keep her out of his life. The last thing he wanted was a weeping woman yearning for his shoulder. He felt an irrational anger rising in him, and he pulled down on the long handle of his shovel, grunting with effort as he turned the rich, black earth. The point of the blade sliced into the soil under the weight of his foot, and he worked steadily, slipping into a rhythm of thrust lift turn, thrust lift turn, progressing along the rows.

The physical exercise kept him fit and he would later be tired, but without aches or pains. In physical work he invariably exerted himself to the full, expending more effort than was required, to compensate for the long hours he spent at his desk. The sweat ran into his eyes as he worked, and his muscles felt loose and supple over his body. He worked aggressively, sweated out the anger, until the plot was turned. He was angry with himself, for he had tried to work the thoughts of Louise Fern from his mind and failed. Don't be a fool, he told himself. She's looking for a father confessor. Forget it. But he kept remembering that other night, the desire in her eyes, the yearning of her body. She's too young. You'll make a fool of yourself. Today she had been utterly sexless, all the desire gone, yet he was still drawn to her and knew that it was all physical. There was something in the remembrance of that frail body that still excited him. The incident was lingering in his mind like an unanswered challenge.

'Ah!' he said aloud as he turned the last spit of soil, 'it's only because she's so young. You're flattered. If she were twenty years older, you wouldn't want to know.'

'I don't want to know now!' he answered himself, and went into his cottage to soak away the sweat and grime in the steaming water of his diminutive bath.

In the evening he had some letters to write, in his atrocious handwriting, about the development at Penavon, then to copy them on his typewriter. He became absorbed in his work and forgot her. The evening descended with the light all going to the west, throwing the headland into black relief against the yellowing sky. There were clouds moving in and the sunset would be obscured, but he went out to lean on his gate to watch and sense the night falling on the hills behind him. It had been some days, he realised, since he had seen Beth and Sam, and he was about to open the gate, with the intention of walking over there, when he saw Louise coming towards him, on the road. She had seen him too, and there was no escape for either of them, so he waited and watched her approach.

She was wearing the same jeans and fishermen's smock (specially made for tourists, only five quid from the harbour market) that she had worn before. He had never seen her in anything else. The plait of long black hair, hanging almost to the waist, was loose at the nape, and on her head was a hand-knitted woollen cap. She's copying all Beth's clothes, Barny thought.

'Hello,' she said, slowing her pace, but not stopping.

'It's a long way to town,' he said, and she paused at the gate, evidently wanting to talk.

'I was in the way,' she said apologetically. 'I came out to let Beth have some peace.'

'Did they say you were in the way?'

'No.'

'Then you weren't.'

She kept looking at him, dropping her eyes whenever he returned her look. He found it disconcerting. Whatever was the matter with her? They exchanged further mundane pleasantries, all lies, until she finally looked straight at him and they stared at each other in silence.

'You're looking better,' Barny said at last, for she was. There was colour in her cheeks, and her green eyes had a glint in them that he had never seen before. 'The sea air must be doing you good.'

'I think it is. I went right down to the headland this afternoon.'

'Miles.'

'It is for me. I'm not used to walking.' She smiled, then laughed as her lips parted. 'It was great.'

She was a different person when she laughed, but her laugh was fleeting, as if she considered it unseemly. 'Come in,' Barny said. 'You've probably walked enough for one day. Come in and talk to me.'

He opened the gate and held it so as she entered, saying in her timid voice, 'I won't stay long.'

And he closed the gate behind her, ensuring the latch was caught, muttering, 'The sheep keep coming in.'

In his little room, Louise stood like a slender aspen in the still air at the centre of a storm, drooping slightly at the shoulders. He did not know, again, what to do with her and almost regretted the impulsive invitation to come in. He was afraid of her, of what she could do to him, yet could not deny the attraction she had for him. He wanted to hold her, to rid her of her sorrows. She sat on the sofa, with her hands still in the pockets of her smock.

'You can take your hat off,' he said, and she did so immediately, with a gesture of submission, as if obeying his will rather than her own. Even in a little thing like removing a hat she needed encouragement and support. What a state, he thought. Does she never relax?

He went into the kitchen and returned with a bottle of wine and two glasses which he filled without asking if she wanted any. 'Here,' he said. 'Drink some of that. It's boughten stuff, better than mine.'

She took it without protest and drank most of it in a couple of gulps.

The fire was low, a glowing bed of red ashes, and Barny knelt on the floor to place a couple of pieces of dried driftwood among the embers. He was on his knees before her, watching the flames engulf the wood: tongues of red and orange and blue, with licks of green from some copper nails embedded in the timber. The flames rose, dancing, and illuminated the room. He slipped to the floor on his haunches, one elbow on the sofa, and sipped some wine, seeing images of fabulous creatures and strange faces in the flames, while Louise watched the glow illuminating his greying hair and beard.

There was nothing to say for a while. Perhaps he should put some music on. Mozart caressing a clarinet? No, he thought, not now. They watched the flames in silence.

The sun had set, the room was getting dark and the flames gradually subsided again to a warm glow of cinders until he placed another log in the grate and they were once more bathed in a rich amber glow.

'I'm leaving.' Louise said. 'Home, I mean. I can't stand it any more. I don't love him, Barny, and I just can't go on pretending any longer. I'm not going back. Tomorrow, I'm going to see about a room in town.'

Her voice was flat, monotonous, and Barny waited for her to continue, not knowing how to respond.

'I don't seem to exist when I'm with him. I'm either somebody's wife, or somebody's mother, as I used to be somebody's daughter or sister. I've disappeared as a person, and I can't cope with that.'

She needs a break, he thought, that's all, some time on her own to get herself together, something to make her laugh. What could he tell her? All this was none of his business.

'Why don't you just come here for a long holiday? A month, say; be on your own for a while.'

'He won't let me. He would have to employ a nanny, he says, and can't afford it. I wanted to get a job, but he won't let me do that either, even though I offered to pay half a child minder's wage.'

'There are no jobs here,' Barny reminded her. 'Hundreds on the dole or social security.'

'It's different here. The people seem to know how to live without being involved with the rat race. Beth and Sam don't care about money.'

He wondered if she realised how hard they worked, how little they had left over at the end of each month. She was seeing the prospects here through the same rose-coloured spectacles that so many others had viewed the place through from their distant predicaments. So many dreams he had seen shattered here, but she might settle in, if she could find the right person to love and protect her.

But that's not me, he thought.

CHAPTER SIX

Yn kever an den... . Concerning the man... .

After she said that she was leaving her husband, Barny, for some reason which he never expressed to himself, did not mention Louise to Sam and Beth. Her name would never have arisen in conversation if Sam had not said, on the day after he saw her, in that hesitant way of his, 'So... Louise.'

'Yes,' Barny said. 'Louise indeed.' And he left it at that, not expecting to see her again.

He continued with his settled way of life, earning just enough to live on by doing odd jobs for friends, or a bit of labouring, or farming and, when persuaded by persistent requests, some electrical work. He avoided the latter as much as possible, for he was aware that he might well find himself in business again, having his time taken up earning money he did not need. People, especially those who did not know him too well, told him he could make a fortune at his profession, and those who had come down here to escape the rat race said he was a typical local yokel, too dimwitted to see the opportunities under his own nose.

For four hours every day, he tried to write. That is to say he sat at his table for those hours, although the writing was merely the expression of thoughts which may have preoccupied his mind for days, weeks, and there were many occasions when he produced nothing but a basket of waste paper.

Steve Trevorrow came out to look at his roof and windows two months or so after Barny spoke to him about the job, during which time those who did not understand the way of things would have gone to another builder in exasperation. Barny forgot about it, in the knowledge that Steve would turn up all in good time and there was no point in doing anything during the winter.

Steve brought his old friend and crewman Uncle Joe, who came along for the ride and to see a part of the countryside he rarely visited, although it was only twenty minutes away in the van.

'Who would live out here?' Joe said. 'Miles from anywhere.'

They put a ladder up through the trap-hatch, and Steve examined the roof. He stuck his knife into the woodwork of the windows and door.

'It's all rotten,' Uncle Joe said, pre-empting Steve's pronouncement on the state of the property. 'Must be the fog down here. D' never get a chance to dry out.'

Barny produced some home-brewed beer. 'Here,' he said. 'Drink that, and shut up.'

Joe had all the signs of ageing. His skin was lined and weather-beaten. He had lost a couple of teeth and his hair was mottled with white, although still thick and wiry. He was still very strong, but he did not look fit. Too much time spent in the pubs, Barny thought, and no responsibilities. He had never had anyone to care for and had not taken care of himself. Too much freedom, Barny decided, can be more pernicious than certain constraints. Joe had avoided the commitments of life, such as marriage, when he was a young man, refusing to compromise his independence, so it seemed, and had lived the whole of his adult life alone. He had his share of women in his youth, for his rugged looks and dry wit attracted them, but he had never, apparently, been in love or, perhaps, could never admit it.

The roof was not too bad, Steve reckoned; might last for years. On the other hand, a strong gale could take the lot off at any time. The windows were sound enough for a few more years and the draught through the door would stop the chimney from smoking.

'You can't expect these old places to be like a nice new bungalow.'

'You can keep them,' Barny said. 'Sterile boxes.'

'I heard on the wireless,' Joe muttered absently, 'that these old houses are full of this 'ere radon gas. Wouldn't catch me living in one of them.'

He lit a cigarette. His eyes were not old, Barny noticed, and his wit as cynical as ever. Joe's own house was even older, as they all knew, in the narrow old streets of down'long.

'Your place,' Barny said, 'is built of driftwood and wreckage. It's been all around the world. The woodworms get seasick every time the tide d' turn.'

'Character,' Joe mused. 'It's a character cottage in the fishermen's quarter. Tim Penberthy said so, and he ought to know. He's one of these here estate agents.'

'Experts,' Barny agreed.

They eventually came around to discussing the cost of renovating Barny's cottage. Steve worked it out, roughly, by allowing so much for timber, new purlins and rafters, so much for the chimney flashings, a bit for sand and cement and lime, and so much for slates and copper tingles.

'As much as that ?' Barny said. 'Is that what asbestos slate costs these days? How much is Delabole, for God's sake?'

'Hell of a price,' Steve said.

'How don't 'ee have corrugated iron ?' Joe asked. 'My old man built a chicken house with galvanised iron down Bamaluz sebmty years ago and it was still there, good as new, till the council knocked 'n down. Coat of tar now and then. Last for ever.'

'Take no notice ob'm,' Steve said. 'His house has a new roof, so he can laugh.'

'Have a grant,' Joe said, as if there was really no problem over money. But Barny was not eligible for a grant. His house was not in a 'Conservation Area' and he was not a pensioner or on any Social Security. Whatever he spent, he would be obliged to find for himself.

Steve thought it was time to go. Barny would make his own decision regarding the roof. 'I'll send 'ee the estimate,' he said, 'near enough. When I've worked 'n out exactly.'

Despite his derogatory remarks, Joe was in no hurry to leave; he liked the ambience of Barny's cottage and the flavour of his beer even more. 'This stuff cheap to make, is i'?' he said.

Barny refilled Joe's glass and offered some to Steve, who accepted a mere topping up of a small glass from which he had barely sipped.

'I'm driving,' Steve said. 'That stuff will blow your head off. I've had some before.'

So they stayed a bit longer, drinking and yarnin'. They were not fishing that day although conditions were ideal, for they had fished their quota.

'Always the same,' Steve said, 'when there's no fish you can go out when you mind to, and when there's fish you aren't allowed to catch them. Used to be the markets, always closed in a glut because they couldn't handle the quantity. It's always been the same.'

'Where's Boy Steve ?' Barny asked, 'Home studying the language?'

'Language? No. Lifeboat practice this mornin' and he's gone over to Penavon 'safnoon. Some of the chaps are having another meeting about the fishing industry. Quotas and one thing and another. And now we have the environmentalists saying we're killing all the birds and dolphins. Make 'ee sick!'

Barny knew that he and young Katie were included in that category. 'Why are they going over there? Why not in town?'

'Simon Sweeting is attendin'. He's got plans to reopen the port and for a fish processing plant and facilities on the quay.'

'What about the sand bar?'

'You musn' ask,' Joe said as he lounged back on the sofa, 'about the bar. Thought you would a' knowed that.'

Barny had no need to ask about the bar as it was. The sandbanks across the mouth of the river shifted with every tide, had always been dangerous, and had claimed enough lives already.

'He's got big plans,' he said. 'Mr Simon Sweeting. Big plans.'

'There's to be a public meeting,' Steve said. 'With all the plans on show. He's spending millions of pounds, so they say. New houses, shops, a marina, brea thing.'

Be a brea thing all right, Barny thought. The old port had been derelict for a hundred years, gradually deteriorating as the industry which had vitalised it declined. First the mining went, then, with the improvements in road and rail services, the shipping trade, and finally the shut-down of a big timber yard which imported logs from Scandinavia. The place was dead, with the quays falling down and the sandbar beginning to block the harbour through lack of sluicing. It was an ugly remnant of its former glory.

'I heard,' Joe said, wiping his mouth, 'that you have a new woman, Barny.'

'Oh?'

'You've been seen.'

In town, of course, the day they saw the man overboard and Boy Steve with Sarah Stevens. He would also have been seen with her on her last weekend visit, and they might have seen her since she moved down, which Barny had not. Joe merely wanted confirmation of rumour that she was indeed Barny's 'new woman'.

'Leave it alone, my 'ansome,' Steve said. 'Bring tears to your eyes and rags to your ass. Leave it alone, I tell 'ee.'

Nothing changes, Barny thought. Yet everything changes. Time passes and leaves people stranded in their era, like shells cast ashore by a receding tide. They stay where deposited by the most violent turbulence in their lives, unless overwhelmed by further waves, when they are once more dragged into motion by an irresistible undertow. Steve had weathered such an emotional storm, had been thrown high and dry, well beyond the reach of further tides. He was safe.

Barny knew that both these old friends had taken stock of their lives, made profound decisions, just as he and Shimshai had done, but these two made no attempt to impart their philosophy on others, would, indeed, deny such a concept in their lives. They were complete in themselves, now, having no desire to communicate or expose themselves in order to find proof of their existence. Maybe, especially in Steve's case, they had revealed too much in the past. They spoke to each other of the superficial, home-brewed beer and money, yet were able to impart their deepest feelings without compromising themselves. It was a talent he did not share, so he said less.

They knew all about him, however, despite his reticence, and they made fun of his poetry with remarks which were intended as implied admiration. Steve, in particular, occasionally said something revealing, to those who understood him, like: 'Don't knaw what you d' find to say. Too many hours in your own head will drive 'ee mad, my 'ansome.'

There were times when Barny appreciated the truth of this. The hours in his own head were dangerous times and brought the thing upon him. Yet, it was only by risking the dangers that he could induce the agonies and ecstasies which were his secret, creative life. Did these two suffer it, he wondered. They had been speaking to him but he had not heard.

'What the hell's a like ?' Joe said. 'Gone off in a bleddy trance.'

'I was listening,' Barny lied. 'I was just thinking of something.'

Steve evidently thought he was thinking of the cost of his renovation work, and to cheer him up said, 'There will be jobs across the river very soon, for everybody. You can always get a few bob together. A man of your experience.'

Jobs across the river! At what cost? He didn't want any of it.

'It's not that,' Barny said, correctly interpreting the unspoken implication behind Steve's remark. 'I could probably manage to have the job done without the help of Simon Sweeting. No. I was thinking about something else.'

'Your new woman,' Joe said, still anxious for confirmation of the rumour.

'I don't have a bleddy woman,' Barny insisted, 'new or old. What do I want to be bothered with a woman for?'

'Tall,' Joe said, as if he had not heard. 'Long black hair. Thin as a lancie. A fine craft, so I was told.'

She was a fine craft all right, Barny thought. But there was no way I could have had her. She was sick, gasping for sex as a substitute for love, and would have taken it from anybody who showed her the most spurious signs of affection. He had never known a woman so desperate for it, but to have taken her would have been like abusing a child. He remembered the things she had told him through her sobs on his sofa, such intimate things, and there was more, much more, that she had concealed. He thought of her white, emaciated body, the starved ribs, thin arms, weak shoulders, bony hips, the bushy black mound and those pathetic, beautiful little breasts. Poor little maid, everything about her was small except her size. No, she was wounded and vulnerable, would become dependent on any who offered her affection. He had got out of it very well, considering how he had allowed himself to be enticed by her, and she had not felt rejected. Women like that were trouble, and he was relieved to think that she had gone out of his life. Yet, and yet.... She was the most female thing he had ever seen, so vulnerable, so submissive, so desirable, the very smell of her was redolent with sexuality. She was the most concupiscent woman he had ever touched, and he felt himself hardening at the memory of her gasping orgasm as her body shuddered under the touch of his hands. By God, he had to admit that he had wanted her. But she was so thin, so pitifully thin. With skin like a peach, he thought, and eyes as green as the sea, with tears as wet. He was annoyed with Joe for reviving memories which were beginning to fade. He wished to forget her, but could not.

'Oh,' he said. 'Her! She's the girl you saw down on the beach. She's a friend of Sam and Beth, across the road,' he reluctantly informed them. 'She's years younger than me... .'

'Aw 'ess,' Joe said.

Barny had said too much, given something away in the intonation of his voice. He looked at Steve, who was suppressing a grin in the knowledge that Barny, the poet, was, for reasons unknown, on the defensive against the illiterate Uncle Joe, and whatever he said could be construed, or misconstrued, as ever Joe should wish. He said nothing until the silence became prolonged, and then... .

'She's come down here to live,' he said. 'Somewhere in town. I don't know where.'

He was not likely to see much of her again, so it hardly mattered what Joe thought. It didn't matter what Joe thought under any circumstances, he concluded in irritation. What did Joe know about women? He had always maintained that women, like jobs, were to be exploited while they lasted, but marriage was like a career, demanding commitment and dedication before getting the sack and a gold watch after outlasting one's usefulness. 'I can tell the time by the bleddy sun,' he once retorted when asked why he had never married. And some thought he had been drunk.

114

'Leave it alone,' Steve said. 'You're old enough to know better. Tears to your eyes and rags to your ass, my 'ansome, so sure as God made little dudgels.'

True enough. They had both suffered at the hand of women.

'That's what I thought. Best left alone.'

He remembered his hands on her delicate skin. 'Best left alone.'

Joe put his glass down, with a sigh of appreciation, and smacked his lips. 'I must have a go at making that stuff,' he said. 'Not bad, is i'?'

'Not bad at all,' Barny agreed, with a quick glance of amusement at Steve.

''ess,' Joe said. 'Well. Ha! P'raps I shall have a go at 'n.'

'You'll have to,' Barny said. 'Because that's the last, or I'd give 'ee a bottle.'

'Come on,' Steve said. 'Time we were making tracks.'

He rose from his chair and turned to Joe, who drained the last dregs from his glass.

'Wus that light flashin' theer?' Joe said, indicating the hi-fi in the corner.

'Oh,' Barny said. 'I left the recorder on.'

He rewound the tape, pushed play, and they heard Steve's voice say, 'Leave it alone, my 'ansome. Bring tears to your eyes and rags to your ass. Leave it alone, I tell 'ee.'

They laughed, and Joe said, 'I cain't see the point of writing things down, if you've got one of they things.'

'Neither can I,' Barny said.

He went out to see them off, and they paused in the garden to look at the neat rows of crops, flower beds, his camellia, piles of seaweed rotting down, and he was pleased by their nods of approval.

'I s'pose,' Joe said, with a face as bland as lettuce, 'You d' enjoy producin' all this orgasmic stuff.'

Barny suppressed a grin, for Uncle Joe was not as inarticulate as he pretended. 'For me, Joe,' he said earnestly, 'inserting the seed is the climax of the year.'

He saw them out to Steve's old van, all laughing, and, as they climbed in, said, 'I'll brew some more beer, Joe, and you can have a drop next time you're passing.'

God knows when that would be, he thought as he watched them drive off. Joe had seen more of the world 'out foreign' than he had of his homeland, for he rarely went anywhere merely for sightseeing or from curiosity. There was nothing down this way to interest him, just farms and old mines, of which he knew, and wished to know, nothing.

All gone, he mused as he returned to his chaotic table and removed the empty bottle and glasses. All gone! The old days, the old ways. They had gone faster than any of them had imagined possible. Even in their awareness of change they had been overwhelmed, and were beyond bewilderment. The past was receding like a man overboard, lost in the wake, to be drowned before their helpless eyes. Gone. Sunk! Lost forever under the waves of change. They had not mentioned times past in their conversation, yet it could not have taken place without their mutual antecedents, for theirs was now the conversation of absences, the unspoken. 'Jobs across the river'. He smiled ruefully to himself and sat down at the table, reaching for his note pad and pencil.

There was an idea, engendered by no more than that laconic expression of Steve's, which had stirred his imagination. Jobs across the river. He wrote it at the top of the page, trying to restrain his hand and keep the writing legible. It was when the work was going well, when he found the confidence to get it down on paper, suck it out of his head and squeeze it into these squiggling symbols of sound, that Barny was happy.

As he wrote, the thoughts and memories of Louise Fern were diluted as a tributary is diluted on entering a river. The sediment and particles from its source are carried into the main stream, held in suspension until filtered out, cast upon a bank or swirled to the all absorbing ocean. He forgot about her as he sat searching for words and, during the ensuing weeks, she faded from his mind like a white sea-mist dispersed by the rising sun.

There were times when Barny doubted himself and his ability as a poet and considered abandoning the whole struggle as a pretentious self-indulgence. Steve was right, as usual, no one ever read it. Everyone was their own poet, experiencing their own emotions, which were not diminished or less intense for not being communicated to others. Why bother with it? Sometimes there was more fulfilment in growing carrots or wiring an electric plug. Nevertheless, he went along to the monthly meetings of the poetry group which, for him, were social rather than literary occasions. They met in each others' houses, although some members thought it would be better to meet in the pub as alcohol would be more relaxing and they might accumulate an audience with whom to communicate. They were out-voted on the grounds that houses were 'more intimate'.

'If it's intimacy you want... .' Barny had once said to a staid old maid who wrote poetry about, and dedicated to, her cats, '...No, never mind. Tea it is.'

He had some good friends among them, however, for they at least knew of the difficulties in trying to say something important in an individual voice. The next meeting was to be in his own house, and he went into town to see his father and pick up Anne, who sometimes came to the readings. His father thought he was off his head to give up a lucrative job to write poetry, but he never said so, just mentioned, now and then, that there was a good job going with so-and-so, or that wha's-his-name was doing well, with a new car and all.

His father had never been without work since the 1930s, when he and his young wife knew what it was to have no job, no money and no prospects. This, though, was rarely mentioned, for he lived in the present, letting the past recede into the distance where it belonged. He had done everything, anything, that came along, and work became his life, for the insecurity of those early days hung over his generation like a blanket of fear.

'With all the thousands out of work now,' Barny said, 'I'm doing somebody a favour by not getting a job or starting a business. I'm all right. I have enough to manage on.'

'Well,' his old man said doubtfully, 'you know best.' Implying that his son knew nothing of the sort.

Anne was one of the few women he knew who never wore trousers or jeans. She dressed in long skirts, with shirts or blouses, jumpers in winter, and had a way of walking, with long confident strides, which was far more enticing and feminine than those arses constricted by contrivedly provocative denim. They went back to his place early to prepare all the cups and mugs for the fifteen or so people expected to attend.

'It would save a hell of a lot of work if we met in the Tinner's Arms,' he grumbled.

'Don't be such an old misery,' Anne said.

They all read their latest work, some good, some bad, and some terrible, and congratulated each other on the effort before joining in discussion and criticism from which Barny abstained, considering himself unqualified to comment on other people's work, and he tried not be be influenced by them in return. He knew that there were hundreds, thousands, of similar groups of poets and writers meeting all over the country, turning out millions of words which would be unread after these initial airings, kept in drawers until thrown out by spouses and children when the writers were safely beyond indifference, in their graves. The meetings were part of his routine, however, and he enjoyed the discussions. There was only one rule in this group, and this had been at Barny's instigation: that they could say what they damn well liked, for an inhibited poet was a contradiction in terms, a castrated bull, and might as well shut up as attempt to bellow in a whisper.

His was, as usual, the only local voice, reading his latest, 'Across the River,' which they thought was about water, and he listened to evocations of familiar scenes from people who thought they appreciated their new surroundings far more than the locals who took it all for granted or were hell bent on destroying it. For this reason he did not speak with his strongest voice, breaking his own rule, and read stuff which would not offend the newcomers. As he read, he heard his own accent and, in this company of English literates, did not know what to do with it. He would not, could not, hide or repress it; yet the voice categorised him, placed him beyond accepted authority. His voice was from outside, even in his own house, from the uneducated fringe, and would never be attended to as carrying prestige or influence. His poem was listened to in silence and evoked no response.

When they had gone, he filled a couple of glasses with elderberry wine, put one on the table in front of Anne and slumped into his ancient chair.

She saw one of his depressions on the way as he pressed his temples between fingers and thumb, sighing deeply. 'Can't they hear me? he said. 'Is my accent too broad, or something?'

'If it was, people would listen,' Anne said. 'That wasn't you speaking. The poem was fine. You were afraid of it.'

'Oh G... od,' he sighed.

She had disclosed, once more, her total perception of him, which he found so irritating. She was another one who knew him too well and made him wonder whether he was too open, whether he would ever have anything to say which was not obvious to those who knew him. No, it was not that. Over the years Anne, like Steve and Shimshai, had become part of him, an inseparable element of his identity, like his manner of speech or walking and the lines on his face, without which he would have been a different person, someone else.

'Why don't you marry me?' he said. 'You know me well enough.'

'No. I'll never marry you. I love you, but I won't marry you. You are too difficult.'

'Stay here for the night.'

'No. Take me home.'

'I'm difficult?' he said in exasperation. 'Then you're impossible. Making me drive all that way when I have to go in again tomorrow morning. Stay here! You can sleep in the bed, and I'll stay down here on the sofa, if you like.'

'No.'

'Well, sleep with me then. Come to bed with me, I mean.'

'No. We can't do that any more. Not these days.'

He considered what she meant. 'All because of those African monkeys?'

'Yes. It's too dangerous.'

'Oh, for God's sake! I haven't been anywhere.'

He thought, now that he had suggested it, how comforting it would be to sleep in her arms, to feel her warm body against him in the night.

'We needn't make love,' he said. 'Just sleep with me.'

'No. Don't be silly. We would do it. You know we would.' There was suddenly a note of sadness in her voice. 'I must go home.'

She was right, as usual. The days of casual sex were gone, even with old partners like Anne. He would never convince her that it would be safe with him, but said again, 'I only want to sleep with you... hold you in my arms... .' His voice diminished as he checked himself, giving too much away again.

Anne shook her head, unable to rely upon her own voice before saying, 'We can't.'

And he knew that they could; that he could have fondled her, taken her by the hand and led her upstairs to his bed, that it would have been perfectly safe, for neither of them had been anywhere else. Neither of them was promiscuous, so why had their passion died? He sighed, and said, 'All right, then. As you wish. I'm too tired to argue.'

As he looked at her he found himself thinking of Louise, comparing the two of them, the practical common sense of Anne, the nervous insecurity of the other. He was thankful that she had gone out of his life and would probably soon return to her family, where she belonged. What a life she lived, if her disclosures were true, but how much of it was? She was in such a state that he suspected she would have said anything to have elicited a little sympathy. She was off her head, poor little thing. If anyone was near to a nervous breakdown, she was. The sudden tears, the hysterical laughter over the silliest of his jokes, the desperate desire for sex as a means of emotional release, all the signs were there. He thought of her lying naked on the bed, offering herself with apologetic revulsion for her emaciated flesh, believing herself fat when she was obviously starved, the fear and lust both in her eyes. What a state!

Anne was talking, telling about a visit from her ex-husband, but Barny did not hear her.

'I was thinking... ,' he said, but faltered, admitting it would be a breach of trust to tell Anne about Louise, even to mention her name. 'No, it doesn't matter.'

'You're not listening to me.'

The voice of Anne dispelled the unwelcome memories of the thin body and tremulous confessions. He was forced to concede that he could not get the damned woman out of his mind. The conversations of those few hours impinged themselves into his thoughts like memories of disturbing dreams. Despite himself, he he heard his own voice say, 'Anyway, there is someone else.'

Anne looked at him with a bland face. She's no good at hiding her feelings either, Barny thought. She's thinking I said that to make her jealous, to come to bed with me. She *was* jealous. He suppressed a grin. 'Lovely bit of gear,' he said, watching her. 'Not like you.'

'You're lying.'

'Am I? If you won't go to bed with me, I have to find somebody who will.'

'Who is she?'

'You don't know her. A bit of young stuff.'

Anne laughed. 'You are lying,' she said. 'Girls are not interested in you. You're too old.' She released another peal of laughter at calling his bluff.

Women! he thought. They think they can say anything to a man, any insult, or make any comment on his deficiencies, his looks, balding head, clothes, age, with impunity, while similar remarks in the other direction would be regarded as male chauvinism. How could men ever wish to be entangled with any of them, the selfish bitches? He looked at her without retaliating for he had no wish to be cruel, no wish to point out her lines, the loss of lustre in her hair, the breasts showing the first reaction to the forces of gravity. She was still an attractive woman, but her physical attributes would not last forever, no more than his.

'What's she called?' Anne asked. 'Fifi? Or Carmen? It would have to be something sexy.'

'I wasn't thinking of her. You ought to be going.'

There was something in his voice which was dismissing her, and Anne realised that she had upset him without knowing why. There was also something which told her he had not been lying about this girl. She was apprehensive, for his own sake as well as her own.

'You can tell me her name,' she said.

Why not? he thought. The damned girl was gone from his life, so what did it matter.

'Louise,' he said indifferently. 'She's called Louise.'

The name seemed to astonish Anne. She looked at him with an expression of near disappointment in her eyes, as though she had been thwarted in her intention of further deriding Barny's new acquaintance.

'Louise is a lovely name,' she said with an involuntary catch of sadness in her voice. 'I have always thought so.'

Anne would not lie to him, even to score points in their teasing games of banter.

'You *are* jealous,' Barny said, and saw her mouth pucker in a defiant pout which amused and puzzled him.

'Only of her name,' she said. 'I expect she's fat and ugly.' Laughing once more.

'ess, well, it doesn't matter.' He found himself disconcerted at the possibility of revealing even the most insignificant information about Louise to Anne. 'It's time I was taking you home, if that's what you want.'

That was no longer what she wanted. She wanted to stay, but he held up her coat in an unambiguous gesture and she slipped her arms through the sleeves, saying, 'Bastard!'

She doesn't know, he thought, that Louise is the same girl she saw down at the beach.

They drove back along the winding road in virtual silence, not in animosity, for there was no irreparable breach between them, but because there was nothing they wanted to say. He dropped her at her door, with a perfunctory kiss, and drove back along the familiar road thinking of what they had said. As a few early moths passed through the beams of his headlights and the eyes of a badger sparkled in the hedge, he became lost in abstraction, driving without thought around the bends. He remembered their conversation, of tonight and nights past, and realised that without her, without his friends and acquaintances and the influence they had on him, he would not exist. He would be as a painting with different pigments, a house with different windows... another scene.

He concluded, however, that they were both too difficult to live with, to marry. But that was not really the obstacle, for they got on very well in fact, and it was their respective independence that neither was willing to compromise. He was quite happy living alone, and so was she. His cottage and fertile garden, after the years he had spent on improving and planting, were now his retreat and sanctuary, where he could live and work in peace.

One day, probably, he and Anne would marry, or live together. The time would come when one or the other suggested it, expecting refusal, and was accepted. What a shock that would be. They had been near it tonight. 'I do love you,' she had said, 'but... ,' ostensibly as a refusal, yet, if he had said the same to her, taken her to bed, they would be faced with the prospect of decisions which neither wished to make. It had always been like this, one saying, 'I love you,' or 'Will you marry me?' expecting, hoping for, rebuttal. Neither had yet said in the same breath, 'I love you and want to marry you,' at a time when it was obvious the other wanted it.

I am still behaving like a silly child, he thought. At my age. How absurd.

When he parked the car outside his cottage, he was smiling to himself. Inside, he placed the poem he had read that night among the other finished work in the folders. Despite their fights, the stings inflicted by mutual candour, from which he smarted more than she, he was invariably invigorated by her company and was smiling at her rejection of his proposition that she sleep with him. Did he love her? he mused as he threw his hat to its accustomed place on the arm of the sofa. In a way, yes. But he liked her more. He sat down for a few minutes, utterly content with his life, his friends, and his prospects, such as they were. Then he climbed the winding stairs to his bedroom, smiling to himself again in the realisation that he was a happy man. He was not yet fulfilled, or even content, for he still had too many ambitions to achieve, but he was happy in that he was free to work toward his aspiration, which was to say something worth listening to. His smile became a cynical chuckle and he called himself a 'big-headed bastard', immediately changing the phrase written in his mind to 'I am a pretentious solipsist,' as he opened the door.

In the darkened bedroom, he looked out over the sea, as he did every night before turning in, and counted the intervals of the revolving beam radiating from the lighthouse.

Seen from the shore, the beams turned over the ocean like the spokes of a gigantic wheel, slowly sweeping the horizon before being sliced from a complete circle by the shield in the lighthouse which prevented the beams from shining inland and directly into the windows of the cottages. In the distance he could see the lights from passing ships to whom the lighthouse was an anachronism, a relic for which they paid but never used, for they took their bearings from the radio beacon on the hill two miles inland and had no need to look out of the windows on the bridge, so they thought. Barny lay down in his bed with both curtain and window wide open and fell instantly asleep.

It came upon him, as always, as if in a dream, in that he was unaware of the processes of the mind which induced the images. They were there when he awoke with fear in his heart and the sweat on his body dampening the sheets. There was no instant when it could be said that he woke. The thing was in him while he slept, yet there was no memory of a dream, for the emotion was deeper than the level of dreams. The images were like some primitive ore beyond the reach of the miners who followed the lodes beneath his house. Something from deep down in the depths had risen to grass to torture him, and stayed hidden in the dark so that he could never identify it. It was fear itself. Of what the fear was he did not know, for there was nothing in his life to be afraid of. It was the knowledge of what the fear was about to manifest itself into that filled him with terror. There was no way of stopping it, nowhere, in some quiet niche of the mind, to where he could escape, no sanctuary to which he could leap from his bed and run.

Still unaware of whether he was asleep or awake, he flung his head from side to side saying, 'No, No,' in an attempt to force the thing to leave him alone, trying to fling it from his head, knowing that it would not go until all the terrible images had passed through his mind to leave him filled with the horror of the inevitability of death. It was death itself that crept out from deep in the bal to torment him in the night.

He opened his eyes, staring at the ceiling where the rhythmic illuminations of the lighthouse intensified and diminished in slow pulsating regularity. In an attempt to force the terrible thing from his mind he sat up, holding his head, but the images, the forms, the thoughts, were still there; now memories, now ideas, recollections of visions which were as lifetimes lived in pain. He lay back with a groan of despair, naked, the bed clothes tossed aside, with his eyes wide open in a waking nightmare of terror as the horrors passed through his mind like a grotesque, silent mime.

'No. Oh no!'

The voice was a mere breathless croak, a denial of the instruments of exquisite torture his mind kept stored away in its black dungeons. He watched the progression of scenes until the final disgusting climax appeared and he flung himself aside in an attempt to escape and screamed for help.

'LOUISE!'

Her name came involuntarily to his lips, and the cry of anguish broke the succession of images as if they were shattered in a splintered mirror.

It was the worst one he had ever endured. Why? He buried his face in the pillow, sobbing, 'Louise, Louise,' and drew the sheets around himself with the wet hem between his teeth.

Louise, he thought. Why her? Of all the people, demons, spirits and saints he could have invoked, hers was the last name he would have expected to burst from his lips in one of his terrors.

He turned on his back and watched the silent pulsations of light illuminating his bedroom as the fearful images imploded into the black holes of his subconscious.

Louise! And he fell asleep, exhausted yet relieved, as if the tremors in his mind were the result of some seismic shift of tension deep in the bedrock of his conception, and he woke the following morning with no thought of her in his head.

CHAPTER SEVEN

Fleghes hep skyans a vyn gul aga syansow. Senseless children will compose their fancies.

'...And what about your sister?
She was prettier than me...'

The girls shared a bedroom in a small rented flat in the less affluent end of Harrow. Their surname was Fern: Bruce and Valeria the parents, Louise and Heather the daughters. Heather always resented her name, and as she grew older said it sounded like acid heathland. Louise regarded her appellation, coupled with their address, as befitting her intellectual superiority over her contemporaries at school. She often omitted the ignominious 'Flat six' from her address and included only the name of the block. *Louise Fern, Elizabeth Court, Harrow-on-the-Hill,* she wrote in her exercise books, and later on her letters, with satisfaction. The postman knew which flat the Ferns occupied, as there were only ten in the block.

Heather was not as industrious in her school-work as Louise. She was bright and gregarious, even rebellious at times, and more precocious and worldly than her older sister, mixing effortlessly with other children while Louise became shy and withdrawn. Heather was often spoken of by her mother as 'the pretty one,' which caused Louise to withdraw even more, not appreciating that the remark was intended to compensate Heather for her lack of academic achievement. Louise came to believe herself ugly and unattractive.

Their mother was a highly-strung, sparrow-like woman who suffered a near breakdown on her husband's departure, and continually instilled into her daughters the necessity of providing for their own future as men could not be relied upon for anything. The flat was cramped, but Valeria kept it clinically clean and tidy, rising early to do the housework before going off to her job in a chain store, instructing the girls on their duties to be performed before her return in the evening. 'Coma straight home from school and don'ta talka to no strangers. Don'ta forgeta the ironing. Keepa the doora locked.'

The girls reacted to their parents in opposite ways. Louise followed her mother's counsel, becoming meticulous in her appearance, seeking approval. Heather became resentful of continual admonition, untidy and careless about her appearance and regarded her older sister as a narrow-minded prude and her mother as an old fuss-pot. 'What does it matter, for Christ's sake?' she said on one occasion, after Bruce had gone, and sent her mother into hysterics about blasphemy before God. 'Whata become of you? Witha no Papa?'

Whereas Heather was disobedient and unindustrious, scornful of the nuns' unworldliness, Louise conducted herself with proper demeanour and deference to her peers. She was superior to her sister in her virtues, and resented her carefree, irresponsible attitude, and especially con-demned her in her attitude to boys. She could not understand why one so naughty could be so popular. Even their father seemed to prefer Heather's disrespectful company to her own, which was most unfair when she unfailingly tried to please him and held him in such high esteem.

The differences were exacerbated by the conditions under which the sisters lived. In the bedroom, Louise resented Heather's indifference to order, and fumed with resentment when she borrowed a book or clothes without asking. She became possessive and territorial, laying her possessions out with meticulous care, everything in its place and labelled. Her books were arranged on her shelves under authors in alphabetical order, or occasionally changed as to subject matter, as in the library where she spent much of her time. She kept notebooks, in which she made lists; of her school subjects, marks for exams, her schoolfriends' names, and a diary in which, by means of a secret code, she recorded her daily routine and aspirations: 'Read *Wuthering Heights,* an excellent novel in my opinion, but a little long-winded. B.T. spoke to me on the way home from school. He is good-looking but a little coarse in his speech, I shall not encourage him...'. She kept them hidden from her sister, under the neatly folded clothes in her bottom drawer.

Despite their parents' warnings of the the consequences of mixing with 'the wrong sort' of children, and their continual exhortations to 'maintain their standards' they never seemed to have any close friends of their own age. Neither did they have any money. Bruce refused, as a matter of principle, he said, to get a job apart from acting. He said there was never anything suitable, and the only time the girls ever saw him lose his temper with their mother, apart from the final night, was when she suggested that, while waiting for a part, he could work part time on the sales floor of the store. He suddenly turned on her, saying she had no respect for his talent and that she was trying to destroy him. For the first time, despite the aggression of his attack, Louise saw her father on the defensive. There was more in her mother's calm proposal than was immediately evident. She remained composed, and her dark eyes condemned him before their daughters. He had always been right in everything he said, there had never been any argument to refute his ineluctable logic. His statements and conversation were all carefully considered before utterance. He had, he told them on frequent occasions, been obliged to work hard in his younger days to eradicate a socially unacceptable and professionally reprehensible East Side accent and learn to control his voice under the emotional stress of performance. Despite the long elocution lessons, with a shabby woman who had slipped down the social ladder to meet Bruce on the way up, the clipped vowels now emerged from regression in his anger.

'For Chrise sake, woman,' he cried. 'I have to be available. You know dat.'

Louise sided with her father. He was an admirable man to stand by his principles, and, one day, she knew, they would all have occasion to be proud of him. She was upset at being forced to defend his ideals, and a little disconcerted to see the grim determination on her mother's face. She found herself watching the argument as one would watch a play, believing it to be mere deception, yet aware of the dreadful truth.

Now and then, he did get something, bit-parts in short-running plays and television commercials. The ideal part never seemed to come along. He was too tall, too slim, he said, for supporting roles. He read some short stories and then had parts in a couple of plays on Radio Three, which were well reviewed, but there was never anything for very long.

'My Father is an actor,' Louise said.

'He's bone idle,' Heather retorted, and they fought over him, each trying to impose their interpretation of his character upon the other.

'I think he's wonderful,' Louise said. 'People write for his autograph, so he must be famous.'

'Do me a favour! He's had ten letters in his life. He'd be a lot more famous and a damn sight richer if he'd play a Yank, instead of arsing around waiting for Hamlet all his life.'

Louise scolded her. 'You are totally irresponsible. You should have respect for your parents.'

His work, when he had any, obliged him, he said, to spend nights away from home, and to Louise the house seemed empty without him. He was always engaged on some project to improve his mind and, after reading up his latest subject, he expounded his knowledge and enthusiasm to his daughters, but, whereas Louise listened dutifully and tried to improve herself, Heather said he was a bore and she had better things to do than listen to him waffling on for hours on end.

'You are disgusting and disrespectful. You are common.'

Louise used an extensive and precocious vocabulary, emulating Bruce in her speech and in her writing, but there was never any spontaneity. Her utterances were cliche-ridden repetitions of the only speech she ever heard without finding fault in it, her father's, the nuns at the convent, and Radio Three, which Bruce listened to when Valeria was at work. The bad language of the streets embarrassed her. She pretended not to hear it, or to know the meaning of the filthy expressions used by some of the girls in the convent and by her own younger sister, of whom she was thoroughly ashamed.

At school, Heather always managed to pass her exams. Only just passed, but she passed, and that was all that mattered as far as she was concerned. Her parents attempted to improve her performance by pointing out that, with a little effort, she could attain the same standards as her sister.

'I passed, didn't I?' was her reaction. 'What more do you want? I'm no genius, you know. Not like Miss bloody-perfect-Louise.'

The sisters grew to dislike each other intensely. The cramped room and the bickering between their parents induced a secrecy between them as each tried to retain an identity. Louise was jealous of Heather's beauty. The younger sister had outgrown her in physical development and, in their early teens, acquired an adult figure with full hips and firm, rounded breasts. Louise grew taller, stayed thin in the belief that she could control her height by dieting, despite exhortation from her mother to 'eata mora da pasta'. She remained flat chested and did not menstruate although she informed some of the girls to the contrary by ambiguous statements about her reasons for abstaining from vigorous games and swimming. She spent time, when Heather was out with her boyfriends, massaging her breasts in an attempt to make them grow and to feel the tightening nipples as a sign that she was normal. This made her feel guilty, as if she was dissatisfied with 'the body God had given her', as one of the nuns put it on the one occasion when she had dared to mention her fears. She felt, after a while, that her body was controlling her mind, and her earthly desires were subjugating her intellect and that she was becoming obsessed by lust.

Bruce assumed that Valeria had educated the girls in this respect, as it was out of his domain, but as her own frustration increased Valeria found herself repulsed by the subject and could talk about it to no one, especially her own daughters, who she would prevent from ever participating in the whole disgusting business if she could.

Louise achieved high academic standards not through genius, as Heather had implied, although she was undoubtedly intelligent, but through a grim determination to succeed and prove to her family, the nuns at the convent, and herself, that she was worthy of their respect. Conversely, she developed a morbid fear of failure, dreading her parents' strictures should her standards drop, and worked herself into a state of physical stress and mental anxiety before examinations. Bruce, in particular, would go through her work with her in his quiet, authoritarian way, and point out the danger of letting her standards fall if she dropped behind in a subject. Her mother might add, with a tremor of desperation in her voice, that her eldest daughter was becoming as lax as the younger.

'Why donta you worka no more?'

When Louise had been in, night after night, exhausting herself with study unknown to any of them.

One day, Bruce announced that he had been offered a part in a television series. He was to play the part of a languid, effeminate son of an eccentric English nobleman in the 1920s. Rehearsals and recording necessitated, he said, his staying with a friend in the city occasionally, to be near the studio. At home he became cheerful and confident.

Louise was very proud of him when the first of the series was screened. All the girls regarded the Fern sisters with new respect, to which Heather was indifferent while Louise exploited the opportunity to scorn those who had, in her opinion, rejected her in the past because of her social inferiority. Her few close acquaintances at school were now asked home occasionally, for she felt that she could be indifferent to their flat now that their father was soon to be rich and famous. He promised to take them on holiday, and she told her classmates they were going to Italy to see her mother's home, which they could never have previously afforded.

And then he was gone. Louise was working for her A levels and Heather her O's when, one night after he had been absent for a couple of days, there was a tremendous row. The girls lay in their beds listening to it in horror: their mother's hysterical sobbing, their father's low monotones of anger. Each sister pretended to be asleep, hiding their fear from the other, until there was a splintering of crockery and a cry of pain from their mother. Bruce went to the bedroom, from where they heard drawers opening and closing as he packed his belongings.

Valeria followed him into the room. 'Leave me alone.' they heard him tell her, and her impassioned plea for him to stay. 'You don't want me.' he said.

'I ado. I needa you. The girls, they needa you.'

The door closed and they heard him say, 'You don't *want* me!'

'I ado,' she sobbed.

From behind closed doors there came the sound of further acrimonious words and then a violent struggle. They heard the bed creak and gasps of exertion, the slap of a hand on flesh and an oath from their usually prudish father and their mother crying, 'No, Bruce. No. Oha, my God.'

The girls cowered in their beds, terrified and guiltily fascinated, listening to the muted sounds of struggle. As the voices ceased they heard a chair fall over and their mother's cosmetics spill from the bedside table.

Louise felt her body trembling as her capacity for emotional stress became overloaded, and she curled up, as if asleep and thrust her clenched fists between her thighs, with her legs trembling involuntarily against her wrists.

There was silence from the bedroom, then the creaking of the bed again, becoming louder. They heard the knocking of the bed-head, as if against the wall. It stopped. All was silence. They heard their mother say: 'Oh. Oh, Bruce. Aghh. Aghh.' They could hear them breathing, both of them, and grunts of effort from their father.

Louise pressed her wrists against herself and squeezed hard with her legs, trying to force the sounds she was hearing from her understanding as she felt the damp tenderness against the beating pulse in her wrist. She trembled all over, with her muscles tensed, saying to herself in silent despair. 'No, no, no. Please no, no, no.' as the wetness spread against her arm.

They heard their mother's voice again, a slow rising crescendo of gasps, and she emitted a low moaning, almost a groan in its intensity, and they heard their father collapse on the bed and burst into tears.

Louise shuddered as her mind tried to shut out the happenings around her, waiting for the front door to slam, but he left quietly, and she buried her face in the pillow. Heather climbed out of bed and went to her mother. 'Don't cry, Mamma,' she said, and put her arms around the trembling shoulders.

Louise could not go to her, for fear of her own sin which was driving her ever nearer to the fires of hell.

The next night, the girls lay on their beds, expecting him to return, while their mother watched the television in their living room with a blank unseeing stare.

'Do you think he has another woman?' Louise asked in an attempt to find some empathy with her sister in this tragedy.

'No,' Heather said, bluntly. 'He's got another man.'

'Oh, what a horrible thing to say.' She was not sure, exactly, what Heather was saying, but she hated her for saying it. 'You evil little bitch.'

'Look!' Heather said. 'It's time you grew up. He's a bloody poofter.'

The vehemence in her voice and the ardent expression in her eyes were the immediate manifestation of Heather's belief in the statement which Louise could not accept.

Louise sat up. 'I don't believe you,' she said, smugly. 'You would say anything against him. You hate him. You always have.'

Heather sat up too. She reached put and put her hand on her sister's knee, a gesture of affection. 'He is,' she said, earnestly.

'Don't touch me.'

Louise thrust the hand away. She was distraught at having to accept that which had been resisted for years. She wanted to cry, to throw herself on the pillow and cry, cry, cry. To run and run and run and throw herself down, on grass, in a field, beside the sea, in a wood, on a beach, anywhere but in this cramped house in the middle of a city where everyone was your enemy, and cry. Even to cling to Heather, holding her tight. She could not do it.

Heather, slighted by the abrupt dismissal of that gesture of friendship, rose and put on her coat. 'Got a date,' she said.

'Dates.' Louise said in despairing anger. 'That's all you think about. Sex!'

Heather turned and re-entered the room. She closed the door lest her voice be heard by that dejected figure in the living room, and approached her sister. 'No!' she said. 'Wrong again, Miss bloody prim. I don't think about it. I do it. It's you who thinks about it. You even dream about it. You talk about it in your sleep. What you need... ' she leaned over and put her mouth close to Louise's ear. '...is a bloody good fuck.'

Louise screamed with rage and tried to grab her. 'You disgusting, filthy...'. But her sister dodged away and rushed through the door, and could be heard shrieking with impudent laughter as she left the house.

Louise cried then. Her tears were of grief at loosing her father, and of rage and frustration over the truth in her sister's words.

Valeria did not come up to console her. She did not hear. She was staring at the image on the screen. He was playing himself, like many supposedly good actors.

He came to see them occasionally, and his visits were accepted grimly by Valeria who would have preferred the odd ten pounds now and then to help her out. She tried to remain aloof and indifferent, but sometimes broke down into hysterics, complaining of her hard life while he was free to do exactly as he wished, a lazy layabout with no sense of responsibility. He took the girls out, not to zoos and fairgrounds, but to museums, art galleries and select restaurants, where he expounded his knowledge of eastern and continental dishes, explaining that there was more to education than academics and that they must learn how to behave in sophisticated society. He impressed upon them the value of culture and the love of books, once scolding Heather for laying a paperback face down with its pages open. Heather was bored by these excursions, preferring to spend time with her friends, while Louise was at great pains to receive his praises, and would return to the bedroom and pore over the literature he had procured during the day. He never laughed, and never took them to his home. They were not sure where he lived, or with whom. A flat in Town, he told them.

The public meeting in the town hall at Penavon was so well attended that people were standing up at the back. In the entrance there was a large 'architect's impression' of the appearance of the proposed development of the harbour and environs. There were workshops on the quay, a fish-processing plant, housing for local people, a supermarket and marina, together with improvements to the crumbling quays and a 'Wildlife Centre', which looked suspiciously like a hotel, built out into the estuary. The plan represented an investment of millions. Most of those present listened to the speakers in stony silence, not wishing to disclose where their sympathies lay, for during the past months there had been much controversy over these proposals.

Among those on the platform were the chairman of the district council, Daniel David Johns, known as Dee Dee Jay; Tim Penberthy, representing the traders; the Planning Officer; and Simon Sweeting and his agent, David Langley. There was a large map of the area on the wall behind them, and all were smiling at one another and at the audience.

'It's him!' Beth said. 'Langley, the agent. He's the one who killed our Guinea fowl.'

'So he is,' Sam said. 'Well well.'

Tim Penberthy stood up and introduced Simon Sweeting. 'For many years,' he said, 'we have witnessed the sad decline of this once prosperous port. I remember, as many of you will, the ships coming in and out, the busy quays bustling with life, the fishing fleet landing their catch.'

There was a murmur in the hall, and Boy Steve gave Katie a nudge with his elbow. Nobody else could remember such things.

Tim waffled on, as was his wont, and eventually introduced the millionaire developer, Simon Sweeting.

He was a tall, gaunt man, with thick black hair and narrow shoulders, although he looked tanned and fit. He used half glasses for reading from his notes. He had developed a great empathy with the local people since buying his house on a south coast creek, and admired their industry and ingenuity in the past and their optimism for the future, despite the difficulties facing them at present. He wished to thank the district council for their co-operation and, in particular, the planning officer for all his help and advice over this, the most important development in the area for over a hundred years. He himself, he reminded them to laughter from the audience, was only a poor millionaire, and most of the day-to-day administration of the development would be undertaken by his agent, Mr Langley. Were there any questions?

Katie Stevens wanted to know about protecting the Sites of Special Scientific Interest. What about dredging the bar, and who was going to pay for this and all the other conservation measures included in the plan?

Langley watched Katie intently as she was speaking. Boy Steve noticed that he continued his scrutiny of her long after she had spoken, and he reinforced his dislike of the man. He was too smart, immaculate in his restrained suit and dark tie, quite unlike the drunken slob they had seen in the restaurant.

Katie's questions prompted other doubters in the audience to query some of the proposals. What about the County Structure Plan? What about the possibility of asset-stripping? Would the council ensure that there was some proviso in the planning to ensure that the scheme was completed in its entirety, with no cost to the taxpayer? How would the small traders fare if there was a large supermarket built? Wouldn't the development completely destroy the character of the town?

The voice of Ezekiel sang out, 'Are you dolphin friendly?' And there was laughter in the hall.

D.D. Johns was the last to speak. He was a tall, elderly man who had served on the council for many years. His face was gaunt, with thin lips, drooping jowls and eyelids, and deeply lined.

'I've heard some things in my time,' Dee Dee said. 'but I've never heard such tripe as I've heard tonight from these protesters.' He turned to the assembly. 'They who d' come down 'ere, tellin' we what to do Outsiders, goin' on about our history and one thing and another. These here environmentalists, all these conversationists, ought to think a bit more about the prosperity of local people. They ought to think a bit less about a few sparrows and dandelions and old stone walls and more about the unemployed. I for one support the scheme wholeheartedly, and anybody with any sense will do the same.' He sat down to the cheers of his supporters.

Katie Stevens and her suporters were furious.

'My God,' Katie said, 'Outsiders, are we?'

'My family were here,' Barny laughed, 'when his were washed ashore from a shipwrecked cattle-boat.'

Even Boy Steve was sympathetic. 'Silly old tuss,' he said.

David Langley and the planning officer had nothing to say and, apart from much smiling in appreciation of Dee Dee's remarks, Langley maintained a blank expression throughout the proceedings, glancing occasionally in the direction of Katie Stevens.

'He's jumping the gun a bit,' Katie said as she left with Boy Steve after the question and answer session. 'He hasn't got planning permission for anything yet.'

'He will,' Boy Steve said. 'It's too big a project for the council to refuse, Especially with Dee Dee Jay and Tim Penberthy backing him. It will bring a lot of money and work into the area.' He turned to Zeke, who was scurrying past them. 'Hullo, Zeke. What 'ee think of it.'

''loh, Ste,' Zeke said. 'Going home'long are 'ee? I could do with a lift.'

'So could I,' Katie said. 'I walked over.'

'Sure,' Boy Steve said.

'Proper job,' Zeke assured them. ''loh, Sarah.'

'I'm called Katie,' she said, with a smile.

'Well, 's all the same. Here! What do 'ee think of it? Marinas! My hell. What about the bar? Never said a word about the mines. Ha! What do a want to go buyin' a pile of rubbish for? Tha's all Penavon is. A pile of rubbish. Bleddy rogues. Tha's all they are... . Bleddy Rogues, and Dee Dee Jay and Tim Penberthy as bad as any of them. Houses for local people. Ha! What local people? Sprat to catch a mackerel, tha's all that ezz.'

His eyes darted about with brilliant flashes as he looked from one to the other of them, at the other people emerging from the hall, at the traffic as they crossed the street to Boy Steve's car.

Katie smiled at Steve as she sat beside him in the front, and Zeke kept up his monologue from the back seat. 'Here! Some smart car 'en brother. Well, good luck to 'ee.'

He was well known as a bit of an eccentric, with views on everything forcibly expressed. Nobody took much notice of him. Some said he wasn't properly made fast, was a bit slack at the moorings, and tolerated his extreme views as the ramblings of a fool. But physically he was well built, broad-shouldered and stocky.

'Here!' he said. 'You're both my cousins, you knaw that do 'ee?' And then, after one of his rare silences. 'Now, you two mind what you're up to.'

Boy Steve dropped him off at the bottom of the hill in town and drove up to Sarah's house to drop Katie. 'You didn't ring me about going down the mine,' she said. 'It's time I had another look.'

'Well, I didn't forget. I just haven't had time.'

'Well, what about Sunday ?'

'Next Sunday ?'

'Yes. You won't be working!'

He thought about it. There was really nothing to it. You just asked, or phoned up. But he had put it off, afraid of refusal, thinking she might not really want to go down the mine or anywhere else with him if her mother was opposed to it

'O.K.' he said. 'I'll ring you on Saturday.'

'I hear you've joined the lifeboat crew.'

'Do 'ee sure 'nuff?'

Katie smiled at his evasive response. 'Bloody mad-brain,' she said.

Sarah Stevens came to the door as her daughter watched the car drive off up the terrace. 'Who was that, Katie?'

'Steve Trevorrow. Boy Steve.'

'How did it go, ?' Fehther Steve asked.

'Well,' his son said. 'There's a lot of money to be spent over there. It'll make a big difference to us if we have a processing plant on our side of the coast. He plans to improve the mooring for fishing boats, with fuelling facilities and stores on the quay. There seemed to be a lot of opposition, you could tell from the response, but nobody said anything against it as a whole.'

'He's a powerful man,' Mary said. 'so of course people are going to be careful what they d' say. They might want jobs over there, pembye.'

'Zeke was over there,' Boy Steve said. 'Ranting on, as usual.'

He wasn't sure if he ought to say anything. Nobody wants to admit insanity in the family, especially his mother, he knew her well enough for that, but his curiosity got the better of discretion.

'How is Zeke related to we ?' he asked.

'Related to we?' Mary said, evidently highly indignant. 'He idn' related to we!'

'Very distant,' Steve said, and gave her one of those looks which Boy Steve had seen them exchange from time to time when there was evidently some risk of discussing family history that he should not know about. He was determined to discover what skeletons lay in the family cupboard but was in no hurry about it.

'Not distant enough, if you ask me. 'Mary stated. 'He's a damn Stevens, and that's that. Idn' none of we in 'n.'

'He said we're cousins.'

'You're second cousins,' Steve said. 'Your mother's Great Aunt Gerty married a Stevens.'

'Married her, did he?' Mary said. 'Got her in the family way for her money, you mean.'

Steve said. 'She had a cheeld.'

'The bleddy rogue,' Mary said.

'It was all a long time ago.'

'You still haven't told me where Zeke comes into it,' Boy Steve said, by now thoroughly intrigued by the tale.

'Their maid grew up and married Zacharias Endean and had a pile of cheldern,' Steve said. 'The last one was Zeke. Ezekiel. He's just like his fehther. Mad as a bleddy hatter.'

'So, I'm no relation to Katie Stevens,' Boy Steve said eventually, about to determine that which had really been on his mind.

'No!' Steve stated.

'What do you have to do with she ?' Mary asked sharply, after a quick glance at her husband. 'You want to keep away from that crowd. The Stevens's have done enough damage to our family.'

'What are you talking about ma? All that was three generations ago, for God's sake.

'They're no damn good,' Mary said. 'Why, Katie is illegitimate! Her mother was after every man she could lay her hands on. Why nothin' more than a damn slut. And she so bleddy pious, going to chapel every Sunday as if butter wouldn' melt in her mouth.'

'Oh, Mary,' Steve said, losing his patience.

'She seems like a very nice girl to me.' Boy Steve said. 'I'm meeting her next Sunday.'

'What?' Mary cried. 'You'd better not, my lad. You needn't think you'll have a home here if you mix up with that crowd. I'm tellin' 'ee now.'

Boy Steve looked at his father with raised eyebrows. Whatever was the matter with her? he asked by a gesture.

Steve nodded to the door, asking his son to leave, and Boy Steve backed through the door, looking at his mother.

'I'm a grown man,' he protested, but Steve pushed him gently out, shaking his head.

'Say no more,' he whispered.

CHAPTER EIGHT.

Spavnell kens an teweth. Calm before the storm.

'It's pretty grim,' Sam said, 'but it will do for the time being. It's an attic room: one skylight, a chest of drawers, no bed; bathroom and kitchen in the basement three floors down shared by two other tenants.'

'She won't like that,' Beth observed.

'You know what she's like. She wants to be on her own. Freedom, she said, from any restrictions, and she doesn't want to impose.'

Beth looked down at the baby, whose head fell drunkenly from her breast. 'Full up, frog-face?' she said. 'Horrible little slug.'

The baby's mouth twisted in a lop-sided smile, dribbling milk that Beth wiped away before hugging the child and kissing its ear. This is what she's avoiding, Beth thought. No belching babies and squalling infants to remind her of her own, abandoned somewhere up'long. But at least Sam had resisted the temptation to offer her a temporary home here with them.

'Does Barny know where she is?'

'I haven't told him,' Sam said. 'Haven't seen him. He seems to be preoccupied with the developments at Penavon, and is spending a lot of time in town seeing his father.'

'And Anne,' Beth said. 'His girlfriend. Well, sort of.' She and Sam had never met Anne, for they went into town only when necessary, and Anne rarely came out here. Like most of Barny's friends, they knew of each other, but were as if in separate compartments of Barny's life and, despite his frequently saying to all of them, 'You must meet', they had never done so.

'You would have thought she would have written to him,' Sam said. 'If only a note to say she was coming.'

'She is funny,' Beth said. 'Poor Loopy.'

She cleaned the baby up and laid it in a cot in the kitchen. She was well aware that Barny had not mentioned Louise during the past weeks. This could only have been deliberate on his part, possibly, she suspected, because he felt himself falling in love with her. Neither he nor Loopy had told her of such a thing, but that look in their eyes when they said goodbye after the last weekend visit was unmistakable. Beth had also deliberately refused to mention Loopy Louise Fern since she had moved into her flat, partly in retaliation for Barny's own reticence and partly in the hope that he would forget her. If Loopy Lou was vulnerable, she told herself, then Barny was infinitely more so, for he regarded Louise as weak and himself as strong, a dangerous assumption in love as well as war.

'We shall have to go and see her.'

'Not today. Goldie is coming for a session on the guitars.'

Beth smiled, but said, 'I'm not sure about him,' as she cleared the table. 'When is he coming?'

'This afternoon. He phoned. He said Simon Sweeting is proposing to open a night-club on Penavon Quay and has asked him to manage it. Meanwhile, we might have a gig at The Chestnut. Barny is writing some lyrics for my new music.'

'Well, let's hope something comes of it this time. Goldie is always promising something. Are you sure he's not using you? What does Barny think of him?'

'I don't know. They don't say much to each other. Goldie likes Barny's lyrics, that's the main thing.'

She doubted if Barny liked Goldie's voice, but said nothing. Sam was a talented musician, but his compositions were too experimental for her tastes. She was not, on her own admission, in the least musical, but Sam's enthusiasm she loved and she shared his delight when he had composed a piece he was happy with. Even with Sam, however, she would not pretend. 'I don't understand it,' she would say, ' but if you like it, that's all that matters.'

Beth said, 'We'd better invite Loopy over sometime. She won't come unless she's asked.'

'Strange girl,' Sam said. 'Why don't we invite her over to hear some music when Goldie and the others come for a session. She might like that.'

Beth doubted it, but such an occasion should mean that she did not have to bear Louise's despondency alone. 'Good idea,' she said, 'It's going to be fine today. I'll take the sprogs out of your way.'

'I was hoping you would,' Sam laughed. 'We might frighten them. Goldie doesn't like children very much.'

No, she thought, and they don't like him. 'I'll go over and see Barny,' she said.

But Barny was out, that afternoon. He had gone into town again, to see Anne, and Katie, and as he was walking down Fore Street was astonished

139

to see Louise there. She was emerging from Blight's, the furniture shop, laden with two full shopping bags and a large parcel. She did not, to his consternation, appear particularly pleased to see him, being almost indifferent in her greeting. As he spoke to her, he saw lines of tension around her mouth, and thought she was thinner than ever, with her narrow shoulders straining to support the weight of her purchases. If she doesn't want to talk to me, he thought, then to hell with her. He would continue on his way, see Anne, have some laughs with her, feel her leg, get his face slapped and take her out for a walk along the harbour. He was was about to leave Louise, feeling somewhat disencumbered from any obligation to her, when the handle snapped on one of her bags.

'Can I help you with that ?' he said.

'I can manage, thank you.'

But she could not. With the weight all on one strap, the stitching ripped and she was obliged to let the bag rest on the ground. Barny picked it up, and watched her eyes in perplexity. All that, all those intimacies, might never have occurred. She was looking at him in fear, as if he were some kind of interrogator to whom she had been forced to confess some crime, or sin, of which she was ashamed.

He cradled the bag in his arms and waited. He could not leave her here, helpless in the street. Zeke came scurrying by and acknowledged Barny with a nod.

'Hullo, Zeke,' Barny said. 'All right?'

Zeke stopped and looked at Louise. 'I'm all right,' he said as he scrutin-ised her. 'Nawthen wrong with me, you. It's the other buggers.'

' 'ess,' Barny said. ' 'ess, well, there we are, Zeke.'

He did not want to speak to his old friend at this moment, for Zeke was a man with problems, and had the gift of seeing them in others.

'Heard the news, have 'ee?' Zeke asked earnestly. 'About he over to Penavon?'

'No. What's that, now?'

'He's going to fill in the creek and build a g'eat shop.'

'Never.'

'Oh 'ess 'e ez, my 'ansome. It's in the *Echo*.'

Louise ignored Zeke, and he looked at her suspiciously, appraising her with a rapidly nodding head. Zeke could see more problems for all hands looming up here. 'Well look,' he said. 'I'm gone... '. And he was off down the street, muttering to himself and anyone who would listen, 'Bleddy rogue. Ought to be put going.'

Louise turned away with a resigned sigh, and said, 'I'll show you my room.'

It was an attic, with the walls showing stains where rain leaked in from the chimney and the skylight. There was a mattress on the floor and a small chest of drawers with the legs cut off so that it could be manoeuvred up the narrow stairs. There was a bookcase, crammed with the classics, Homer, Catullus, The Annals, Plato; all, he noticed, in pristine condition, with no evidence of much use down their spines. Her toiletries and a large round alarm clock were arranged neatly on an old orange box beside the bed. There was a copy of *Spare Rib* lying on the floor. The table was a large packing-case, in which she had brought the remnants of her existence, now draped in a brightly-coloured cloth. It bore the weight of a figure of Krishna, the playful eighth reincarnation of Vishnu, entwined in erotic embrace with a Gopi. Beside them, a fat, brass Buddha condoned their behaviour with a patronising smirk. She had hung large posters on the end walls, to hide the damp. They were of pop-stars and cult figures of her university days, evidently kept somewhere, rolled up and waiting, for the past fifteen years or so. There was the smell of joss sticks and he saw dead ash spilling from a brass burner between the Buddha and the perpetual orgasm of the Hindu lovers entwined forever in ecstasy. This, he thought, was the pathetic sum of her years. It was as if she had renounced them all except for those spent at university and intended starting afresh from that time, to begin her adult life again. He wanted to welcome her back into his life, hold her in his arms, but she was distant, bearing the weight of her isolation, and he watched ineffectually as she emptied her shopping bags. She did permit him to help in putting a new cover on her duvet, spread over the mattress on the bare floor.

She can't live like this, he thought, but when she was satisfied with the arrangement he stood up and said, 'Well. I'll be going,' obliged to stand only in the middle of the attic, the apex of beams like a tent over his head. 'You seem to have settled in all right.'

He went to the top of the stairs, which fell like a narrow precipice to the silence of the house below. The carpet on the stairs was worn to shreds and hung over the treads between chipped paint. At the bottom, where the flight led up from the landing, was a sharp twist and a small door with a flimsy lock, not strong enough to resist the paws of a cat.

'You ought to have a lock,' he said. 'A proper lock, on that door.'

'I've asked the landlord to do it.' She was waiting for him to go. 'I'm

141

sorry,' she said off-handedly, 'I can't ask you to stay, but I'm expecting company.'

Pretence, he concluded. She was alone, had nobody, and was rejecting him in an attempt to assert her self-sufficiency. She would inflict this punishment upon herself in an endeavour to prove her independence. Perhaps, for her, it was the right course of action but she would suffer for it. She came to the top of the stairs, to lead him down to the street.

'Louise!' he pleaded. But she refused to look at him. 'Louise, be careful. Be careful about who you invite up here.'

'I am quite capable of looking after myself, thank you.'

She had told him nothing about the circumstances of leaving home, her husband, children, what she planned to do with her life... . No reference to those intimacies she had divulged, the passion she had shown. Perhaps she regretted them, was ashamed of revealing herself in weakness, and wished to deny them. Those hours he had spent thinking of her, wanting her and assuming that she wanted him, had been passed in illusion, as he should have known when there had been no letter, no phone call, not a word, since she moved in. Ah well. So be it!

'I'll see myself out,' he said.

His father's model was progressing well. She was decked-in and he was working on the hatches of the fish and net rooms.

'You caint git the damn wood,' the old man said. 'I wanted a bit of yella pine. Nobody ab'm heard ob'm these days.'

He seemed well enough, happy as he complained about every inconvenience of the modern age. 'You caint even git the proper glue,' he said. 'Anybody would think cows never had no bones no more. All I can git is poxy resin, whatever that ez. Bleddy awful stuff, like the poxy wood.'

But the model was already a beautiful thing. Every plank lay snugly against its neighbour, and the stem and stern rose from the keel in elegant curves. She was a work of art, in design and execution, although such a notion would have been denied by the old man. 'Work of art, my ass. She's only a model.' But the expression of pride as he cast his eye over her, or ran his hand along the rounded bulges, was of more than the craftsman in him. 'Whatsoever thy hand seeketh to do,' he said, 'do it with thy might.' 'Tha's all there ez to en,' he explained to his son. 'If you're going to do a thing, do en proper, no good fartin' around with things.

And there then came upon Barny a chill of apprehension. This was the last model to be fashioned by these old hands. He foresaw, in a nebulous instant, that, by reason of age, his father's death was near, and the revelation immediately transformed itself into a vague recollection of events experienced beyond the confines of time. He did not know if he was experiencing memory or premonition and, as he watched the hands at work, was unsure whether the thought had occurred to him at all. No, it was a foolish notion. Those confident hands were surely destined to continue working for years to come. He stayed, watching the shaping of miniature planks of wood, until the old man said, 'What you hanging around here for? Ab'm 'ee got no work to do?'

He left him contented and totally absorbed in his work, perhaps the happiest state of men, and went to see Anne. She was out, so he left a note.

Loopy Lou came out by bus on the day Sam arranged a session with some of his musical friends, including Goldie, who was to be what he called 'vocals and link' before the potential hordes of adoring fans. He was tall with a proportionate body, long fair hair and beard and dull grey, insipid irises. On the occasions when Barny had sat in on the sessions he thought that Goldie's flamboyant clothes and suggestive hip movements were a contrived substitute for the lack of lustre in his eyes. He also thought that the group's presentation was as far behind the times as theirs were from his own. Goldie, in his central role, was impersonating the idols of his teens, though he was now in his thirties. When Barny heard Sam playing alone, on one of the several instruments he had mastered, then, he thought, he heard the true expression of emotion, and it was for the sake of these solo performances that he agreed to write lyrics for the group.

After Beth had made Loopy welcome and taken her in to meet Sam's friends in his music room, one of the spare bedrooms crammed with mikes, mixers and synthesisers, she took the children out of the way and went for a walk along the lane, down to the sea. Her music was here, in the breaking surf, the songs of wrens, the lowing of cows in Denzil Trethewy's fields. If ever she wanted canned music, she had a couple of tapes which she played to herself now and then, dismissing her musical ignorance by saying with a grin, 'It's Bach, I think.' She pointed out a ship and a line of gannets to Susy, who said, remembering a young friend in the village, 'I yike Jannet.'

The noise was still pounding from the bedroom when she returned, so she gave them all a tea of goose-egg omlettes and home-made cake, noting that Loopy had withdrawn into silence but was exchanging glances with Goldie across the table. She fed the baby, put him to bed, bathed Susy, put her to bed, cleared the table, washed the dishes, fed the animals, locked up the poultry, swore at the gleenys, decided she had done enough for one day and told Sam she was going over to see Barny, for the children were accustomed to noise and slept through natural and synthesised storms alike. Loopy gave not a glimmer of recognition of Barny's name as she sat on the floor next to Goldie.

Beth found Barny listening to tapes of songs in the old language as he read through a story called *Jowan Chy an Horth*, the beginning of which translates as... *In the time that is past, there were settled in Saint Levan a man and a woman, in the place that is called The House of The Ram*. He read it aloud to her. Listen to this: *yn termyn ys passyas, yth-essa tryges yn Plu Selevan den ha bennen, yn teller yu cries Chy an Horth...* and said, 'isn't that lovely? Every sentence is melodious and lyrical, no wonder we are accused of speaking "sing song" English. The intonation transcends translation.'

'It sounds nice,' Beth said. 'Why don't you write in it ?'

'I will, when I am able. Sometimes I wish I was born when it was still widely used. Huh! I suppose I would have been like everyone else, ashamed of my birthright, regarding it as the language of the ignorant.'

'It was,' Beth said. 'Wasn't it?'

'Yes,' he said, briefly annoyed by her apparent lack of empathy with the past. 'Ignorant of things English. In the way that a broad accent is regarded now. Which is why I don't know how to speak any more.'

'But we can't live in the past.'

'No, I know that, but it would be a pity for it to be lost. *...mes, trueth vya mar pe kellys...* . But, pity would it be, it to be lost.'

'You could write in dialect.'

'No. Written dialect makes the speakers seem comic, stupid. Yet that too is as much part of our heritage as the landscape.'

'That's going too,' she said, treading common ground.

'There are too many damned strangers here,' he said, and reminded himself of the strangest stranger he had ever met. He had to ask, as casually as he could, 'What is Loopy up to? I haven't seen her.'

'She's over with Sam and the others.' Beth made a face, raised brows over wide eyes and a tight-lipped smile, to hide what she might be thinking, as Barny saw full well.

She was thinking precisely the same thought that now entered his own head.

'Now?' he asked in astonishment. 'Isn't she coming over ?'

'Don't think so.'

She could not tell him of those looks exchanged across the table, the inviting glances and the speculative response briefly animating the dull eyes as Goldie's voice confidently outlined their impending rise to fame under the patronage of Simon Sweeting.

'Goldie was using your lyrics, I think.' She laughed apologetically. 'I can never understand what he is saying. Too much gasping and shrieking for me.'

'And for me too.' As he thought, it's up to her, and Beth thought, you're better clear of her, Barny.

'I'm not sure about Goldie,' he mumbled.

'Neither am I,' Beth said.

'Oh ? You've never said so.'

'You never asked.' With that exaggerated grin to mask her opinion of the man.

'Goldie! I ask you. What's his real name ?'

'Don't know. Don't know anything about him.'

'He's from the South East, Kent, Essex, fringe of London, it's in his voice, one of those places where they believe they have no accent. Anonymous people, there's millions of them up there.'

'He says he's been offered a contract to play in Simon Sweeting's leisure complex, when it's built.'

'God,' Barny said. 'A leisure complex. What the hell is that? Is there anything around here that doesn't depend on Simon Sweeting's development?'

The tape ceased playing with a click of the auto stop. They had not heard the last song. He reached out and pressed the 'play' switch on the CD, waited for the opening bars. 'Let's listen to this,' he said, 'It's a new one.'

'What is it ?'

'Haydn. Sonatas for violin and viola.' He swung his feet over the end of the sofa and rested his head on her thigh. 'Let's see if you like it.' He looked up at her brown, weather-beaten young face and smiling eyes. 'You mean a lot to me, Beth,' he said.

She brushed the hair on his temple with her forefingers, and he could smell the rich earth on her clothes and some kind of skin lotion on her callused hands. 'How can she live in that place?' he said.

'She'll be all right. Just relax and listen to the music.'

It was Sam who said, on a day when Barny had been helping on their land, hoeing the long rows of vegetables, tying-in the peas, pulling the first tender carrots and cleaning out the chicken house after collecting the eggs. 'We can take some in to Loopy,'

The eggs were piled up in layers between packing, large, dark brown from the Welsummers and Marrans, smaller, paler from the hybrids they had bought cheap, as year-old naked neurotics from a battery, and introduced to the terrifying prospect of free- range. They were taught the rudiments of life in the open by three Silky bantams tending broods of chicks sired by a couple of arrogant roosters who occasionally engaged in ferocious fights over members of harems already too numerous to subjugate. After a moult and a diet of worms, they became prolific layers but never went broody.

'We have more eggs than we can use,' Sam told Barny. 'It's all or nothing in the self-sufficiency game.'

They knew that Barny intended to go into town the following day. He could take some eggs and fresh vegetables in for her. They were aware that she had little money and thought she might be grateful for them. It was three weeks since he had seen her on that brief visit to her attic when she had dismissed him. Their encounters, he decided, had been one of life's transient interludes, which, like a single daub of paint applied to a canvas, becomes an essential element of the whole picture only by reason of its inclusion. His life would have been just as complete if he had never met her. Some other incident would have influenced his destiny, brushing him with pigments of another hue. He could live, as previously, without her, as if he had never known her. Life was too short, too sweet, and he could not permit the rest of it to be disrupted by memories of an insignificant incident .

'She's been seeing Goldie,' Sam said. And Barny's heart became as lead as he replied with a non-committal 'Hmm'

On the following day, he worked in the morning, managing to banish all thoughts of her as he typed the final copies of work in hand. It was drizzling, the horizon obscured by grey mist, but Sam was out in the fields when Barny went over, and Beth gave him the eggs, saying, in a tone of voice that implied her appreciation of his predicament, 'You don't have to.'

'But I do,' Barny said. 'Don't I?'

'I suppose.'

He took the eggs and a large bag of vegetables into town, could find no nearby spaces for his car, and was committed to driving all through the crowded one-way system to the car-park on the hill overlooking the narrow streets and slate roofs, bright with yellow lichen. Although he was a little apprehensive about seeing her, he had become resigned to her indifference on his previous visit. If she were to live in the area there would certainly be occasions when they met, at Sam and Beth's or even in the street, so he might as well establish how their relationship was to be, friendly or otherwise. He could not expect a young, attractive woman to stay interested in him when he had so little to offer. He was poor by her standards, with no prospect of acquiring the wherewithal to provide a prosperous future for two. His own life-style, he mused as he descended the hill among the crowds of tourists mooching about in the rain, was of his own choosing, but not one to impose upon another.

She had been obliged to treat him with caution, to save them both from further, irretractable commitment. He could, however, offer friendship free of complication, which was what he offered all his acquaintances

When he reached her house, after weaving head-down through the wet people and dripping launders, he saw her in the kitchen in the basement with a young, unknown man, so he went down the steps past the window of what had once been the cellar, and she let him in. She introduced the man as a fellow tenant, an accountant who used the room as a base when visiting clients locally. Barny removed his sodden hat and explained the purpose of his visit, placing the onus on Beth as he gave Louise the produce, 'She asked me to drop these in.'

'She's very kind. Please thank her for me.'

The remark was a formality from Louise, for the eggs were loaded with chloresterol and the vegetables grown in shit. She would never eat them, although, despite a suntanned face and a shine among the folds of her plait, she looked starved.

Barny sat at the table, although not invited to do so, deliberately imposing himself upon them, so that Louise would have the options of conversing in the presence of the stranger, inviting him up to her room, or asking him to leave. The young man, Barny had forgotten his name as soon as told it, was preparing something at the cooker. A kettle reached boiling point, emitting an ear-piercing shriek. The man poured it into a tea pot, saying, 'I'll put it on again for mine,' implying that the tea was for Louise.

She was obliged to invite Barny up to her room, carrying the pot, milk and mugs on a tray as she led the way up through the narrow staircase to the attic.

There was a new lock on the flimsy door, Barny noticed with some satisfaction and, as she preceded him up the stairs, she asked him to secure it behind them as a precaution against intruders. There was nowhere to sit, except for the mattress on the floor.

He did not know what to say to her. Cursed himself for forcing her to invite him up here.

'How are the children?'

'All right. They don't seem to miss me. They never ask how I am.'

A bit much, he thought, to expect from kids that age. 'Have you phoned them?'

'Yes.'

She did not wish to discuss children. Too painful for her? 'I see,' he said, 'that you've been out in the sun.'

She poured the tea, which he did not want, as an excuse to avoid his eyes, with her hips straining the denim of her jeans as she knelt on the floor. 'I've been out walking every day. '

'Do you good.'

She could not hide the stress, although her hand was steady as she filled the mugs.

'With Goldie,' she said.

'Oh yes. Out walking eh? Goldie hardly seems the outdoor type.'

What does this damned woman mean to me? he asked himself. What does it matter who she goes out with? 'You like him, do you? I find him a bit... .'

He fumbled for words. He found Goldie, if truth be told, a bleddy tuss. A thick, self-opinionated, bleddy tuss!

'....difficult to get on with.'

'How is your friend?' she asked.

'Which friend?'

'The woman we saw on the beach.'

'Oh, Anne! I don't know. I think she's been away.'

'Do you like her?"

What was she getting at? 'She's a very old friend.' he said, avoiding the question. 'I don't see what you find so attractive about Goldie.' He could not see how this intelligent girl could find anything in common with the doubtful talents of that third-rate aspiring entertainer.

'I want to make friends. He knows a lot of people of my age.'

'Ah, yes.'

'He's very popular with women.'

'Is he sure 'nuff?'

What women? he thought. Silly teenaged girls bestowing their

148

adoration on a substitute for fear of the reality. They must have gone to his head, filled him with delusions of grandeur. What was Louise doing consorting with such a man?

'He said,' Louise went on, 'that he's not interested in me. Only my body. He said that, deep down, women only want men to screw them anyway, so it's all for sexual equality as far as he's concerned.'

'A real charmer. So sensitive.'

Was she so desperate for attention, for flattery, however crude, about the desirability of her body? The poor soul, he thought, she must be so lonely. He looked at her with concern, unable to fathom the depths of her mind.

She turned to him, half sitting, half lying on the mattress, and reached for his hand. 'Im sorry Barny.'

It was intended as a statement of her determination to relinquish him, but he drew her hand towards him and they fell back on to the soft duvet and he put his arms around her.

'Oh God.' He said 'I do worry about you.'

'I'm so lonely,' she sobbed. 'So lonely.'

'You have me,' he said, 'and Beth. Why don't you come out and see us?"

'I have to be strong. I have to stand on my own two feet.'

'But we all need friends,' Barny said, kissing her on the temple. 'None of us are too strong for that.'

And he held her for a long time, he was not sure how long, resisting the desire in him to slip his hand under her smock and fondle those delicate breasts, to kiss her on the mouth. If they stayed like this he would be unable to withhold himself, the desire to make love to her, smell her body, taste her skin, would overcome his wish to help her stand alone. He could sense her own desire growing in her as she moved against him and he disengaged himself from her embrace, pretending not to notice.

'You have friends,' he said. 'You're not alone. I'll come and see you when I'm in town, or you can come out on the bus. Give me a ring if you need anything. I don't ask anything of you. You won't be making any commitment.'

'You are so good to me, Barny.'

'As long as you need me, I'll do what I can for you.' It seemed an easy way out. No commitment on either side. 'I'll call and see if you're in when I come into town.'

'Yes please,' she sobbed.

He stood up, declaring his intention to leave, and Louise collected the cups of unconsumed tea and put them on the tray beside the matress on the floor.

'I saw your friend,' she said, 'the other day.'

'Anne?'

'Yes, but I didn't mean her. The little man with the moustache.'

'Oh.' Barny said, with some relief. 'Zeke.'

'Who ?'

'Zeke! Ezekiel The Man.' Barny was as eager as she to discuss matters other than her problems, to divert her attention from morbid introspection.

Louise settled on the mattress again, there was nowhere else to sit. Barny remained standing, aware of the probabilities should he settle beside her.

'Why did you call him Ezekiel The Man?' she asked. 'Is it a nickname?'

'Oh no. He's called Ezekiel Emanuel Endean. Endean means 'The Man', in the Old Language, *'An Den'*

'He looks a bit odd,' she said. 'Not very bright. He made me nervous, the way he looked at me, straight into my eyes.'

Barny knew what she meant. Zeke knew how to scrutinise people, and Louise would have been disconcerted by his gaze. 'You don't have to worry about Zeke,' he said. 'He's too angry with humanity to hurt anybody. He's a very gentle man, although you might not think so at first. And he's bright enough. He's an inventor.'

Louise had her doubts. 'What does he invent?' she asked.

'Oh, all sorts of things. He's very eccentric. Gets some crazy ideas.'

Barny remembered some of Zeke's more outlandish schemes and smiled to himself. Louise would never believe him, if he told her.

'One of his projects, one he's working on at the moment, so he tells me, is a contraption for measuring variations in geomagnetic impulses in the Earth.'

'It's been done before.'

'Not quite in the way or for the reasons that Zeke is working on it.'

Barny remained standing, looking down at her. In telling her of Zeke's eccentricities, he was delaying his departure, using his tale as an excuse to stay with her for a while.

'He hopes to compile maps and tables of geomagnetic fields for the benefit of his pigeon-fancier friends, among others. He lugs his gear all the way from the tops of the hills to the bottom of mine shafts to measure variations in the magnetism. Pigeons navigate along lines of magnetic force, apparently, so, with enough data, he reckons, it should be possible to arrange pigeon races over particular lines of flight at optimum times, so that birds don't get lost.'

'That sounds feasible.'

'Maybe. But he's also using the same apparatus for measuring the magnetic impulses in people's heads.'

'Brain waves? That's been done before too. He sounds a bit odd to me.'

'Yeah,' Barny laughed. 'He's odd all right. You'll get used to meeting oddballs down here. The place seems to attract them.' Like a Christmas Stocking all right, he thought, and here's another nut gone to the bottom. 'Mind you, Zeke is a local.'

'Well,' Louise conceded in Zeke's favour, 'it's remarkable how often some of these crazy ideas are eventually proven to be based on scientific fact.'

Barny had not implied that any of Zeke's theories were not likely to be proven. 'Well, some of Zeke's ideas are too outlandish for credibility. And I hope he's wrong about the brain waves.'

'Why?'

'What he's done, you see, is to get hold of some old encephalograph monitors, video recorders and old television sets, which he has wired up to sensors and electrodes that he sticks all over his head. I don't know where he gets all the stuff. He's a paradoxical chap, no doubt about that, but I don't know whether he's very clever or just daft. He tells me it works and I have no reason to dispute it. The electronics are all beyond me and I'm an electrical engineer. When he's wired up, he thinks along certain lines or tries to feel a given emotion, and the impulses are all monitored and recorded on the screens and tapes. I've known him sit for hours. It's a form of meditation, or a trance, he goes off into. Then, at a later date, he reverses the process, to put those same thoughts and emotions back into his mind from the electrical impulses of the recordings, chosen, he says, at random, so that he doesn't know which ones he's using. He says that music, cinema, television, radio and all kinds of vicarious experiences do this already, even story-telling, and he's merely trying to identify the subliminal elements which induce given emotions.'

Louise was horrified. 'What a horrible thing to do,' she said. 'The thoughts of millions of people could be controlled if such a thing was invented.'

'Zeke says it's only a matter of time before it is, if it's not been done already.'

'But why should he want to invent such an evil thing.'

'Ah, well. That's where his genius is countered by his simplicity. He wants to patent the invention and thereby prevent anyone else, so he thinks, from using it. He's incredibly naive.'

'Are you telling me the truth? I never know with you.'

'Neither do I,' he said. And she laughed with him, standing up under the low roof. The drizzle had thickened to steady rain and was pattering on the slates and skylight 'I'd better be going,' he murmured, 'my father is expecting me.'

'You'll get wet.'

This might have been an invitation to stay, to lie among the billows of the duvet. 'It's not far,' he said, and put his hat on. What else could he do? She was much more relaxed now and she had to learn how to live alone. 'And you will be careful, won't you? You'll remember what I said about inviting anyone up here. You know how that would be interpreted by... by some people?'

'Yes.'

Anne was in her kitchen, where the table was strewn with little heaps of prepared vegetables and chunks of meat, with her hands deep in a mixing bowl of flour.

'Ah,' he said, 'pasties,' as he stood behind her and put his arms around her waist. 'How are 'ee?'

'How haven't 'ee been to see me ?' she said, ignoring both the embrace and the comment.

'I haven't been in town. Last time I came, you were out. I left a note.'

'Yes, and I made some stew for us. You said you were coming back.'

That was when that maid had upset him, he remembered, when she had made him feel so despondent, but that was over. 'Sorry,' he said. I spent longer with father than I expected. I had to go straight home after I left 'n.'

'You liard !' Anne said. 'You were with that maid. I know she's here. I've seen her. Like one-in-a-dream walking 'round town.'

'I've just seen her again.' Barny said, to avoid comment on the previous occasion. 'She's in a brea state. But I think she'll be all right now.'

All right now that she has that bloody tuss of a singer, he thought, but she was not his responsibility any more.

'I suppose you want a pasty,' Anne said.

She had forgiven him.

She made the best pasties Barny had ever tasted, apart from his mother's of course, but everybody's mother makes the best pasties. He slipped his hand up to her ribs, feeling the curve of her breasts against his thumbs. 'Yes please.'

'Well, get your hands off and peel some more taties and onions and I'll do some more pastry.'

He stayed with her, talking, as she rolled out the pastry into circles, filled them with the ingredients, crimped the edges and put the pasties in the oven.

There was no one with whom he felt more at ease. The time fled while they waited for the pasties to cook, ate them, drank tea and discussed mutual friends. Life could be good with such a woman.

He left her late at night, after promising to bring her some of the produce of his garden, for he often brought her a selection of vegetables and whatever flowers happened to be in bloom, and he went home to bed without a further thought of Louise Fern crossing his mind.

Louise did not come out to Sam and Beth, or Barny, and neither did she phone, so they assumed she was coping with life and continued with their daily routines. Barny went once to the stones. He walked across the moors one evening to see the sunset from the hill, and stopped at the circle. He touched the stone with both hands, after ensuring that no one was in sight up there on the slopes, and closed his eyes with the red glow of the sun on his face. Wordlessly, with only the flow of emotion and the love of the ground in which these stones had lain embedded for four thousand years, he told the earth of his devotion, and went upon his path, to sit on the carn and watch the end of another day.

That night, as he lay reading before going to sleep, he became aware of thoughts of Louise in his mind. They were of nothing specific, no more than a sudden awareness of her existence, but reminded him that he had promised to visit her, a promise he had all but decided not to fulfil, so, on the following day, after seeing his father, he went to call on her. He wanted to reassure himself that she was well, yet felt uneasy at the prospect of being alone with her in the intimacy of that lonely attic and hoped, in a perverse way, that she would be out. He would have fulfilled his obligation without further involvement.

There were children playing on the street as he approached Louise's house. Several young women were gathered at a door, enjoying the sunshine and a bit of a chat as they watched their offspring. A ginger cat lay on its back, with its eyes closed and legs limp as the sun warmed the white, vulnerably exposed belly. Barny knocked the door, wondering whose daughters and grandchildren all these people were. There followed a long wait, during which he doubted if she could hear the knock from so far up in the house. He knocked again, louder, and the house sounded empty, uncarpeted, unfurnished and unloved. He heard the inner door being opened, then her voice, loud insistent.

'Who's there?'

Why didn't she open the bleddy door and have a look? He stooped low, to confide in the letter box, conscious of the women watching him.

'It's Barny!' he told the hollow interior.

Louise opened the door and stepped back into the hallway. She looked ghastly. Her cheeks were pale and drawn, her eyes red and dry, although she became convulsed with further tears at the sight of him. He hastily closed the door behind him and stepped towards her.

'What's the matter?' he asked. 'You look awful.'

'I've been raped.'

He hated her. The stupid woman led him up to her room, where she fell upon the mattress and he stood over her, almost as distraught as she, as she told him who had done it.

He had warned her. And she should have heeded his warning. She had asked for it. A man like that! To invite him up here, a man like Goldie who had told her he wanted her only for her body, only to fuck her, the silly bitch. She was sex mad. It was all she ever thought about. Rape! With three people in the house to whom she could have screamed for help He removed his hat and threw it viciously to the floor.

Barny listened to her hysterical sobs and incoherent words, trying to find some compassion for her after she had rejected him in favour of that masochistic poser. What had she expected of him if not this? He imagined the aggressive advances of the man, how she would have reacted to his lust, how much she had encouraged him before the situation became out of control and violent. Was this what she wanted? To have a man so roused by desire for her body that he would overcome her token resistance and take her by force, so that she might gratify her own desires without compromising her hypocritical morality?

As he watched her, he despised himself for his doubts. The poor girl was so desirous of affection, so starved of love, that she would be beguiled by flattery and unable to resist perfidious advances. She was so vulnerable, so much more so than she was aware. But she was not his responsibility, he had done what he could for her.

And then he remembered the cry of anguish he had raised to her in the time of his dreads, when her name had wrenched itself from his throat in the night of terrified desperation. It had been an irrational cry, one that should have been directed at Beth or Anne, who had the strength to succour him, not to this hopeless neurotic lying in a heap upon the floor. But he knew her needs, her pain.

He dropped to his knees and stroked her hair. 'You poor thing,' he said. 'You poor little maid.'

Louise turned and clung to him, her face a red mess of tears and fatigue. 'How can you touch me? I am so dirty.'

Barny felt the tears welling in his own eyes, and he put his arms around her. 'You're not dirty. How can you think that?' She smelt of soap and shampoo, and he kissed her hair.

'He forced me,' she said between sobs. 'We went to the cinema and I asked him back for a cup of coffee. He raped me. I didn't want him to.'

Barny was on his knees, holding her awkwardly as she lay across his legs. He kicked off his shoes and sat on the bed, with his back against the wall as she tried to control her sobs. The position was still too uncomfortable to hold her so they lay down, heads on the pillow, and he cuddled her, uttering soft terms of endearment and support, then anger. 'I'll murder the bastard,' he said.

'I didn't know what to do' I had no one to go to.'

That was not quite true, he thought. She could have phoned from the kiosk across the street.

'I went to the hospital. Three nurses took care of me. One of them held me in her arms. I felt so dirty. They washed me out. It was horrible, but they were so kind.'

She told him how Goldie had made advances which she did not want, then forced her, saying at the end 'That was not so bad, was it? Why did you struggle? It was what you wanted.'

'I didn't.' she wailed. 'I didn't want it. I didn't even come.'

There was, Barny detected, an element of astonishment in her voice, as if she had expected to be ravished into an involuntary orgasm which had not occurred. What a disgusting business. She would have to come to terms with herself, and seek gratification in love, or her life would be forever fraught with anguish. It was almost as if her sexual desires were so associated with dirt and pain that it was only when accompanied by

155

revulsion that she could release her libido. What a state. What a neurotic. But Barny was in no position to diagnose such a condition. She needed help, but from whom? To suggest psychiatric treatment, even now, in the form of counselling, would only add to her insecurity, convincing her that she was even more loopy than she was.

Her sobs finally subsided and she began shivering with nerves. He told her to get in bed, while he went down to the kitchen to prepare something to eat.

'I don't want anything.'

'A cup of tea, then.'

She acquiesced and he went below, locking the door behind him as she requested, thinking, it's a bit late now, my 'ansome.

When he returned she was under the duvet, still shivering. She was obliged to hold the mug in two hands until she had drunk enough to swallow some aspirin which, he said, not believing himself, would help to calm her nerves.

She sank down into the bed, a pathetic waif, and said, 'Will you cuddle me, Barny?'

Barny lay beside her, holding her as she was intermittently convulsed by deep shudders, and drew her close. He kissed her temple and she clung to him, pressing herself close, and he felt himself rising at her proximity, ashamed of his involuntary desire for her. She had taken her jeans off and he was aware of her bare legs against him. He put his hand on her waist, feeling her skin, so soft and smooth. She suddenly burst into tears again, saying 'I love you, Barny. I love you...' and as she pressed against him his erection was hard against her thigh.

'You won't want me now,' she said. 'I'm dirty. I'm defiled. How can you touch me?'

He was confused by his own desire, utterly disconcerted by his want of her at such a time. He drew away and she said, 'You don't want me. No one will want me now'

'I do,' he said. 'I do. I can't help myself. But I couldn't, not now.'

She held on to him, drawing him back to her, with her wet, familiar tears on his cheek, desperate for his proximity, for release from the anguish.

'Do you want to come?' he whispered.

'Yes.' In a voice so soft he barely heard it. 'But I'm dirty. I don't want you in me while... there's still... .'

'Oh my darling.'

It would relieve her. Release her from the stress. Put her to sleep as he held her. He slipped his hand down, down through the hair, and said 'You are beautiful. You are lovely.'

'How can you touch me?'

He did it inside her knickers as she clung desperately on to him, gasping at his touch. 'Let it go,' he said. 'Let it go, my darling. I love you. Oh, how I love you.'

CHAPTER NINE

Aga hensa profyans a garensa. Their first loving.

You say you hated men...

Except for Barny. He was the only one who understood me, my needs. I mean, my desires. Lust. All the wickedness. And he never condemned me. I was afraid of him for knowing me so well. I eventually felt I was becoming dependent again... .

They never saw Goldie again. Barny went looking for him and discovered that he had already made plans to move away, back where he came from, so he did not have the opportunity to murder him. Sam and Beth were not told of the incident in Louise's attic and were astonished to learn that she had moved in with Barny. He could not leave her there alone, he told himself, too frightened to go out or open the door, lying awake at night in terror of imagined intruders.

Barny did not tell his father either, but was not surprised to hear him say, some weeks later, 'Who's that party you got livin' with 'ee?'

'Who told you about she?' Barny asked.

'A little bird told me,' he said as he cut the saffron cake and shoved it, on a plate, in front of his son. 'Time for 'ee to grow up. You're old enough to know better.'.

Barny sighed in resignation. 'I s'pose you're right,' he said. 'You usually are.'

He had no intention of quarrelling with this father over Louise. That she was living with him as one apart no one would believe, for they could not imagine what suffering she endured, the revulsion she seemed to feel at physical contact. Whenever he touched her, as a gesture of affection or reassurance, she visibly tensed, as if in fear, so he left her alone for the wounds to heal.

It was unlikely that the old man would come out to Barny's cottage to see her. He had been a couple of times; once when Barny had first moved in, just to see the place, and then on the first occasion when he had been taken ill following the death of Barny's mother. A slight heart attack, which he denied, saying, 'Bit of heartburn, indigestion. Bleddy doctors, making a damn fuss.'

Since then he had learned to live alone, believed his son had done likewise and could not understand the need to become entangled with a woman. 'Damn strangers,' he muttered. 'Don't know who they are, nor what they are.' And, after sitting for a while in contemplation, 'I heard she's n'more than a cheeld.'

'She's a married woman with two children.'

'Two cheldern!' he cried. 'You must be off your bleddy head.'

I could live to be a hundred and ten, Barny thought, and he would still regard me as a boy. Sooner or later he would meet her and then, perhaps, approve, for it is always the unknown which causes most anxiety. Only the spilling of a little tea into the saucer, as he poured it into the china cups, indicated the father's true agitation at his son's folly. 'Mind what you're about, booy,' he said.

Barny was foolish enough to tell Louise of this, intending to share it with her as a source of amusement, but she was not amused. She saw it as rejection, not only by Barny's father, but the whole local community. 'I will never be accepted,' she said. 'They will all hate me, for enticing you.'

'Some of them might wish you had enticed them instead.'

She smiled, and he put his arms around her and kissed her on the temple. 'That's better,' he said. 'Let's have a drop of wine.'

Alcohol would probably make her more depressed, he thought, but he needed some. The incident in that attic seemed to be preying on her mind, leaving her desolate, as if she would never recover.

He fetched two glasses, filled them to the brim, led her to the old sofa and sat on the floor beside her, holding her hand. Since she had moved in with him, he felt exhausted from continually reassuring her. Her despondency was beginning to drain him, infecting him with her contagious tension.

As he watched the flames, he became aware of the gentle touch of her hand upon his shoulder, the slip to his nape, the fingers exploring his locks. Her touch was like the touch of an innocent child, tentative, exploring, questing knowledge. He could not imagine what tremulous thoughts were in her mind.

They were all of love and the need of him. As he turned to her, a whimsical smile hovered on her lips and she drew him towards her until his head was resting on her knees. She stroked his hair, wanting the comfort of his touch. She loved him. She wanted to tell him so, tell him how she had ached for him ever since that night of her first visit, but restrained herself, slowly stroking his thinning hair, asking herself, why? Why him? Why Barny? The reasons were irrelevant, illogical and inexplicable, but she had loved him, she remembered, from the minute she saw him. His eyes, his voice. And now she was dirty, touched by evil, and he would never want her in his arms again.

She bent over him, running her hands over the strong back beneath his navy guarnsey, and Barny raised his head to look at her and saw that she was suppressing tears of happiness.

A great surge of compassion seized him and he turned and held her around the waist, with his head against her breast, saying, 'Oh, you poor little maid. What have they done to you?'

She had opened her legs and he was kneeling between her thighs, with tears dropping on to his head. 'Oh you poor little thing, cry it all away. Let it go. I'll hold you.'

He raised himself until his face was against her wet, slippery cheek, and he kissed her on the lips to absorb the trembles. 'It's all right,' he said, 'Let me hold you,' and he brushed the tears from under her eyes with a finger, recalling all those revelations of that previous embrace, here in this same room, on this same sofa, with the same glow of firelight illuminating her streaming cheeks.

Louise put her arms around him and hugged him tight, sobbing into his hair. There was a solid strength to his wiry body, and she tried to draw it out of him, to nourish herself on his vitality. She felt she could embrace him so fiercely that he would become part of her. She wanted his strength, his body, his manhood, in her, deep inside her. She pressed his head down against her breasts, overcoming the resistance she felt in him, and heard him say, 'What are you doing to me ?' as he nuzzled into her. 'Be careful, Louise.'

The desire for him overwhelmed her. She felt her thighs involuntarily clutching his kneeling body in slow quivering pulsations. Her tears gradually ceased, becoming occasional trembles between her regular, deepening breaths. Her head fell back and he raised himself to look at her. She saw his eyes narrow, as if questioning her, asking if she knew what she was doing to herself and to him. She placed her head against his neck, to hide from him, and opened her lips against his skin, breathing her wet breath upon him. There was a strong pulse beating beneath his ear. She could taste him on her tongue, clean and fresh, like brine from the sea. His hands slipped to her waist, she arched her back as they slid up under her clothes, and they felt warm against her bare skin. She wanted his strong, gentle hands on her breasts to caress and soothe her and make her better.

But he drew away from her. There was an expression of doubt and interrogation in his eyes, as if he considered her not responsible for her own actions, as if she was behaving in an impetuous manner which she would later regret, and her passion subsided as rapidly as it had arisen. Once again she had gone too far. The animal within had taken control of her, that other, primitive being that continually emerged from her subconscious to excite and then humiliate her. When he realised that she had drawn him on, he had become repulsed by her, she could tell. She had alarmed him with the ferocity of her lust, as she had alarmed herself. She was ashamed, and finally looked at him in penitence, feeling vulnerable and exposed. There was nowhere to hide. His body was between her legs. She could not turn away nor bury her face in his chest; she must endure the scrutiny of those questioning eyes.

'I'm sorry,' she said, as the tears fell again from her eyes, tears of shame. Could he not see that she wished to reveal herself to him, to give herself entirely, that there be no secrets withheld from him, that she wanted him to take the animal within her, the rampaging tiger, and tame it, bring it to submission?

The woman was forever in tears, Barny thought. She had so much emotion pent up in her, suppressed, more than she could cope with. It was more that he could cope with too, but he wanted her. Against all his instincts, his reservations, the certain knowledge that she was capable of involving him in her predicament, he still wanted her. It was madness! He drew away from her and stood up, slightly trembling with fear.

'I can't,' he said. 'I mean... it wouldn't be right.'

He could not explain his reluctance, and became inarticulate before her imploring eyes. 'You're too vulnerable,' he sighed. 'You don't realise... . I mean, don't you see the danger?'

It was the danger of his own passion, his own needs, of which he was warning her. 'I could destroy you,' he said.

Louise interpreted his vacillation as being aversion. 'I'm sorry,' she said, acutely aware of him examining her, searching for her eyes, but she denied him, staring into the fire, with her eyes expressionless and inscrutable.

Now he was contrite, afraid he had humiliated her. To deny her would be too much of a rejection. 'You haven't finished your wine.' She sipped from the glass, conserving the dregs as an excuse to stay the conversation. The silence became constrained, with both of them suppressing desires which threatened to engulf them. Barny felt himself trembling slightly from nervous tension.

'Let's listen to some music,' he said in desperation. 'What would you like?' He rose from the sofa and went to his hi-fi, keeping his back to her, hiding his arousal. It was entirely involuntary, he told himself, the animal in him wanting to take advantage of her.

'Do you have Carl Orff's Carmina Burana ?' she asked. 'I like that. It's so sensual.'

There was some element in her voice that implied he would never have heard of it, that it would be something beyond his musical repertoire. She was trying to impress him; so he inserted the disc and returned to the sofa without replying.

He sat beside her, with his head thrown back, and let the music saturate his mind.

At the end of *Fortuna Imperatrix Mundi* Louise stretched out on the sofa with her head resting on his thigh, and they listened to the rich voices with their eyes closed. Through *Primo Vere* he stroked the long hair draping over her shoulders, and during *Uf Dem Angec* she put her hand above his knee, the long fingers stroking his leg. To the rhythm of *In Taberna* he could pretend no longer, she held him through the faded denim and his want of her was enormous.

Ego sum abbas. Ego sum abbas, sum abbas sum abbas. The music expressed all his longing for her and he slipped his hand under her jumper to hold the delicate protuberance of her little breast. With his eyes still closed he heard her saying, 'On the floor, Barny. On the floor.'

He could resist her no longer. He stood up, tore the old bedspread and cushions from the back of the sofa and spread them on the floor. He threw off his clothes, then hers, strewing them carelessly about the room, and they lay entwined in each other's arms to the chiming of bells at the opening of *Cours D'amors.* He kissed and caressed her to *Amor Volat Undique*, exploring her body, arms, long legs and fervent lips. During *Dies, Nox et omnia*, he lay upon her body with their mouths seeking each other in gasping desire.

This time, he thought, I must have her. This must be the time. He forgot the music in listening to her breathing against his neck, anticipating her abandonment to sensuality and desire. Suddenly, she held him tightly, constricting his breathing.

'They're coming,' she said.'

'What? Who are coming?'

'The demons. I can hear them. Talk to me, Barny. Oh, my God. Talk to me.'

'Talk to you? What do you mean.'

'They come to take me to hell if I sin. Help me to fight them.'

She fought against him, thrusting herself at him in rage at the unknown terrors which seized her, fighting him as representing the sexuality and sin within her which must be subjugated, and for which she must be punished.

'Talk to me. Tell me what you will do to me. Drive them away with your voice. Let me hear you. Oh, God, they're horrible.'

He told her. Fighting for breath, he told her of the lascivious titillation to which she was about to be subjected.

'Talk to me,' she said, 'Keep talking. Drive them away,' And he told her of the evils in sex which excited and humiliated her, the obscenities for which the demons had come to punish her, and of the excitement which would suppress them, as she fought him to a mutual screaming climax of physical and emotional conflict.

'My bogey men,' she said. 'They always come. Oh, my God.'

The music drew to its pulsating climax and the cottage was silent, as if all noises had been driven out except for those in their unsound minds.

Barny's greatest difficulty lay in facing Anne, and he avoided her for some time, hoping that she too would hear of his involvement with Louise from elsewhere. After his father had spoken of Louise he could assume that Anne knew of her too, so, some weeks after she moved in with him, Barny went to see her, dreading the confrontation but dismissing his vague feelings of guilt as irrational. There had never been any commitment between them, he told himself, and Anne had consistently refused any deepening of their friendship, so why should she be concerned? However, despite his resolution that his life was his own affair, and that he had no obligation to anyone, he approached her door with some trepidation.

Her greeting was casual, although there was a slight catch in her voice. She was attempting to change a light bulb, the glass of which had become detached from the bayonet, and she was standing on a chair, struggling to remove the fitting from the holder.

'Let me do that for you,' Barny said, quite relieved to find her engaged in a task in which she could pretend to be absorbed, thinking that previously, in such a situation, he would have slipped his hand up her skirt as she stood above him on the chair, unable to escape. 'Your fingers aren't strong enough. Have you got any pliers?'

'I can manage!' she said defiantly. And then, with a laugh of resignation, 'No, I can't,' as she stepped down from the chair.

'This flex is dangerous,' Barny said after he had stepped up. 'It's perished. The wires are bare.'

He went down to the shops, bought some flex, and then to his car for tools. The whole place needs rewiring, he thought as he replaced the flex, removed the broken bulb and put the new one in. She can't afford to have it done and I can't afford a new roof, but between us we could be well off. He tried the switch. 'There you are.'

'Thank you,' she said.

And suddenly there was nothing to talk about except Louise, whom neither wished to mention.

'Will 'ee still come and see me?' Anne said at last.

'Of course I will. Why not?'

They each contemplated the numerous reasons why not. Their friendship could never be the same. They had been too close for a third party to tolerate, and now must remain distant. Anne's absence would be a great loss in his life, he conceded, but he had fallen in love with Louise, who needed him so much. He had told her he loved her, that day in the attic, yet now, as he saw the consternation in Anne's eyes, he began to have doubts. What had he let himself in for?

Anne came to the door with him and he left her without a kiss, without having touched her at all during his visit, for the first time in years. She watched him join the holidaymakers walking up the street, and closed the door. She went back to the kitchen, flicked the switch a couple of times, and sat with her elbows on the table, her cheeks in her hands, considering the prospect of life without him until he came to his senses.

Barny found Louise speaking on the telephone when he arrived home. She was talking to her children, so he went to look around the garden that she might continue to speak freely. She joined him some time later when, he observed, she had washed and dried the tears from her face.

'I have no one but you, Barny.'

Somewhere, he discovered during the ensuing weeks, she had a mother and father, although she saw them even less frequently than they saw each other, for they had been divorced for nearly twenty years. The mother was an Italian whose family had left home to escape the regime of Mussolini, and from whom Louise inherited her black hair and temperament. It seemed that she was inclined to be 'highly strung', as Louise put it. Her father, from whom she had inherited her stature, had been brought up in America, and was very tall, an actor, she said, who she rarely saw because he was always travelling. From time to time she revealed these details about herself as they were walking or sitting in the sun in the garden. She gradually became stronger, although she found the sea too cold for swimming and would stay in the shallows, her arms wrapped around herself as Barny swam in deep water or rode the breaking surf in their favourite cove. There was one occasion when he dived from a high rock and swam back to find her watching him with admiring eyes.

'You are just the kind of man I've always wanted,' she said as he hauled himself up to sit beside her. 'I've never been so happy. All I need is a job.'

'Don't worry about jobs. There aren't any. Just enjoy your life.'

'But what will the inspector say?'

As Louise had no money, literally none, she was drawing Social Security Benefit and, while in the attic, had received a rent allowance. She had filled in the form to the effect that she was now renting a room in Barny's house without declaring that they were living together, cohabiting.

'It's not, strictly speaking, honest,' Barny teased her. 'You ought to tell them we are screwing each other day and night.'

'That's none of their business,' Louise said. 'If they were prepared to pay the exorbitant rent for me to live in that poky attic, why should they object to paying less because I'm living with you? It's silly.'

They had agreed between then that some of the rent should go toward their shared living expenses and the remainder was hers. Barny would be obliged to declare the rent to the inland revenue but, as his income was so low, it did not matter.

'It's exactly the same,' Louise said, 'as I see it. If you came and slept with me in the attic, or I came out here and kept the other place on, they would pay without quibble. They are not going to lose anything.'

'Don't worry about it,' Barny said, detecting the anxiety in her voice. 'It's English money.'

'What do you mean?'

'Money they owe us.'

She did not understand. 'But what about the inspector they are sending out, to check on the living arrangements.'

'We'll sort that out.'

They put all her things in the biggest bedroom, while his stuff was moved into the small bedroom at the back, and Barny fixed a new lock on her door.

'I might lock you out,' Louise said.

'I have another key, in case of fire.'

'In the loins,' she said, with a provocative smile.

She had fire in the loins all right. It was like a raging inferno, and was burning her up, for she could not quench it, and neither could he. It was as if she was stifled by her own heat and could not love without fighting the flames and the bogey men which haunted her. There was much she had not told him.

On the day the inspector was due, Louise wore a dress, with a soft scarf over her shoulder, and Barny told her he would be working in the garden. He went out to the shed and put on an ancient pair of baggy corduroys, a stretched and much-darned jumper and a filthy old trilby hat he wore while cleaning out Beth's chicken houses. The inspector was a woman of Louise's age, or younger, from up country. She came to the gate and he went to let her in, with his hands grimy and a dusty old pair of wire-framed spectacles under the limp brim of his hat. She had a slight accent, Reading, Oxford or somewhere thereabouts, Barny reckoned, probably very nice, but a townie.

'She's in theer,' he said. 'Some 'ansome young woman, you. Ab'mt got no home nor habitation. She d' remind me,' he said confidingly, 'of that maid to Daniel Oates, you knaw, the one who used to live next door to Emily Pender and they, down the peeth.'

He called Louise out and grinned at her before going back to his smoky bonfire, saying, 'I'll leeb 'n to 'ee.'

Louise turned into the cottage, leading the woman to the sitting room, hearing her say, 'What a dear old man.'

The woman waved to Barny as she left, and he went to the door, where he found Louise in a fit of giggles just inside, out of sight from the road.

'You look awful,' she said.

'What did she say?'

'Not much. She didn't even ask to see the bedroom. She must think you're well past it.'

They fell about each other laughing, until Louise said, 'You even smell horrible.'

He changed back into his usual clothes and threw the old things on the bonfire before coming in to sit with her on the sofa.

'You're so good for me,' she said. 'I am so happy, now that I have enough to survive on, but I do want to get a job.'

Barny doubted if she was ready for the demands of a responsible job, yet could see, as he came to know her, that she would soon be bored and frustrated with anything that did not stretch her mind.

The summer passed, and they spent their time together, walking over the moors, sharing the gardening and going down to the cove to relax beside the sea. She was still reading feminist literature, as a means of self-assertion, she said, and then books on the role of women in history and religion. Usually, she did not discuss what she was assimilating but occasionally read aloud some particularly revealing passage; the discrimination against women in commerce and medicine, the domination of men in the hierarchy of the Church, the persecution of witches. All feminist wisdom and knowledge, together with their influence, had been ruthlessly suppressed, she asserted. Though vaguely aware of all this, Barny had never thought much about it, for there had been no reason to do so. Most of his own female acquaintances, from his mother onwards, had been stronger than himself in many respects and he regarded them as equals. He told her on one occasion when she was prepared to discuss the subject, 'There were some pretty powerful and competent women around when I was young. They would have laughed at Women's Lib.'

'As long as they were happy being housewives,' Louise said. 'The girls of those days would have found it impossible to join the professions, to become a doctor or a priest.'

'ess,' Barny said. 'Tha's true.'

And so too, he thought to himself, would all of the boys I grew up with.

This was one of the occasions when he disputed some of the extreme assertions made about men in the books she read, but Louise immediately took these comments as personal affronts, as if her own opinions were in question, so he became non-committal, believing that anything which helped her to gain confidence was worth fostering, even if he didn't agree with it.

He found her changing temperament a constant enigma. The slightest stimulus could induce a complete reversal of her moods, from gaiety to gloom and vice versa. When she laughed, her whole face became animated, her eyes sparkled and the full lips of her rather large mouth relaxed into a sensuality of which she was totally unaware. At such times, his heart opened to her and he was determined to rid her of the dark demons which fought for possession of her mind.

These demons grasped her most firmly in their clutches when they were making love. They lurked in the depths, like leviathans, submerged and out of sight until she was at her most vulnerable, when she should have yielded to her passions and slipped into ecstatic oblivion. It was then that they rose up and seized her, held her back in cold claws of fear, and she cried out for Barny to drive them away. 'My bogey men,' was the only way she could describe them, these fears that gripped her then.

After she had settled in with him, arranged some of her possessions about the place, and he had built yet another bookcase for her precious classics, which she never read, although saying, 'Home is where the books are,' she devoted much of her energy to searching for work. Barny had hoped that she would have spent more time with Sam and Beth, learning from them how to be content with life, but she rarely went over there, even with Barny, who continued to drop in regularly despite suspecting that Louise was jealous of his easy relationship with Beth.

Louise was even more jealous of Anne, and was always suspicious when he went to town alone, asking if he had seen her. The matter reached a crisis one evening when Anne phoned as they were sitting together on the sofa. Anne's ex-husband had been to see her, she was upset at his abuse, and, after he left, all her electrical fuses had blown, leaving her without light, heating or cooking. Barny knew she must be desperate to have phoned, so, despite Louise's protests, he took some tools and drove in to repair the fault in her wiring. He returned very late, leaving Anne in no doubt that although he had obliged her this time he was no longer available for such emergencies, and found Louise in a distraught state of anxiety, asking if he was tired of her, did he love her, and it took an hour of soothing to assuage her doubts.

Each time Louise went to town she visited the job centre and looked through the cards arranged on stands around the hot, thickly carpeted office. She began keeping a list of all the jobs she applied for, with the name of the company, date of application, details of the work and, on the rare occasions when one was received, the reply. One day she went into town alone early in the morning and returned late at night, exhausted. She had been into every shop in town, she said, working her way down one side of the main streets and back up the other. There was nothing for her, not a single job in any shop in town. On another occasion, she perused the whole of the yellow pages in the phone book, listing every company where there might be the remotest possibility of a job, and spent her entire social security cheque on postage. There was nothing here either, as any local could have told her, indeed did tell her, for many of them had been through the same procedure, but she had to discover it for herself. For the menial jobs she was too highly qualified, and for those requiring skills she had no experience.

Throughout all this, whenever Barny wanted to write, Louise left him alone and took long walks or occasionally went to see Sam and Beth, to leave him undisturbed, and his poetry flowed as never before. His notebooks were filled with ideas, lines which came into his head during conversations with her about the area, its history and destiny. She offered to type them for him but he did it himself, as always, and rarely showed her anything, for he was aware of the energy that is dissipated in discussing work in progress. It is as if the discussion itself becomes the means of communication, leaving no further need for the expression of the thought or emotion in writing.

One evening she came in utterly despondent and Barny comforted her, kneeling beside her as she lay on the sofa with her cheeks running in tears.

'There's no hope for me,' she wailed. 'The locals get all the jobs down here. I'll never be accepted.'

Barny said, 'There are no jobs for anybody, my flower. Being local has nothing to do with it. You'll get something. Don't worry about it. Use the time to do all the things you won't be able to when you are working.'

He thought, but didn't say, that she was being unreasonable in expecting to find work so soon. He knew of people who had been months, years, looking for jobs, and there was little prospect of finding something suitable for someone of her intelligence and education. So many similarly talented young people were forced to leave, against their will, because there was nothing for them here. It was also an unreasonable resentment she was expressing. If there was a grain of truth in her assumption it would, in his opinion, be justified, for why should people be forced from their communities by waves of incomers? It was happening all over the world. Crazy! People moving, shunting about the globe, buzzing around like blue-arsed flies looking for the juiciest piece of meat to suck.

'I can't live on Social Security,' she said. 'It's costing me a fortune just applying for jobs. I can't even afford to buy a new pair of shoes.'

'You don't have to worry about money,' he said. 'You have somewhere to live, and you're safe here with me. I'll take care of you. Something will turn up. You'll see. Wait till Simon Sweeting's venture gets under way.'

'Oh, Barny,' she wept, 'You're so good to me. Without you, I have nothing, nowhere to go. Don't ever throw me out. Promise!'

There was a desperate, appealing look in her eyes, and he reassured her for the hundredth time. 'As long as you need me,' he said, 'I'm here.'

'You're so strong,' she said, putting her arms around him. 'I wish I were like you.'

He stroked her long hair, running the thick plaid through his hand. 'It's lovely,' he said. 'Beautiful.'

'Is it?'

She was asking for a compliment. 'Don't ever cut it off,' he said.

'No. I won't, if you like it.'

The summer ended in a gale that Louise thought was a storm, and she listened to every gust in dread, fearful of the roof. The gale blew up quickly and was soon past, while the wind stayed in the west, drenching the countryside in a thick drizzle through which Barny peered at the cement-washed slates. There was no damage to the roof but it would not last forever. They were confined to the cottage for several days, and Louise became fidgety with nothing to do.

Eventually the rain cleared, to be followed by a period of cold nor-westerlies which dried the rusting bracken before dying away to a light breeze under skies so intensely blue that the shallow puddles in the moorland peat reflected the colour like sheets of lapis lazuli embedded in the earth. They appeared solid enough to skate upon, yet so fragile that a thrown pebble would have shattered them into splinters of clear crystal.

He stood at his gate, one morning, looking at the hills, envious of those with the ability to capture the quintessence of the landscape in pigment, its moods and atmosphere in smears of paint. Over in the distance he saw the postman's van approaching like a drunken red ladybird meandering around the tortuous bends of the narrow road, an extra blob of pigment in the brilliant landscape.

Louise came to the door. 'What are you doing?' she asked.

'Just having a look - at the colours. It's always so much clearer after rain.'

But she had seen the red blob, trickling down the picture, and he saw her eyes following its progress towards them.

'The bracken is turning,' he said. 'The slopes will soon be sheathed in copper.'

'Yes.'

The van approached, and the driver changed gear as it passed the cottage. They heard it pull off the road onto the scrunchy gravel of the farm. She turned to him with a wry curl of her lips and, while it was obvious that once again she was disappointed at there being no offer of a job in the post, said nothing. Barny thought she was becoming obsessed with this business of getting work and beginning to lose her enthusiasm for her new surroundings.

'Shall we go out?' he suggested. 'Both of us could do with some fresh air and exercise. Let's go up to the moors.'

He knew that she had not yet learned to value her leisure, and that the time would come, while she was employed in some boring job, when every minute of her spare time would be too valuable to waste in brooding over her imaginary imperfections and misfortunes. A long walk in the autumn sun might stimulate her mind and tire her physically, so that she would relax and stop deprecating herself.

He took her along the coast road and then inland to follow a narrow track that led to the summit among the massive rocks outcropping at the highest point of the peninsula. They could see the sea below them to the north, while to the south, beyond the moors and fields, the sunlight glinted on the calm waters of the opposite coast. The long, southernmost pro-montory was visible as a flat featureless profile in the distance. They could see the hamlets dotted along the coastal plain below them. They could see Sam and Beth's farm and the roof of Barny's cottage, tucked away among the distorted sycamores. It was a sparse, hard landscape, with four thousand years of man's endeavour manifest in the arrangement of stones, one upon the other, to form walls, houses, places of habitation, work and ritual. They could see the towers of three churches set among the stones, where now the people dwelling here filled but a pew or two on the forgotten Sabbaths.

Despite Barny's attempts at conversation, Louise was unresponsive, as if her vision was as obscure as her thoughts. He abandoned any notion of pointing out salient features in the landscape, and let her discover her own curiosity. They sat in the autumn sunshine for some time in silence, until Barny rose to lead on through the dry, white grasses of the high moors before she changed her mind about going further.

Abruptly, when he thought her mind quite empty of conscious thought, she said, 'We're very lucky to live here.'

'Lucky?' he said, astonished that she had been thinking of anything but her deficiencies, 'There's no luck in it. I am part of this. It's my birthright. And you are here from conscious choice. Where's the luck?'

'You could have been born somewhere else,' she said, showing some irritation, 'and still appreciate it.'

'Well, yes. But if I had been born somewhere else I would not be me. The assumption is a contradiction in terms, an impossibility.'

He was trying to stimulate her, but was misunderstood.

'Why do you always contradict me ?'

'I'm sorry. Just trying to be clever.' He rose to his feet, thinking that her polemical curiosity was as jaded as her appetite. 'Shall we move on? It's a long walk.'

He led her across the undulating plateau at the top of the hill, where they were obliged to walk in single file between the scattered pools remaining from the rain. He thought she might have seen the colours... in the lichen glistening in the sun, in the white grasses and in the blue water, but she made no comment. Despite her height and long legs, she had difficulty in keeping up with him, so he slackened his pace. There would be no benefit to his fitness in this walk and he resolved to toughen her up, develop some stamina in her. She was as weak physically as she was in her mind, and would require discreet encouragement or she might become reluctant to accompany him on these excursions into his fields of inspiration.

About five hundred yards from the summit, the moors sloped away to the south and met the highest of the cultivated fields where, on the edge of the moor, there was a ruined building, long abandoned, with only the crumbling walls remaining. It stood in isolation among the heather and gorse and encroaching bracken, blending into the landscape, its stones encrusted with lichen as nature reclaimed her own. They stopped to look at it. Originally it had been a single-storey longhouse, with living quarters at one end and accommodation for domestic animals at the other. All had been constructed with equal skill. The granite stonework was as carefully laid for the the animals as for the humans. Only the massive chimney breast indicated which section of the building has been used for the family, all traces of timber and plaster had long since vanished.

'I can't imagine,' Louise said, 'anyone living up here. It must have been intolerable.'

'Pretty tough,' he agreed.

'No running water, no bathroom or toilet... .'

'No electricity,' he interjected, 'no gas, road, fridge, washing machine, telly... . It must have been hell.'

'So cold,' she said, not seeing the irony in his eyes, 'in the winter.'

'Not inside. The walls are three feet thick, look, and the roof was thatched.'

'How do you know that?'

'There are no old slates among the debris inside. In any case, all the cottages were thatched in those days, only the posh houses had slate roofs.'

She looked doubtful but he assured her this was the case. 'And they had plenty of fuel,' he said. 'It was all around them. Furze and bracken. They used to be valuable commodities. It may have made economic sense to live up here. Who knows? People always choose easy options, so there must have been some advantage in it or they would never have built the place. It involved an awful lot of work.'

They walked on. In the fields further down the slope there was a more recently abandoned dwelling, a small farmhouse, with barns and granite pigsties under rusted corrugated iron. The house roof was still intact, but the timber of the windows and doors was beginning to rot. Soon it would succumb to damp and gales and collapse into a ruin like its neighbour.

'What a shame,' Louse said. 'Somebody could easily do it up and live in it.'

'It has no water, no electricity, no road leading to a double garage with automatic up-and-over doors. It would cost more that it's worth.'

'People up country...' She was already beginning to use the local colloquialisms, '...would pay a fortune for it.'

'Yeah,' he said, remembering how she had cowered in the gale 'And after the first winter it would be up for sale again.'

The air now was utterly still, with only the calls of meadow pipits, strutting and flitting before them as they walked on, piercing the silence between them. Louise made no attempt to initiate conversation and he could elicit little more that monosyllables in response to his own observations, so he postponed the impartation of his knowledge. There would be other times when he could talk to her, reveal his sentiments toward this ancient landscape. They went into the fields, green, too green, he noticed as his feet fell upon the even sward, not a clover leaf, not a weed to be seen. In one of the larger fields, they came upon a tall stone, higher than Louise, standing in isolation.

'What is it?' she asked.

'Damned if I know. It wasn't here yesterday.'

He immediately wished he had not said it, for she seemed to believe him, yet, in retaliation against her lack of communication, he enjoyed a smug satisfaction in teasing her.

Upon closer inspection of the stone she could see it bore an engraved inscription. 'There is writing on it,' she said. 'What does it say?"

'RIALO something, I think,' Barny said, tracing the inscription with his finger, although the letters were barely discernible. 'Yes, RIALO! RIALO... BRAN... CUNIVAL... FILLS. I think its an advert for a high-fibre diet. Fancy stickin' it up here.'

He put his hands upon the stone, feeling the warmth absorbed from the sun, and with a sudden change of mood said, slowly and quietly, 'It says, Royal Raven son of Cunival.'

She looked at him. There was an expression of profound humility in his eyes, of a man perplexed beyond his comprehension. His hands caressed the hard crystals in the granite.

'*Maen Scryfa,*' he said. 'The Stone of Writing.'

'Royal Raven?' Louise queried. She realised that he had originally been making fun of her and that now he was deeply moved by some emotion evoked by the proximity of the megalith. '*Rialobran Cunival Fills*. Of course. It's Latin. Was Royal Raven a person?'

'Who knows ?' he said, relinquishing the touch of the stone on his hands. 'Some chief, perhaps. Some Roman Legionary. Or perhaps the carver couldn't spell. "*Cunival Fills*". *Cunival* doesn't sound like a name, does it ? Perhaps it says, *Rialobran Cuniwal Fills,* Royal Raven, son of Cornu Weahlas.'

'You would like to think so, wouldn't you?'

'I can think what I like. Nobody knows anything about it, even the archaeologists disagree. Nobody knows anything about anything... up here. It's all mystery.'

She smiled at him and he put his arms around her as she leaned back against the stone. 'Almost as much a mystery as you,' he said, and kissed her on the cheek. 'And your hair is as black as a Raven. Perhaps... .'

He looked beyond her, to where a rutted track led up from the road to the coast.

'What... the hell is that?'

Turning to see what had attracted his attention, she saw nothing which might have caused alarm.

'Over there,' he insisted. 'Coming up the track.'

Following his gaze, she saw them, a party of people walking towards them in single file. They were walking slowly, evenly spaced, and were draped in long hooded cloaks of a heavy dark material. Their heads were bowed and their hand clasped together before them, in the manner of monks and nuns. Eventually they came to where the track sank between high banks following centuries of erosion from the hoofs of mules and wheels and shoes of horses, and began to pass out of sight.

'Who are they?' Louise asked, evidently disconcerted at seeing this macabre procession when she had thought that she and Barny were so completely alone, up here on the moor.

174

'Come on,' Barny said. 'while they're out of sight. We'll find out.'

He took her by the hand as they ran through the fields to the concealment of the hawthorn trees bordering the track. He was giggling, and put his finger to his lips as they crouched behind the scrub. The hooded figures were intoning a monotonous chant, of which they could interpret not a single word. As the procession passed, the two eaves-droppers lifted their heads to watch. The robed ones went up the track and then turned off to the right, over a stile. Some of them were evidently not so agile and there was some disruption of the orderly procession as they were helped over, with their long robes becoming caught up in brambles and gorse.

'Who are they ?' Louise demanded for the second time.

'I don't know. Bloody cranks! Going to the *Maen an Tol* for some stupid ritual. As it said in the paper the other day, I remember it... "The growing spell of the mysterious stone not only draws thousands of tourists to wonder at its meaning but troops of astronomers, geomantics, dowsers, occultists, mystics, UFOlogists, folklorists, and many others...". 'What have we come to?'

He now felt somewhat embarrassed at being concealed and, when all had their backs to him, stood up, saying, 'Come on. Let's go and see what they are doing.'

'There are thirteen of them,' Louise said, and he knew what she was implying.

'Oh, don't be silly,' he said. 'Not this lot. Come on.' He pulled her arm and she followed him, reluctantly.

Twelve of the hooded figures had formed a circle around a group of three stones, the centre one of which had a large hole through its centre. Pools of blue water lay in the eroded earth about their feet. The thirteenth figure stood in the middle, talking and mildly gesticulating towards the stones and various features among the distant hills and rolling moorland. He had thrown back his hood to reveal himself as a middle-aged man with a handsome face, long hair, silver and wavy, and a neatly trimmed beard.

'Oh!' Barny said. 'It's him!'

'Who is he?' Louise whispered, for they were approaching the circle.

'I don't know.'

She glanced at him, her exasperation surpassing trepidation as the man smiled at them. He had a confident, serene expression and, after Barny and Louise had stopped and stood watching, he continued to address his retinue. They too removed their hoods and were seen to be mainly middle-aged, although there were one or two younger people, in their thirties maybe. They were all plain, the men nondescript, the women scrubbed pink, with no make up.

'And of all the holy sites we have visited,' the man said, with his hands resting on the stone, 'this, *Maen an Tol*, is that which has the most powerful curative powers of all. The local inhabitants have invoked its energy for generations, bringing their children here for the ritual cure for rickets and themselves passing nine times, widdershins, through the stone to cure their own physical, emotional and mental illnesses. You can see the alignments. There is no doubt that the ancient people placed these stones exactly on the lines of energy.'

He raised both hands high, turned to the four points of the compass and said, 'If you will now walk slowly around in your circle to absorb the energies from all directions, I will offer the prayer.'

He closed his eyes, with both hands brought to rest on the stone, and the party, somewhat hesitantly and self-consciously, began to circle around him with their robes, which were now seen to be made of old woollen blankets, catching in the gorse. A vicious bramble, with thorns hardened in the summer sun, grasped a woollen cloak and brought its wearer to a halt, revealing, beneath the blanket's coarse fibres, a trim pair of legs right up to the crutch of a short pair of shorts. One elderly devotee on the opposite side of the circle was distracted from his devotions and tripped, falling against his predecessor, who in turn stepped on the hem of his blanket, fell into the pool to finish on his hands and knees, covered in mud, while he at the centre continued his low chant with eyes tightly closed, unaware of the chaos in the circle.

Barny gave Louise a nudge and turned hurriedly away. She followed him to the stile, having difficulty in keeping up with him, and as he climbed over he too appeared to stumble and fall.

'Oh,' she said. 'Are you all right?'

He brushed her away and at last turned to her with tears streaming down his cheeks. He was helpless with laughter, and could neither speak nor stand. 'For God's sake,' he managed to say. 'Leave me alone. My sides are splitting.'

At last he controlled himself and wiped the tears from his eyes. 'Oh God,' he said. 'What next am I going to see?'

He rose to his feet and looked back at the stones. The circling had ceased and the man at the centre was speaking, although they were too far away to hear him. Those in the circle listened intently and then one stepped forward, removed his cloak, crouched before the stone and attempted to crawl through the hole. He tried to keep his hands and clothes clean but was obliged to put both hands and knees in the mud in order to squeeze through the orifice, smothering his knees in filth. He rose to his feet in triumph, however, for now the others could not but follow his example. The white-haired one embraced him, and he returned to the periphery as another, she of the very short shorts, came forward to crawl in that humiliating struggle through the hole.

'Who are they?' Louise persisted. 'Who is that man?' She could see no ridicule in the proceedings but Barny was scathing in his mirth. He led her away, saying, 'Silly buggers!' And in answer to her question, 'I don't know who he is. I've seen him around for the past year or so. I'll find out about him.' And, as an afterthought, 'the bleddy tuss.'

Their circling walk led them down the rutted track and on to the road, which they followed back to his house. At the junction of the track and road, they passed three expensive cars parked on the verge. Barny looked inside them, and at their number plates, but said nothing about them to Louse. He stepped out along the tarmac, forcing the pace a little, and when they arrived home her face was flushed with exertion and the cool, fresh air.

The evening would be cold so, after eating, Barny lit the fire, and he heard Louise humming to herself in the kitchen as she prepared the coffee. It was a little thing, to be ignored in anyone else, but she had gone in there and got on with it: no questions as to whether it should be black or white, mugs or cups, sugar or not, no fuss about irrelevances. He avoided any intimation of the change he perceived in her, and she seemed to radiate happiness. 'Who's Shimshai, Barny?' she called, the first time he had heard her raise her voice in normal conversation. She was usually too controlled, even for that, unless in one of her total collapses. She was evidently remembering some conversation they'd had about his friends.

'He's a writer. An old friend of Steve and Joe. He based some characters in one of his books on them and various other locals. I thought they'd never forgive him, but they did. You'll meet him. He's coming home.'

They sat together on the old settee and, for a while, she looked at one of his books, something she rarely did, despite professing such an interest in literature.

'I've not seen any of your poems,' she said later on. 'May I read them, sometime?'

'One day.' Barny said as he sat looking at the flames, with his mind still up on the moors.

'I suppose I shouldn't laugh at them,' Barny said. 'They're probably harmless enough.'

Louise remembered the expression in his eyes as he had placed his own hands upon the stone. She put her arms around him and drew his lips down upon her neck. 'I love you so,' she said. 'But I wish you wouldn't laugh at me. There are so many things I don't understand.'

'I'm not laughing at you. Not really. I'm trying to make you laugh with me. And as long as you know how much I love you and that I would never do anything to hurt you, then perhaps you will learn to laugh with me, at me if you like, as long as you love me too.'

'Oh I do,' she said. 'You are the one. The one big one I've been looking for all my life.'

Barny raised his head and brushed her cheeks with his lips, and Louise searched for his mouth with her own, closing her eyes with pleasure as she parted her lips and tasted him with the tip of her tongue, drawing away only when they were both in need of breath.

'I love the taste of you,' Barny said. 'The smell of you, the feel of you. You are the only woman who has ever roused such desire in me.'

He wanted her, for she had excited him with a single kiss, but they drew apart and watched the flames.

There were things unsaid between them, and each recollected the day, remembering their conversation and changing moods. He would have liked to know what was in her mind, what barrier was between them when she retreated inside herself, distant and inaccessible. She wanted to understand his affinities with the stones on the moors, what had been in his thoughts when he placed his hands on the monument to the Royal Raven, the reason for the ostensible frivolity when it was obvious that he held the stones in considerable reverence. Why did he dismiss others visiting the stones as 'bloody cranks' when, as she surmised, he himself went to them for revitalisation? He was withholding himself, as if he could not trust her. At risk of rejection, she asked him

'I don't know what you mean,' he said.

He was lying, and failing in the art, of which he was no master. Louise felt snubbed, rejected from some part of his entity, yet intrigued by the mysteries in his mind. Some expression in her eyes informed him of her pique and he relented

'I'll tell you,' he said. 'One day.'

'Why not now ?' she asked, with a hurt expression. 'Don't you trust me? Don't you love me enough?'

'More than enough.' He took her hand in both his own and brought it to his lips. 'When you're ready,' he said. 'When you're strong enough.'

The next time Barny went into town, he made enquiries about the man and learned that he lived in one of the larger houses overlooking the bay. It had been the home of nineteenth-century gentry and was now a guest house, from which all the vulgar paraphernalia of commercialism had been removed. There were no signs here informing the passer-by of B.B. and E.M.(opt), colour telly, en-suite loos or parking spaces at owner's risk, although all of these were still provided. There was merely a small plaque, of solid polished brass, bearing the simple inscription 'Holistic Health'. It was quite hard to see, for the mottled leaves of an overgrown laurel all but obscured the granite gatepost to which it was fixed. There was no 'off-the-road' trade here.

The man himself was a qualified doctor who had abandoned conventional medicine up country upon realising that most of his patients were either sick with the normal illnesses of approaching senility, and therefore incurable, or, and these were in the majority, were suffering from varying degrees of self inflicted ailments which were the manifestation of subconscious stress or repression... neurotics!

His establishment ran residential courses in 'Sacred Healing,' which enabled him to charge exorbitant fees for getting people to wear themselves out in unaccustomed exercise, ie traipsing around the megaliths in old blankets chanting gibberish, preparing their own cheap vegetarian food, and washing dishes.

He never advertised himself as 'doctor', but managed to let it be known he was qualified as such when people visited him, and he was still able to cure as many patients as when he was a registered practitioner. The difference was that he was now free to screw the richer ones out of their money and the young female ones out of their minds, which, he concluded, was what many of them needed anyway, and get well paid for it.

His own problem was that he had come to accept the validity of his treatment, seeing himself as divinely guided, and the most incredible thing was that it all worked. They went home, a few hundred pounds poorer, believing themselves renewed, 'healed by the Cosmic Whole' as he put it. What they did, in fact, was to have a week or a fortnight's exercise away from work, spouses and the telly, and have something to talk about in the office for the rest of the year.

The less Louise knew about him the better, Barny decided. She might be another nut come to the bottom of the stocking, but she's best away from all the others who were crackers.

While in town he bought the local paper, full of news about people he had never heard of, controversy over Simon Sweeting's plans and what to do with all the shit that the burgeoning population of incomers was producing, as if it was a matter for a private company to deal with. The local supermarket was advertising jobs on the check-out and filling shelves. Care assistants were needed in old people's homes. Carpenters were wanted by a high-quality double-glazing company of international repute. Only first-class tradesmen need apply. Must be self-employed. Oh yeah? There was nothing for Louise but he handed the paper over to her eager hands.

'Nothing,' she said, 'as usual. Today I counted how many jobs I have applied for.'

So, what's new? Barny thought, you count them every day.

'Eighty-six.' she said. 'And only twenty-five bothered to reply.'

He had not realised that there had been so many disappointments and he put his arm around her. 'Don't worry,' he said, 'something will turn up.'

She burst into tears, her face reddening. 'I'm useless,' she sobbed. 'Nobody wants me.'

'You're not useless, and I want you.' He cuddled her, and wiped the tears, but she was despondent.

'I shall have to go away,' she said. 'Go back up country. And I've nowhere to live and no money. Oh, Barny, you won't throw me out, will you? Do you love me ? Will you love me for ever?'

'As long as you need me, I'll take care of you.'

She looked at him with wet, imploring eyes. 'Oh,' she wept, 'you're so good to me. I couldn't live without you.'

'Silly,' he said. 'Of course you could. Look at yourself. You're good-looking, intelligent, well educated, very articulate, much more so than me. You don't need a job to prove all that. You need to prove all that to get a job. Perhaps you are undervaluing yourself. The people who turn you down don't know you, so you have to come across from a letter or questionnaire, it's not easy.'

'Some people manage it. Why can't I.'

'Perhaps you're trying too hard, being too honest. The world turns on a lubrication of the essence of bullshit, you know. Bullshit baffles brains, always has, always will, so you'll have to spread some around.'

'I couldn't tell lies about myself,' she said, insistently, and Barny summoned all his self-control to ignore all the lies she told *to* herself, to continue with, 'You don't have to tell lies about yourself. You tell lies about the person they want to employ. If you were to apply for a job washing dishes or emptying bed pans or filling shelves, would you tell them you had a degree in Classics?'

'Well no, it would be irrelevant. But I'd still be the same person.'

'But they wouldn't want you as you are, to do that kind of work. They'd call it "being over-qualified" and turn you down no matter how efficient you might be. They'd be scared of you, because they couldn't keep you in the dark and feed you on bullshit, like mushrooms as they say. What I'm trying to say is that you have to realise that all your qualifications don't mean a thing. You have to sell yourself to the people who are buying your labour, time and skills. The small, local firms know so many people that they don't have to take risks with unknowns. You can't blame them. It has nothing to do with your not being a native, well, not directly, I mean. You'll have more success with big companies. Lay on the bullshit and they'll gobble it up like nicey.'

He could have told her of some firms who wouldn't employ local people because they were too 'laid back' and couldn't be pushed around, or be terrified of losing the job, but she wouldn't believe it.

'What's nicey?' she asked. And he doubted if she had heard a word he'd said.

'Nicey ? It's dialect, sorry, meaning sweets.'

181

CHAPTER TEN

An kynyow dystrewys. The spoiled dinner.

...raped you?
'Yes,' she sobbed, 'it was awful.'

They were in the flat. It was Saturday night. Heather was in the kitchen ironing her clothes in preparation for going out with her latest boyfriend. Louise was reading in the living room.

'How long are you going to be before you use the bath?' Louise wanted to know. 'I want to wash my hair.'

'Oh?' Heather taunted her. 'Where are you going?'

Louise was going nowhere, as Heather well knew, while she was off to the disco with her latest. 'He's crazy about me.' she said. 'Really dishy.'

All her boyfriends were crazy about her, and, at first, she was crazy about them, telling her sister how wonderful and handsome they were, but she soon tired of them and they were discarded in favour of another. 'He's boring,' she would say, 'He's a pain,' unwittingly confirming her sister's original opinion of most of them. The latest, however, she had not been able to dominate in quite such an indifferent manner. He was tall, as tall as Louise, much taller than Heather, and a few years older, for her partners tended to be so now that she sought more satisfying relationships with more experienced men. As always, the unattainable had become the desirable, and she had not been entirely truthful in saying he was crazy about her. This time, she was crazy about him and wanted to keep him.

Louise had always been envious of her younger sister's popularity with the opposite sex, but now, seeing Heather's happiness, she felt a seething jealousy. She feigned her usual indifference to her sister's love affairs, trying not to allow her jealousy to show. Heather saw this, and could not refrain from taunting her prudish older sister.

'Why don't you come with us?' she ventured. 'You might get picked up.'

'I'm not a slut,' Louise said, 'interested in nothing but men. They disgust me. All the horrible stupid leering beasts that you bring home.'

'None of them leer at you! You put men off. You're like ice.' All of this said through the open kitchen door.

If only they knew, Louise thought. If only the men knew of her carnal desires, her wicked lusts, her shameful self-gratification when she yearned for the touch of a man. Unlike her sister, she knew that these things were the temptation of the devil, and she resisted them, controlling her temptations by willpower and not letting her body dominate her mind.

Heather came from the kitchen and draped an ironed and folded dress over the back of a chair. She saw her sister's drawn lips, the tight mouth which was becoming her normal expression, and, in her own happiness at the prospect of an evening out with her boyfriend, permitted herself some charity.

'Sorry.' she said. 'I didn't mean that. People think you're cold, that's what I meant. You ought to relax, enjoy yourself.' She saw the tight mouth soften. 'Why don't you come out with us?'

'I'm not ready. And he'll be here soon.'

Louise could not accompany her sister and boyfriend to the disco. Everyone would see that she had been invited only from pity, in the hope that some fellow or other would take her off their hands.

'There's tons of time,' Heather said. 'Go up and bath while I finish my ironing.'

At least she could do that. Have a bath and get away from her sister's patronising comments. Stirring herself from the sofa she placed a marker in her book and took it upstairs. She wrapped her long hair in a towel and lay in the warm bath. She soaped herself, under the arms, over the small breasts, round the tight belly, along her long legs. She laid back, lapped water over her body, slid the smooth cake of soap between her legs. Oh. Her fingers. Oh no! Later, when she had the bedroom to herself.

With an effort of self-control she swilled herself and rose from the water. She carefully wiped the bath and wrapped herself in her blue towelling robe as she heard Heather call, 'Nearly finished?'

'Yes.' She unlocked the door, saying, 'I'll dry myself in the living room.'

Heather was naked. She was carrying a towel and a bag of toiletries. Louise saw that the nipples on her sister's full, firm breasts were hard with sexual arousal, and she blushed as she felt her own rise against the material of the robe. Heather laughed at her and, after throwing her things on the floor, turned to face the long mirror on the bathroom wall. She had a firm, sturdy body with strong shoulders, smooth skin and a rather small cluster of fair curls on her pubis.

'Not bad,' she said, 'am I?'

Louise thought Heather did these things to humiliate her: to compare her own fully developed body with Louise's small breasts and thin, weak shoulders and broad hips. She had never admitted to envy of her sister in any respect, especially in her precocious physical maturity, but now, instead of retreating in shame as previously, she stood beside her sister, watching the images reflected from the mirror. Heather turned a little, to see the outline of her buttock, inhaled deeply to thrust her breasts forward. Louise repudiated a curiosity within herself, denied a desire in her to reach forward and caress them, perhaps to put her lips around the nipples; evil thoughts! She said, 'I'm not that bad myself.'

'Let's have a look, then,' Heather replied indifferently as she ran her hands down over her ribs to her waist and rounded hips, expecting Louise to flee in horror.

Louise decided to retaliate, to call the bluff of her sister's provocative behaviour. She pulled the cord of her robe, ran her hands up the front hems and slipped it from her shoulders, allowing it to fall to the floor. The whiteness of her skin emphasised the bush of black hair on her pubis. Her breasts were small, but, compared to her sister's large round mounds, were delicate and pink from the warmth of her bath. Heather had not seen her sister naked since they were children, and she gasped involuntarily at the sight of the voluptuous hips and female thighs with the luxuriant growth of black hair above them. They looked at each other's bodies in silence for a minute, each envious, in some respect, of the other.

Louise allowed her sister to scrutinise her body, saw her own nipples in the mirror, hard and tingling. She ran her palms over her breasts, rolling the nipples between finger and thumb and felt an exquisite flush dampening the secret depths of her vagina as Heather watched in astonishment.

Heather suspected that this was a show of bravado intended to shock her, but she had never seen her sister behave anything like this before, and involuntarily responded, despite herself, becoming aroused at the sight of her sister's lascivious exhibition of her sexuality. She felt her desires rising like a wave of sensuality. 'Oh, my God,' Heather said, thinking of Louise's chastity. 'How can you live without it?'

Louise drew away and picked up her robe. 'How do you know that I do?' she said. 'You don't know what I do.'

Her sister was so aroused, Louise saw, that she was almost beside herself with lust. She could have done anything to her, with her. She could have touched her, caressed her, kissed her and tasted her, taken her to the damp rug and brought the both of them to a gushing orgasm such as she had only imagined in her wildest fantasies. She slipped her arms into her robe, her expressionless face watching the misted mirror. She had enticed her sister into an awareness and realisation of proclivities which neither would ever mention again, but which she could use as a weapon in their future battles. All those shameful desires that she had subdued in the belief that they were her own sinful lusts, she had discovered in her sister. As she tied the cord on her robe she watched Heather standing before the mirror with her legs apart, shamelessly stroking herself with her fingers.

'You'll make yourself sore,' Louise said as she closed the door. 'Why don't you wait for your man, if he's so wonderful?'

The door opened behind her as she went along the narrow hallway. Heather called after her. 'And what are you going to do when we've gone out? Play with yourself with that candle you keep hidden in your drawer?'

Louise felt the blush spread all over her body. 'Or are you a bloody lesbian?' Heather cried as she returned to the bathroom and slammed the door. 'Waiting for the right woman?' Louise went into the sitting room, angry with Heather and disgusted with herself.

'I used to fool myself that I was virtuous. Now I know that the nuns were right. Even as a child, I was always a sinner. I was evil. Barny was fortunate to be rid of me. Even as a child...' She collapsed into tears. '...I killed him. I killed him.'

When the letter came asking Louise to attend an interview for a job in a supermarket, she panicked. There was no running around like a blue-arsed fly as anyone else would have done. Oh no. First she collapsed in Barny's arms. Then she became contrivedly calm and collected, making lists. Lists of the clothes she would need, of the books to borrow or buy on retailing, of the positive and negative consequences of working. She bought several types of cosmetics, according to the image she deemed it necessary to project, but tried none of them on her face. She extrapolated every aspect of her future in relation to the job, even checking on train time tables to ascertain how she could visit her children at weekends, when she had not seen or mentioned them for months.

Before the interview, of which she had two weeks' notice, Barny took her around all the shops, trying to find suitable clothes. There was nothing she liked locally, so he took her to the city, where she bought a plain skirt, dark blue, and a stylish jacket to match. When she tried them on, she looked a different person, imposing and elegant, and he was astonished by the transformation, assuring her that she would make a good impression. She also bought pairs of black tights and took them back to the car, smiling with satisfaction, but on the drive home relapsed into doubt, wanting to go back and change them. Barny refused to take her, and eventually she accepted his assurances that they were exactly right for the interview.

'But I've spent all my money,' she wailed. 'And if I get the job I'll have to buy suits and blouses, more shoes, tights, no end of things.'

You haven't got the job yet. So don't panic. And if you do get it, I'll lend you the money. Don't worry, I'll look after all that.'

'I'll pay it all back.'

He suggested, not wishing to remind her too emphatically of that which should be a willingly undertaken duty, that she might like, perhaps, to visit her children, that there would be less free time if she did get the job. She declined, saying that her ex parents-in-law were taking them away for a while. Barny did not press the matter but did wonder what fear she harboured of her own babies, for despite her declarations of guilt at leaving them and insistence that she missed them terribly, there was inevitably some spurious excuse for not visiting them.

'I merely thought you would like to go,' Barny said, 'while you have the chance.'

He ignored the the tale about them going away. Perhaps they were. But then again perhaps they weren't. That was not what he was discussing. 'They'll need to see you now and then.'

'They don't seem to need me,' she said with some resentment. 'They never want to talk to me on the phone. And last time I went to see them they were more interested in going out to play with their friends.'

Evidently she did not wish to discuss visiting her children. When she was working, she said, she could afford to go every month, so there was no point in rushing off there now, when she had so much to do in preparation for the interview.

Barny shrugged the matter off as being of little importance, while thinking privately that she was taking a lot for for granted. She hadn't got the bloody job yet, hadn't even attended the interview.

He tried to give her confidence while refusing to show, or share, too much enthusiasm, for he could see how shattered she would be when rejected. Staff Manageress, by God. She couldn't organise her own life, much less a hundred others... .

He went over to see Sam and Beth one day when Louise went to the library in town. Sam had already gone in there, to buy some fence posts.

'She could have had a lift,' Beth said, 'if only she'd called in,'

The baby was crawling about the kitchen floor, rolling earthy potatoes under the table with gurgles of satisfaction.

'Loopy has an interview for a job.' Barny said. 'Did she tell you?'

'No. Not a word. What's it for?'

He told her, Staff Manageress, and they laughed. Poor Loopy. She had No Chance. He also told her about the worries over clothes and details of irrelevant trivia, pushing everything but the interview from her mind: her children, friends, even him, concentrating her whole effort into the prospect of employment.

'She's already been in and bought a whole load of books on interview techniques and spent half the night reading them as if they were the latter-day Book of Revelations. I looked though them. It's all bullshit for people with no intuition. No...' He hesitated, even before Beth, '...no telepathy.' He shrugged. 'You know what I mean?'

'Funny Maid,' Beth said, putting her arms around him. 'Don't worry about her, she'll be all right.' She kissed him. A gesture of affection.

'Am I worried?' he asked.

'I think so. You are not as relaxed as you usually are.' She pushed him against the table and kissed him again.

He felt a tingle of arousal that had nothing to do with desire, it was the relief of tension of which he had been unaware. He pulled Beth close to him. 'Well, I don't suppose I am very relaxed. I don't know how I'll cope with her if she's rejected yet again. She's put so much into it.'

They were holding each other around the waist. He made no effort to conceal his involuntary arousal and, when she felt it, she wiggled against him, looking him straight in the eye with an expression of appreciation that he should respond to her. Barny laughed.

'Why don't you have a day off?' Beth said. 'Go to see your friends in town.'

A day off! From what? He never had days off. A 'day off' was like snipping a day off from one's life as far as Barny was concerned, but he knew what Beth meant. Go into town and forget about Loopy for an hour or two. She had implied, but would never say, that he was beginning to give a bit too much of himself to Louise. He looked at her.

'Do you good,' she said simply, and was exactly right. It would do him good. He cleaned himself up and drove in about mid-day, just as Louise was returning on the bus, loaded down with books.

The tide was rising. Boats were casting off their moorings, coming astern, all bright colours, with red and green plastic and brilliant hulls. They were all black, Barny mused, when I was a boy. Well, lots of them were; the old luggers tarred, with the sails tanned, and the nets were made of string.

There was the *Morwennol*, Boy Steve at the wheel, Uncle Joe and Father Steve on deck, surrounded by mounds of green, monofilament nylon. Boy Steve waved through the window of the wheelhouse.

Katie was on the quay. She waved, and Uncle Joe waved, and Boy Steve waved again. Father Steve got on with stowing the lines and did not look ashore.

'What's all this about the Stevenses and the Trevorrows?' Barny asked his father when they were sat at his table.

'All what?'

'You know what. The trouble between the families.'

The old man pursed his lips in doubt. There are some yarns best left unspun.

'Well... ,' he said after after considering the consequences of telling or not telling, '...wudn the Stevenses and Trevorrows. Was the Stevenses and Trenowdens, Mary's people.'

He would have left it at that, but Barny said, 'Yes... go on.'

The old man drew breath and let it escape with a sigh of resignation.

'Mary's grandfehther had a young sister, Gertrude. She was a bit, what 'ee call it, why wild, by all accounts. The other Trenowdens were all very conventional, like Mary. Gerty fell for one of Sarah Stevens' great-uncles, John Henry, who was another mad heathen. They made a very good pair, I've heard them say. Wild as the wind.'

'Can you remember them?'

'Not Gerty. I remember her husband, John Henry. He was deffernt when I knawd 'n. An old man. No fool, mind.'

'Well what were all the ructions about?'

'Well... you don't like to say. Families d' go through hard times.'

'You can't condemn people because they are poor.'

'Wudn only that. John Henry's fehther couldn't do nawthen but drink whisky and make cheldern. Of course the Trenowdens objected. There was ten of they Stevenses in that house, with nawthen more'n a bucket to shit in. The Trenowdens didn' want Gerty to go that. Her fehther said if she went off with John Henry Stevens he would disown her.'

'And did she go?'

'ess. She went. She married John Henry and went to live with them.'

'Good for her, if she loved him.'

'She had one maid, Janie... and died of consumption two years later. The Trenowdens, Mary's people, said John Henry had murdered her... . Living in squalor.'

'Oh. I see. Did her father forgive her?'

'She asked to see him, on her death bed. He wouldn't go. John Henry despised him till his dying day.'

'And the families have hated each other ever since?'

'Ever since.'

'And Zeke is Janie's son! Which makes him a cousin to Katie, and Boy Steve.'

'And to we.'

'How come?'

'Why because my uncle William Uren Endean married Janie, tha's how. And she was another dammee mad-brain. Zeke d' turn after her. Mad as a bleddy hatter. He idn like none of our party.'

'Of course,' Barny told Anne. 'We don't have any nutcases in our family.'

'Only you,' she said.

Louise was at home when he returned. He put his hand upon the garden gate and felt her, was aware of her presence in the house. His immediate impulse was to rush in and take her in his arms, to share his day and the jokes of his friends, and he was smiling to himself as he closed the gate behind him and paused to look at his camellia. Too late now for flower buds to form, he decided. These were all too narrow, not shielding embryonic flowers, and were the progenitors of all the future branches which would determine the shape of the shrub over its lifetime, fifty, or maybe a hundred, years. They were more important than flower buds at this stage of the shrub's development but it would have been gratifying to have a few blooms to look forward to. It would now be another year and a half before he could hope to see the lovely delicate pink but, perhaps, if the coming summer was warm, the next bud initiation might incline to flowers. Some signal, some instruction, would come from the plant's intangible heart and induce it to blossom. From somewhere deep in the tissues the mysterious directive would spread: that the branches should grow in such a way, that the leaves should be evenly spaced in the manner

189

of camellia leaves and be the particular shape of this variety and no other, that there should be the embryonic bud which would open pink, that particular shade of pink, not red or white.

He stood with his head bowed, looking down at the little plant, thinking that the day might come when he could see the flowers at eye level and then, in his latter years, look up at them as they shed their petals around his door. He thought that by removing one or two of those tiny buds he could predetermine its future development, train it, force it into a shape of his own choice. No, he thought, not with a camellia. It must be allowed to develop naturally, with the minimum of restraint and pruning and shape itself as it will.

'Just like we,' he said to himself as he turned to the door, aware that he was thinking in dialect after spending a few hours with his friends.

Louise had dropped some books on the table. There were two more on interview techniques, one on body language and one on self-assertion for women.

'Lord!' he said to himself as he glanced through the blurbs, 'these are all best sellers. 'Hulloooo.' he called.

She answered from the bedroom, 'Hullo. Don't come up.'

'I'll put the kettle on,' he said, craning his neck up the stairs. 'You OK?'

'Yes.' The voice was less than confident.

She's bought some new clothes, he thought. She's trying them on and will want my approval. The kettle boiled and he brought the tea into the sitting room to wait for her appearance. Although she was jealous of his time away from her, and there were occasions when he felt stifled and needed to break away to recharge himself, he missed her, even during his shortest absences. Her dependency was such that she often became irrationally possessive, resenting the hours when she was excluded from his thoughts, perhaps when they were in the same room and he was working or if he tended the garden without her, as if she were not whole without him. Some bud, some delicate point of developing independence in her seedling days had been bruised or cut away, although the profusion of the auxiliary growth had obscured the wound. He knew of no remedy but nurture and support.

She came down the narrow winding stairs, along the passage and entered the room, where she stood waiting at the door.

It was gone! All the lovely, black, cascading hair, was gone. She stood there with apprehensive eyes and a short, bobbed hairstyle which was the height of fashion and made her thin neck look weak and her nose too long.

Barny's immediate response was one of anger. What had she done to herself? What demon of doubt had undermined her confidence to such an extent that she had lost faith in her most glorious asset? All the months of his encouragement and confidence building had been to no avail. She still had no faith in herself as she was, and was attempting to create some persona grata beyond herself, to be someone else. He stifled his anger and managed a smile. He could not berate her, not now, when she was at her most vulnerable, when she had need of compliments.

'Turn around,' he said.

With her back to him, he closed his eyes and shook his head in despair before managing to say, with as much sincerity as he could muster, 'It looks very nice.'

All her character was gone. She looked like a thousand other women walking the streets or wedged behind a desk in some building society or bank, anonymous in their compulsion to conform with the demands of convention. Whereas, previous to this delaceration, she had borne an aura of individuality, and heads turned to look at her, she would now walk down the streets unseen, invisible in the drab, compliant crowd. He desperately sought some compliment to pay her, not wishing to lie, for the truth would eventually out and she would regret this impulsive cut.

'It's just right for the interview,' he said, 'But I still prefer it long, myself.'

How banal, he thought, how trite, but it was just what she wanted.

'I can always grow it again,' she said.

She never would. He was certain of that. 'What have you done with it?

'It's upstairs. I can sell it, to wig-makers.'

'Oh no,' he cried, losing control. 'Don't do that!' And, regaining his composure. 'I would like to keep it. Let me buy it.'

She gave it to him. It was in a plastic bag, like a braided coil of black silk, and he hid it away amongst his chaotic papers in a drawer where he knew the whereabouts of everything. As he closed the drawer, he thought, she must have had an appointment with the hairdresser. It was not such an impulsive cut.

On the morning of the interview, Louise rose early when the new alarm clock emitted its electronic pulse beside the bed. She had slept deeply, still glowing in the satisfaction of Barny's loving, entwined in his arms. She bathed and washed her hair. She ironed her clothes in the bedroom while half-dressed and made up her face while sitting on the bed as Barny watched, with his hands behind his head, perplexed that it could take two hours to prepare for an interview.

Barny offered to take me to town, but I insisted that I went alone, for this was something I wanted to do entirely on my own, to assert my independence. I was glad that it was not raining, and that there was no wind to ruffle my hair. There had been no necessity to rise quite so early, I conceded, but better to allow more than enough time than to arrive flustered with haste. Here was a chance to prove myself, to step on that all-important bottom rung of the ladder to success, upon which I was determined not to stumble. I took an early bus, permitting Barny to drive me to the stop by the village shop. There was time to kill when I arrived in town, so I went into a café and drank a small cup of coffee. My watch seemed to have slowed down, or stopped, and I kept checking it against the clock on the café wall. A violent pain momentarily cramped my stomach, a pain which I attributed to having eaten no breakfast, so I ordered a bread roll and another cup of coffee. Then I wished I had brought my toothbrush, as I remembered the techniques of self-assertion and image projection in the manuals.

I met the assistant manager on the shop floor and told him why I was there. He was ten years my junior, a good-looking young man in a smart suit. The office to which he escorted me was small, with a large window overlooking the shop floor. I thought it odd that I had never noticed it while shopping in the store. There was one desk and several grey filing cabinets. It was shabby, somehow, with marks on the walls where notices or charts had been stuck, and the carpet was threadbare. The manager was a short man, in his forties, with tired eyes and dark hair groomed flat over his temples. His name was Miller, and he introduced an elegantly dressed woman as Mrs Crocket, the regional personnel manager. She was a woman of about forty with large businesslike spectacles and neatly cut fair hair immaculately groomed. I felt some satisfaction in the style I had chosen for myself. It was just what this woman would have worn had her hair been of my type.

The manager stood at the window, looking down at the shop floor as Mrs Crocket addressed me from behind the desk. I realised the window was made of one-way glass, so he could see all that was going on in the shop but the customers and staff could not see him. While Mrs Crocket was looking through my c.v. I glanced down at the crowded aisles, with vague people pushing trolleys, boys in men's bodies filling shelves, girls with resigned faces pushing buttons on the tills. I saw that weird friend of Barny's, Zeke, examining tins of fish and pursing his lips like a half-wit.

When Mrs Crocket spoke, there was self-assurance in her voice, an authority which intimidated me a little, and I thought, this woman is not much older than me. I could be like her in five years, when I am her age. These people in the office had power and authority, and I was on the threshold of joining them. I could be up here, a woman of substance, or down there, a shop girl, or unemployed, looking for cheap food past its sell-by date. Where do I see myself in five years, Mrs Crocket asked me. I knew the answer, for I had read it in a book.

The whole interview went well and I had no difficulty in answering the questions put to me. I recognised them as standard interviewing techniques and responded as required. They were impressed by my academic qualifications and by my assurances that I had always wished to be in retail management and would still be with M&S were it not for an unsatisfactory marriage which had interrupted my early career. They hardly mentioned my family, however, but enquired about my present circumstances.

'I'm staying with a friend,' I told them.

She justified her denial of Barny by telling herself that her private life was none of their business and went back to him on the bus, gazing disconsolately through the window at the darkening moors, feeling utterly exhausted after the strain of the interview. While being sure that she had presented herself well, had made all the right noises and spoken with the required body-language, she still felt that those people in the store were alien to her. She was aware that she had presented a false image, as advised by Barny and her books and, if they were as skilled in the techniques of interviewing people as they should be, they would have seen through the deception.

She also felt incongruous in her smart clothes as she sat among the local people on the bus. The women all looked so poor, wearing old, unfashionable clothes, and the men shabby, with dispirited eyes. All of them, she thought, must be unemployed from the redundant mine, or pensioners, unable to afford their own cars, yet all of them were probably richer than she, who was wearing all of her most expensive possessions. The thought depressed her. She had invested so much, cut off her beautiful hair, changed her personality, all for the sake of a job she wouldn't get.

'It went well,' she told Barny, unable to concede defeat until forced to. 'But they have others to interview. There's sure to be someone with the experience they are looking for.'

'You did your best,' he said. 'Now you must forget it until they contact you.'

He seemed distant, responding to her remarks about the interview without enthusiasm. She interpreted this as a means of quelling unreasonable expectations on her part, especially when he suggested that she keep trying for something more suited to her education and intellect. 'I can't see you working in a shop.'

This merely increased her despondency. She believed he was belittling her predicament and was in a jovial mood which he was trying, unsuccessfully, to conceal from her for, despite his solicitations, his eyes were twinkling and an irrepressible grin enlivened his face as he held her in his arms.

'Have you done the dinner?' she asked wearily, aware that there was no smell of cooking in the house.

'No. I've been down town.'

He might have prepared something, she thought. He should have known how tired and hungry she would be after such a gruelling day. 'Oh. Then I'd better change,' she sighed.

He held her tight, saying, 'Don't ever change,' as the grin widened to a laugh, 'I love you just as you are.'

She went up to the bedroom, and Barny followed her, suppressing a momentary doubt of the truth in his own words as she turned away from him in indifference. Sitting on the bed, he watched her remove her smart clothes and hang them carefully in the wardrobe. Wearing only her pants and bra, she came to the chest of drawers by the bed, avoiding his eyes and grin. She felt that he was putting her under scrutiny and began to suspect his reasons for doing so, perhaps to compensate for some indiscretion of his own, with Beth or Anne.

'Did you see Anne?' she said as she took a jumper from the drawer.

'No, I didn't,' And, as she began to put her arms in the jumper, 'You needn't put that on.'

'Oh,' she said. 'Not now Barny. Can't you see I'm exhausted ?'

He grabbed her, and pulled her down on the bed, his face alive with glee. 'We are going out to celebrate.'

'What's there to celebrate? It was only an interview. I haven't got the job yet.'

He reached into his shirt pocket, gave her a letter. 'We've won!' he shrieked. 'The Poetry Prize. I've won it.'

Louise also screamed with joy, and hurriedly scanned the letter. 'You crafty old devil. You didn't even tell me you'd entered.'

'I've been dying to tell you for the past hour.'

She hugged him, and they rolled back and forward over each other on the bed, laughing until the tears mingled on their faces.

Suddenly she pulled away from him, her face crestfallen. 'You won't want me now.'

'What? Whatever are you talking about?'

She swung her legs over the bed and sat up, shoulders drooping. 'You'll be famous,' she said, 'and I'll be a nobody. You'll be able to have any woman you want.'

'I already have,' he said as his own elation subsided, 'the woman I want.'

She burst into tears, and he too sat up, holding her around the shoulders. I've picked the wrong time, he thought, to tell her. She is still in a state of anxiety over the interview. But why couldn't she simply let go and be happy for an hour or two, for his sake. It was almost as if she could not value anyone, or their merits, without comparing them to herself, her own predicament. Now, as a reaction to Barny's success and her doubts about the interview, she was regressing into insecurity. After the initial, brief elation she was already seeing his achievement as a threat. He let her cry the tears away, reached for a tissue from the box by the bed, gave it to her in silence and thought about the prize. There might be some prestige in it, if only from other poets, and even there some envy and resentment among the congratulations, for such esteem is a matter of opinion after all. It was not going to change his life.

'I've booked a meal,' he said, phlegmatically, 'at Jennifer's, for eight o'clock.'

When they were ready to go out, Louise looked delightful in a long-sleeved dress that he had not seen her wearing before, and she had used her make-up with skill, but her eyes were dull. Barny tidied his beard and dressed in his rarely-worn sports coat, slacks, shirt and tie. He complimented Louise on her appearance, but could not rouse her from despondency.

'Jennifer's was a quiet restaurant in the village, with seating for twenty or so. ('What they d' call covers,' Barny said) run by a local wife-and-husband team. The husband knew how to prepare the locally-produced food to be eaten, not looked at, and the wife had a manner at the tables which made the customers feel welcome, because they were. It was that simple. There was a bright fire burning in the grate, and the whitewashed (well, DIY emulsioned, to be absolutely correct) walls were decorated with a few old prints. There were no horse harnesses, carriage lamps, old miners' hats, boots, candles or fishermen's balls (glass) hanging from the beams. It was somewhere to eat food, not to taste the flavour of industrial archaeology.

They sat at a table in the corner. Barny thought he would have a steak, for he did not eat much meat at home now, and Louise chose the vegetarian dish. He accepted the wine Jennifer recommended, telling her, 'The only wines I know about are elderberry and dandelion, my han'some so I'll leave it to you.'

He remembered a time in his early youth, he told Louise, when he had asked for a bottle of dry sauterne from the wine merchants in town. 'You g'eat cuddle!' from the girl in the shop had cured him of any snobbery in that direction for the rest of his life.

Louise was not amused. It was a sign of sophistication to know about wines, she said, and now that he was to be a 'public figure' it would be expected of him. He drank nearly all the bottle himself and, after the meal, had a large brandy and one of those little cigars which are supposed to bring women flocking to the smoker's side, and became quite tipsy while Louise sat opposite him in virtual silence, preoccupied with her own thoughts.

When they walked back in the cold starlight, under the trees overhanging the lane from the village gardens, he put his arm through hers. There was no response; her arm felt like lead. At home, he removed his jacket, tie and shoes and flopped on the sofa, thoroughly fed up with her. She had not mentioned his triumph all evening, had not even asked to read his winning poems. He was exhausted after the period of intense elation, and fuzzy with drink, so he stretched out, with his feet up and closed his eyes. Like a spoilt child, he thought. She's sulking like a bleddy kid.

He wondered why he loved her. If, indeed, he did love her. After all this time she should have learned to trust him, to relax in the knowledge that he would not abandon her, no matter what successes came his way, but there you are, she couldn't, or wouldn't. How different the evening would have been had he but spent it with Anne. They would have been in fits of laughter by now. Damn the woman.

He descended, momentarily, into the abyss of troubled, inebriated sleep, until his body and mind relaxed in fatigue, only to be woken, cold and shivering, by the sound of Louise's voice. His eyes refused to open and he wished he did not have to face climbing the stairs, that he was already in bed, oblivious to her presence, or that she would cover him with a blanket and leave him to sleep by the warmth of the fire. He stirred himself and sat up, bleary eyed and bewildered. She had made coffee, and was putting it on the low table, saying, 'You probably need this.'

He did not. He needed sleep, and thought she was forcing communication for the sake of it, fearful of isolation and silence.

'I saw your friend,' she said. 'When I was in the shop. The inventor.'

'Oh, yes,' he mumbled. 'Zeke. I'm surprised.'

What the hell did she want to talk about Zeke for - at a time like this?

'He didn't seem to buy anything.'

Barny forced himself to consider the relevance of that. Zeke bought everything he needed to eat from friends, like Sam and Beth, or scrounged from Barny, and his clothes were from Oxfam, so what was he doing in a supermarket? 'Probably checking the tuna tins,' he offered wearily, 'to see if they were dolphin friendly.'

Her remarks, he decided, were a route back to her own crossroads, the events of her day, which she regarded as being of more significance than those of his.

He roused himself and put some wood on the fire, a piece of sycamore brought down in a gale. It burned too fast and didn't smell all that good. He remembered when the apple tree died. There was a smell of woodsmoke as she ought to be.

'Is he an environmentalist?' Louise asked.

What about my bloody prize? was in his head. I've waited all my life for this, you selfish bitch. For Christ's sake make me laugh.

'Yeah,' he said. 'Zeke's an environmentalist...'

And an anarchist, a communist, a pragmatist with a shopping list and I'm fuckingpist. Let me go to sleee...puh! ...Zeke organises all the bottle and waste-paper collections. Another bloody crank.'

Barny was speaking ironically, including himself in the category, but Louise took exception to the remark.

'What do you mean, "crank"? I've done all that. As an environmentalist yourself, you shouldn't deride his convictions by calling such people "cranks". Recycling is the only way of conserving non-renewable resources.'

'Yeah. You're right.'

He wondered what had made her change to Zeke's side in the discussion as he tried to focus his eyes on her.

'I'm sorry,' he said, 'but there are limits to what can be recycled and Zeke is obsessed with it, gone over the top.'

She was about to argue, adamant in her defence of the environment, gathering her case before Barny went on, speaking through an alcoholic haze.

'He wants to make felt hats from recycled fluff collected from belly buttons.'

There was not a glimmer of amusement in his eye as he stared, bleary eyed, at the flames.

'Don't be ridiculous!' she said.

'It's true. He reckons that everybody accumulates enough belly-button fluff in a lifetime to make a pair of felt boots, like they wear in Outer Mongolia.'

'You fool.'

'He has it all worked out. He has reams of calculations on the potential crop, according to the clothes worn and the ambient temperature. I've seen his samples, all saved in match-boxes and graded by colour and texture. He's really serious about it. Says he can find no scientific reason for it all being in shades of blue, regardless of the colour of the clothes worn.'

She didn't know whether to believe him, for his expression was so earnest. She tried to verify the truth of the matter by calculating how much fluff she had picked from her own navel, digging it out with the long nail on her little finger. There had been times when she had made herself raw, trying to retrieve the last little bit from the interior folds of the crevice.

'I don't believe you,' she said.

'He's only made one, so far, from his own fluff, which took him a month to collect when he wore his jumper next to his skin as an experiment. It was a little skull-cap for his neighbour's son's Action Man, to be worn under his tin hat to prevent it chaffing his forehead. The prototype model, Zeke calls it. He wrote to the Ministry of Defence about it, suggesting that all ranks attend a daily fluff parade, when the M.O. can go around with a plastic bag and a pair of tweezers, picking it out. He's estimated that a regiment of infantry could supply enough material for a hat a day. In a year, every man could have one and save the taxpayer thousands on arctic clothing. Eighty per cent of heat is lost through the head, according to Zeke, but I would have thought he was exaggerating, myself. The Ministry never replied. Zeke says it's because the textile industry is full of vested interests.'

'You idiot! You can't expect me to believe that.'

'I don't. As I told you, Zeke is a crank. There's hundreds of them down here. You wouldn't believe half the things they get up to.'

She was believing him now. 'It's a bit far out,' she said.

'Yeah. In outer space, some of them. Poor old Zeke has got into a lot of trouble over it, actually. He tried collecting fluff from his friends but they either forgot or said it blew away on their breath, so he let his fingernails grow and went down on the beach accosting holiday-makers as they began undressing. He had the cops after him for causing a public nuisance. Sad, really, he meant well.'

'The poor man,' Louise said. But I suppose there is some logic in his idea. There are all kinds of things we waste.'

Barny could keep it up no longer and broke into hysterical giggling, doubling up with a stitch in his side.

Louise took it badly, angry at being made fun of.

'I don't know,' she said, indignantly. 'It could happen. It's not impossible.'

She was attempting to vindicate her gullibility and found that she could not; he had strung her a skein of nonsense which she had believed instead of sharing his sense of the absurd and, in retaliation, she hit him below the belt.

'It sounds no more outlandish,' she said, 'than writing poetry about a dead culture.'

Barny's laughter died, like a twinkling star obscured by a cloud, as he took his arms from around her, stinging from this personal attack on his work.

'I thought it was quite a good yarn,' he said, wondering if she had any sense of humour at all, for he had hoped to make her laugh with him. He could not be angry with her, however, so childlike was she in her response.

'Come here,' he said, taking her in his arms again, 'you silly hap'orth.'

She reluctantly cuddled into him and he held her with a hand kneading the taut knot of muscle in her nape, under the shorn hair, wishing she could learn to relax.

'I'm sorry,' she said.

He was not sure for what she was sorry this time, and was too exasperated to enquire.

The next few days, waiting for the results of her interview, were strained and tense. Barny spent some time talking on the phone to the organisers of the poetry prize, making arrangements for appearances when the winner was announced publicly. There was to be a reception at a posh hotel, a famous author to present the prize, and interviews with the press, radio and television.

'I'm going to lap it up,' he told Louise, 'cus it's only a nine-day wonder. I feel like a seal, coming up for breath after all the oxygen in my body has been used up, enjoying a few minutes of fresh air before diving to fish for sustenance in the obscure depths beneath the surface of life.'

'You'll be famous,' she said.

'I doubt it.'

He had hoped for some comment on his metaphor, but it was not forthcoming. Ah well.

Sam and Beth were delighted at hearing the news, and asked Barny and Louise over for a celebratory drink, during which Louise sat in silent contemplation. 'Funny maid,' Beth said.

Anne, as expected, took it all very stoically when he called in to tell her the news and see how she was. Her immediate reaction was a blank stare, and he had no idea what she was thinking but, after hearing some details, she said, 'It'll go to your head.' Giggling at the prospect. 'You'll become a pompous old fart,'

His father said, 'Five hundred pounds waint keep 'ee for long.'

'It's not the money. It's the prestige.'

'Who from ?'

Barny had not a clue who from, he realised. The literati? The common people? Generations yet unborn? He could not answer his father's question. 'I thought you'd be pleased,' he said.

'I am. Pass me one of they screw-eyes theer, will 'ee.'

Everything was relative. Barny read through his winning entries one evening and underwent an intense crisis of confidence. It was all rubbish! The other entries must have been appallingly bad if this stuff could win a prize. He woke up that night with the dreads about to engulf him in despair, and he clung to Louise in terror.

'Loopy,' he choked. 'Hold me.'

She was immediately awake, turned to him and held him as he fought against panic, the futility of life and achievement when every success was anticlimax, the knowledge that all his ambitions had been attained only for this despondency and fear to continue plaguing him. He clutched her and she soothed him silently, with her hand massaging his spine until it passed away. He wanted to cry, to be her baby, let himself be totally revealed in his weakness, and could not, no more than she. He was just as loopy as Louise.

She held him until he slept, loving him for suffering a weakness so akin to her own.

CHAPTER ELEVEN

Kynweres dyworth an veyn. Succour from the stones.

...You said he raped you?

The silent clock on the psychiatrist's desk transformed the passing seconds into pulsating digits of light... .

'Yes... . He came to the door while Heather was in the bath. I was still ashamed. I mean, it must have showed... that I was sexually aroused, but it wouldn't go away. I wanted it to. I was still wearing only my bath robe, and I was combing my hair. I let him in and he sat beside me on the sofa. I didn't ask him to. He just did it. He said I smelt nice and put his hand on my leg and opened my robe and leaned over on top of me. He was heavy and I couldn't push him off. I was afraid Heather would come in.'

She sat on the sofa combing her hair. Her robe was untied. It fell open. She ignored it, letting her long legs show. She pressed her knees together in a muscular contraction of her thighs and looked at Heather's boyfriend. He was good-looking, well built, with long brown hair. He wore tight jeans. Louise saw that he was roused by her and that Heather was not the exclusive object of his interest.

She could have her revenge on her precocious sister, and steal one of her boyfriends for a change. She was just as attractive to him as Heather was, and could prove it. She reached to the back of her head with the comb and the robe fell open down the length of her body.

'He raped me. I couldn't stop him. I couldn't cry for help because Heather would say I seduced him.'

The devil came into me and filled my blood with evil. It surged through my body like a flood of sin and took my breath away, leaving me gasping in the wake of his depravity. It was the first time I had felt the full force of his power.

Heather went out for the night with her boyfriend, leaving me to cry in despair on the sofa.

'I am worthless,' she said. 'I taint everybody.'

One morning, when Barny and Louise had gone into town for the weekend shopping, Barny stopped to speak to Zeke in the street. He had to admit that Zeke looked an odd character, with his long drooping moustache, haunted eyes and the incongruous assortment of second-hand clothes he was wearing. Barny addressed him cautiously.

'How's it going, Zeke?

And Zeke said, 'If everybody was like we, it would be going fine, but they aren't. The world is full of morons. Hello, Sarah.'

She was walking past them, and stopped. 'I'm called Katie, Zeke. Hullo, Barny.'

'Where 'ee off to? ' Zeke said before Barny could speak.

Katie was dressed in anorak, jeans and walking boots, with a pack slung over her back. 'Off to check the bats.' she said.

'Well you mind what you're about. You shudn' be going down the bal by yourself. Git Boy Steve to go with 'ee. He edn gone to say.'

'He was supposed to phone me.'

'Ah. He might be gone over Penavon.'

And Zeke went on his way, muttering. 'Bleddy morons,' he said to a passer-by who looked at him in alarm. 'Tha's what they are. Bleddy morons. Ought to be dammee put going.'

Louise made no comment on the encounter until they were back in the cottage, when her curiosity overcame her code of etiquette. The strange little man intrigued her.

'He looks unstable. Is he violent?'

'Who, Zeke?' Barny said. 'No. He's harmless enough.'

Louise had her doubts, 'I'm not so sure,' she said.

Katie left Barny, Louise and Zeke, and walked up to the car park. She stopped to watch the *Morwennol* leaving harbour before she drove away. She had not seen Barny's lady friend before, although she knew about her, and was concerned that Barny was not looking his usual hearty self. That he should not have asked her for more information regarding the rumours about the mine was, in itself, of some significance. She would visit him, and ask Boy Steve to go with her. That would cause a few more ructions if their families got to know. There was another car parked in the lay-by, a car with an unfamiliar, not local, registration plate. It was a very clean car, a new and expensive car, incongruous here in the countryside with no occupant, and roused her suspicions quite illogically. There was nobody in sight, on either the road or footpath over the moors. She made a mental note of its number, and trudged down the footpath to the cliff.

In a patch of mud by the last gate, she saw clear new footprints, probably of welly boots, and they showed again, from time to time, as she followed the path to the mine, where they were not separable from the many others at the entrance. She paused there, reluctant to enter the mine alone after her fall, despite her familiarity with the adit, and looked along the cliffs. To the west there was nobody, and she saw spiders' webs spanning the path. Eastwards, there were dark tracks in the dew, whether of man or beast she could not tell. She sat on a rock, removed her backpack and took out her torch, feeling uneasy.

Where the path rose steeply, among an outcrop of greenstone, there was a movement, as of a head withdrawn, or it could have been a fox that drew her attention. She stared at the rocks for minutes but saw nothing more.

The *Morwennol* came around the head. There was only one man aboard. Katie took out her binoculars. It was Father Steve, alone in the boat. She swung the binoculars quickly to the outcrop. Nothing. Nobody to be seen. Back to the boat. Old Steve was preparing handlines.

There was less water dripping now. The mine was drying out in the summer drought. Katie went in as far as the chamber, where the bats were roosting in the crevices of the roof. There seemed to be fewer each time she came. She turned up the volume of the detector and walked around the chamber. On the ground, pressed into the earth, there was a cartridge, new, still shining. She knelt to pick it it up and smelled it. It had been recently fired.

A powerful torch shone right in her eyes, blinding her, and Katie rose to her feet in fear.

'Well, just look,' said a voice that she did not immediately recognise as that of Langley, Simon Sweeting's agent. 'It's Batwoman herself.'

Her own torch was just powerful enough to enable her to see his face. He was leering at her, showing his small teeth.

'Take your light out of my eyes.' Katie said. 'You're blinding me.'

'You're trespassing,' Langley said. 'This mine is private property.'

'What are you doing here?' She held out the cartridges. 'Who's been shooting the bats?'

'There are no bats,' Langley said. 'Only naughty little girls who interfere with other people's business.'

'Don't be ridiculous.' Katie was afraid of him. He could do as he liked with her down here and no one would know. 'Of course there are bats.'

'If there were, they couldn't be disturbed, and all our plans might be held up, for the sake of a few flying mice. The conservationists have made that clear. It is against the law, apart from the stupid sentimentality of silly girls.'

'I am a scientist.' Katie said.

'You...' Langley paused, and flicked his torch down over her body before bringing it back to her eyes. '...are a trespasser.'

Katie switched her detector on. The clickings of the noctules echoed in the gloom of the chamber. 'What about these bats, are they trespassers too?'

'I can hear no bats. There are no bats. No one has ever claimed to see bats here except you.'

'Sorry,' Katie said. 'That won't do. Barny Baragwaneth has recorded them here for years. Now we can prosecute you for disturbing them with shot-guns.'

'There are no bats. There are no cartridges, no shot-guns. You are mistaken.'

'Steve Trevorrow has been down here with me and seen and heard them too.'

'We can deal with him. I haven't settled with him for that unprovoked attack in the restaurant yet.' He came close to her. The light was in her eyes. 'He has good taste, for a peasant, I'll give him that.'

She could see his face, in the reflected light from her own. Everything else was in total darkness. His arm around her came too suddenly for her to kick him in the balls. They fell to the ground and the torches rolled away, shining their beams to black walls of rock around them. She felt his mouth against her neck as he forced her arms behind her. He was a big man and she could not throw him off. He held both her hands in one of his, behind her back, and reached for her belt buckle with the other.

'You should know better,' he hissed, 'than to come down here alone. It's very dangerous. You could easily fall down a shaft and never be seen again.'

Katie screamed. Her voice reverberated around the blackness of the mine. She heard the echo come out of the adits and off the roof of the chamber. No one would hear her from in here. She screamed again. It was terminated by Langley's hand hitting her across the mouth. He pulled her belt through the loops of her jeans, and tried to wind it round her wrists.

'I've wanted you since I first saw you,' he said. 'And what I want I get, one way or another.'

In desperation, Katie wrenched a hand free from the belt behind her back, and as she thrashed around under his weight her hand found a rock. It was bigger than her fist, and struck his skull with a barely audible crunch. He fell upon her, momentarily stunned, and she felt blood run onto her face as she pushed him off her and struggled to her feet.

'You little bitch,' Langley groaned.

He stood up and staggered towards her. There was blood in his eyes. Katie stepped back, turned, desperately looking for a weapon, and picked up his torch. He lurched towards her, but she backed away. With the beam straight in his eyes, she picked up her own torch and edged towards the adit. He staggered after her and Katie turned and ran, with a light in each hand. In his dazed condition he could not keep up with her in the dark and, as soon as she had gained some ground, she smashed his torch against the rock. Using only her own torch, which she dimmed with her fingers over the glass to deny him light, she ran, crouching, towards the faint illumination reflected on the walls from the mouth of the adit.

She could hear him shouting, the words indistinguishable, as she struck her head on the roof and fell.

'Found her s'afnoon,' Zeke said, 'On the bleddy cliff. Thought she was dammee slaipin.' Had a fall, I reckon. Brought her round.'

'Where is she now?' Boy Steve asked.

'Home. I took her home to Sarah's. She's all right. She drove the car home. Said she wanted to see 'ee.'

'I'll come down right away. Thanks Zeke.'

Boy Steve put the phone down and turned to his parents. 'Katie Stevens has had an accident. Zeke found her unconscious outside the adit of Wheal Dowr. She wants to see me.'

'See you?' Mary said. 'How d' she want to see you?'

'Don't know, but she do.'

He had never, he suddenly realised, been inside Sarah Stevens' house. He doubted if any man, other than his own father, had been inside her house since the death of her parents and the birth of her child. She had lived on her own as an enigma, a quiet, chapel-going woman who had borne an illegitimate child late in life and never disclosed the identity of the father. There was talk, and talk only, mere speculation, and best ignored, his father said, as idle gossip. Father Steve had always done her work, everything from odd bits of carpentering to the complete renovation of her kitchen when the girl, Katie, went away to college. A surprise, Sarah had said, for when Katie came home. She was, as everybody knew, very fond and very proud of her daughter. Blatant, some said. Why, darin'.

He was invited in by Sarah, who answered the door, and led into the front room, where Katie sat in an armchair, facing the window.

His first reaction was one of shock. There was a large bruise on her temple, another on her cheek, and her left eye was partly closed and black.

'What happened?' he said. 'Did you fall again? I warned you about going down there on your own.'

'Calm down,' Katie said. 'Take a seat.' She told him what had occurred in the mine. 'It was Langley, and it was my own fault. His car was parked up on the road and I didn't realise it was his, but afterwards I remembered. It was the same car they all turned up at the restaurant in. I haven't told anybody else, not even Ma. I told her I fell.'

'Why? Why not tell her?'

'Because someone got me out of there, and they don't wish to be known.'

'It was Zeke.'

'No. That's the point. Zeke said he found me outside the adit. But there was somebody else there. I saw somebody, just before I went in. I remember falling down in the adit. That's where I struck my head and knocked myself silly, and when I came round I was outside. I couldn't have got there by myself.'

'Well Zeke must have got 'ee out.'

'He says not. I mean, he said he found me on the cliff path. I didn't question him. I wasn't up to it. By the time Zeke had helped me back to the car, I could just about drive.'

'Well, Zeke could have brought 'ee out, all the same. He might have reasons for denying it. You know what Zeke is like. And what about Langley? Perhaps he was struck by conscience and brought you out before getting his head seen to.'

'Possibly. His car was gone when we got back to the road. But I doubt it.'

'Why?'

'I just do. The mood he was in, I think he would have raped me as I lay there unconscious. Whoever got me out must have seen Langley and have been seen by Langley.'

'What are you suggestin'?'

'Well, nothing, really. But what if somebody was there? What if they clobbered Langley to protect me?'

'I'll murder the bastard when I see him.'

'That's why Mother objects to me seeing you. She says you're too old for me, but what she really means is that you are too hot-headed, unreliable... .'

'I might be hot headed... .'

Sarah came into the room. She must have been just like Katie, Boy Steve thought again, when she was her age. Even now, she had that same quiet dignity, the same smile, an openness that revealed nothing she wished to conceal. For the hundredth time he wondered who she could have slept with, who she could have copulated with, to produce Katie.

Her accent was so strong, all the vowel sounds so long and melodious, yet her voice so soft. 'She's promised me not to go down there again,' she said. 'Unless there's someone with her. I shall ask Barny Baragwaneth.'

Boy Steve looked from mother to daughter, smarting under Sarah's rebuff. He was unreliable, she had implied, not suitable company for Katie. All right as a casual acquaintance but no more. He saw the pleading glance in Katie's eye, and held his tongue, wishing he had phoned her instead of coming to this house.

'They've got the nerve of the devil,' Mary said.

'Who?' Steve asked, absently turning the pages of the *Echo*. 'Who are you talkin' about?'

'You know who. The Stevenses, that's who. The very idea. Ringing up here for Boy Steve to go and see her. It's like I said, she's just like her mawther. Man mad.'

Steve laid his newspaper aside. Mr Sweeting, it seemed, was pressing the local council for planning permission for blocks of flats and a superstore to be granted before any other development. It was to finance the improvements to the harbour, he said, and to bring immediate employment to the area. Steve had had a hard day, working the boat by himself, and was intending a relaxed evening reading the paper and watching the telly. He glanced at the clock on the wall. It was nearly time for the news. 'Katie Stevens, you mean?'

Mary was doing the ironing. Her hands turned shirt sleeves and pressed the steaming iron as she spoke, her face expressing a determination to have this out, not knowing where to begin.

'They've always been the same.'

'He didn' have to go,' Steve said. 'He's a grown man.'

'He's a very good catch.'

'I want to watch the news and weather forecast.'

'Too good for the likes of they.'

Steve turned the television on. The international news was of wars between races and religions, the national news of the battle against inflation, the local news of growing unemployment. There was trouble in the Balkans, the Middle East.

'Nawthen will come of it,' he said absently. 'She's too young. She'll want somebody her own age.' The news was the same as it had been for twenty five years. He sighed.

'Reports are coming in,' the regional news reader said, 'of growing concern about the whereabouts of Mr David Langley, the local agent of Mr Simon Sweeting, the millionaire entrepreneur... .'

'I expect Sarah's encouraging it.' Mary said.

'Hark a minute.'

'...His car was found, late this afternoon, apparently abandoned, at the end of a remote lane high on the moors, and it is feared that Mr Langley may have fallen into one of the many old mineshafts in the area. A search was initiated and called off when darkness fell. Police say it will be resumed at first light. Meanwhile, anyone who may have seen Mr Langley during the day is asked to contact the police immediately. Mr Simon Sweeting, whose multi-million pound development...

'Hu,' Steve said. 'Done a bunk, more like it.'

'You're more concerned about they party than your own son,' Mary said. 'To hell with Langley, and Sweeting too. What are they going to do for the likes of we?'

'Of course I'm concerned about my own son.'

'You don't seem to mind 'n getting mixed up with Sarah Stevens's bastard.'

Steve looked at his wife, waiting for the mortification at her own words. It did not come.

'Sarah waint allow Katie to marry Ste',' he said. 'So forget it.'

'She waint, waint she? Don't you believe it. The mother couldn't have the man, so the daughter must have his son.'

Steve was aghast that she could have said such a thing, although he had no doubt it had been on her mind for weeks. 'Don't be so bleddy stupid, woman. Think what you're saying, for Christ's sake!'

It had been a long time since Mary had heard Steve cursing and swearing. He had grown mellow in his ageing, and rarely raised his voice. His angry face glared at her but she saw it as defiance, a denial of the past, and must have it out.

'You're the stupid one,' she shouted back. 'You can't see what's going on under your very nose.'

'Don't you realise what you are saying? What kind of woman do you think Sarah is when.... God damn it ...when you've always thought the bleddy maid was mine!'

They stared at each other in silence for minutes, each defying the other, challenging, daring the truth.

'Well,' Mary said at last. 'Idn she?'

The job was offered, and Louise accepted it. Loopy Lou was to be the staff manageress of the biggest store in town.

She took it all very calmly, only panicking when buying clothes. She had difficulty over the shoes again. Something low-heeled, comfortable yet smart, she wanted, and, to be sure, there are not many such shoes. There were some, all more or less the same as far as Barny could see, apart from an odd bit of bow or a strap or two. His main task was to assure her that the pair she did eventually choose were the most suitable. In one shop she became breathless with anxiety and he doubted if she could have bought anything if he had not been accompanying her.

'Are they too expensive ? Are they to high? Do they make me look too tall? Are they too low? Are they smart enough?' The ones she did choose, eventually, pinched her toes after a week but there was no way in which Barny could have foreseen that she was trying to deny the size of her feet.

He suggested another celebratory dinner at Jennifer's, and Louise agreed to go, this time with enthusiasm. The proprietors greeted them as old friends which, in Barny's case, they were, and Barny chatted with Sydney about the new road-widening in front of the premises as Louise chose the wine, saying that she knew more about that sort of thing than he did, being half continental and all.

'Do you have Chateauxneuf du Pape?' Louise asked.

'No. I'm sorry, my 'ansome. We used to stock 'n but decided it was never worth the money.'

Barny was aware that Louise had remembered the name of a wine that her father had bought some years ago, and winked at Sydney. Eventually, on Jennifer's recommendation, she chose a bottle of Sauterne which, Barny noted smugly to himself, was the one he would have picked.

'You can't go wrong with that,' Jennifer said. 'For a ordn'ry night out.'

There were only two other tables occupied and, when they had eaten, Barny and Louise dawdled over their coffee. She looked vibrant and beautiful in the dim light (not so damned dim that they couldn't see what they were eating or who they were with) and smiled at him, with her eyes shining to match her hair. 'Thanks,' she said. 'That was a lovely meal. Sorry about the last time.'

He shrugged the last time off. 'Are you happy now?'

'Oh yes.' She reached for his hand. He wasn't quite sure about that, in public. It was the age difference, people might think he was her sugar daddy, or worse. To hell with them. He caressed her fingers in his own, loving the feel of her.

'All my dreams,' Louise said, 'come true. I have the man I love, and a good job in the place I love. Everyone is so natural down here. This restaurant is so typical of it. There's no pretence. I feel I can be myself.'

There was pretence over the wine, he thought, but she was learning. Be like one of we before long. Her fingers gripped his hand, and she leaned across the table.

'There's only one more thing I want now,' she said.

'There's no hurry, we have all night.'

There was only one thing he wanted at that time too, but alone with her, not with the bogey men lurking and waiting to leap out at them from the depths of her subconscious.

Although there were one or two occasions in the next fortnight when Louise clung to him in tears, fearful of that to which she had committed herself, he convinced her of the futility of worrying, asking her what she had to lose.

'Just give it a whirl. You're on three months' probation anyway. And just remember that you're not dependent on them. You will always have a safe retreat here with me.'

She hugged him in silence and he said, 'You are strong enough for anything now.'

He took her up on the moors again, walking through the lanes, where they saw the first golden stars of the year pressing through the grass.

'Celandines!' Louise cried when she spied them. 'I've been with you for almost a year. Where has it gone?'

He took her hand. She could keep up with him now, her legs were getting stronger and she had more breath.

'The year has gone on ahead,' he said, 'to wait for us.' And she merely smiled as he paused, knowing that he was sorting out some ideas which came too fast to grasp. 'It has gone forward into the future,' he said, 'so that we may meet it there, look back and remember our love.'

'I shall never forget it,' Louise said, 'wherever it goes.'

He had taken her over new ground, to a part of the moor she had never seen before, and he led her along a narrow track through the heather until they reached the highest carn, overlooking the coastal plain, with the horizon clear under the strands of cumulus in the distance. The carn was a peak of jagged granite, and they climbed to the top, from whence Barny pointed to the low profile of the islands in the distance.

'Are they the lost land,' Louise asked, 'of Lyonesse?'

Barny had climbed to the highest peak of granite where he stood precariously with his arms spread wide. He cried aloud, in a booming voice:

'When King Arthur stepped in Lion's Mess, A mighty crispy thing.'

'What did you say?' she called.

'When King Arthur slept in Lyonesse,' he cried again, 'A mighty Christian king... . It's my school song.'

She was not certain she had heard him correctly the first time, and looked at him in annoyance until he broke into laughter and said, 'Come on, let's go a bit further.'

After clambering down from the carn they walked over the moor until they came to a shallow depression in the white grass, where, by reason of the peculiarities of the contours, they were hidden from all sides yet still on the open moor. There were boulders protruding from the shallow soil. They seemed to be set at random, quite naturally but, in the approximate centre, there was a taller stone, leaning slightly to the east. The crystalline structure of this was unlike anything around it. The granite was black, flecked with silver.

'What is it?'

'Magic.'

She waited. Nothing further was forthcoming. He put his hands on the stone. 'Yes,' he said at last. *'Ottomma bukkyas gwyn.'*

'What are you talking about?'

'Try it,' he said, stepping aside. 'See what happens.'

Louise stayed where she was, with her gloved hands deep in her pockets of her smock. She was wearing a woollen hat and a scarf around her neck, for she felt the cold without her hair. There was a look of expectation on Barny's face, as if he perceived something in her that was unknown to herself. It was always the same, up here on the moors or in

211

the vicinity of the megaliths; he seemed to draw apart from her, as if the landscape claimed him. It made her nervous, like being in the company of a stranger.

'Go on,' he said. 'There's nothing to be afraid of.'

He had read her mind again. 'I'm not afraid,' she protested, remembering how he had caressed the stone of the Royal Raven. 'What's there to be afraid of? It's only a stone.'

'Touch it! Put your hands on it.' And, as she began to comply, 'Take your gloves off.'

She put both hands around the stone, and held it for a while. It was strangely warm, although the sun was weak. She was facing east, with the stone leaning away from her, so that she had to lean forwards slightly to reach the top. She ran her hands down the stone, one on each side, and up again, over the rounded top. Barny was watching her, and she tried to humour him, although uncertain of what was expected of her.

'What am I supposed to feel?'

'I don't know.'

But he did know, Louise thought. He was trying to tell her something, to share something of which she had no conception.

The heat radiating from the stone warmed her hands as she pressed them against its rough surface. The warmest part was near the top and she held it there, one hand on either side, as she stretched to reach it. A faint smile flickered around Barny's eyes. She pressed herself against the stone, with her knees straddling the hard granite, while her hands embraced the rounded contours of its extremity. Slight protuberances of crystals pushed against the denim of her jeans as she felt the warmth permeating her clothes, and she put her arms around the stone, pressing her cheek against it, her mind empty.

Barny was waiting for her. She said, 'Was it supposed to be erotic.'

'I don't know,' he said. 'What you mean. It's only a stone.'

'I think there is magic in them, don't you ?'

He didn't answer. Louise took his hand and gazed around her at the familiar landscape, seeing it for the first time.

They walked slowly home, in a silence that was in no way constrained. Where the path was wide enough, and when back on the road, they linked arms, occasionally smiling at each other. They called in to see Beth, who seemed to sense some new affinity between them, kissing them both as they left in the darkening evening.

After their meal they sat beside the fire, listening to Mozart, talking of neither his work nor hers, until she said, 'Tell me about the stones, Barny.'

'You already know, now.'

'I don't understand.'

'And that is the knowledge. There is no understanding.' He turned from the flames. 'All these people, that lot we saw at the *Maen an Tol*, going up there for healing, enlightenment, knowledge, drawing upon the energy, like leeches sucking blood from a drowning mother, are the same as speculators coming here to drain off the remaining resources. They will never be cured, or rewarded. The earth will curse them.'

He believed it. There was no emotion in his voice. He took hold of her hand, opened it out, straightening the long fingers, and placed it against his cheek. She caressed his face, and in response he kissed her fingers. 'You see what I mean ?'

'No, I don't. Or at least, I'm not sure.'

'When you hugged the stone, when you loved it, it gave you its love and wisdom in return. That's all there is to it.'

There was far more to it. There was all of the mysticism, of God and man's place in the scheme of things, and the path to awareness, which she must follow alone, although Barny would be there to guide her. She felt that their minds were as one, with their thoughts simultaneous and mutual as they gazed at each other in the firelight.

'Zeke,' Barny said at last, 'tries to measure the force with all his weird equipment. He took it up to *Boscawen Un*, one of the stone circles - I'll take you there sometime - together with a length of wire. The idea was to join all the stones together and take a reading of what he calls the geokinetic energy.'

Louise saw the twinkle coming into his eye and prepared for another of his improbable tales. 'Go on,' she said.

'He took it all on the bus, in a huge cardboard box, and then lugged it over the moor to the circle. He became quite excited when he told me about it. "I'm not one to exaggerate, Booy," he said, "as you d' knaw, but the energy coming off they stones was enough to peel the skin off your bleddy hands. It was the spring equinox, see. Then, all these fellas turned up. Bunch of bleddy weirdos. Would you mind leavin' they said. Leavin' I said. 'ess they said. We are about to conduct a ceremony. Ceremony I said, what kind of ceremony? The equinox they said, they wanted to catch the sunset. So did I, but what could I do? Couldn't do nawthen with that crowd there. All right, I said, How long will 'ee be ? I had to take all my gear away again. Hid behind the furse, I did. Heard them all chantin' and wailin', and had a look as it was getting dark. All dammee starkers, now, with one of them lashed up with coloured ropes around his ankles and neck, like a bleddy chicken trussed up, you. One was wearing this g'eat black cloak, and nawthen else, and he had a broomstick, it's true you, and a sword, and they had this here five pointed star on the ground. And damn me if he in the cloak didn kiss the other fella on the feet, on the knees, his cock, and his nipples, and then on the mouth. Bunch of bleddy ass-bandits if you ask me. And then he with the cloak up and lashed to 'n with a bleddy rope, and then he had this here home-made knife with a black handle which he waved in the air as he led the poor bugger around the circle. And then they went home.

To hell with them, I thought. I lugged my gear back, and do you knaw, Barny, theer wudn't a ounce of energy left in they stones. They had taken the bleddy lot! How do so many queer people come down here, Barny, do 'ee knaw? Anyway, the energy gradually came back and I set up my gear, pitch black by now, mind you. I unwound my wire, got scratched all over my legs from the damn brambles, and passed 'n from stone to stone around the outside of the circle... and do you knaw what...?"

'You blawed a fuse in a light bulb,' I said.

'No. Don't be stupid. The bleddy wire was a foot too short. I had to walk all the way home in the dark for nawthen. What a crant!'

Barny was in tears of laughter, remembering Zeke's adventure. 'It's a good job he's strong, carrying all that gear.'

'Is that all true?' Louise asked. 'I never know, with you.'

'Oh yes. They were pagans, witches.'

'Witches ?'

'There's all sorts here, my flower.'

He went out to the kitchen, still laughing, leaving her to decide for herself whether he was lying, and returned with two wine glasses.

'Let's try some of last year's elderberry,' he said and, as he poured it, resumed the narrative of Zeke's encounter at the circle. 'What Zeke saw was the initiation rite into the second degree of a male coven. Yet more of them trying to suck the last blood from my dying motherland.'

'Does it bother you?'

'Not much.' His hand fell to her nape, slender as an aspen beneath the shorn hair. 'She will drive them insane, in the end. I always want to touch you,' he said. 'I hope you don't think I'm pawing you.'

'I love it,' she said. 'It's what I need, the way you brush my hair as you pass me, and hold my behind when we walk together. It makes me feel loved and wanted. I can't get enough of it. I have never wanted it from anyone else. I love it.' She took his hand and placed it on her thigh. 'I love it.'

He smiled a rueful smile. 'I hope you love it as much as I do.'

They sat sipping the wine as he stroked her, brushing the hard seam of denim between her legs. 'It's not all sex,' he said. 'I want to show you my affection.'

Louise drained her wine and placed her head upon his shoulder. 'You do it just right,' she said. 'You always know what I need.' She closed her eyes and reached for his hardening cock, squeezing it through his trousers.

She smelt faintly of her elusive perfume. Her forehead was cold against his cheek. 'Are you happy now ?' he asked, and she nodded. 'Are you warm enough?'

'Nearly.'

'Oh', he said. 'you are lovely.' And in a moment of doubt, 'I don't know what you see in an old man like me.'

'I love you, you old bugger. You exasperate me, but I love you.'

A breath of contentment escaped from his lips. He loved her. He loved the touch and smell of her, all her fears and phobias, her beautiful black hair and weak body. Surges of emotion flowed through him, and he took his hand from her thigh, stroked her temple and slipped it under her jumper to feel her soft breasts and warm belly. Louise unzipped his fly, saying, 'You're big,' and took it out, rolling her thumb over the tender skin.

'We don't have to make love,' Barny said, wondering if she was merely attempting to demonstrate her love for him rather than feeling a genuine desire.

'Oh...,' she urged, squeezing him, 'I want it. I want it.'

He rubbed her thighs again, saying, 'And I want you.' He unbuckled the belt on her jeans, dropped the zip and ran his hand over her belly, with the fingers under the elastic of her pants. The tangle of black hair was tantalisingly close but the jeans were too tight for him to brush his hand down over the pubic bone. A delicious female scent arose from her, rousing him further in her rhythmically pulsating hand. By firmly pressing down on her, he could just reach the folds but she stopped him. 'Take your jeans off,' he said.'

'No.' She took his hand away. 'I don't want to.'

'Yes, you do. I can feel your lust. I can smell it. He reached for her again, laughing, 'Let me stroke your beautiful black pussy.'

215

'No! No!' she cried. 'I need a wash. I want to wash. I'm dirty. I'm smelly. I don't want you to touch me until I've had a wash.'

'You're not smelly! You're secreting so many female pheromones they make me feel like a rutting stag.' He leaned down and kissed her belly. 'I could eat you.'

'I can smell myself,' she said. 'It's horrible.' She drew his head away. 'Shall we have a bath, together?'

A bath! he thought, she had a bleddy bath this mornin'. No wonder her skin is so delicate, it's all scrubbed away. 'All right then. If you want to.'

He pulled the zip up over his flagging erection, all spontaneous desire deflated.

For some perverse reason, which Barny could not justify to himself, he remained downstairs after she went up. He washed the glasses and put things away in the kitchen, deliberately making her wait as he heard the water flowing in the bath and then stop. Louise came down in her robe and went to the loo. He did not look at her as she passed through the kitchen. He looked for additional tasks, cleaning the sink, putting all the cutlery away in drawers, jobs which he would normally forget when there was the prospect of making love to her. He wanted her now, but not on her terms, with the necessity of continually relating pornographic fantasies in order to bring her to a climax. That demon in her head would have to be exorcised and he did not know how to do it. He paused at the sink, staring blindly at the wall before his eyes.

What a state! he thought.

She came back into the kitchen, stood behind him, and wrapped her arms around his shoulders and chest. 'Are you coming up ?'

'In a minute.'

'Don't you want me? Don't you love me?' She pleaded. 'You're thinking of someone else aren't you ? Is it Anne?'

'I'm not thinking of anyone else.'

He finished wiping the sink and dried his hands, turning away from her to hang the towel back on its hook.

'I'm not good enough for you, am I? I'm not woman enough for you. You could have any woman you wanted. Are you getting tired of me?'

He was getting tired of her self-denigration, but he relented. It was the only way of preventing a flood of tears. He embraced her with his hands inside the robe.

'I already have the woman I want. The woman I love. How can I convince you? I'm not looking for anyone else, Louise, I love you.'

'Do you?' she pleaded. 'Will you love me forever?'

'As long as you need me,' he said, and felt the wet trickle of a tear on his cheek as he drew her close to him, with his hands feeling the bumps down her spine and the rounded contour of her behind. 'You have a lovely ass. Come on, the water is getting cold.'

They undressed in the bedroom, for the bathroom was too small for them both to stand in, and the bath was too small for Louise to lie in, so she sat with water up to her waist as he soaped her back. Then she slipped down, with her knees drawn up, as he leaned over the rim and washed her belly and breasts. He ran the soapy cloth down between her legs as he said, 'And what's this?'

'My vagina.'

'My what?'

'My pussy.' She admitted.

'My what?'

'My beautiful pussy.'

She had put weight on; her ribs were no longer protruding like corrugated iron and her little umbonate breasts were firm as peaches. There was now a covering of flesh on her thighs.

'Yes,' Barny said. 'Your beautiful pussy. And you are a very beautiful woman.'

They changed places when she was quite satisfied that she was clean. She dried herself as Barny sat in the bath, now fully aroused again. She washed him and swilled him down with a jug of water. 'I can't keep my hands off you,' she said.

In the bedroom, she spread a smear of body lotion over her skin. 'I want to smell nice for you.'

'I would rather have your own scent. You smell like a bouquet of meadow flowers. I want to bury my nose in you, and become intoxicated on the perfumes of your lust.'

'Come on then,' she said, suddenly quivering with excitement, 'come and love me, have me, take me,' as her hand squeezed him painfully in her enthusiasm.

He dropped to his knees and nuzzled into her, stroking her curls with his cheek, drawing deep breaths of her in through his nostrils until she took him by the hair and clutched him tight. And Barny was aware that the demons and bogey men were at bay, and he could keep them there,

217

forever cowering and unable to torment her, if only she could let herself come out beyond their reach.

She was dribbling on his beard, and he became almost out of control in his lust for her.

'You are the most sensual, responsive, delicate, sexy woman,' he gasped, 'that a man could ever dream of.'

She fell back on the bed, and he crawled after as she wriggled her head up to the pillow, enticing him with her open legs. He went into her with a slow lunge, determined to wait for her no matter how much he roused her.

'Can I go on top?' she pleaded. 'Can I? I want to.'

'Whatever you want.' And they rolled over, legs entwined, until she was sitting astride him with her long legs clasping his waist. She bowed her head and began kneading him with her hips and he sensed the desperate struggle was about to begin again, that the bogey men were coming, as her body began to writhe. He relaxed himself, stopped thrusting up at her, and murmured softly, 'You don't have to fight me. You can't fight me and love me at the same time.'

'They are coming,' she said. 'I have to fight *them*.'

'Are they there now ?'

'No. They've gone.'

She fell on him, with her breasts against his chest. 'Love me gently.' he said. 'Do it for me. Give me your beautiful pussy, and I'll keep her safe.'

Louise collapsed completely, her full weight on him, and let her breathing subside. 'You're so good to me,' she sighed.

'Let me kiss you,' he said, and she brought her full lips on to his mouth, too hard, and he drew away, holding her head in his hands as he brushed his lips over hers in slow lingering enticement to passion.

'I want your cock,' she said when she drew away for breath. 'I want to kiss your cock.'

That's not the way, Barny thought, not this time. 'You are kissing it,' he said. 'You are kissing it with your cunt.'

The word sent a shudder through her body and she sat up on him, dribbling so much juice he felt it running over his balls. He thrust up against her as she worked her body against him, encouraging and controlling her with his hands on her hips. She was magnificent, and he let out an involuntary laugh of delight in her sensuality.

'Oh,' he said. 'How I love you, my gorgeous woman.'

It came over her like a terrifying wave of emotion that threatened to engulf her, drown her as she was pounded against the rocks. She would have to struggle against it or be dashed to pieces. She took a deep breath, to cry out in terror, and heard Barny saying, somewhere on the safety of the shore. 'Go with it, ride it, let it take you to me', and the breath escaped in a cry of exhilaration as the wave lifted her beyond any height she had reached before and threw her passively forward in a surging glide onto the throbs of the man beneath her. She emitted a cry of pure, untainted pleasure as her body became out of control and took over her mind. She had no mind. There was only feeling. The pleasure of the flesh.

She collapsed and broke down into great sobbing spasms of emotion as Barny held her close to him, comforting her. She released a long, wailing sob, the last, and said, 'No bogey men! I didn't know. I didn't know what it should be like. There weren't any bogey men.'

'Don't talk about it,' Barny said. 'They won't bother you again.'

'Not as long as I have you.'

'Just hold me. Hold me tight.'

CHAPTER TWELVE

Beunans bysy. A busy life.

There were no buses at appropriate times, so Barny ferried her back and forth as she was too nervous to drive his old car. They rose early, allowing at least an hour for Louise to prepare herself, and Barny would have a meal ready for her return in the evening.

He listened to her talking about the job for hours, and the names of her colleagues became almost as familiar to him as to her. She rarely asked him about his own days. What was there to tell her? he asked himself. He did his writing, thinking, gardening, saw friends, did things about the house, like making a built-in wardrobe for her accumulating clothes.

As the days went by, however, he began to miss her during her working hours and was always eager to see her outside the shop when she left work. At times she was delayed and, as he waited, he could see her through the window, among the customers in the aisles beyond the lines of waiting trolleys and bleeping check-outs. Tall and elegant in her smart suits, with a clipboard under her arm, she appeared the quintessence of efficiency, and Barny felt too scruffy to wait for her inside, fearful of shattering her image.

She was invariably anxious to relate the day's events although never, she told him, could she disclose personal information about the staff. He was happy to be spared that! There was an almost impossible amount of work to do, she said, for the previous staff manager had been hopelessly incompetent and had let things slide. In fact none of the records were up to date and there was even a case, she could not mention names, someone well-known in the district, of a sacked employee who had gone on receiving a pay cheque for weeks after his dismissal because no one had told the computer in central accounts he had gone.

Barny thought that was hilarious, the only funny thing she had told him after three months in the shop. There had always been something to laugh at in his jobs.

There would have been trouble all round, she insisted, if she had not discovered the error. The manager would have been given a 'written warning' but Louise had dealt with it by informing the anonymous staff at head office, and no one in the region would ever know anything about it. Nearly all the staff were part-timers and turnover was high, so Louise was always having to advertise vacancies and interview applicants. She met a lot of people.

Once in the vehicle, or even walking down to the car park, she would slump with exhaustion, become another person, the one the company never saw, the tender girl he loved as she rubbed his thigh on the road to home. Apart from the strain of the job, Louise seemed blissfully happy, although Barny was concerned that she was giving too much of herself to the company. If she finished work early enough he helped her to relax by walking down to the lighthouse to see the revolving beam or listen to the reverberating blast of the foghorn, or they might stroll through the fields or walk over the moors before sleeping contentedly in each others arms. He rarely gave Anne a thought.

After one such excursion, when Barny had spent the day in the garden, they had seen the setting sun illuminate the clouds with scarlet. It was a sunset such as she had never seen before and she was awed by the magnificence of the sky, remaining in a pensive mood after they returned to the cottage. Barny lit the fire, for the evenings were getting cold and, when they had been sitting in silence for a while, he heard Louise say, 'May I read your poems now?'

'You mean you haven't read them?'

'No. None of them.'

'Not my book ?'

'No. You said you would let me read them when I was ready.'

'Did I?'

'May I read them now? Those in your book.'

He fetched a sheaf of papers from the bookcase and handed it to her, saying, 'Read the originals, corrections and all.' She read in silence for half an hour, while he gazed in abstraction at the fire.

They were all of love: the love of rocks, the love of trees and weeds, of humanity and The Mother Earth, defiled by her own sons. She read them in silence,

He did not look at her until the last page dropped from her hand to join the others scattered on the floor. There were tears in her eyes, the first he had seen there which were not of despair or despondency. They were of sheer, detached emotion, aroused by the poems' sentiments and her own inherent compassion.

'I didn't know,' she said. 'I thought you were writing about your local culture.'

'I am. Not everything here became extinct in the seventeenth century.'

'Oh, Barny. You are a lovely man.'

During the ensuing interval, while he gazed thoughtfully into the flames, she thought that she knew him at last, as he knew her, and loved him the more for the public exposure of his passion and tears. She wanted him for her own, to have him and love him, to be hers. A physical desire arose in her and she expressed her hunger for him with her lips, brushing his cheek as she sought his mouth.

'Shall we go to bed early?' she asked.

'It's too late to go to bed early. And I think I'm too tired,' he laughed, 'judging by the look in your eye, to go to bed with you at any time tonight.' He was reluctant, fearing the demons which could re-emerge to shatter their equanimity.

'You're never too tired,' she murmured. 'And you won't have to do any work. I want to show you how much I love you.'

There was a fire of confidence in her eyes such as he had never seen before and he was instantly excited, yet scared, by it. He studied her in the glow from the hearth. How could one so thin, so small-breasted and weak, be so voluptuous? He knew not, cared not.

'Come on then,' he said. 'Show me.'

She took him by the hand and led him like a child to the stairs. When they were in bed, she insisted that he lie passively while she kissed and fondled him and loved his body. He had never seen her like this before, and was apprehensive lest she suddenly become ashamed of her salaciousness and revert to trepidation in fear of her bogey men. She massaged him, kissed his nipples until they tingled from the suction of her lips. She would not allow him to touch her anywhere, not her hair or breasts, neither her elbows nor her knees. He became so tumid he thought he would burst, but she would not let him have her, even kiss her. 'This is all for you,' she said as she put her hand around him. 'I love your cock,' she said, contorting her face in delight, 'I love it. I love it.'

It seemed to Barny that all his strength and energy became concentrated in his sex, for his body became limper with the hardening of his erection, and he lay back sighing with pleasure as she tasted his juices with the tip of her tongue.

'I wish I had one,' she gasped. 'I would play with it all the time.'

'You can play with mine,' he said, but she stopped her sucking and sat astride of him, playing with herself.

'And what is this ?' she demanded in mock aggression as she mimicked his voice, caressing it as she hovered over him.

'*Dha gathyk*,' he said, teasing her.

'My what ?' as she rubbed her slippery finger across his lips, 'My what?'

He tried to bite her finger, to suck her secretions off her, but snapped air as she snatched it away.

'My what?' she insisted.

'*Dha gathyk!*'

'My what ?' She reached behind her with her free hand and took hold of his balls, hanging vulnerably beneath his towering cock. 'My what?'

'*Dha gathyk*,' he gasped. '*Dha gathyk teg. Dha gathyk whek. Dha cons fyn. Dha cons marthys.*'

She squeezed him, saying, 'In English, you old bugger.' and he capitulated.

'Your kitten,' he said. 'Your beautiful, sweet, pussy. Your delicate, wonderful, vagina.' And she shuddered with passion at the sound of his words. He thought she was going to climax as her knees clamped against his ribs but she threw her head back and stroked herself, sensuously, with her fingers slipping in and out, moaning with pleasure. Barny expected her to cry out in terror at any minute as her bogey men crept out from the dark depths of her mind to subjugate her liberty. He held her breasts, gently rubbing against the tumescent nipples, watching her hand, her wet fingers, her pulsating ribs. 'Give her to me,' he said, and she leaned over him with her hands spread across the pillows, and lowered her beautiful pussy on to him.

Barny the Bard, he loved her. He cherished her. He worshipped her body and her petulant mind, all her defects and growing confidence. He adored the sensuality that he had released in her. He was hers and she was his, as they had been no other's. He had made a woman of her, liberated her from the terrors, inhibitions and guilt, which had suppressed her ardour for years. She was free at last to give of a self which was confident and generous, and in giving herself so completely to Barny she had acquired in return all the love he had hoarded for one such as her, only for her. He would do anything for her, in life as in bed. He would die for her.

The motions of her body ceased. Those short, slow strokes gradually lessened, and she was still, silent, until she whispered, 'Don't move.' almost as if she were in exquisite pain, 'I'm coming. I'm coming.'

He stroked her hair and she let it envelope her, let it take her, silently, breathing deeper with every shuddering wave as her hands gripped the pillows and her head hung loosely from her shoulders.

'Barny,' she said. 'Oh, Barny. I'm coming. I'm coming.' Her voice dying away until barely audible in her ecstasy. 'I'm coming.'

With her eyelids drooping, she slowly eased herself away from him and gently placed her head upon his chest, until he became limp and drew her up on to the pillow and covered their cooling bodies with the duvet, holding her in his arms, stroking her hair as she asked in a briefly querulous voice, 'Am I woman enough for you? You will be faithful won't you, while I'm at work or away? You won't have anyone else ?'

'How could I,' he sighed. 'I'll love you for ever. You have utterly ruined me for anyone else.'

'And you have ruined me,' she said as she fell again into a contented sleep. 'Ruined me, you old bugger.'

Steve Trevorrow was beginning to feel his age, yet he often forgot how many years he had lived in this same town of cobbled streets, cottages, beaches and the harbour. Always the harbour. He had existed, he sometimes thought cynically to himself, as part of the scenery: been painted, photographed, visited like an antiquity by perennial tourists, written about by Shimshai; as if he were an animal in a nature reserve, a rare species, solitary, declining, unable to adapt to a changing environment. He watched his son becoming more like him every day, and it worried him.

He was leaning on the railings with Joe, watching the boy working on the boat, refastening the leads running down the mast from the radar and radio. They had been having a bit of trouble with the electrics. All beyond me, Steve thought, this modern gear. Thousands of pounds lying at anchor there. It would never be paid off in his working life but Boy Steve didn't worry, so why should he?

Joe was also thinking: close-hauled on another tack. It was time to wind up the lines, he decided, to come ashore. He had worked long enough, and there was no need to continue. The trouble was that he liked it. He liked the cold morning air as they set out, the salt on his lips, the dangers, working with his friends. He also knew what happened to boats, and people, when they were laid up for long - the rot set in. Uncle Joe had lived a good life, so far, and had all that a man could ask for. Some just didn' seem to recognise their good fortune. Steve here, with a fine son like that, and he d' come down here in the mornin' as miserable as sin.

'What the hell's the matter with you?' he said. 'You're as miserable as sin.'

'Oh,' Steve said. 'Nawthen. Well, we had words last night, Mary and me. She objects to the boy going out with Sarah's maid.'

'Nawthen wrong with Katie,' Joe said. 'Lovely maid.'

'It's all that old stuff between the Trenowdens and the Stevenses. Rows about people dead and gone. I'm sick of it.'

That's not the whole of it, Joe thought. What about all that old stuff about you and Sarah, years ago? Mary wudn ever going to forget that. I know who she d' think the maid's fehther is. He watched his friend's face. My hell, he thought, he d' give less away than me.

'I heard they've been going off together,' he said. 'Very fine pair, I thought. Just right for each other.'

'I hope not,' Steve grumbled. 'It could lead to all sorts of trouble.' Suddenly he laughed, and Joe laughed with him as Steve said, dismissing the prospect of a marriage between them as unlikely. 'You can imagine Mary and Sarah at the wedding.'

'Haw.' Joe said. 'The champagne would freeze in the bleddy glasses.'

They turned, laughing, put their backs to the railings and faced another aspect of the day.

'Here comes the poet,' Joe said. 'Wonder how he's getting on with his woman. We don't see much of her.'

'Too posh for we,' Steve said, grinning.

'And for he too, I shouldn't wonder.'

Barny knew they were talking about him and thought their laughter had also been at his expense. He looked at them suspiciously as they said in unison, ''loh Barny.'

''loh, Steve,' Barny said, cautiously, ''loh Joe.'

'Surprised,' Joe said. 'you d' talk to the likes of we.' He chewed on his lip, waiting for Barny's reaction.

Ah! They had heard of the prize. It had been in the local paper.

'S'pose,' Steve said, 'you'll be world famous now, down the lodge.'

They all laughed. His friends had congratulated him in the only way they knew, and Barny was grateful to them.

'What did 'ee write about?' Joe laughed. 'Bleddy pirates and smugglers, shipwrecks, and wreckers putting cows on the cliffs with lanterns tied to their tails? Ghosts and piskies and witches? Bleddy ballads of lore and legend. Hee hee.'

'I shan't tell 'ee,' Barny retaliated. 'You'll have to wait until the book is out.'

Steve raised his eyebrows at Barny's retort. They were all aware of Joe's problem. Steve would have to read the poems aloud to him, which he would not relish.

Boy Steve was rowing ashore, pulling the skiff with regularly dipping oars, and they watched him go alongside the quay.

'They had a call out yesterday,' Steve said. 'Brought an injured man ashore. '

'Oh? We don't know what's going on, down where I live. Who was it?'

'Stranger,' Joe said. 'Off a Spanish trawler. You wouldn't know 'n.'

They all grinned again. 'You silly bugger, Joe,' Barny said, forgetting for a moment Steve's religiousness. It was all OK for Joe to swear in Steve's company but he didn't like it from anyone else. He caught his friend's eye, saw only a continuing amusement at the conversation, and then Barny suddenly remembered his absurd premonition, which he could not mention for fear of ridicule. It seemed that Boy Steve was now one of the regular crew. What would Mary think of that? And did she know that the boy was seeing Sarah's maid?

'What's the news over to Penavon, now?' he said, deciding not to declare his anxiety.' I suppose Sweeting is still carrying on with the developments.'

'They've put plans in for the supermarket. Nothing else.'

'Nothing at all? That'll bring a lot of prosperity to the town, I'm sure. Perhaps he's waiting for a new agent.'

'There's plenty more where Langley came from.' Joe said.

Why weren't they down there? Barny thought, helping Boy Steve? They must have had words, over Katie.

'Don't 'ee ever worry about 'n?' With a nod in the direction of the boy. 'In the lifeboat, I mean.'

'Somebody got t' do it.'

'I've ben glad of them,' Joe said, 'afore now.'

He had been all over the shop, Joe had, had experienced more adventures than most dreamed of, and never spoke of them. He was as close as a tier of punts when he had a mind to be.

Barny was late, and he wanted to see his father before going home, so he left them, considering why it was he never asked Steve about Mary. She must be all right or Steve would say so. He had not taken more than a step or two when he turned about, remembering something.

'I think I'll have the house done,' he said. 'When you have the time.'

'After the season. I'll give 'ee a shout.'

'Now look,' Joe said as Barny was leaving them for the second time.
'Yes ?'
'Mind what you're about.'

Barny knocked on Anne's door, not sure of his reception, and opened it tentatively, calling to her before entering.

'Come in,' she said. 'I won't bite you.'

She seemed to have forgiven him, or was holding her condemnation in abeyance for a while. 'Have you seen the paper?' she asked. 'Langley has disappeared. Here, read it.'

'AGENT VANISHES' the headline blared. 'There is still no news of Mr David Langley. The much respected agent of developer and new owner of Penavon, Mr Simon Sweeting, has not been seen since his car was found abandoned on the moors and, despite extensive enquiries, no trace of the thirty-nine-year-old executive has been found... .'

'Oh,' Barny said, 'how about that then? Do you think he's gone off with the loot?'

'There isn't any loot,' Anne said. 'Not until they get permission to develop the port. Or dump nuclear waste in the mine.'

'Why do people keep on about nuclear waste? No application has been made. Sweeting hasn't mentioned the mines.'

'Exactly. So why has he employed a highly-qualified nuclear physicist and a geologist to go poking around in there?'

'Perhaps he's hoping to re-open the mine.' Barny said, although there was little conviction in his voice.

'With the price of tin what it is? Come on! People are getting suspicious of him. I saw graffiti on the harbour wall.'

'I didn't see that. What did it say?'

'I don't know. I can't speak the language.'

'I'll go and look.' Who could have written that, he thought, Boy Steve ?

Something was bothering her, he could see, but was reluctant to ask what. There was a certain reserve in her manner, and she was cold towards him, despite her assurances. There was no humour in her eye and she had not made fun of him. He had to admit a degree of guilt at not visiting her more often, as he had promised.

'Anyway,' he said when the silence became prolonged. 'How are you keeping?'

'I'm fine, but you don't care.' She was abrupt as ever, pushing him aside as she went to fill the obligatory kettle.

227

'Of course I care,' Barny said. Then, forestalling the tea, 'I can't stay long. I have to see Father, and then pick Louise up from work.'

'She's got you, hasn't she?'

'What do you mean?'

'You're becoming like a little lap-dog, running around after her. Does she pat you on the head when you're good? Throw sticks ?'

'Why do you have to be so cruel to her? She's never done you any harm.'

'No,' she said, her irony melting, 'but you have. In your subservience to her you won't have anything to do with me. You're only here now because you feel guilty.'

'Rubbish!' he said, colouring at the truth of her words. 'We're living together. I can't go off seeing another woman.'

'I am not,' she cried angrily, with a tear appearing in her eye, "another woman". I'm *me* And...' her voice tailing off, '...I need you.'

'You need me.'

'Yes,' she snapped.

'But why?'

Anne turned away from him, doing things at the sink, unable to face him with what she was going to say.

'Because I'm lonely. And because somebody else is after me and I don't know what to do.'

Barny felt only relief at her words. If there was another man in Anne's life, although he was not sure that he believed her, then he could tell her he loved Louise and wanted to marry her. He would have no more res- ponsibility to Anne.

'I don't believe you.' he said facetiously in an attempt to elicit more details of her new man, who he was. 'Or is it Uncle Joe?'

She faced him. 'Someone I knew years ago. He came down on holiday and came to see me. I went away for a weekend with him. You didn't even know I'd gone.'

An irrational jealousy stung him. Had she slept with the man? It was none of his business.

'You're jealous,' Anne said, with a sudden change of mood. 'He's very rich.'

'Oh, Annie.'

'He's asked me to go and live with him. He's fallen in love with me and wants to marry me.'

'You wouldn't marry me.' he challenged her.

'You never asked me.'

'I did! Lots of times.'

'No, you didn't. You only said it. That's not the same.'

He capitulated. 'Well, all right, but you wouldn't have said yes if I did mean it. And, I don't understand. If this bloke wants to marry you, why do you need me?'

Anne's voice dropped, as if in a confessional. 'Because I still love you. I would wait until Louise leaves you, I know she will, and then begin again, as long as you kept seeing me, but you won't. She won't let you.'

'You can't blame her,' he said, ignoring her first statement, 'under the circumstances.'

'No. And you can't blame me. I'll have someone to take care of me.'

'But you don't love him.'

She refused to comment on that, and Barny was afraid for her, that she would get herself in an impossible situation because of him.

'Can he mend a fuse ?'

She slapped him, a hard right-hander that sent him reeling. Too hard for play, it stung with all the force of her pent-up frustration. He too lost his temper, and went out through the door before he should slap her in retaliation. In the street, he remembered his hat, and turned back, to find her on the doorstep, about to hurl it after him, her arm thrown back in defiance. They stopped, a few paces apart, fuming with rage, and broke down into giggles at the sight of each other's faces.

The probationary period passed successfully and Louise was told that she would be attending a staff training course in the near future, an arse-about-face way of doing things in Barny's opinion, but then, it's a crazy world out there, fehther. She was working long hours, far more than the so called 'thirty-nine minimum' of her contract, but she assured him that when all the backlog was caught up she could relax. 'They expect it, for the salary I'm getting,' she said. There was no chance of her seeing her children for a while for she worked every Saturday. Barny didn't think it was worth it, the salary was not all that generous. 'More than twice what the girls on the shop floor get,' Louise pointed out. What did that prove?

She was not eating enough, he told her. She ate, she said, at work, which he knew was a lie, or a lie by his definition of eating: just a lettuce leaf or a bread roll. She had gone off meat altogether, she said, which meant that he either had to cook two meals or forego meat himself. He chose the former.

On her day off, which was often reduced to half a day, or none, because of pressure of work, she seemed to be entirely preoccupied with preparations for another week. Her clothes demanded an inordinate amount of attention and she spent hours ironing. Every little crease in every little garment had to be totally eradicated before she was satisfied that it was fit to wear. Her suits had to be ironed every night and dry-cleaned after a week's wear. She'd have a bleddy fit, Barny thought, if she could see the several little creases in the back of her coat after sitting in his car in the mornings.

'I have to set the standard for the whole shop,' she said. 'I can't tell people they are not suitably dressed unless I am myself faultless.'

He was sure she was losing weight, but she insisted that her thighs were thickening, that her skirts were getting tighter. 'They're shrinking,' he said, 'with all the cleaning.'

The arrangements were eventually made for Barny's big day, the presentation of the poetry prize. These included having Louise by his side at the top table, where she would meet all the celebrities present. He was looking forward to showing her off, was even thinking of proposing in time to announce their marriage there.

'You might as well enjoy it,' he said. 'It's only a nine-day wonder and will be all forgotten in a week or two.'

'I won't be coming.' she said.

'What?' He was flabbergasted, unable to believe her. 'Why not ?'

'There's too much work to do. I can't get the time off.'

'Surely,' he insisted, 'they'll let you off for just one day. They owe it to you. You always work overtime for nothing. I thought you were supposed to work thirty-nine hours a week, not fifty or more.'

'My contract says thirty-nine minimum. The regional director is coming and I have to be there. I'm sorry Barny.'

She did not sound very convincing. He swore to himself. What kind of job was it where even one day off, for something as important as this, was an impossibility? 'Go sick,' he said.

'I can't. They'd notice. My photograph might even be in the paper with yours. They'd say I had no dedication. I can't risk it. There is too much depending on my being there that day.'

'Oh well. I'll go on my own.'

Barny was devastated. What did it all mean if she were not there to share his acclaim. But why not? Her excuses were lies, obvious lies.

By the time he returned from the presentation, sitting in the train with the gloom of anticlimax falling around him like the drizzle on the trackside trees, he had decided to tell her nothing about it. He had not presented himself well; had been inveigled into making 'controversial' comments about much of the popular fiction set in his country, which, while being true, should have been avoided before the media. In retaliation to what he saw as Louise's indifference to his success, he did not even give her a copy of his little book, pretending that he had forgotten to in the preoccupation with the launch. If she wanted one, with a declaration of love and gratitude written on the flysheet, she would damn well have to ask for it, which of course she would never do.

There was still a signing session to be undertaken at a promotion in a local bookshop, and one or two 'readings' in the ensuing weeks. Louise made merely the most desultory enquiries about the presentation and the readings, which went well and renewed his confidence. For the final appearance he had to travel away and stay overnight and this induced a violent objection from her. She said she was afraid to be abandoned in the house alone, that he was glad to be away from her and that he would find some adoring woman to go to bed with.

There was nothing to fear in the house, he told her, he would miss her and was staying on in the hotel only because the next train after his appearance arrived back in the early hours of the morning. Would she like to drive the car and meet him at the station at five in the morning? No!

A red rose, with a message of love, was delivered to the venue, and another to his breakfast table the following morning. He found them embarrassing, suspecting that their message was not genuine, merely a device to advertise her presence in his life, but he carefully packed them with his belongings to take back and put on the table until they faded.

As their second summer together approached the longest days, when the swathes of thrift clouded the cliff-tops in flamingo pink, and the yellow kidney vetches, trefoils and dyer's greenweed dotted crumbs of saffron between the white clusters of ox-eye daisies, when the bog pimpernel flowered among the damp sedges, and the sea plantain extruded spikes from salty fissures in the rocks, when the eyasses in the peregrine's eyrie were losing their down, Louise was too busy catering to the needs of tourists to see them.

Barny could not imagine why many of the hordes of tourists bothered to come on holiday at all. They seemed to spend most of their time indulging in the same activities that preoccupied them for the rest of the year. They appeared to be forever quarrelling among themselves, and seemed unable to visit the beach, the countryside, or even the cinema, without continually stuffing themselves with inordinate amounts of food. For what they did, as opposed to where they did it, they might as well have stayed home and watched the telly. They could have sat in their cars for hours on end, as they did here, with pictures of beauty spots stuck on their windscreens and have been just as happy. Barny didn't care what they did, really, except that the time they spent mooching around the shops, unable to break the behaviour patterns of their daily lives, buying fast foods and instant dinners which would give them even more time to waste, meant that Louise worked longer hours than ever. The sole aspiration of the frantic manager was to ensure that turnover and profit were increased to comply with directives from central office; inflation plus ten per cent. No chance of that in these times of depression, slump, temporary blips, homelessness, poll tax, council tax... no chance! Up on the moors the tiny blue flowers of milkwort hid away in the grass.

One morning, when it promised to be a lovely day, Barny stood at the door planning to hoe the vegetables and go for a swim. Louise was all ready for work and he was waiting to drive her in. She came halfway down the stairs and suddenly cried out in pain, collapsing in a heap upon the treads. She was in agony, and he could do nothing to alleviate the pain; neither could she move from where she had fallen, sprawled against the banisters in a contortion of twisted limbs. She could not speak and her eyes were wide with in fear. The pain was vaguely down in her abdomen, she said, where she clutched herself with both hands, moaning between her teeth as her body tensed in slow convulsions. He tried to get her back upstairs to bed but she could not move; the slightest turn increased the pain. He merely managed to get her to sit on the treads while he telephoned the doctor, with a tremble in his voice that he could not control. The doctor arrived within half an hour. He had been just about to leave his home to attend other patients in the area, so came straight there. Louise was still cramped upon the stairs, and Barny expected an ambulance to be called, but the Doctor persuaded her to ease herself slowly back up to the bedroom where he examined her while Barny waited anxiously below.

'Bleddy doctors,' he cursed fifteen minutes later, 'are all the same! They'll never tell 'ee anything.' He had left some pills, and she would need more. There was a prescription upstairs and would Barny go into town for the medicine. Barny saw him out, thanking him, and was left feeling he had panicked over nothing: indigestion from food she had not eaten, or wind from one of her suffocated farts. He went upstairs, finished the undressing the doctor had begun, and got her back in bed.

'I can't go to work,' she said. 'Will you phone the shop ?'

Barny knelt beside the bed and took hold of her hand. 'Is the pain gone?'

'No. But it's much better.' She suddenly turned and clung to him and he held her head, stroking her hair.

'What did he say it was.'

'He said he wasn't sure, but he thinks it's irritable colon.'

'I see.' Barny had never heard of irritable colon. 'You've taken something for it, have you ?'

'Yes. Will you phone the shop ?'

She was getting drowsy. The doctor must have knocked her out. Barny could not fault him in that. By the time he had phoned the shop she was out like a light, so he left a message by the bed and went to get her pills.

He thought of calling in to see Beth, ask her to come over and take care of Loopy while he was gone. Beth had enough on her hands. He drove over the moor too fast and had to wait for the chemist to open. While standing in the doorway, he saw Katie coming up the street.

'Hullo, Barny,' she said. 'Are you all right?'

It was because he was waiting outside the chemist, he thought, but Katie looked at him with concern.

'You don't look very well.'

'I'm fine. Louise has been taken ill. I don't think it's anything serious,' he lied. 'Where are you off to?'

'To the council offices. There are more rumours about them dumping nuclear waste in the mine. They've been sending geologists and a nuclear physicist down there. People are beginning to doubt his intentions openly. The euphoria has dwindled, and there those who are secretly organising opposition to him. I want to confront Dee Dee'

'Be careful, Katie. There's a lot at stake in this for some people. You're getting a reputation as a trouble-maker.'

'I only want the truth,' Katie said.

He knew the girl who served him in the chemist - he had been to school with her mother, Jessie Perkins that was, old James's maid - and he asked her about irritable colon.

'It's nerves,' Jessie's maid said. 'Colic. One of they stress-related syndromes, what they d' call. They're all the fashion.'

233

Barny managed to share a smile with the girl while wondering if he was the cause of Louise's stress. No. She had been keeping something from him. He might have known it.

She was still asleep when he returned. Damned doctors, he was thinking, why couldn't he have said what was the matter with her?

It was not until mid-day that she awoke, and Barny took a tray of tea, toast and a boiled egg up to the bedroom.

'I'm not hungry,' she said.

'Doctor's orders,' he lied. 'He said I'm to make sure you eat something as soon as you wake up. He said if you don't eat, the pain will be worse than ever tomorrow.'

'I'm not hungry.'

He poured two cups of tea and began munching a piece of toast. 'Please yourself.'

She ate the lot, drank two cups of tea, and he left her alone to sleep again. She's just exhausted, he decided, knackered!

Barny went out and worked in the garden. The sun was warm on his back and the soil was drying out, so he prepared seed beds and hoed between the rows of beans, shallots and cabbages, but his mind was on Louise. He was working away his worries, and finally cleared and turned the soil where the brussels sprouts had yielded the last of their crop. He was finishing the last row of spits when he sensed Louise watching him from the doorway. He left his tools and went over to her, with beads of sweat trickling from his brow, and his muscles tingling from exertion.

'Are you better?'

'I'm all right,' she said wearily, 'the pain has gone. I feel weak, that's all.'

She looked tired, with lines under her eyes, the effect of her long sleep, from which she appeared not to have completely awoken.

'I've been watching you. I love to see you working.'

She was going to disregard her illness, pre-empt his solicitous enquires by claiming to be recovered, which he could see she was not.

'Come out and sit in the sun,' he said. 'I'll get some drinks.'

He fetched some fruit juice from the fridge, and they sat on the bench at the back of the house. Best thing, Barny decided, is to keep quiet; she'll tell me what she needs to tell me. I still don't know what goes on inside that head of hers. She's almost as much a mystery as when she came to me.

There was a prolonged silence which he pretended not to notice as he rested his head against the wall and gazed at the cumulus clouds slowly changing from India into Africa over the brow of the carn. He could see Nigeria, where, in some respects, all this began, where the money was made to buy this house and forge this way of life. The continent split as the tributaries of the Congo reached in like probing fingers and wedged open the valley of the Nile from Burundi to Wadi Halfa, and the whole of the Ethiopian region drifted over the hill before Louise reached for his hand in that tentative way she used to do when he first met her. He closed his eyes from the glare of the sky, with her fingers like pliant sensors exploring his palm, as he waited for her to speak.

'I'm not what they think I am, Barny,' she said at last.

He didn't need to be told that, so remained silent, the warm sun drying the last of the sweat from his brow. He would have a bath, cook something nice for dinner, maybe open a bottle of wine, the blackberry should be worth trying now, and get her to relax.

'They think I'm efficient and reliable but I'm not. I just don't seem able to catch up with all the work. They keep piling it on and I just can't cope with it, Barny.' That tremor in her voice again.

He kept his eyes closed. If there was so much work, why didn't she tell them? He would have done. She had not said anything about all this before. She had said how much she enjoyed the job, not minding about working all those extra hours for no extra pay, not minding bringing the job home every night, not minding never knowing when she could have a day off so that her private life could be planned in advance, not minding never having a weekend to go and see her children. Well, the last wasn't quite true; she used the uncertainties of her free time as an excuse. Not minding being so tired that she was losing her enthusiasm for love making.

'Pack it in,' he said. 'Tell them to stuff the bleddy job.'

'I can't,' she moaned. 'I need the money.'

He pushed himself upright and drank the cold juice, looking at her with exasperation. She was fighting tears.

'Oh,' he said, yielding to her. 'Don't worry, my flower. You can do the job with your eyes shut. You're expecting too much of yourself. Has anyone ever complained about your work ?'

'No.'

'Well, then.'

'Barny, I was fired from my very first job! ' She said it as if it were a confession of some heinous crime.

She was talking about something that happened, what, fifteen years ago. He suddenly realised that she had been carrying this shame with her ever since, and wondered what felony she could have committed to warrant it. She had been newly graduated, intelligent, keen. He decided not to ask.

'It was constructive dismissal, as it's called. They said I was unsuitable for management.'

He imagined her, a twenty-one-year-old highly strung girl trying to prove her worth. Betraying herself by being over-zealous, losing control in a crisis. Was that the way it wa ? Perhaps they could see that she would crack up under stress and responsibility, or perhaps they simply didn't like her, her face didn't fit. God knows, she was not easy to get on with and not everyone would be prepared to nourish her potential. He refused to be shocked by her revelation. There was more in it, for one thing, than she had told him. It was all a long time ago, so why bring it up now. 'Probably the best thing that ever happened to you,' he said.

'Mr Warman was supposed to come yesterday,' Louise said. 'Miller was in a panic.'

And who else? Barny thought to himself. Who else worked herself up into a state of collapse? 'So?' he said.

'He's the regional director.'

'Yeah, I know that. So what? He comes every month, more or less. Why the panic?'

'Someone is trying to stitch Miller up.'

'And about time too, the hours he makes you work for nothing. What's it got to do with you ?'

'You know we have this grapevine, whereby all the shop managers let each other know where Mr Warman is? Well, somebody got it going around that he was coming to us yesterday. Miller spent the last three days working till midnight to make sure everything was all right and then Warman didn't come. I phoned his secretary on a pretext and found he's at a conference all this week. Somebody is trying to make Miller crack up.'

'Serves the bastard right. He's doing the same to you.'

The last thing Barny wanted was to concern himself with the cut-throat duplicity of over-promoted counter-jumpers. That was quite good, he thought to himself.

'They're nothing but a bunch of over-promoted counter-jumpers,' he said, 'None of them has half the brains you have.'

'Miller had a nervous breakdown last year when he was in charge of a big store in Devon. Warman came and bawled him out in front of the assistant manager and staff managers. He cracked up. Had six months off sick and was demoted to one of the smallest stores in the region.'

'So what's his problem? He must be on thirty-thousand a year, and no worries.'

'More like thirty-five.'

Barny whistled. 'That's nearly seven hundred quid a week, and he begrudges people in the store taking eighty for what's virtually a full-time job. Pack it in,' he said. 'It's never worth it.'

'I can't,' she wailed. 'I need the money. And if I gave it up voluntarily I couldn't even claim unemployment benefit. I'd have nothing.'

'Look,' he said. 'you don't have to be a slave. No company has the right to destroy people, and they couldn't do it unless people were willing to be destroyed. I can keep you until you find something else.'

'You don't understand,' she said. 'I want to succeed. I want to be something. Do something with my life. The firm has big plans for this area. They plan to build a new superstore for Simon Sweeting's development at Penavon, and I can be the staff manager. Warman said the job is mine if the local authority grants planning permission.'

He had it then, another premonition, terrifying in its absurd uncertainty. There was a path to death here, not life. Somewhere there was death in this. The vision was as clear as the blue skies over his head, but so fleeting that he had not assimilated the images, for they were subliminal in their transience. He was alarmed by what he had almost seen.

'That's fine,' he said. 'As long as you remember that it's your own life, not theirs.'

He tried to recall the vision but it eluded his memory like a faded dream. It was gone. He began to doubt that the thought had even flashed through his mind. 'Don't let them destroy you,' he said.

The training course was to be held at the company's residential centre in a converted country house in Berkshire. It was over five days, meaning that she would travel up to attend the course from Monday to Friday and spend a weekend with her children while she was up there at the company's expense, staying six nights away.

On the day before she left, he took her to the beach, swam briefly in the still-cold sea, lay in the sun and returned home as it was setting. She had been relaxed and contented all day, it seemed, not mentioning the prospect of being under critical scrutiny for the duration of the course. They prepared a meal together and sat, as in the beginning, on the old sofa, cuddling and rousing each other. He was gratified that her enthusiasm for lovemaking had not been permanently retarded and, although the bogey men came lurking he was able to beat them off with words of assurance and love.

He took her to the station and saw her aboard the train with her suitcases and kissed her goodbye as she said, 'I don't want to go,' with a tremble of fear in her voice. 'I hate hotels.'

'Phone me when you get there,' he told her. 'Let me know how you are. I'll wait at home for your call.'

Every day there was a letter for him. He had never received such declarations of love and desire, and there was also a greater self-awareness than he had expected.

...Day one, and I want to come home. It is really strange here. I look at some of the 'successful' women and feel relieved that I failed. (What did she mean by that?). I am not like them, They are glamorous, confident, ruthless, hard and totally committed to the company. Many of them are divorced. In a way I am sad that I can not share the same confidence and attractiveness, but when you actually listen to them, and see how unnatural their permed, dyed hair and piles of make-up are, then I'm reassured, because there's little depth or real value in them. I have to be cheerful, which is a strain because I hate the whole charade. Do you still love me? Do you still want me? I suppose being tired has left me feeling low and sad, and I get colic every day. I need one of your very special cuddles rather urgently... .

He wondered how long she could keep it up, and looked through the local papers for another job for her. There was nothing, as usual. He had seen the way such women as she had described finished their lives: bitter harridans, with their glamour vanished under the strain of competition, bullying all beneath them in attempting to regain their confidence before retiring each night to their elegant, lonely apartments and a bottle; unwanted, unknown beyond the company parameters. This was not for Louise, he hoped.

She did well on the course, she told him on her return, but the weekend with the children had not been successful. They did not seem to care whether she was there or not, although the little boy kept running to her for a cuddle with his thumb in his mouth. The little girl was distant, as she was, Louise's husband said, with everybody. They had discussed divorce, and, she said, he had agreed to one on the grounds of his unreasonable behaviour provided he had full custody and control of the children, with unlimited access for her. No maintenance on either side. It was exactly what she wanted, she said, and immediately broke down, crying, 'I've lost my babies.'

She was so distraught, really distraught this time, that Barny too was upset and summoned considerable self-control to stem the flood of his own tears. He was able to console her with assurances that she had not lost them. They were still there, still hers, to visit whenever she wished and later they could spend their holidays here. How they would love going to the cove, learning to swim, catching crabs in the pools.

'Did you miss me?' she enquired. 'I suspected you were looking forward to a week without me. I thought you were tiring of me.'

I was, he thought. Fed up, and exhausted by your continual emotional demands, glad to see the back of you for a while.

He told her, 'I was. I wanted some space on my own.'

Her face clouded with gloom before he could continue with: 'But I missed you from the first half hour. When I came home from putting you on the train, the house was dead without you and the nights were awful. I looked across the fields for the postman's van every morning, waiting for your letters. I shall keep them all.'

He had bundled them up in an elastic band and put them with the plait of shorn hair. He could not tell her he had taken this from its secret hiding place and slept with it on his pillow to clutch when the dreads engulfed him, breathing the lingering fragrance of her perfume.

'You've become such a part of me that I can no longer manage life without you,' he said, confessing his dependence.

'You'll never have to,' she sighed. 'I'll always be with you. I'll love you for ever.' Looking into his eyes with an incredulous frown. 'Will you love me for ever?'

'As long as you need me.'

As the result of her training course, Louise was awarded a higher grade, a rise in salary and, it seemed to Barny, even more responsibility at the store. She began complaining about her male colleagues, accusing them of inefficiency and discrimination against women. Her reading, on management procedure and feminism, increased to the extent that she read everything on the subjects in the local library and she bought books from a small shop specialising in esoteric literature. Barny looked through them now and then and said nothing, noting that her reading matter became concentrated on the role of women in history, religion, persecution of witches and then on the concept of God as female. His own concept of God, such as it was, was of an utterly genderless imponderable, and he would have enjoyed debating the implications with her, but could not, for she was not yet confident enough to argue without regarding his views as derogatory.

One evening, he had been dutifully listening to her account of some dispute in the store between the union, representing an employee, and the management. Louise's role in such cases was supposed to be impartial, not to take sides, merely to ensure that correct procedures were followed. There was no doubt, however, in Barny's mind, where the pressure came from, for her actual role, as was made abundantly clear, was to ensure that management did not screw up their case by default. Go by the book! Cover your ass!

'But I can't see,' she said, 'Why the unions are so opposed to us.'

Ah, Barny thought, what a revelation in the use of that 'us'.

'Well,' he said, 'can you see why the management are so opposed to the unions ?'

She could not. 'I assume,' she said, 'that it's just prejudice,' and Barny assumed she was evading the issue.

Perhaps he should have made a non-committal remark or changed the subject, instead of which he began thinking aloud, always a dangerous practice.

'I think it's more basic even than prejudice. It's the old class struggle continuing, the endeavours of the ruling establishment to maintain their power and of the working classes to grab a bit of the action. There's always opposition between the classes, whether they adopt fascism or communism. The ideology is irrelevant.'

'How can you say that?' she demanded. 'The desire for dominance or equality is ideology, whether between rich and poor or men and women. Feminism is ideology.'

'Is it now? As I see it, the only desire for equality has lain in the equality of wealth, money. Everybody wants something owned by someone else. I think the working classes are too blinkered to see that all the money in the world will never make them equal to the ineffable presumption, inherent in the upper classes, of their right to rule, to control the lives and minds of others. They *allow* themselves to be treated as inferior beings by their inferior behaviour, squandering their intelligence

240

and talent, which is exactly what's expected of them. Their only aim is to destroy those that they have been indoctrinated to regard as their superiors. Iconoclasts! And you feminists,' - this was the the first time he had referred to her as such - 'are just the same. You can never be men, or equal to men, so you try to destroy them instead of developing your womanhood. It's women who hold themselves in serfdom, just like the working classes.'

He expected a violent diatribe against his argument and was disappointed when she remained silent. He went to the window, irritated by her lack of defiance. Eventually, she said, 'What does 'ineffable' mean?'

He turned and gazed at her in exasperation. She had apparently not been listening to a word he said, and he realised that he would never be able to wrangle over ideas with her; she was too introspective.

'Ineffable,' he sighed at last, 'means a morbid fear of dirty words.'

The shop was open seven days a week and, while Louise rarely had to work on a Sunday, a full weekend off was not allowed. She could not perform the normal tasks of her job on Saturdays because head office, the job-centre and most other organisations involved with the recruitment and management of staff, were closed. Nevertheless, Miller insisted that she be there. 'If I have to do it,' he told her, 'why shouldn't you? You are management, the same as me.'

As far as her own work was concerned, it seemed a wasted day, she told Barny, 'Yet he insists that either I or the assistant manager is there all the time. Sometimes I think he can't cope on his own.'

'It's absurd,' he said. 'Why do you put up with it? Does the man have any idea how much you earn? How much your hourly rate is with all this extra time for no money?'

'It's expected of me.' she said. 'To show commitment to the company. What have you been doing today?'

'Louise,' he said, 'what's happening to you. The job is changing you. They are taking you over.'

'I'm merely acting the part, just as you told me. I have to sell myself.'

'You're giving yourself away,' he said. 'You don't know your own value.'

Barny saw her attitude as the beginning of total subservience to corporate identity, for she was beginning to believe in the creeds, trying to get noticed for future promotion by showing complete dedication to the company. 'Sometimes,' he said, 'you remind me of a child in school, trying to get gold stars to impress the teacher.'

'It's the only way to get on,' she said wistfully, as if she were but taking a reluctant step over a minor obstacle on the path to success yet, Barny noticed, in tacit agreement with his remark, like a child in school.

'There's nothing wrong in trying to get on,' he assured her. 'But you shouldn't believe all the crap they throw at you. Don't get brainwashed.'

He held her by the hands. 'What's happening to my lovely Loopy Loo? The one who was so passionate about the quality of life, the planet, conservation and Green politics as opposed to the exploitation of people by giant conglomerates. Where is she? Where is she going?'

Louise drew away from him. 'I'm still the same person,' she said. 'I still believe in those things. And if I get on, I can press Green issues from inside the company. It's important for people like me to achieve positions of authority.'

How high, he wondered, does she think she's going? How high do you have to get before your Green issues can influence pounds, shillings and pence? Well, pounds and p's, then?

'You want to be a real high-flyer, do you? he said, with a smile.

'Why not?' she demanded, defiantly.

'No reason, if that's what you want.'

'I do. But you want me to be weak and vulnerable, dependent on you. You don't like women to be strong and assertive. It threatens you.'

'Oh, I see.'

Maybe she was right. But he could not see why strong, assertive women should threaten him any more than strong, assertive men, of whom he had no fear. 'I would just like you to be yourself, that's all. I don't think this corporate identity is good for you, or anybody else for that matter. Just give them what they pay you for and then come home and forget the bloody job. None of the board of management are going to lie awake at night worrying about you if you crack yourself up with work and worry. It's only a fucking job, for Christ's sake!'

'I can't stand non-professionalism,' she said haughtily, while Barny wondered where the hell she had come across that bit of company jargon, 'and I wish you wouldn't swear.'

'Yeah, well, I'm sorry. It's the poet in me.'

At the height of the season, the company decided to reorganise the work rotas and three of their most experienced female staff left on the same day, saying they were unable to work the new split shifts suddenly imposed upon them, because they had family responsibilities which took precedence over their time. What they wrote, as 'reasons for leaving' on their termination papers, which Louise had to process, was 'To further my career' or 'For personal reasons' while what they said, to Louise, the manager, or anyone else who incurred their wrath, was that they were not going to be buggered around any longer, and that the company could 'get stuffed.'

One of these, a Mrs Jory, had been with the company seven years and practically ran her department as an unpaid supervisor. The other two were people whom Louise had recruited in the first days of her employment, and she was reprimanded for engaging unreliable personnel, with the insistent, 'You had better get replacements pretty damn quick', before pressure on the remaining staff induced more of them to leave.

'And,' she was told, 'don't employ any more dozy locals.'

Louise worried about it for days, refusing to accept that the company was at fault for arbitrarily changing the working hours, and censured herself for inefficiency. On the following Monday the assistant manager gave notice that he too was leaving, because the job was wrecking his marriage. The boss was furious, and she heard him on the phone to the regional director, swearing and denouncing the young man, who had been working sixty hours a week without a day off for three months. 'The bloody wimp. He's fucking useless. Can't stand the pace.'

'Why don't you pack it in too?' Barny asked. 'The place is a ruthless madhouse behind the façade of corporate benevolence they try to project. From what you tell me, they don't give a shit about any of their employees.'

'The regional director has offered me promotion,' she said.

'You'll be promoted to glory if you don't take care. They'll be the death of you.'

'I may have to go away.'

'Go away?'

He could not believe that she had said it, and looked at her with incredulity.

'What 'ee mean? Go away?' He uttered a hard, dry laugh. 'Go where ?'

'Nothing is definite,' she said.

Barny assumed that the offer of promotion and the promise of the job in the new store was nothing more that a ploy to induce her to work even harder, a promise of another gold star for 'A good effort. You can do better,' for she made no more mention of it.

Louise's divorce was made absolute at the end of summer, and she was then able to take a long weekend to visit her children and, now ex-husband. He was now involved with another woman, he told her with some satisfaction, and said that in future it would not be convenient for her to stay with him on her visits, which Louise interpreted as just another way of making access more difficult. She telephoned Barny each night, from a phone box in the street so that her husband could not hear the conversation, sounding desperately unhappy and fearful of some violence towards herself.

'I hate it up here,' she said. 'I can't wait to get back to you.'

Barny was gratified to hear that she still missed him during her absences, and met her at the station, watching the tall figure carrying a suitcase coming down the platform. Like, he thought, a fugitive from a disaster zone. She barely mentioned her weekend but asked him about events in his own life during her absence. How were Sam and Beth? His friends in town? When were they coming to do the roof?

'Langley is dead,' he told her. 'His body was found in the old mine.'

'Who is Langley?' she said.

'The agent. Simon Sweeting's agent. The one who disappeared last autumn.' Surely she knew that. 'It was on the local radio.' The radio told them even less that he had heard in the street and had merely confirmed the gossip.

'Did he fall into a mineshaft?'

'Seems like it. He was found at the bottom of the shaft where the collapse occurred, where my grandfather was killed. Their geologist went in there with a party of men, intending to clear the rubble jamming the shaft, so that they could get to the lower levels. Seems that Langley's body, or what was left of it, was lying on top of the debris.'

He also told her he had come to acknowledge that the bathroom and loo were a bit primitive, and that Steve and Joe were about to begin work on the renovation of the cottage, which pleased her. This meant the commitment of a mortgage to pay for it, which was worrying him a bit as he had sworn never to go into debt.

'We can manage,' Louise said. 'I'm earning a good salary now. And it will be a relief to you, not having to worry about the roof.'

'True. And it will be more convenient when the children come down. Did he agree to it ?'

'He said he wasn't sure.'

'He will be. He and his new girlfriend will be glad of a break from them now and then.'

September was a fine month. With most of the tourists gone, Louise's working hours were reduced and she even managed to get another whole

Saturday off. They spent two days down in the cove, soaking up the last of the summer sun. After the stress of the season, toward the end of which he had been unable to rouse her, she now seemed hungrier for him than ever. There had been something about the visit to her ex, it seemed, some reminder of how her life had improved, that had re-stimulated her passion for Barny and even while soaking up the sun on the beach, among the few remaining tourists, she kept touching him, lying so close that her thighs were brushing against him, saying, on one occasion, 'I want you now.' And he had laughed in delight at her impatient whisper, with her lips close to his ear, 'Will you fuck me tonight?'

'You haven't wanted much of me lately,' he said afterwards. 'I was afraid you were going off me.'

'I know. I've just been too tired. Sorry.'

When he lived alone, Barny thought, he slept for weeks without thinking much about making love, and years without doing it, but to lie in bed with Louise, wanting her when she seemed utterly indifferent to his presence, was a strain he could not endure indefinitely. He was physically unsatisfied now, but the release of his emotional desire for her was as fulfilling as a physical climax and he held her through the night, as in the past, content in the knowledge of her love for him.

'You are all woman again,' he murmured. 'You are wonderful.'

Sarah found it disconcerting to accept that her daughter had developed into almost exactly the person she had hoped for. She was proud of her, as her father must be, despite there being the impossibility of acknowledgement. It was only in the matter of religion that she gave Sarah cause for concern, for science, she believed, might well explain the wherefores but not the whys of our existence. However, Sarah had known others who had left the chapel only to return, and was sure that Katie would eventually come to accept the love of God and his creation as her family had done for generations, despite their sins. She could see her from the window, running up the street with her hair flying, and turned to her as she entered, breathless and distraught.

'Zeke has been arrested, Ma.'

'I know. The police have been here. They want to see you.'

'I went to see them. They are investigating Langley's death. They questioned me and have arrested Zeke on suspicion of murder.'

Sometimes, when her eyes flashed, or when she turned her lips in a cynical smile, Katie was so like her father in mannerisms that Sarah thought people must be blind not to see who she was. I s'pose, Sarah said to herself, I brought her up to be like 'n without knowing it. Well, there's plenty worse than he.

'What did they say, exactly?'

'He's being held for questioning. Fancy arresting Zeke. He wouldn't hurt a fly.'

Sarah smiled and then laughed, as she said, 'Can 'ee imagine it? Questioning Zeke? He'll drive them mad.'

CHAPTER THIRTEEN

Fros a eryow. A torrent of words.

'...and did you enjoy your job?'

'I worked hard in that shop, and came to realise that I was more intelligent than any of them. I discovered that Miller was almost illiterate and I had to correct all his letters: bad grammar, spelling mistakes, but the second manager, at the bigger store, was more educated and helpful and was keen to push me on. He set me projects to get me noticed by regional management.

Visiting directors started talking to me... what did I see my role becoming, where did I see myself in five years time, what problems were there in the current job? None, I said, the need for greater intellectual challenge was my priority. They made me feel important.

It was about this time that the manager of the larger store, Mr Brown, cracked up. He was a nice man, the only gentleman I've met in the whole hierarchy. I knew that Miller had suffered a nervous breakdown, but he was incompetent. To see Mr Brown go under put a strain on the whole shop. He was very efficient and worked hard, liked by everybody except Warman, who hated him. I think, now, that Warman saw him as a threat. He was always checking on him, always on his back. I remember one incident. Mr Brown had already been off sick for a month, suffering from stress, and only been back a week. It made me disgusted with the whole lot of them. There was a produce manager, a fresh fruit and vegetable specialist, fat man, full of bullshit, claimed to be Warman's best friend but was actually terrified of him, who came to the store for the day. He said Warman was 'on the region,' terrifying managers up and down the area; no telling where he'd turn up next. We phoned all the other shops, trying to find out where he was. No one had seen him, so we thought he must be coming to see us to twist the knife in again. It should have been a normal working day for me, leave home at seven, an hour in the train, finish at six, get home at seven thirty but, because Warman was coming, I stayed on to support Mr Brown and stop Warman from bullying him. Mr Brown was busting a gut ensuring that everything was right in the shop, screwed up with tension and strain. I stayed until closing time, and Warman never showed up. I'd missed the last train and Mr Brown told me off, after I'd tried to help him. The produce manager offered to take me home and I thought that was very generous, it was forty miles, but on the way he tried to chat me up, asking about my 'elderly grey-thatch' meaning Barny. He said that Warman had gone on holiday. There was no way he could have visited the shop that day. It was the same ploy they'd used on Miller to crack him, he said, when he was past his sell-by date. He was laughing at Mr Brown. He said the company sorted the men from the boys, implying that he was a man and Mr Brown a boy. I was furious, arrived home at ten o' clock and had a row with Barny, who said I'd sold my soul to the company store.

I didn't tell him that the company had finally recognised my ability and potential. The regional director himself had told me that my efficiency had already been noticed by visiting directors from head office and, if I played my cards right, the sky was the limit for me. The next step was a temporary position in the largest store in the area, to sort out the mess left by an incompetent predecessor, a spell setting things up in the new store at Simon Sweeting's development, and then to go for the top with an application for a job in head office myself.

The regional director and I had a long discussion in which I stated my ambition and told him something of my private life. By this time, he treated me differently from other senior members of staff, and said that as a skilled manager he utilised different techniques to motivate different individuals. People like Miller required pushing, and only functioned efficiently under pressure, like little squirts. I could see some truth in this and, although I would never mention such a thing, I was now fully aware of that individual's shortcomings.

Mr Warman asked me about Barny and his prospects, and, while I did my best to present him in a favourable light, I could see that Mr Warman was not impressed. Barny was poor, with no future, and was so much older than me that sooner or later he would become a burden to me. I went so far as to say that Barny wished me to resign from the company, and Mr Warman laughed.

'What does he expect you to do?' he said. 'Hang around while he writes his fucking nursery rhymes? Take him cups of tea for Christ's sake?'

I always considered it a compliment that Mr Warman felt sufficiently at ease with me to be totally uninhibited in his speech.

I recognised, even then, that I was torn between the alternatives. The career prospects were what I had always dreamed of, available to me at last, and I could find fulfilment in becoming committed to the company in a way that Barny would find reprehensible. My love for Barny was undiminished, although it had changed. In staying with him I could find the emotional contentment that no one else had ever given me, and he loved me more that I had ever dreamed any one would: I knew that, yet I felt that the very intensity of our love was restricting me. While I was with him, I would never develop as an individual, for we were beginning to function as a dual entity, always dependent on each other, and this frightened me. I felt that his strong personality was undermining mine, that he was trying to mould me according to some preconceived notion of what *he* thought I should be. All my life I had been obliged to conform to the wishes of others, and I wanted my own space. If I came to see him as restricting my development I would begin to resent him, and he was too important to me to allow that to happen. It was all very confusing.

It was the regional director who said I should apply for a job in head office whenever I felt ready. He promised quick promotion, an interesting job, pleasant working conditions, more responsibility and more money, away from the stress of the retail side of things. The sky was the limit for people of my calibre, he said. It sounded like utopia, from which only Barny was holding me back. And I destroyed him. It was me. I killed him!.'

The fine weather lasted for weeks, right into October, with a light easterly breeze and, at night under the clear starlit sky, they could hear the call of the migrating redwings coming in off the sea from Iceland. The bracken turned to bronze, then copper in the evening light. Barny gathered the last of the summer crops, dried the onions, froze the beans, turned the ground, made blackberry wine. They almost forgot the sound of the foghorn, although, as autumn progressed, the valleys were sometimes obscured by ethereal mists which dampened the grass and fairy rings of mushrooms in the fields.

With more free time, Louise began reading again, nearly all feminist stuff, he noticed, and still more on women in industry and business. He ignored it and sat at his desk as usual, writing every day.

She said, 'Have you always been a poet?'

The question startled him in its alacrity; they had not discussed his work for some time and he wondered what thoughts in her mind had induced this precipitate question.

'No.' he said. 'Not always. Well, perhaps I was. It's difficult to know.'

'When did you begin writing ?'

'About ten years ago. I don't think that has anything to do with it. The two are not synonymous.'

He looked at her. She was not really interested, he thought, just pretending, for the betterment of concord in their relationship.

'Steve Trevorrow and I became poets when we were children, he collecting Saturday pennies from his grandmother, or watching his mother count fish, and me collecting horse-shit from the streets for my great-aunt's garden.'

He smiled in reminiscence. 'I used to see Sammy's father riding his cart horses... . It was another world, he said, *'Yn termyn ys passyas.'* He smiled at her, and translated. '...In times gone by.'

On Saturdays, they had their Saturday pennies, money of their own to spend on marbles and clidgey nicey in No-Cocky's shop. Some had to work for their Saturday pennies, others got them for nothing, but they all had them, their precious Saturday pennies, although some had only one between two, for the thirties were hard times, while Tim usually had a tanner which he shared with the others. Some were given the money and told to git out and stay out, for their cottages were too small for all hands to be home at once unless some of them were in the bed.

Steve earned his pennies by running errands. He fetched the shopping for his mother and granny. The trouble with Steve's mother was that she was absent-minded. She forgot things, so that he would have to go down twice to the same street or the same shop. 'Look,' he told her, 'you ought to have a *list*, a proper *list*.' But her mind was far away, over a distant ocean where men were striving to kill each other.

'What I ought to do, and what I do do, is two deffernt things,' as she rummaged absently in her purse with fingers wet from the washing board dripping bubbles on the coins.

'Now here, run over to Jan Biscay's for a quarter of cream for your mawther.'

On some Saturdays it was ten or eleven o'clock before the errands were done and they were all gathered under the arches of the old quay to count the money. Some could get out to play early, for they didn't run errands but merely went from one relation to the other, saying, 'I've come for my Saturday's penny.' Steve couldn't do that. Not just tell them he had come for his money, take it and go. With each, there was a ritual of greeting that never varied. With his Granny it was: 'Now hark, how's your mawther? Has she heard from your fehther?' and 'Will 'ee have a mo'ssle of bread?'

'No, thank you.'

'A bit of nicey?'

'Well, iss, you mind to.'

'You should say "Yes please".'

And she would lavish wet kisses on his cheeks, engulfing him in the folds of her cotton pinafore, exclaiming 'My flute! My flute an' arrow,'

Later, after the telegram, she might say, 'And wheer's your fehther now, my cheeld?'

'In heaven,' Steve told her.

'That's right, my 'ansome, in heaven.' As she went about the kitchen chores with her old head shaking and her wet cheeks wobbling, with all hope of the future now invested in the only son of her only son. 'In Heaven.'

Barny's mother, on the other hand, was too efficient to have many chores for the boy to do, so he went to his old aunt who lived in one of the few houses in the jumble of down'long cottages to have a garden, and it was in this sheltered courtyard that Barny became a poet. It was surrounded by houses on three sides, and on the north by a natural bluff of rock which shielded it from all the winds, and there was never a frost so close to the sea. His aunt's plants were grown in a series of tubs and pots, old earthenware sinks, chimney pots and low retaining walls around the cobbles. From the imported soil of these receptacles grew geraniums, fuchsias and nasturtiums in profusion. They covered the walls with fiery explosions of colour throughout the summer and spread in an annual surge over the roof of the linney, which was part the court, covered in a scantle-slated roof.

In winter, the sun was too low to reach the cobbles and struck its warmth only on to the face of the blue-grey cliff of stone, part of the great Carn Glaze which once shielded and dominated the natural cove which is now the harbour. This same Carn Glaze which still thrusts, here and there, a spur or shoulder through the streets and walls of down'long, bearing in its crystals the legend of the Celtic Silures which proclaims, 'I am five hundred million years of age.'

As the winters of Barny's *flogholeth* passed into his tremulous springs, and the sun rose higher and dropped its beams like a lever balanced on the fulcrum of the red-ridged roof, the warming light crept daily lower, down the face of Carn Glaze until one day, *yn termin us passyas*, the first shaft of light shot beneath the ovice and launders of the linney.

For a while, only a day or two each spring and autumn, there would be, at midday, a plane of light like a sheet of yellow glittering glass sloping down through the dark shadows under the overhanging roof. The boy would walk beneath this magic thing, ducking his head to avoid piercing the even flow of wondrous glittering dust and particles of pure golden colour planing through the gloom and shadows of the linney. And, after bringing his eyes closer to this marvel he would slip his hand through the solid light, flicking it with his fingers, or rise through it, standing with the sun a circle, a pierced membrane, around his waist, swirling with both hands the particles of sun-dust all about him, warming him as he swirled the light to the dark corners of the linney, scooping the coming summer with both his hands.

As the sun rose with the advancing spring, the back of the linney was in shadow again, and the gear of his grandfather's calling lay, as it had lain for years, gathering dust in his memory. There were odd bits of tackle and rope, a gurrie, a tanned mizzen sail draped over a folded net hanging from a spar lashed to the rafters. Nets gone rotten. 'They've lost their nature.' 'Sell them? Who d' want nets now? Edn no herrin'. There's no herring now.' A couple of oars lashed to the wall, cork bu'ys, and a dan lamp, the black balsh rope of their lashing hard and brittle with age. Here was his Granny's cast-iron mangle, and her wash-tub and flasket hanging on the wall. Stood out of the way, under tables and on shelves, there were chests and boxes of ancient artefacts, the jetsam of a life-time, bits of clocks, button hooks, fine bone net-needles fashioned by hands so long since dead, an ivory-handled pocket-knife with hard steel blades still sharp, and, permeating all, the smell of nets and pickled ropes, and the lubrication of blocks and tackle, fish oil and tanning... bark, they called it, bark, from the oak trees, don't 'ee know.

'Do the arrants? Why they're all done, you. But you can go out to the Island if you mind to, for a bucket of earth for the garden.'

Barny didn't mind fetching earth from the Island, but when the fish had been landed and taken to the wharf in carts his aunt might send him out with a bucket and shovel to collect the piles of dung, wet and steaming, from the cobbled streets. And the other kids would laugh, crying 'Tit tit tit, pickin' up shit. Ha ha ha.' His aunt would look at it and know which horse it came from.

'Don't want any of Matt Pearce's,' she would tell him. 'Nawthen but straw. He don't feed them proper. Dicky's hosses are the best, cus he d' take them out to the fields.' With a sidelong glance at the child. 'But he's a terrible man, my cheeld.'

'He d' swear,' Barny said.

'Terrible!'

Although she preferred horse dung, as long as it wasn't from Matt Pearce's skinny nag, sometimes, when she had been making marios perhaps, she would bury a bucket of fish guts in the garden as well as the horse shit, and the boy would wonder how the plants made such lovely smells from all this pong.

Matt had a little wagon which he loaded with fruit and vegetables and took from door to door, walking at the head of his pony with his peculiar rolling gait caused by one leg being considerably shorter than the other. He was a little man, with sharp features accentuated by the peak of his shabby cloth cap, and his trousers and jackets were invariably several sizes too large, so they hung loosely from his bony frame as if from a hook behind a door. A cigarette, sometimes lit but as like as not cold and stained with saliva from his mouth, hung from his bottom lip, jerking spasmodically when he spoke to the women at their doors or, leading his pony by the reins, he announced his presence with a shrill consumptive cry. Haa...ples, rooo...ties, cabbage, laa...tice, ripe tomaaa...ties.

And the women used to stand by his cart for a while, gossiping in the broad, musical dialect, that they never knew they had, before returning to their cottages with earthy vegetables held in the folds of their pinafores, as if they had all the time in the world and as if this way of life would go on forever.

The horses were busy when the fish were landed, and, on dull November days when the herring came back in the days of the war, they would be hitched to the shafts of two-wheeled carts and driven up to their bellies in the sea. They were taken alongside the gigs and luggers where baskets of the previous night's catch were heaved overboard and brought ashore to be counted. As the carts took the weight, the wheels sank into the sand, and as the horses waited patiently for the carts to be loaded they shifted their hooves from time to time as they too sank, and the water swirled with clouds of sand in the ebbing tide. Then, with a 'Yik' and 'Yeah' and a 'Heaaaagh heeaaagh', the carters flicked their reins and the great horses leaned their weight against the harness and pulled the heavy loads to the slipway, dripping water, and gathering speed when the wheels reached solid ground.

'Heaaaagh! Come on, come on.' And the voice of Sammy's da, Dicky-drive-'osses, the mad bugger, above them all, 'Yik! Come on, you sods. Gitup! Yeeh Yeeh.'

The carts were unloaded on the wharf, the fish prepared for the women to count, and as the hosses waited they often dropped their dung, and if Barny's aunt saw it he would be sent down there with a bucket and shovel.

'Nawthen to be asheamed of in that, you. Goest on with thee.'

Sitting beside the gurries, the women picked up the herring and put them in baskets, counting and gossiping simultaneously, while the old mothers kept tally in a book. All along the wharf, when Steve was a little boy, every boat had its place and, among the continuous scatter of boxes, baskets, barrels, gurries, horses, carters, lorries, buyers, onlookers, idlers and children come to watch, the wives and crew from every boat counted out the catch in scores. Six score made a hundred, eight hundred in a gurrie, with every fish counted and, at every twenty, the cry of 'Score!' sang out, so that amid the bustling and clatter, the clop of hooves and the grating of ironbound wheels, there was the continuous chorus of, 'Score! Score, Ma!' And Ma made another mark in her book. One score, two, three, four, five, and six, with a line drawn through to mark the hundred. Six score to a hundred, eight hundred to a gurrie, and you can count them, weigh them, measure them, do what the hell you like with them, and it's always to the buyer's advantage. And an omer is the tenth part of an ephah, don't forget!

And when Steve was really small, before Willy Lawry told young Uncle Joe he was an idiot and that Jesus was not real, he used to play with pieces of ice spilled from boxes being opened in the road, or stand at his mother's side as she sat on a barrel counting fish. The scales of herring are readily shed and were everywhere when the fish had been landed by Dicky-drive-'osses in his cart. They were on the boy's hands and face, the boxes and baskets, the sou'westers and barwells of the men and on the cobbles of the wharf. And when the haze of the winter mornings cleared from the eastern shore, the scales around the harbour sparkled with translucent fire, as if the scene had been scattered with sequins and tinsel.

Young Steve saw the sunlight catching the women's hands, chapped and split to the quick as they dipped again and again into the thousands of cold fish and, as he stood there at her side, he saw the accumulated scales on his mother's fingers and wrists twinkling with opalescent light, encrusting her hands in pearls.

When the fish were all counted, they had to be loaded back onto the carts and taken to the railway station, but they had lorries to do most of that before long and, were it not for the fear of getting them stuck in the sand, they would have used lorries to bring the fish ashore from the boats too, and Dicky-drive-'osses had no doubt that the days of the carters were numbered. He and his family had been carters forever, and while there had been fish to pull, they had pulled them, as they had pulled broccla from the farms, granite and blue elvan from the quarries, tin and copper from the mines, and any other mortal thing that needed pulling from one place to another.

And when the loads were heavy, they hitched up two, four, or even six horses and had gangs of men pushing and shoving to get them up Tregenna Hill, laying sand to catch the slime dripping from rays and skates, with the waggoners garmin' and blaytin', 'yey! yey, yey, Sheilah! Giddup Duke. Come o... on, you sods.'

Barny was afraid of Dicky-drive-'osses, even though he was Sammy's da, and after the work was done would watch in silence as Sheila and Duke were led away to their stables with Dicky-drive-'osses talking more softly to them than he ever did to his brood of children. He would water them, feed them, brush them down, put them in the stable and go to the Sheaf of Wheat. On Saturdays, when his boy, Sammy, and Steve and Barny and they, were collecting their Saturday pennies, Dicky-drive-'osses used to go out to the railway station with a clean trap to collect the luggage of the gentry staying at the big hotel outside the town. He loaded their suitcases and leather hatboxes into his trap, listening to their raucous English voices and the accents he had obeyed through fear and hatred after suffering Field Punishment Number One for dumb insubordination.

As a disillusioned, under-aged volunteer, when his polished leggings were up to the knees in the guts of horses and men in the mud of the Somme, he had looked at one of them with condemnation. So they had tied him to the wheel of a field gun during a bombardment. Two days, with only water and noise, and a trouserful of his own shit. And he would take their tips on Saturdays and go into the Sheaf of Wheat and drink silently in the corner. Dicky-drive-'osses had seen things that men had done to each other and to their horses and, sometimes, while burying shreds of flesh, he had not been sure which was which. He would drink lots of beer and then walk from the pub to the stables with a wild look in his eye which meant that he loved his horses more than he loved his fellow men, and his fellow men avoided his eye and gave him room to pass. He would mount his gelding, Duke, or his mare, Sheila, and ride them out to the fields, galloping like a madman, cracking his whip over people's heads and swearing terrible: 'Eeyaah. Yeeh! Out of the way, you bleddy sods. Out of the way!'

When the boys saw him go galloping, whipcracking, swearing by, and he had loads of beer aboard, they hid behind the gate and then went to play in the cart-shed where there was a wagon, two carts, a trap, a hearse with its magnificent brass carriage lamps and, best of all, a horse-drawn, hand pumped, fire engine. The cart-shed was behind the cottages in the Stennack where he lived. The cottages are nearly all gone now but all up the Stennack, in those days, *Yn termyn ys passyas*, there were rows of miners' cottages. It's strange, how the fishermen lived in clusters, while the miners lived in rows: short rows, of four or six small dwellings with two rooms downstairs and two up. The best of them had a scullery over the Stennack river, from whence everything dropped into the water and was carried away down the valley to the sea. They nearly all had a water tap, mind; they were quite modern for their day, and a shallow clome sink with a brownish-yellow glaze which was to become an art form in the future, further up stream, in the pottery.

In places the Stennack was so narrow that only one vehicle could get by at a time but then, when it took half an hour to get to Hellesveor, a few minutes' wait was neither here nor there. It was only when the motor car enabled people to get up there in three minutes that speed became imperative and the drivers so impatient that the cottages came down, one by one, stone by stone, memory by memory. Ma Jennings, who lived in one of the cottages, was mazed as a gurgy, couldn't understand it, but realised one of her life's ambitions when she bought a fur coat with all of her compensation money and wore it day in, day out, for what remained of the rest of her life.

Dicky-drive-'osses had a hand-driven hair clipper, which he used on the horses to cut their coats, trimming them up smartly to match the polished brass on the harnesses. The clipper stood on a tall portable stand and was worked by a flexible drive driven by turning a handle on the stand, which made it difficult for one man to use: he couldn't wind and clip too, don't 'ee see? And when Dicky was trying to clip the horses on his own, he used a vocabulary that the boys at first thought was German, 'Goddammenblast thesoddenthing', and they kept out of his way.

At first the clipper was a fascinating piece of machinery. It made a soft whirring noise which rose in pitch the faster it was turned and the boys longed to have a go: to turn it round and round and listen to the whirr. But later, when they were big enough to turn the thing properly, Dicky would make Sammy, and Barny, or anybody else who happened to be handy, wind it until their arms were aching and curse them when they tired and wound too slow. So, when they heard the clippers they crept out past the stables, unseen, and, knowing that Sammy's old man would be busy for an hour or two, went to play in the hearse.

When they played in the hearse, they could hear him coming, and they kept quiet until the hoof beats died away. Then they took the long whip from its tubular holder on the side of the hearse and cracked it over the heads of imaginary horses pulling the whole gang of them on wild journeys through injun country with smuggled brandy for the cossack sultan. And, after Steve's mother told him yet another war had started, they shot lots of Germans with their bows and arrows for what they had done to Sammy's da, Dicky-drive-'osses, being ignorant of irresponsible British staff officers in the War to end Wars which ended just a few years before they were born.

Lots of kids lived near Sammy, and they were all in gangs. But only Sammy's gang played in the hearse, because the hearse was Sammy's old man's and Sammy was chief of his gang. The gangs had fights and bobbed tubbins at each other, which made everybody beastly dirty, caggled in earth and grass, but they only used stones in serious fights, between up'long and down'long. The kids who lived at the top of the Stennack reckoned Sammy and Barny were down'long kids, and those who lived below the market place reckoned they were up'long kids, so they had a brea many fights, one way and another. However, none of the other gangs played in the cart-shed or the stables or the hearse, because they were afraid of Dicky'-drive-'osses who used to crack his whip over their heads and gallop up the Stennack, swearing like buggery.

The child, Barny told Louise, is the father of the man and the poet.

He saw the two policemen sat in their car at the top of the quay, and thought nothing of it. One of them was Richard, the son of Sam-the-taxi-man, who was the son of Dicky-drive-'osses, the other a plainclothes, CID, or whatever they are. He decided to go down and wait for Joe and Steve and Boy Steve to come ashore. It didn't seem much of a catch they were landing. He wondered how much there would be to share out among the three of them. Not a lot, by the look of it.

The sand bank at the harbour mouth was accumulating all the time. There was now only a narrow channel, close to the quay, to be negotiated at half tide or less. A few feet out and they were ashore on the bank, too close and they hit the granite quoins of the quay. Below half tide the harbour was inaccessible, with all the boats aground. It was becoming a dangerous entrance, though not as bad as the bar across the bay. Simon Sweeting's yacht was anchored outside. Perhaps the cops were there to look after him following the threats. No chance of him risking his paintwork by coming in here, much less crossing the bar. Marina, he thought. Some hopes.

They landed their fish, moored up, and came ashore in the skiff. Barny met them at the top of the quay steps. They looked tired, but not from physical effort, he discovered. They had caught their quota and were allowed to land no more.

'We were throwing them overboard,' Steve said. 'A boatload of prime cod. Only kept the rubbish. That's all we're allowed to land.'

'At least you had fine weather,' Barny said.

'Too damned fine,' Joe said. He was in a bad mood, something unusual in Joe.

'What do you mean? How can it be too fine?'

'He'll take something big to shift this high pressure,' Joe said, 'We'll have a blow dreckly, you wait. How's your fehther?

'A1, really, considering his age.'

'Seen Anne, lately?'

'No.'

'She's a good old maid.' Joe said.

Barny resisted the desire to look into Joe's eyes. What was he saying?

'Mr Trevorrow?' the plainclothes man said. 'Mr Steven Trevorrow?'

'ess.'

'We'd like you to come with us, if you wouldn't mind.'

Boy Steve said, 'What you ben up to 'en, fehther?'

The constable, son of Sam-the-taxi-man, said, 'The other one, sir.'

'We'd like you to come up to the station and answer a few questions, sir,' the inspector said to Joe.

'You don't have to call me "sir",' Joe said. 'I was a working man myself, once,'

'This one,' Sam's boy, Richard, said. 'He's the Steven Trevorrow you want.'

'Wus this all about?' Boy Steve said.

'Just a few routine questions, sir,'

'What about?'

'Just step into the car,' the plainclothes man said. 'We don't want any trouble.'

Joe said, 'Have 'ee got a 'rest warrant?'

'Kindly keep out of this, sir,' the inspector said.

Sam-the-taxi-man's boy said, 'Best to come with us, Ste' Boy, make 'n easier for 'ee.'

'Now?'

'Right now, sir.'

'As I am?' Boy Steve said. 'Can't I even go home and change my clothes?'

'Just as you are, sir.'

Boy Steve looked at his father and shrugged before walking up the quay to the car, with one policemen on either side of him and his father and Barny and Joe following close behind. They were seen by half the town as pedestrians all along the harbour stopped their perambulations to watch the procession.

Steve's boy waited while Sam's boy opened the car door and the inspector said 'Get in the car, sir.' Then, Boy Steve climbed in, to be followed by the inspector whose smart suit was thereby smeared in fish slime and scales left on the upholstery from Boy Steve's waterproofs.

'What ever you say, constable,' Boy Steve said.

'I'd better go home and tell Mary,' Steve said.

'Tell her not to worry,' Joe said. 'I spect it's all over nothen.'

Richard, the young police constable, came round the back of the car before getting into the driver's seat. 'Don't worry, Steve,' he said. 'Nothen to do with the boy. They've done a post-mortem on David Langley's body. He's been murdered.'

'But what has it got to do with Boy Steve?

'They say,' Anne said, 'that he threatened to kill Langley. They had a fight over Katie Stevens.'

'Who said so?'

'The people down at the restaurant and the geologist, Thorpe.'

'What's the latest about Langley, Joe? Any news?'

'No,' Joe said. 'Nothen.'

Steve said, 'They keep taking the boy in for questioning. He's "not been eliminated from their enquiries". They say Simon Sweeting's putting pressure on for his arrest. Demanding results.'

'What's the news about all the developments?'

'Nothing at all.'

'Perhaps he's trying to find a new agent.'

'There's plenty more where Langley came from,' Joe muttered. 'The likes of he are ten-a-penny, up London.'

'Why don't they come and do the roof ? Louise asked.

'They're worried about the weather,' Barny said, gazing about him under a cloudless sky over the garden. 'Steve said he thinks there's a storm coming. The area of high pressure is so well settled that it will only be moved by a very deep depression. Come and look at the camellia, I think it's developing flower buds. Too early to tell for certain.'

'They've had all summer.' Louise protested,' to do the roof. Why wait so long?'

'Steve and Joe are busy in the summer. There's no hurry.'

'It's very inconvenient,' she grumbled, 'having to go down to that freezing loo at night in the cold, and there's hardly room to undress in the bathroom. I hope we don't have to put up with it for another winter. Can't you get another builder?'

'No. Steve'll do it when he's ready. All in good time.'

After so many years, he thought, there's no rush for a few more weeks. 'The last thing we want is a storm when the roof is off, with buckets of rain pouring in. It would ruin all our books.'

'I hope the existing roof withstands the storm,' she said. 'Why do you people always procrastinate?'

'We don't. It makes you go blind.'

'I wish you wouldn't be so frivolous. If there was any damage, you could claim off your friend's public liability insurance.'

'Yeah. That's right. So I could.'

While they were arguing, the depression began as a tropical storm, a whirling vortex that drew millions of gallons of Caribbean sea-water high into the air while the last of the summer tourists were enjoying the warm sunshine in the still October air of the town's sheltered harbour.

'It's going to be a bugger,' Joe said. 'Be a brea thing here dreckly.' He was looking at the boats lying quietly at their moorings. 'Time they were heaved up out of it.'

It was the same every year, boats left out too long and then smashed up in the first of the autumn storms. 'You can't teach them nothen,' Steve said. 'They never learn.'

'True,' Joe agreed. 'I've taught them all I knaw, and they still don't knaw nothen.'

The three of them, Joe, Steve, and Boy Steve, decided to make one more trip to sea before the storm came, for there were large shoals of bass north of the islands and the price was high. They could gross as much as two thousand pounds if they struck them right. Joe had his doubts, but Boy Steve pointed out that the forecast was fine for the next few hours, with the wind slowly veering southerly, just what they needed to fish in the lee of the islands. With plenty of warning from the forecast, and a fast boat, there was nothing to worry about. This, Steve thought, was what they had spent all that money for, and the decision was up to Boy Steve, for he was the Capm, now.

Boy Steve, Joe admitted, had more enthusiasm than his father, was more ambitious, but with less of his caution, and took risks, as he was about to do now, because of financial necessity. Well, not risks exactly, he just had more faith in his boat and the gear, although there had been times when, if the decision had been Joe's, they would have stayed ashore. 'Life,' he said, 'is only one time round, my flute.'

When they did put to sea, early in the morning, the weather was fine. As they left the harbour with the ebbing tide, high cirrus veiled the sun, a warm southerly blew lightly off the land, and the sea was flat and green with a slight mist pouring out from the estuary across the bay. Joe looked about him, saw the beautiful morning, the sleek lines of Sweeting's yacht lying in the shallows, and old Baragwaneth, leaning on his stick, on the end of the quay.

Barny's father was an early riser. He had come down for a breath of fresh air while waiting for the shops to open. He wanted a bit of fine twine to finish the rigging on his model of the *Ebeneezer* and rued the changing times when even the fishermen's co-op no longer sold skilliven, when everything was plastic, even the twine, and they did not open until half past eight. 'Half the damn day's gone,' he said to himself as he watched Boy Steve in the wheelhouse steer the *Morwennol* around the quay head.

On deck, Joe caught father Steve's eye, and jerked his head to shore. 'Look who's up theer.'

Steve looked up to the receding quay, waved his arm, and the old man raised his stick in farewell. 'Good luck to 'ee.'

'Gone mad,' Steve grinned, receiving the old man's thoughts, 'to go out in this weather.'

Joe too, waved his arm in brief acknowledgement, turned his eyes to the southern sky and breathed a resigned sigh. In Old Baragwaneth's time they would have taken all day to reach the grounds Boy Steve could get to in four-hours steaming, and they had no wireless, radar or satellite weather forecasts. On a day like this, with the mercury falling through the bottom of the barometer, they would have read the skies and gone back to bed. Joe leaned against the wheelhouse in the sun, rolled a fag, thanking God there were always men like Old Baragwaneth and Boy Steve to go aboard the lifeboat, and tourists to put money in the model up in her house.

Barny's father, up on the quay, watched them pass, looking at all the gear aboard, trying to figure out what it was all for. They used to be religious, trusting in the Lord. Now, they relied more on their engines and gear, believing them infallible. He recognised the canister on the wheelhouse roof, which contained an automatically inflatable life-raft. Never had no such thing in our day, it was all hands aboard the skiff and heave ho and bail her out. He remembered their day, when there were more fish than ever they could catch, if only they could find them. And he remembered their night, that one night, when the German U-boats and aeroplanes had attacked the convoy twenty miles away to the no'thard and they had gone out theer to lend a hand.

They gave him another wave and Boy Steve opened her up, full speed ahead.

Terrible. What they had seen that night. Terrible! It was a dark, drizzly night, the sea calm, like this, a bit of a swell, but nothen to spake of. They steamed out there, towards what there was, the explosions and the fire, and the sinking ships, and they could hear the aeroplane circling overhead and the bugger dropped a bomb right 'longside them. The spray came over the starboard side. They cut the engine, so there would be no wake to be seen, and covered the white decks with the brown, tanned mizzen sails and drifted among the flotsam and the smell of oil and the corpses floating on the dark, calm sea, and all aboard put their hands one to the other and said, 'God by 'ee, brother', as they waited to be found and blawed to bits like they in the say around them as the droning plane went round and round like a Tom-Harry bird searching for dulkins, invisible and malevolent, dropping bombs around them from the black sky illuminated on the horizon with brilliant explosions from the direction of the convoy before his fuel gauge told the Jerry it was time to head for France and write a letter to his family in Dresden.

He wouldn't have done it, Barny's father thought as he remembered the horrible things they had brought ashore that night. He wouldn't have done it, if he'd a-knawed we was a lifeboat.

As Steve and they steamed out past the head, he turned to walk up the quay, and was obliged to heave to for a minute and hang on to the railing at the top of the steps. The bleddy pain of it all, he thought, as he put the little white pill of nitro-glycerin under his tongue, d' give 'ee hell sometimes.

And all hands aboard had agreed: they ashore should never knaw nothen about it. They would never tell their women. And the little cheldern should never learn of such terrible things: bits, just bits, floating on the say like rubby dubby.

While Old Baragwaneth, then young, had slept away the horrors of the night on the following day, the little children, from whom these horrors were to be kept, were going along the beach. Barny, sent out of the house to let his father sleep in peace, Steve, Mary Trenowden, Young Uncle Joe, Shimshai - he was there, of course - and Jeanie the 'vacuee, all skimming flat stones across the surface and kicking over the seaweed in search of treasure.

Jeanie found a treasure in the fronds of kelp, an unknown object which she turned over with the point of her shoe. It was a white, wrinkled thing among the seaweed and shells washed by the foam-flecked sea. It was a shrivelled, shapeless thing, like a piece of octopus or squid. A wrinkled, parboiled thing with branches and a broad, thick trunk.

'What's this, then?' Jeanie asked, in her broad Cockney accent, turning again the unrecognised object with the point of her shoe, fearful and apprehensive, yet wishing to know all of the wonders in her new surroundings by the sea.

They came to her, formed a circle and turned the thing over, once again on the point of a shoe, to see it from all sides, that there might be no mistake in its identification. They looked at it in silence, in the knowledge of what they were seeing, but unwilling to communicate that shared knowledge among themselves until, to break the timorous silence, Barny spoke their thoughts aloud.

'It's a hand. It's somebody's hand.'

There it was: the palm, part of the wrist with the shattered bone protruding, the five parboiled fingers with the worn and broken nails. Somebody's hand. They stared down at it, letting it lie among the seaweed, unwilling to touch it again, even with their shoes, or the point of a stick.

For a long time, the children gazed down at the grotesque thing that had come from the beautiful blue sea where men were killing each other with torpedoes and bombs. They watched it drying in the weak sunshine and cool breeze until Jeanie slipped her hand into Steve's and they made off along the beach as the flowing tide filled the footsteps of childhood in the damp sand and swept them away for ever, and they never mentioned it again.

Old Baragwaneth stood looking at the harbour which had been his playground, school and workshop for over eighty years, waiting for the pain to subside, one hand on the railing, the other on his stick. It was nearly empty now, compared to what it was, nothing but little toshers and pleasure craft, hardly any fishing boats any more, and those that were normally here all gone 'round Land, to work out of the new harbour. When he was a boy you could hardly see any water, there were so many boats here.

'Oh,' he said to himself, 'dear Lord,' as he endured the pain. It was a bad one this time.

After a while, he began walking up the quay, slowly drawing breath. I'm like an old man here, he thought. 'bout time, I s'pose.

They had none of the fine twine he wanted in the Co-op, so he bought the next best thing, a reel of thread of the kind anglers use to bind their rods. It would have to do, now. He shoved the thread in his pocket and left the shop, bound for the hill and home, and when he paused for breath, he saw that maid Boy Barny used to be friendly with, Anne, Josh Trewella's maid.

He stopped to have a yarn with her, a nice young woman, relieved to have some excuse for a Spell-Oh and a bit of a pause to draw breath again.

'Be'n down for a bit of twine, for my model of the *Ebenezer*.'

'Are you all right?' she asked.

'Why 'ess. I'm all right. And how are you?'

He was not all right, as Anne could see, and she walked home with him after lying about her own destination. 'I'm going up your way.'

They took a long time to get up the hill, and when they reached his door a wisp of a breeze caught Anne's hair, blew up the tail of a cat which went scuttling around the corner, and swung a Bed and Breakfast sign on its hinges with a scream for oil. He opened the door which, Anne noticed, he had not locked when he went out. His face was grey around the smile.

'Aren't 'ee going to show me your new model ?' Anne said, reluctant to leave him alone. 'She must be nearly finished.'

He invited her in, the first time she had seen his house, and she then suggested that she make some tea while he rested after the walk up the hill. He said the hill was nawthen to hurt anybody, had kept him fit and yes, perhaps he would have a dish of tay with her. He sat in his chair and explained his possessions, said who were in the photographs, when they were taken. That china figure had been his mother's, that Crown Derby jug, his wife's. 'Ab'm never had a drop of milk in 'n for forty years.'

He took her out to his shed, where the clean, perfect lines of the model, lying in a cradle of polished mahogany, were in stark contrast to the chaos all about her. The boat rested on a small dust-free part of the bench that he had swept clean. Anne examined the detail, appreciating the workmanship, the full sails, the gear on deck, down to the neatly painted numbers, the name on the sides, and the twine halyards.

'They're too heavy. I'm going to change them.'

A gust of wind slammed the shed door against the jamb. 'The wind is rising all the time,' Anne said.

'Es, he ez. And the glass is very low. I'm afraid the old shed will blaw down. Do 'ee think you could take her in for me? I can do the halyards on the kitchen table.'

She had doubts, but carefully carried the model into the house, while he followed with the cradle, and they set her up on the sideboard.

'I'll change the halyards dreckly and that's that, finished. I shain't do n'more.'

She left him sitting in his chair after he had assured her that he was fully recovered from his 'turn', and he cast his eye over his work for the umpteenth time.

''es,' he said to himself. 'She's a bea'ty, sure 'nuff.'

On the south coast, the breeze disturbed the flat sea and dark clouds lay low over the horizon when Barny went to fetch Louise from work that evening.

She was uncharacteristically quiet during the drive home, saying nothing about the events of her day which, Barny conjectured, was a sure sign of anxiety regarding the job. There was something on her mind too important to discuss casually in the car. Ah well, all in good time. The clouds followed them across the moor, a uniform darkening of the sky, with a few specks of rain, heavy and intermittent, falling to ground in the headlight's beam. It was just as well, he thought, that the roof wasn't off, and was about to say something along those lines, but desisted, lest she interpret his comment as a reprimand for her impatience with Steve. The telephone was ringing as they entered the house. Barny ignored it, turning to take her in his arms. 'I don't want to answer that.'

Louise picked up the receiver. 'It might be the children.' She dropped the instrument after saying nothing except their number. 'It's for you.' Her expression grim and resentful.

'Who is it?' he whispered, picking up the phone. Louise left the room and went upstairs.

'Oh,' he said, 'Anne. Hello. Oh.' As he listened to her anxious voice. 'I see. What did he say? Typical! Yes, I'll give him a ring now. Yes, I will. And how are you? I haven't see you for ages. Yes, I know, I'm sorry.' Louise could hear all he was saying. 'Are they? When did they go out?' And after listening again, 'Well I'm sure there's no need to worry. Steve knows what he's doing. Why don't you give Mary a ring? No, I suppose not. Yes, I'll give him a ring now. Thanks, Anne.'

His father was indignant. 'On'y one of my turns,' he said. 'Same as they belong. What d' she want to go phonin' you for? Down here? I don't want you down here. I'm now going to have my tay.'

'Well, as you wish, Da. Any news of Steve and they? Are they back yet? Yes, I suppose so. I'll see you tomorrow.'

He went up to Louise in the bedroom. She had changed her clothes, and met him with a challenging, 'She'll never give up, will she?'

'It was about my father. He had another of his angina attacks, down at the harbour this morning. She's worried about him, that's all.'

She was somewhat mollified by this. 'Did she she ask you to go and see her?'

'No. She didn't.'

Could Louise not see, Barny asked himself, that he was devoted to her? He gazed at her troubled face, considering how he could convince her that he was so in love with her that she need have no doubts about his fidelity.

'When will you marry me?' he said.

She looked at him, with her expression a disconcerted stare at the abruptness of his question. Barny waited for a reply, hoping that he had reassured her, and watched her eyes, with a slight smile of anticipation.

'It's the wrong time to ask,' she said.

'Is it?'

It was an ill-concealed lie she had told him, and that which remained unsaid an even greater lie, although he had no idea what that lie might be. She had successfully parried his proposal, refused him, refused his offer of total commitment, even if it was unintentional, and in doing so had stung him cruelly.

266

'I'll ask you again,' he said, hiding his pain, 'under more romantic circumstances.'

As they stared at each other, a gust of wind hurled heavy rain against the window, billowed the curtains, and he went to close the sash, blaming Anne's phone call for Louise's doubts. They would pass, however. When he considered what a state she had been in when first she came to him, it was hardly surprising that she occasionally lapsed into insecurity.

'But I love you,' he said, turning back to her, 'under any circumstances.'

To his astonishment, she burst into tears and clung to him, saying, 'Oh Barny. Oh, Barny. How can I manage without you?'

'You don't have to,' he said, and drew her down on to the bed, where he cradled her head against his chest. 'You'll always have me, as long as you need me.'

This brought fresh tears, which she made no attempt to control. They were the first she had shed for weeks, and soon subsided under his assurances before he left her and went to prepare their meal, thinking: now what's brought this on?

As they ate, they could hear the wind rising, the rain getting heavier. There was a whistling moan about the eaves as a gust increased in strength, died away to silence.

Louise looked at Barny. 'Don't worry,' he said. 'I've made everything secure outside.'

'I'm thinking about the roof.'

'So am I. But there's nothing we can do about that. Don't worry about it. I'm much more concerned about Steve and his son and Joe.'

'Why?' There was suspicion in her voice. 'Why should you be concerned about them?'

He told her what Anne had said. 'They're overdue, and have lost contact by radio. No one has heard from them since early this morning.

Louise evidently did not appreciate the significance of this

'They're out to sea,' he explained as the wind rose again. 'Somewhere north of the islands. In this bloody lot.'

'I'm sure they'll be all right,' Louise said. 'You have always extolled their competence at sea.'

How easy, he thought, to be complacent about the predicament of others, with your two feet under the table, a fire glowing in the hearth, a roof over your head, a warm bed to go to. 'Yes. I'm sure they're OK too. It's just that... . It's silly, really, but I've had these premonitions. I can't explain it. Something about Boy Steve. Something tragic. Just that. And the sea somewhere. Nothing more. I know,' he protested, looking directly at her, 'that it's all rubbish. Absurd. I don't believe any of it. But I'm still worried.'

This was the first time he had told anyone about these crazy notions in his head, of premonition which implied that events were pre-ordained, a total contradiction of his own concepts of existence. He thought she might laugh at him, instead of which she said, 'Have you ever had one about me?"

'Yes,' he told her frankly. 'And about myself too.' Especially, he thought, about myself. Those fearful images which the comfort of Louise's arms had driven away forever.

'What? What are they?'

'I'd rather not talk about it. It's all rubbish.'

Were it otherwise, *if* the future *were* predictable, the consequences would be unbearable.

'Have any of them come true ?'

He had told her he did not want to talk about it. 'No more,' he said, 'than can be rationalised as being within the parameters of statistical coincidence.' He stared at her blankly. 'Let's talk about something else.'

'You people are so superstitious.'

'I have never given you any reason to believe that,' he said, smiling at her.

'What about the stones?'

'That's not superstition. I don't know what it is. As I told you, it's beyond explanation.' He was afraid she was about to deny her own experience of the mystery.

'I employed a woman this week,' she said, 'who refused to start today because it's bad luck to begin anything on a Friday.'

Barny laughed outright. 'And so it is, anybody will tell you that. That's not superstition either, it's a fact.'

After they had eaten their meal, Barny suggested they go over to see Sam and Beth, for he thought they might need help in securing their outbuildings against the gale. It was now howling about the cottage continually and Louise was reluctant to go out, but he insisted. Everything was already secured, however, with the animals shut in and loose items put in the barn. They had bolted all the doors, closed the vents and guyed the greenhouses, covered the cold frames and brought in a supply of fuel and food. There was nothing more they could do.

Barny told them of the *Morwennol*, overdue, and Sam said he had seen Sweeting's yacht, that evening, close to shore, moving slowly west, with her propellers nearly out of the water at times, thrashing foam.

'He'll be trying to get 'round Land,' Barny conjectured, 'before the wind veers. He's left it a bit late.'

The forecast is up to force ten,' Beth said, 'as it veers round to north west, and decreasing seven to eight before dawn.'

'He'll never make it.' Barny said. 'He should run back to the bay and ride it out at anchor.'

'Surely,' Louise said, obviously irritated by them expressing opinions about the competence of a professional seaman from the viewpoint of amateur prejudice, 'the captain will know what he's doing'

Beth said, 'Let's hope so.' And Sam, for once expressing his own opinion, added, 'He might know what he's doing now. But he might not know this coast. He's heading for hell, out there.'

Their talk exacerbated Louise's own anxiety and she visibly cringed with each gust that thumped about the house, looking at Beth, who said, 'At least we can be thankful we're not out there.'

'Hadn't we better get back,' Louise said to Barny, 'before it gets any stronger.?'

The telegraph wires were moaning and wailing overhead as they struggled back along the road. Barny's powerful torch illuminated the raindrops, the rushing leaves stripped from the trees, the bracken beaten flat and the grass on the verges waving like the combed hair of mermaids underwater. They clung together, forced open the gate, which was snatched from Barny's grasp as they entered, and passed under the lashing branches of the sycamore tree to the door.

'It's so loud!' Louise cried. 'The noise frightens me.'

'The noise can't hurt you,' Barny said as he leaned back against the shut door. 'Oh, blast!'

The room was full of smoke, billowing into the room as the pressure of passing wind forced down-draughts through the chimney. Barny went outside again and brought back a bucket of earth with which he dampened the fire.

'There's only one place to be on a night like this, he said. 'Come on... bed!

CHAPTER FOURTEEN

Terryans-gorhel Shipwreck.

...and when did you first feel yourself to be a worthless sinner, Louise?

The school impressed upon the girls the virtue of physical fitness - 'A healthy mind develops a healthy body' - and there were daily periods in the gym or on the hockey pitch. Louise was twelve years old when they had first attempted to climb the ropes hanging from the beam across the ceiling. She was weak in the arms, her muscles undeveloped, and she was fearful of ridicule if she failed to ascend the dangling ropes, for she was the tallest girl in the class. A few of the girls arrived at the gym early, changed into their white vests and navy-blue knickers, and swung on the ropes, disobeying the rules as they waited for the nun who was the class mistress.

'I wanted to prove to her that I was keen, and making progress in PT. Developing my strength. I reached up, grasped the hard fibrous rope, and drew my feet up under me. My legs were very long. The trailing edge of the rope was wedged between my feet. I knew how to do it. I hung there, swinging, slowly turning round as I looked at the other girls shinning up and down with ease. The rope passed between my thighs, and I drew them tightly together. Hand over hand I straightened my body and stretched higher and again drew my feet up, beneath my buttocks. The rope between my thighs was hard against my knickers, with the fibres prickling the fine, delicate skin on each side of my crotch. I felt a tremor of apprehension and excitement tingling my body as I swung slowly on the rope and felt my knickers pressing into me from the rubbing of the hard, unyielding rope. I moved my legs, still holding the rope between my shins and feet as it rubbed against me. The tremors increased, I felt a warm glowing sensation around my private parts and a fearful shame that this was happening to me. It was a nice feeling. I felt a spasm of excitement in my vagina. I swung around, breathing as if from the exertion of hanging there from my weak arms. No one was taking any notice of me, swinging slowly back and forth. I tensed the muscles in my legs. The rope hardened against me. I relaxed and the sensation, a tightening of uncontrollable muscles somewhere deep inside me, subsided. I tensed again, the hard rope pressed against my knickers. I had never had such a lovely feeling before. It was the first sexual experience I can remember.'

'Stop that! At once!'

Louise Fern fell to the floor in a flush of shame and confusion, and heard her own voice, as if from another body, saying, 'I couldn't help it. I didn't mean to.' As the sensations of her body lingered on in illicit delight.

'I couldn't help it,' the voice was crying. 'She made me.'

The teacher stood over Louise with her wide cowl haloed against the light of the gym skylight. 'Don't be ridiculous,' she said. 'Don't lie to me, you little sinner.'

The other girls were silent, waiting for the punishment. 'Now get up!' the nun cried. 'How many times do you have to be told not to use the apparatus in the gym unsupervised?'

Louise struggled to her feet and found that she had twisted her ankle in the fall. The pain was slight but she limped towards the line of girls against the wall.

'Oh, good gracious. You can't do gym like that. Go back and change and sit in the classroom. You will write a hundred lines: "*I will not disobey the rules*" - I'll deal with you later.'

As she left the gym, Louise found that her ankle was giving her very little pain - it had been only a slight twist, but she walked with an exaggerated limp to the changing room. It was not fair. None of the others who had been on the ropes were to receive, it seemed, any chastisement at all, so she felt justified in overdoing her hesitant progress. She resented the unwarranted punishment. But perhaps, she thought, the nun had seen what was happening to her, what else she had been doing while hanging on the rope. She had told the truth, however. She had no reason for guilt. Some will other than her own had taken over her body. She could never have done such a dirty thing. The devil had possessed her.

Alone in the changing room, the schoolgirl Louise entered the cubicle with her clothes over her arm. She slipped her vest over her head, and then, curious, pushed the elastic away from her belly and slid her hand down. Her private parts were warm and wet. It was smooth, soft, like silk. She stroked herself and slipped a finger inside. She drew it out over the little hard bit and in again. One gasp of breath burst out of her lungs and she shuddered in horror at the evil pleasure. She dressed with tears

271

streaming down her cheeks and went to the classroom and wrote not one, but two hundred lines, in a self-inflicted punishment to purge the devil from her everlasting soul.

...I always felt the need to prove myself - to be an achiever - even as a child it was very important to me.

The roar of the wind was continuous. Even in the lulls it screamed about Barny's cottage with a malevolent persistence, like a flight of demons searching for vulnerable victims in the night. Barny could sense the tension in Louise's body as he lay with his arms around her. She was terrified of the noise, and on one occasion woke him from a fitful doze, saying, 'How can you sleep ?'

They heard a crash outside, as something broke or was hurled away in a squall. He was not afraid, though increasingly concerned that at any moment they would hear the clatter of falling slates as the roof began to disintegrate. They were in no physical danger and if the roof did go it would be inconvenient, probably expensive, but in a week or two repaired or renewed and the worry of it gone for the rest of his life. The rain was no longer pelting the window. The wind was going around to the north-west, which meant that it would be blowing along the line of the ridge, less likely to suck the slates from the leeward side, where the damage usually started.

'I think,' he said, 'the roof would have gone by now, if it was going at all. Stop worrying.'

She turned away from him and he snuggled into her back. He could feel his hair and soft cock against her bum, and enjoyed a tingle of arousal as he cupped his hand around her breast. They could make love, he mused, still drowsy from lack of sleep and drifting off again, to match the fury of the gale, exhaust themselves in mutual passion. His hand slipped into the warmth of her thighs and his fingers fondled the black pubic hair. They could show how they loved each other, he dreamt, regardless of the tumult in the world about them.

'Get your hands off me,' she demanded.

'What?' he said as he snatched his hand away. 'What did you say ?"

'You are taking liberties with my body.'

'What the hell are you talking about, Loopy?'

'My body. It is mine, to decide what's done with it. I don't have to be subject to male demands.'

'I'm not making any demands, for Christ's sake. What's got into you?'
'It's one o'clock in the morning,' she said.

Barny lay on his back with his hands behind his head, staring at the ceiling. Her irascibility had nothing whatsoever to do with the time of day. She was trying to assert, or deny, some feminist principle she had read about in all that literature written by women with inadequate fathers. She was no longer a woman lying beside him, but a feminist, with whom he knew not how to behave, neither did he want to. A vicious gust of wind struck the cottage. It felt as if the very foundations rocked, and he rose from the bed, looked out of the window and took his clothes downstairs, wishing that the bloody roof would blow off, to give her a taste of life.

He dropped the switch on the kitchen wall, then tried the sitting room. There was no light, no power. The lines must be down somewhere. He filled the kettle, put it on the gas. The house was cold and he sat by the dead fire, worrying about Loopy. When would she ever find a mind of her own, be herself for what she was, instead of forever seeking to be what some other, self-opinionated pedagogue, said she should be? It was time she discovered who she was for herself.

Outside, it was a hell of a night, the rain was coming down in torrents, spluttering on the dead fireplace, leaving black puddles of soot on the hearth. He drank his tea, wondering how he could ever approach her again. Taking liberties! After all the times she had asked for it, demanded it, his touch, so fervently. Bloody feminists! Their mission was to destroy women, make them all become men, yet to hate men, to hate other women and, most of all, to hate themselves. He couldn't cope with it.

The *Morwennol* was steaming back through the falling night, loaded down with the best catch they had hauled all summer. The wind was rising with every gust, and the visibility bad. They could see no land or lights and the wind, veering to the west a few points with every squall, was driving heavy swells under the stinging rain. The boat was heavy with fish, rising sluggishly on the following swells, wallowing deep into the troughs. Boy Steve had tried more power, of which they had plenty in reserve, to race the weather home, in the knowledge that should they miss the tide they would be obliged to make for Penavon, where there were the dreaded breakers of the bar to face, but, after nearly broaching when the boat ploughed her nose into a receding wave, and hearing Joe grumble, 'Bloody mad-brain,' he had eased her down. It was the only way.

Boy Steve had decided that the weather would hold off long enough for one more shut and, despite the reservations of the older men and the sudden failure of the electronic gear aboard, they had stayed out there in comparative shelter in the lee of the Islands. The rapid draw and rise in the wind caught them before they had the gear aboard, and they made the final haul in the worst weather they had ever fished in.

It had been a hard trip, sure 'nuff, and Joe was not happy about it. He had reservations about carrying on with Boy Steve when Steve packed it up. He would not be happy until he was warm and dry in his own bed and, as he peered about him in the blackening night, he continually glanced from the gloom to the compass. They had made a lot of money, and Boy Steve needed it, but one of these days he would have a fright, as Joe had, and as Fehther Steve had, as all hands who spent their lives out here would have, sooner or later. It was not a game for gamblers. The fault in the electronics was probably nothing more than a loose wire or damp got in somewhere, but there was nothing to be seen. Its diagnosis required testers and meters, instruments beyond Joe's expertise, and they were sailing back on the compass and dead reckoning, which he knew about. Joe could see that Boy Steve, despite being at the wheel, was depending on his father to see them home. They were taking the weather on the starboard quarter, running before the wind, and Steve, after three-hours steaming, was getting anxious as the wind continued to rise. As long as it didn't fly around to the no'thard, they would be all right, he thought.

They stared into the wet blackness before them, driving blind, relying on the compass, their watches, and knowledge of the tide and current to ensure that they did not drive on to those rocks along the whole coast, which none of them mentioned. If they went ashore in this weather, out here, they had no chance of survival. Boy Steve resolved that he had made his last trip against his father's counsel.

Steve said, 'Take her a point or two to port, Boy. I b'lieve I can see the Watch.'

They peered ahead, saw nothing, then a stab of light, and another, and another. 'Ah,' Steve said, and the three of them smiled with relief. They had only the north-west tide to go through off An Ebal and Penzausen, where the ebb met the weather and built up into rising rollers. After that it was a clear run up the coast to home.

Joe caught Boy Steve's smiling eye. 'We edn theer yet,' he scolded, remembering the flat calm and the fog, that time years ago when they had run aground on The Stones, and Old William had been lost. 'You idn home,' he said, determinedly, 'until you're home.'

Steve, standing next to his son at the wheel, was staring ahead. 'What's that, up there?' he said, not sure if he had seen anything through the murk.

As they rose on the crest of a wave and caught the wind in its full force, they all saw lights. There was the white mast-head and the red port light of a ship, with portholes lit up under the bridge, rolling in the swell in the full force of the tide.

'What's he doin' in here, now?'

Boy Steve slid open the wheel-house window for a clearer view and saw the other vessel wallowing heavily as her bow plunged deep into the oncoming rollers. Her stern rose high and her propeller came above the sea, churning the surface under her stern.

'Simon Sweeting's yacht,' Joe said.

'She wasn't built for this,' Boy Steve said. 'They'll have a job to maintain steerage in this swell. If the weather goes round she'll be in trouble.'

'She's in trouble now,' Joe said.

There was nothing they could do. They had no radio to contact the yacht, no way of advising the skipper to come about, if he could, and return to the bay before the wind veered.

'Ease her down,' Steve said. 'We'll be in the tide dreckly.'

They passed between the yacht and the shore, with the wind and rain completely obscuring the lights as the squalls swept between them. Boy Steve relinquished the wheel to the hands of his father, who had not asked for it and who took it without comment as they approached the tide race off the head. All three wedged themselves steady as the *Morwennol*, with her stern lifted high by the following waves, plunged and careened forward into the troughs, when the lights from the yacht and the Watch, receding astern, were completely screened by the walls of water all about them.

Whatever made the captain of the yacht believe he could round Land in this weather, they did not know. Perhaps it was on orders. That he would never do it, if the forecasted storm developed as predicted, they had no doubts, and there was nothing they could do for them. Sooner or later he would have to turn back, and God help him if he left it too late.

Joe rubbed his hand over the stubble on his chin. Boy Steve looked straight ahead through the rain and spray curling from the surface in whirls of violence as Steve concentrated on guiding the boat through the turbulence until they left the yacht astern and the sea fell calmer, the tide race behind them.

'I think we left 'n late enough,' Steve said as he looked at his watch. 'We'll just about see water-in to make it to the moorings.'

Joe turned, and looked back through the weather to the Watch, at the lighthouse now clearly flashing behind them as the rain briefly eased. 'I suppose,' he said, 'Barny Baragwaneth in theer, is worried about his roof.'

Steve returned his grin and opened up the throttle. The boat surged ahead as he came to starboard a turn to follow the coast, and they had a bit of shelter for the run home. 'We'll do 'n as soon as the weather d' fine away,' he said.

There was a cluster of people on the quay to see them ride the surf over the sand bank at the harbour mouth, and they saw a police car there. News had got around, it seemed, of their being overdue and Sweeting's yacht in trouble.

By the time they had put the fish ashore in the cold store and caught the moorings just as the tide was leaving them high and dry, it was after midnight. The wind was up to full gale and had turned north-west. They had been lucky, and they thought of the yacht out there in the full force of it. They could not make harbour now, even if they did turn about, for the tide had left it empty except for the swells over the bank.

'We saw her,' they said, 'off Penzausen. God help them.'

From the window of his bedroom where he stood holding the curtain aside, Barny's father could see the lights of the harbour. He could make out the *Morwennol* on her junks, safely home. He wished, sometimes, that he had put his own boy to fishing, believing it might have made a better man of him, instead of which he had put him to a career which he had given up to do dammee nothen. Writing poems, for pity's sake! The sort of thing women d' do. Yet, he was a good son to have and he was proud of him, in a way. He looked at the clock. Five and twenty after one here, and the damn pain wouldn't go away. The wind was blowing steady and the bay was full of lights. He counted fifteen vessels lying in the lee. All right, he thought, as long as the wind don't draw in here to the no'thard. He dropped the curtain, suddenly cold, and decided that he might as well get dressed, so he took off his 'jamas and drew on his trousers and guarnsey and went downstairs, switching on the lights. 'lectric is a blessing, he thought.

There she was, finished. He looked her over, found no fault worth bothering with and grimaced in exasperation as the pain gripped his heart.

276

He put more pills under his tongue. How much longer? he asked. It's dammee two o'clock here.

At half-past two o'clock in the morning, he was sitting in his chair by the window when he saw the arching trail of a rocket ascending into the sky, to be followed by a resounding explosion that rattled the sashes, and he waited for the second one and put out his light, the better to see through the window and out across the bay. He breathed out a long breath, and shook his head.

'They'll never go,' he said to himself. 'Not in this weather.'

When the first explosion rent the air over the town, Anne was instantly awake. She lay in bed with her head raised, listening for the second, not certain if she had heard thunder in her sleep. There was an interval of silence during which even the storm seemed to have abated for a moment to await the dreaded summons to the lifeboat crew.

There it was: the second crack, like a gunshot in the ear, short, without reverberation, clear and instant, shaking her window. She heard the wind screeching along the streets and then the cries of gulls, terrified in the black sky. After what seemed mere seconds there came the sound of running feet, cars being driven very fast and voices calling above the wind. She rose and went to her door, with her coat over her night-dress, where she stopped a running figure with the question.

'Is it the *Morwennol*?'

'No,' The breathless voice informed her. 'She's on her moorings. It's a ship. 'Ashore on Meor.' And the figure ran on, to be followed by a police car with its blue light flashing and its siren briefly wailing as it approached the junction in the centre of town. Wah-wah. Wah-wah. And then the wet, empty street, reflecting lights appearing in the windows, and she thought of Boy Steve and the other lifeboat crew, running from the warm comfort of their wives, and she couldn't stop the tears from mingling with the rain upon her cheek.

The phone rang three times before he heard it, so deep was Barny in thought.

'Aren't you going to answer that?' he heard Louise call from the bedroom. 'I'm trying to get some sleep.'

It would be his father. Thank God the phone lines were not down. 'Hullo.'

'Oh,' he said after a while. 'Oh, God. Yes, yes. I'll come down now. No, I was already up. Thanks for telling me, Anne.'

He put the phone down and rested his head on his arm against the wall in the dark at the bottom of the stairs. The wind hammered on the front door, slamming rain against the glass. They won't go out in this, he thought. But they would. They would go out in any weather. He went upstairs to get his warm clothes. 'I'm going down town,' he said, as Louise fumbled with the beside lamp. 'No good trying that. The power's off.'

'Was that Anne?'

'Yes.'

She sat up in bed, her naked torso a vague shape in the dim room as he used his torch to find his thick guarnsey and sea-boot stockings.

'What did she want this time?'

'There's a ship ashore on the headland.' He paused before leaving her. 'The lifeboat has been called out.'

The swell now would be tremendous, with the gale onshore, the sea a mass of foam. The prospect of going out in that small boat was horrifying.

'But what about the house?' she said.

'Well, what about it?'

'Aren't you worried that the storm will damage your own property?'

'Not now.'

If she was, in fact, afraid of being left alone here, then she would have to say so, admit that she needed him.

'What can you do?' she said, 'down there? You can't rescue anybody. The lifeboat will save them.'

She had no idea, he conceded, what those lifeboat men were having to face, so was silent as she continued.

'I don't see why you have to rush off and leave me alone on a night like this, with no power, no heat or light and the roof about to blow off.'

She was scared, but he had no sympathy. Men might die tonight while she was tucked up in the comfort of this bed in which they had made such ardent love and in which, just an hour ago, she had rejected his affection.

If she bursts into tears, Barny thought, those infantile tears of self-pity, I'll throw her out, naked as she is, into the storm. He sat on the edge of the bed, rolling on his thick stockings, his lips compressed into a resolute twist.

'Just as you said,' he told her icily when he was dressed and stood looking down at her, 'it's your body, and you can do what the fuck you like with it. You can leave it here, or bring it with me. Right now, to be frank, I don't give a shit either way. I'm going down there to see what I can do.'

'I'll come with you,' Louise said. 'I can't stay here on my own.'

The sea had ebbed against the wind, built up the swell, paused, and flowed back again to renew its onslaught against the land. The ground swells were breaking over the sand bank at the harbour mouth and surging up the slipway when Louise and Barny came through the narrow alley leading to the wharf.

'They're not going out,' he said. 'It's too rough, as I thought. Normally, they'd be afloat by now.'

Towers of spray rose above the outer quay, from waves striking the courses of granite on the seaward side before they rolled on to surge across the harbour mouth. The boat was still on her carriage at the top of the slipway, with the launchers standing by, the tractor ready to push her out into the black water. Men's yellow waterproofs gleamed wet under the lights, while all around the onlookers were standing clear, getting soaked, come to help where none was needed, and to offer support, which was. The police were there, the inspector and the constable, Sam-the-taxi-man's boy, called Richard after his grandfather, Dicky-drive-'osses, whose family had used their horses to launch the lifeboat long before the advent of the tractor. Zeke was down there with the launchers, his broad shoulders bent under the weight of a heavy block. There were women among the people, in small groups or standing alone, clutching hoods and scarves about their heads. They saw Sarah and Katie Stevens standing with their arms linked at the back of the crowd, and Barny wondered where Anne might be. Home, perhaps, preparing blankets, flasks of hot coffee, practical as ever. The drunken writer, Natt, was leaning over the railings of the harbour wall, his face pale in the lamplight.

Everything was wet, from both the rain and spray, and the wind howled overhead among the chimneys and aerials as the two new arrivals stood on the edge of the crowd. The thought in everyone's mind was the more obvious because no one had uttered it, except Louise, who was appalled at the fury of the night, experiencing such weather for the first time in her life.

'They can't go out in this.'

'There's Joe,' Barny said, and he led Louise over to the railing where Joe nodded a greeting, his eyes a glitter of fatigue.

'What's happening?'

'The tide is zackly wrong. Not enough water over the bank and too much weather to go in around 'n. All broken water. They'll have to wait.'

They could see it, off the rocks opposite the harbour-mouth, seas surging up and falling back all white in the light reflected from the windows of the houses.

'Is Boy Steve aboard?' Barny asked.'

'He's aboard.'

'He must be worn out.'

'We had a hard trip,' Joe said.

'Where's *he* to ?'

Joe inclined his head, and Barny saw Steve, standing with Mary in the doorway of Trevorrow's-that-was, the nicey shop.

'Steve is over there with his wife,' Barny told Louise. 'I must have a word with them dreckly.'

'Annie Jory got two aboard,' Joe said.

There was nothing that would induce Joe to go to sea on a night like this. If he was in the crew, he would refuse to go, he decided. But then, they who would refuse to go didn' sign on, didn' volunteer to drown their selves attempting to save some bleddy fools in danger because of their own folly. Not that you could ever say such a thing.

'Where's the bleddy helicopter?' Joe said, sniffing rain up his nose.

'There might be too much wind for the helicopter,' Louise said.

'If it's too mooch wind for they, it's too mooch wind for she.' Joe said. Louise didn't understand him.

'Where's the ship ashore to?' Barny asked Joe, in the realisation that, in his concern for the lifeboat crew, he had thought little of the plight of the seamen in the stricken vessel.

'B'tween Meor and Maen Derrens,' Joe said. 'Right in the eye ob'm'

Louise stood there feeling cold and wet, her hands in her pockets, the hood of her anorak dripping water on her brow, with her shoulders characteristically hunched as the symptom of her distress. She looked from face to face among the crowd, seeing many she recognised as customers in the shop, understanding little of the conversation from the people around her, by whom she was virtually ignored.

'Ah!' Barny said, when they had been waiting for some time. 'They're not going, it's too rough.'

Figures were climbing down the ladder from the boat on its carriage, one after the other, down on to the concrete of the slipway.

'Boy Steve ... .' Joe drawled, quietly roll-calling as the crew descended.' ...Danny Jory, Peter Jory... .' He recognised them all, knew them all, from their childhood, pals together, one and all. '...Young William ...Mathew Penrose.

'Oh.' Barny said as he foresaw what they were about to do. 'Oh, my God.' He reached for Louise's arm.

Boy Steve was the first on the slip, followed by Annie Jory's husband and son. He walked up to the doorway of the nicey shop and took his mother in his arms.

The Jorys did the same, the two of them. All of them embraced their loved ones. Boy Steve left his parents and went over to Katie. He took her hands in his and looked into her eyes before turning back to the slipway without a word. There was only the sound of the storm around them as the men climbed back on board: the howling wind, the roar of the breakers at the harbour mouth, the rattling of rigging from the boats at anchor, noises which no one heard through the silence in their minds.

Louise could not take her eyes from Mrs Jory, recognising her as the same Mrs Jory who had been sacked from the shop for refusing to work the new rota on the grounds that she had a family to look after. The look of resignation on the woman's uplifted face, as the tears mingled unashamedly with the rain and she watched her two men take their stations on the deck, brought a shiver of dread down Louise's spine. How could they do it?

A loud belch of exhaust came from the great tractor's silencer, the carriage rumbled quickly down to the sea and the boat slipped away, her propellers throwing a wake behind her.

'Boy Jory's missus,' Joe said, 'is home with their cheldern.' No damn business to be aboard of her, he thought, but what can 'ee say?

As she approached the harbour mouth, the searchlight at the mast-head swept ahead of the lifeboat and illuminated the surf breaking over the bank ahead of her. The propellers sent a sudden spurt astern and she shot ahead, full speed. As she reached the quay-head she swung to port and went out between the surf and the quay, in the narrow channel of deep water cut by the tide. She must have nearly scraped the granite, but she was gone, out into the storm.

'Idn many could do that,' Joe said. 'Jory's a good coxs'n.' He came off the railing and went over to Steve and Mary.

'Come on,' Barny said to Louise, 'you might as well see it all.'

After a night like this, he thought, she'll see other values in her life. He led her down along the wharf, through Quay Street to the vantage point at the top of the quay, joining the other people, some running youths, to watch the lifeboat pass around the headland. Most of the time she was out of sight, deep in the troughs. Only occasionally could they see her lights flashing as she arched over the massive swells rolling before the wind into the bay until, plunging slow ahead, she eventually passed out of sight, behind the headland. All the people then crossed over to the other side of the headland, where they saw the stricken ship, cast ashore on the rocks. She was near the beach with her bow rammed against the reef, her stern rising and falling as the waves crashed onto her. There was the sickening taste of diesel in the air, blown ashore with the spray, discolouring the foam and coating the rocks with a treacherous, slippery film, and they heard the sound of grating iron, tearing through the night.

Cars on the shore had their headlights on, illuminating the scene, and the crowd of watchers looked on helplessly as the big yacht began to go down by the stern, capsizing under the onslaught of white water crashing into her. They saw a light flashing in the sky and heard the rotors of a helicopter which came and hung over the wreck, with a searchlight sweeping the sea, rising and falling, then steady as a kestrel as the computers sensed the variations in the wind.

Barny and Louise had joined the people watching from a low wall, overlooking the beach. The gale was full in their faces, conversation impossible below a shout. As Steve came up behind them, they saw a dark figure descend from the helicopter and dangle in the air. Lowered on a wire, the man hung over the hull, swinging like a conker in the wind and pelting rain of a vicious squall. The lights of the lifeboat came into view as she passed the headland and came towards the beach. She was broadside on to the weather. Barny felt for Louise's hand. There was nothing he could say to her with Steve standing right beside him. He regretted being so angry with her, for such a night was enough to frighten anybody.

They could see three men aboard the yacht. They had opened a door in the bridge, and two came out onto the catwalk. The ship lurched and listed heavily to starboard, the head of her short mast, above the bridge, hanging over the sea, with flailing wires and rigging whipping in the wind. Cascades of water came pouring over the bridge, obscuring the men in the spray. Barny sensed her presence and turned, to see Anne, holding Joe's arm. Louise had not seen her.

The man dangling from the wire was dropped lower, close to the level of the bridge, swinging in the wind. He could get no nearer the desperate men. The mast was in the way, and, should he or his harness get caught up with the rigging, he was likely to be ripped in half as the ship rolled over. He was taken up and lowered again to the port side of the mast, an anonymous figure in black. The men could not get up there without being swept overboard. The conker came down to the gangway, astern of the bridge, just clear of the mast and rigging, and the figure reached towards the rail with his feet as the ship wallowed in the swell, with the wires and rigging lashing the air beside him. A shower of spray completely obscured the dangling figure, so close to the men on deck, so far away from reaching them.

The lifeboat was running in with the swell, out clear of the rocks. The coxswain was trying to see his way in to the wreck, which was no more than twenty-five yards outside the line of broken water where the rollers arched up, with the spume flying off their crests, and crashed into a mighty rolling surf surging onto the beach. When the breakers expended themselves they drew back, sucking sand and shingle in a grinding undertow. No boat could survive in that.

He would have to go in, keeping outside the surf, get alongside in what little shelter was provided by the wreck herself, get the men off without striking either the ship or the rocks at her bow, then go astern, come about while keeping clear of the surf and drive out round the head in the teeth of the weather. A brea job, sure 'nuff, Uncle Joe thought, One of they breakers on the beam and she'd capsize, no doubt about it.

The lifeboat's navigation light changed from red to red and green as she ran in before the surges, then to green as she came about, athwart the weather, the wind on her port side.

Those ashore could hardly see what was going on at times. The car headlights were lost in spray and the searchlight on the helicopter picked out only details of the drama. They saw one of the ship's crew, clambering towards the dangling rescuer hanging from the wire beneath the racket and downdraught of the rotor. There was a harness hanging loosely beside the dangling man. The pilot eased the chopper closer until the winch-line was only a few feet from the mast and rigging, and it seemed to the onlookers that they would surely become entangled. Then, as the ship heaved up from the pressure of a passing wave, the two figures were together and the big black helicopter rose slowly above the wreck, and the winch-line began to shorten as the aircraft dropped to lee, towards the beach.

Two men dangling, rising in the wind towards the square hole in the chopper's abdomen. The chopper tilting slightly and the rotors loud, choop choop choop, slicing the turbulent air. Hands reaching out and a black figure falling, slowly turning, and the splash lost among the raging violence on the surface of the sea.

Barny felt Louise's fingers digging into the muscle of his upper arm. It hurt, but he did not pull away. He looked at her and shook his head. There was nothing they could do for him. He had fallen among the rocks. However, they saw lights down there, beams sweeping the surf, men at the edge of the sea.

The lifeboat was coming in, watching the running swells, slowly easing in towards the ship's side. Some of the stricken crew were coming up to the deck, hanging on to the rails.

Joe, with his arm around Anne's shoulder, wiped the rain from his eyes. Bleddy madness, he thought. No business out there. Who would listen to him, illiterate and afraid?

'Go back,' he cried. 'Get below, you stupid buggers.' His voice was snatched away, unheard in the confusion of the night.

The helicopter was overhead again. They saw, it seemed, one of the men wave it away. They were afraid of it. The lifeboat came slowly closer, into the shelter of the wreck, and then men were leaping, being caught, falling, thrown by the lurching boat, clambering, reaching, as the gap between them narrowed, widened, with the surges of swell in the roaring wind. They had no idea how many crewmen were aboard, six perhaps, or ten, and it seemed that the lifeboat would never come away.

At last they saw her lights slowly coming astern, her green for star-board and her white mast-head, her white decks shining, the mast swaying. Barny heard Joe groaning. She went further astern, clear of the wreck, clear of the rocks, lost in the troughs, and the lights began to wallow as she stopped, came slow ahead, and began turning into the weather, well clear of the wreck and the rocks, away from the greatest dangers.

The swell rose up to weather of her. They could see it from the shore, a massive wall of black water outside the lifeboat, and it broke into a pounding turbulence of fury, completely engulfing her. The mast-head light was all they could see, and it fell towards the shore and disappeared, and they could see the white keel as the boat capsized.

The roar of anguish that rose from the crowd that night came from every throat, yet none heard his own involuntary shriek. They heard but a cry of agony that soared with the wind and carried across the roof tops to those still in the harbour awaiting the boat's return. It was a cry they would hear resounding in their minds for the remainder of their days.

Louise bit into her fist as she heard them crying, 'She's gone! She's gone!' And men were running down the short flight of steps towards the breakers on the beach.

'You,' she heard Barny yell, 'Stay with Anne. And he too was gone, following Steve and Joe, down to the beach.

They stood at the edge of the surf, among all the others on the shore, looking for heads and yellow life-jackets. The helicopter hung low, with the dangling man on the wire sweeping the surface. They saw it drop him into the water to pick up a limp body and bring it back to the beach before sweeping over the sea again, its searchlight illuminating the spume.

The headlights of the cars shone on the sea close to the shore and they could see the white hull of the lifeboat, being thrown like a toy onto the black rocks, smashed to pieces with each succeeding wave. The big yacht lay with her bow wedged among the rocks and was slowly listing to starboard as the waves broke over her. There was a momentary glint of orange day-glo, out there among the white surf. Steve threw off his jacket and boots, saying, 'He's one of ours.' Joe tried to stop him, but was shoved aside. 'It could be the boy,' Steve said.

Joe caught hold of Steve by the front of his guarnsey, screwing it up in his fist. He pulled Steve's body close to his own. Barny moved forward to prevent him smashing his fist in Steve's face. Joe was wild with anger. 'Put on your jacket,' he snarled. 'Do 'ee want Mary to lose her husband as well as her son?'

Steve slumped, the tears in his eyes, and looked out helplessly at the body in the surf. Joe thrust him aside, took off his jacket, kicked off his boots, and went down to the sea.

He waded out, the undertow swirling about his legs, and plunged into the next breaker. They saw him emerge on the other side and begin swimming towards the man in the life-jacket, a struggling crawl through the wind and rain.

'The bleddy fool,' Steve sobbed, and dropped his jacket on the beach. Barny restrained him by the arm and they watched in silence as Joe struggled out. He reached the man in the sea, lifted his head out of the water and began swimming backwards, pulling his burden with him. They had made some progress towards the shore, and Louise thought they were safe, but they watched the next wave break over Joe and twist him like a piece of wet rag, beat the breath out of his lungs against the hard sand, and could see no more of him in the undertow. Barny and Steve waded out into the sea, looking for that bundle of rags, the spray and wind flying about them, and were joined by others, men and women, scouring the surf, some of whom were themselves swept off their feet and washed up on the shore. There was the man in the life-jacket, swirling in the foam,

285

and Steve ventured out and grabbed him, dragged him ashore with the help of other hands. They turned him over and did not know him. He was a crewman from the yacht, a damned stranger, still alive and conscious. They wrapped him in blankets and took him away to a warm bed in someone's home.

Boy Steve stayed under water as long as he could, until the life-jacket brought him to the surface, too close to the rigging on the mast. He turned his back to the shore and kicked out with his legs. The next breaker caught him and he went passively with it, holding his breath until he surfaced again. He could see no others in the sea about him, but he felt a body brush his legs. He reached down, brought the head up to his chest and waited for the next breaker to engulf him. He was cast up onto the beach into waiting hands a hundred yards along the shore, still gripping the sailor from the ship, who was taken to a waiting ambulance while Boy Steve was stripped of his life-jacket.

'Tell fehther I'm all right,' he said, and Katie Stevens ran across the beach as word was passed along.' They've got Boy Steve ashore.' She stood beside him, the tears of relief in her eyes washed away by the rain, and waited for Sarah to join her.

And then they saw Joe, rolling in the surf, smashed onto the sand like a rag doll, and lost again in the grinding undertow. Steve and Barny went out, up to their waists in the foam, and found him when he surfaced on a crest. They grabbed hold of him in the turbulence of the following breaker and dragged him in to the beach.

Hag yn meth an Venen. And quoth the woman.

I went down across the beach, following Anne, who ran ahead. The sand was wet, and streaked with globules of foam quivering in the wind. People were carrying blankets from their beds, hot-water bottles, vacuum flasks, waterproof sheets, as if they knew what was needed, and I felt utterly helpless. Electric blue lights were pulsating from the tops of ambulances on the headland and the road above the beach. The rain stung my face, and I had difficulty in standing on my feet. I saw people in the sea, fully clothed, up to their waists, pulling bodies from the waves.

They were working on Joe. They had taken his clothes off and wrapped him in warm blankets that a woman had brought from her own bed. Steve was rubbing the legs while Barny closed the nose with his fingers and forced his breath into Joe's mouth. He had vomit all over his face. Anne knelt beside them and slipped her hand inside the blanket, feeling for a pulse in the cold wrist, until the ambulance men came and took him away with an oxygen mask over his mouth. They all seemed so familiar, calling each other by name.

Barny asked where Steve's wife was, and they said she had gone home after the launch, to prepare a meal and warm clothes, ready for her men's return. She would know nothing of all this.

Anne took us back to her house, and made Barny strip off his wet clothes in her warm kitchen. He was white and shivering and didn't seem to notice his nakedness as we rubbed him down, Anne on his arms, me on his legs, before being wrapped in warm blankets with hot-water bottles. Anne rinsed and spun his clothes, all together in her washing machine, and hung them in her airing cupboard and in front of the fire. I felt so helpless in the presence of her efficiency. As the first light of day came through the window, and the wind began to die away, I kept seeing Joe's wet face, his hair and open staring eyes, full of sand.

'Will he be all right?' I asked, and they looked at each other, reluctant to answer me.

'No.' Barny said, after a while. 'I'm afraid Joe has gone, my flower.'

I can't remember if Anne had spoken directly to me before but she put her arms around me as I sat at her table trying not to cry, although my vision was clouded with tears of distress. She made us breakfast, I remember, of eggs, bacon and toast, which we ate in silence.

Barny began putting his clothes on, and I pointed out that they were still damp.

It won't take long to go home,' he said, 'and then I'll change again.'

He turned to Anne. 'Thanks,' he said. 'I'll come and see 'ee pembye.'

'You'd better go up'long,' she said. 'See how he is.'

It was evident she was referring to Barny's father.

They found him in his armchair by the bedroom window, facing the sea, with the morning sun streaming in from a blue sky. A few white clouds drifted across the eastern shore, and the bay was calming down, disturbed only by a slight ground swell running before a dying breeze which too would fine away on the ebb. His eyes were closed, as in sleep, his mouth open, his skin cold. Barny fell to his knees and pressed his head into his father's chest, sobbing uncontrollably, while Louise looked at the white, lined face, recoiling in shock. Before this day, she had been unfamiliar with the features of death.

'Help me,' Barny said when he had recovered himself. 'to get him on the bed.'

I forced myself to take the legs, and we carried him to the bed, where Barny straightened the limbs, tied up the sagging jaw with a piece of linen and covered the body with a sheet. I had never seen anything like this before. Barny picked up the phone and called the doctor, the undertaker, and he tidied a few things in the room. We watched the doctor hold the limp wrist and feel for a pulse as he looked at his watch for two long minutes in silence, after saying, 'I have to do this.' And Barny nodded.

The undertaker came. He offered few words of sympathy, it seemed to me, and was highly unprofessional. He wasn't even wearing a suit. 'You knaw,' Barny said, and I had never heard him speak in such a broad accent as in the past six hours, 'what we d' want, Peter. I'll leave 'n to 'ee.'

There was nothing to do in the old man's home. Everything was neat and tidy, although Barny was reluctant to leave and kept picking things up and putting them back in their places. I had never seen a house with so many old-fashioned ornaments. He picked up a piece of shiny metal. 'fool's gold,' he said, and put it in his pocket. He stood before a model of a boat, an old fishing boat, I think, and said, 'He got her dammee zackly. The best one he ever built.' I could see him suppressing a further welling of emotion and he turned to me, saying, 'He was a cantankerous old bugger when he had a mind to be,' before falling on my shoulder, weeping.

'All by himself,' he sobbed, 'all alone.'

CHAPTER FIFTEEN

Wosa an hager-awel. After the storm.

'...so you left him.'

'I maintained that in the following days and weeks too much was expected of me, in the circumstances. On the one hand I felt totally excluded from Barny's community for being an outsider while, on the other hand, he expected me to conform to their customs as well as support him in his personal grief while continuing with my work. I did what I could, considering my predicament, for I also found life difficult. Barny seemed forever in town, either seeing to his father's business or visiting friends, including, although he denied there was anything more than friendship between them, Anne. He said she had a boyfriend now, living up country. I didn't believe him. There were occasions when he could not even pick me up from work, although I was now and likely to remain, the only breadwinner. And yet he still expected me to console him at night. I felt that he was imposing altogether too much of a burden on me and that he should have been aware of it. He expected me to attend the funerals, then the memorial service for the five drowned sailors and Joe, the only local to lose his life. The lifeboat men were all saved by their life-jackets and familiarity with local conditions it seemed, although there were some injuries to rescuers hit by waves while scrambling among the rocks to reach survivors. The most ironic thing was that two crew members were too terrified to make the jump into the lifeboat and stayed below, in the cabin of the ship, just as Joe had said they should. When the sea went out next day they were able to wade ashore, unscathed.

Fortunately, I was able to persuade the company that it would be a good public relations exercise if I were to attend the memorial services as their representative, so was able to get time off from work. Barny was so preoccupied with his own affairs that I found it impossible to broach the subject of my imminent promotion and what this would mean to my future career.'

There was hardly a breeze about the cottage as Barny stood at his door looking at a new life on Monday afternoon. The colours on the moors were dazzling in the bright sunshine. The heather was over, the grasses dry and the shades of browns and whites brilliant beneath the almost cloudless sky. What changes he had to face. Since Friday the world had become transformed, with his father gone, Joe gone, and Louise further away from him than she had ever been. When they returned to the cottage on that beautiful sunny day after the gale and found everything still intact, she had put her arms around him, saying, 'I'm so sorry Barny. I wish I could help you.' Implying, however unintentionally, that she could not, that she wished, indeed, to distance herself from the tragedy.

'I'm sorry,' he said, 'about swearing at you. I was upset.'

Their experience of the night had not, he feared, strengthened any bonds between them, for she had insisted in going off to the shop for the afternoon, despite being exhausted and despite the fact that he needed her here, to comfort him. It was as if the events of the night were too momentous for her to accept and she must continue her life as if she had never experienced them. Perhaps, he thought, like himself, she was in a state of profound shock and would eventually return to him.

'I understand,' she said.

The garden had suffered in the storm. The last leaves had been wrenched from the sycamore, the bean poles blown down, and the brussels sprouts and cabbages twisted off their roots. What did it matter? he could plant more. The camellia, sheltered in its corner, was undamaged, with all its buds intact. He did not look at the roof.

The last person he expected a phone call from was his bank manager. Not now, he thought, I have more important things on my mind. Besides, I have two houses now. The thought brought a chill upon him. No more to hear his father's grumbles, his earthy wisdom and cynical humour. I s'pose that's where I got it from. They wanted to see him. Yes, it was urgent, but they didn't know how important. What rubbish.

The manager, near to retirement, was a Penavon man and had done well for himself, by local standards. He had been in the job long enough to know everybody in the town, more or less, before all the damn strangers came, that is, and he became subservient to a computer in Hong Kong.

'It was deposited,' he said, 'last year. He opened an account with a few bob and has never put a penny in since. Just this, in our safe keeping until his death, when it was to be handed to you in person. He never responded to any correspondence.'

Barny took the small parcel. It was a padded envelope. 'He couldn't read,' he said, 'or write. Apart from signing his name.'

He took it home before opening it to find inside an audiotape, and he sat beside his expensive hi-fi to listen to the voice of 'Uncle' Joseph Curnow, deceased.

'Hullaw, Barny,' the voice said, in that strong accent of Joe's. 'Don't s'pose you expected to hear from me again. Hee hee.'

Barny pressed the Stop button. He wasn't sure he could cope with this alone and might need to wait for Louise's return from work. He fetched bottle and glass, poured himself a large measure of whisky and tried again, standing in the doorway, looking up at the distant carn.

'Now...'

There was a pause. It seemed that Joe too was drinking whisky. There was the sound of clinking glass, and a bottle placed on a table.

'...turn the thing off if there's anybody with 'ee. What I got to say is private.'

Barny closed the door and went inside. He sat in his old arm chair, turned the volume of the tape down low, and listened.

Sarah said, 'I was in love with Steve Trevorrow, and had been ever since I was a girl. He had plenty of girlfriends, but Mary Trenowden had him in the end. I was very shy, in they days, or I might have had him. I reckon I could have, if I'd been a bit more daring.'

'Your Gramma died, then your Granda, after I had looked after them for years. I was thirty-eight years of age, all alone, and likely to remain so for the rest of my life.'

'Just after they died, Steve had an affair, with an artist, when he had been married for twenty years. It nearly broke my heart to see him... making a fool of himself. I began to drink, here, all by myself. Nobody knew. At first it was sherry, then I would go all the way to Penavon to buy spirits. None of us were happy, neither Steve, nor me, nor yet Mary. I used to have Steve here, doing bits of jobs, just to see him.'

Katie felt a chill pass through her as she anticipated what it was her mother was trying to tell her. So, she thought, that's why everybody has advised against me seeing Boy Steve. It would be incest. Oh no! Or would it? she thought. No one else need know.

Her mother appeared to have difficulty in recollection, was obviously finding this disclosure stressful, and so was Katie.

'Ma,' Katie said, to help them both. 'If you're going to tell, you must tell all.'

Sarah had anticipated this day for twenty-three years, looked forward to it, except for dreading the circumstances in which it would happen, and now found it almost impossible to face.

'He helped out when he could,' she said. 'All in cash. Your clothes, money for your education. It must have been very hard for him, not to have had your love.'

I had his, Katie thought, and never knew. And now, I love his son, my own brother.

Sarah said, 'You have to understand that I made the decision. He was in no way to blame. I mean, people might have thought he was taking advantage of me. It wudn like that.'

'Things were very different in they days, when I was a girl. I was never able to be myself. I was ashamed of myself, the real me that nobody knew about.' Sarah looked her daughter in the eye. 'I had lust, you see, Katie, and it wudn allowed.'

She paused for several minutes, thinking about what she had done, what her father would have said. He would have thrown her out in self-righteous indignation for bringing disgrace to the family.

'I asn'd to give me a baby. He said no.'

Katie's jaw dropped in astonishment. She had imagined a moment of indiscretion, unleashed passion and circumstance romantic, in which this quiet woman who was her mother had lost control and succumbed to the passion of a lover against her better judgement.

Old Steve must have been very handsome in his youth, she thought, he was attractive now, quiet, with a certain dignity. It was easy to see why Sarah had been attracted to him, with his twinkling eyes.

'I said, "If you won't, I'll ask somebody else. I'll seduce somebody, I'll have the plumber or the milkman. I'm nearly thirty-nine years old and I'm not going to spend the rest of my life all by myself not knowing what it's like."'

Sarah paused, remembering the circumstances of her life at that time.

'He never said a word, over all the years, not to a single soul. I knew he wouldn't.'

Katie waited for her mother to continue in a quiet, resigned voice, 'He spent the night here. We loved each other.'

Katie had great difficulty in fighting her emotions. She bit her lip, dug her fingernails into the palms of her hands. Only once? she thought, only once in her whole life?

'Was it...? ' she said.

'Oh yes!'

Katie broke down. She fell onto her mother's lap and hugged her, with the tears wetting her skirt. 'And Mary never knew?'

'Mary? What 'ee mean, Mary? Wudn nothen to do with she.'

Sarah rose to her knees. 'How can you say that? Steve is her husband.'

'Steve?' Sarah cried, alarmed that her daughter had misunderstood. 'Wudn Steve!'

'It wasn't Steve?'

'Why no! Wus Joe!'

'Joe!' Katie cried. 'Joe? Uncle Joe Curnow? He's my father?'

'Yes.'

Katie's incredulous face turned to her mother. It was true. She felt a twitch convulse her features, and she laughed. Amid tears and hugs of her mother, she laughed until Sarah pressed her away.

'Not *Steve*. Why, he was a married man. I couldn't have Steve.'

Joe, old rough-and-ready Uncle Joe, Katie thought. I never even considered him. Illiterate Joe, from whom she had inherited half her genes, half her intelligence.

'He was a good man,' Sarah said

'I know.

'He wudn no fool.'

'I know. I know. You won't ever have to apologise for him. I'm glad he was my father. I shall tell everybody.'

'I must answer the phone,' Sarah said.

It was Barny.

'He wants to speak to you.'

'When?' Katie said. 'When shall I come down? No, I can't come now. OK. Tomorrow morning then. I'll bring it with me.'

'He wants to see me. Alone. He asked me to bring the fool's gold.'

'It's still here in the drawer.'

Sarah reached back and opened the drawer behind her. She took out the lump of ore and passed it to Katie. She felt disencumbered of a heavy weight that she had borne too long alone. Light-headed in her liberation, she was nevertheless apprehensive of the burden passed to her daughter.

'You don't have to tell anybody,' she said, 'if you don't want to.'

Katie suddenly stood stock still. 'You don't think Barny knows, do you. Do you think Joe could have told him?

'No. I don't think so.'

The two pieces of ore lay side by side on Barny's table. He picked one up, weighing it in his hand. 'They're obviously the same,' he said.' So I thought I'd better tell 'ee, I took my father's sample to the School of Mines museum to compare it with their samples and there's no doubt about it. It's a nugget of high-quality ore. Iron pyrites is harsher in colour, crystalline, cubic in structure, while the ore in these is smooth, like dross from molten metal, tending to be more homogeneous with the rock, embedded in the quartz.'

He took a small square tile from a drawer, and rubbed the lump of ore across it, leaving a yellow streak on the ceramic surface.

'Iron pyrites wouldn' do that.' He put the sample down, picked up the other and did the same, leaving a second streak on the tile. 'Yours is the same as mine, so it seems that both pieces are gold.'

'Gold?' Katie said. 'I didn't know there was gold in our mines.'

'There's everything in them. All kinds of minerals. Gold as much as two ounces per ton of gozzan.'

'What's gozzan?

'Spoil. From the word *gossen*, rust, or ferruginous earth.'

'Doesn't sound very much, two ounces per ton of spoil.'

'Depends what it's worth. And there might be a lot more. If the price is high enough Simon Sweeting would rip the place apart for it. There'd be spoil heaps all along the cliff.'

'You're suggesting that Sweeting might well have been right in seeing our land as a gold mine.'

'He probably doesn't even know that there is gold here. I am merely saying, at this stage, that we should not say where our specimens came from. Say nothing about them at all.'

'I see. I think.'

'We need to do a lot more thinking.' He picked the nuggets up, felt the weight of them again. 'I should have known all along,' he said. 'As I suspect my father knew, and I'm certain my grandfather knew. As a young miner he would have been aware of its value but unable to sell it before he was killed. I'll put them somewhere safe, if that's all right with you.'

'Yes. Sure.'

'The name of the mine, *Wheal Dowr*, has always puzzled me. It doesn't make sense in that it's no wetter or nearer water than many others. I mean the water wasn't sufficiently significant for the mine to be named after it.'

'What are you suggesting?'

'Well, if it were originally *Whel Owr*, on the other hand, with the intrusive 'd' that came into the late vernacular, *Whel Dowr*, it might well mean 'gold mine'. The older form would have been *Bal Owr*, or *Pol Owr*, as *Pol*, meaning Pool, was sometimes used for gold diggings, of which, it seems, there were quite a few. What I'm suggesting is that the mine might well be developed from one of the ancient gold mines, the name of which has been distorted, and that there could still be rich lodes in there.'

He opened a drawer, wide enough for her to see a braid of black hair in it, and threw them in, saying, 'Safe as houses there,' with a wry smile.

'There's something else.' He turned to her and went to his hi-fi. 'There is something you ought to know, and it might not be easy for 'ee. It's about Joe.'

'I already know.'

'You do?'

'Ma told me.' She was smiling. 'I wish I'd known before he died. But they agreed not to tell anyone, not even me.'

'Who did? When?'

'Sarah and Joe. My mother and father.'

Barny sat down. He rubbed his hand over his mouth, bit the side of his index finger. 'Joe?' he said. 'Uncle Joe?'

'Yes.'

Good God! he thought, Uncle Joe, the old devil.

'Oh. well... . If you already know... . ' He put the tape in the drawer.

'By my life.' Barny said to Steve next time he had a chance to talk to him alone, which was after the funerals, 'you're a dark horse. Always were.'

'Am I?'

'Everybody thought it was you.'

'Thought what was me?'

'You know perfectly well what I mean. Katie.'

'Nobody ever said anything to me, so I couldn't deny it or confirm it. I let them think what they liked. I b'lieve Sarah's been laughing at me all this time. She did it to punish me. She's a very determined woman. She's like her fehther.'

'Did you know it was Joe?'

'No. Not for certain.'

'You don't mind?'

'I'm very glad for them. Katie must have given Joe a lot of happiness over the years, watching her grow up. Huh! You think *I'm* a dark horse.'

'Boy Steve must be relieved.'

'How?'

'Well, him and Katie.'

'Nothen will come of that. Mary's against it, and so is Sarah, from what I gather.'

'Oh?'

'She has her suspicions about the boy being involved with Langley's murder. Well, not really. She thinks Steve is a bit of a mad-brain, and he has still "not been eliminated" from police enquiries.'

'I see. I shouldn't worry about that, if I were you.'

'No, I don't. But Simon Sweeting is pressing for action, they say, and wants the boy arrested and charged. He's put all the harbour dues up double. He's mad as hell because his yacht was stripped.'

'What 'ee mean, stripped?'

'Well.... . You knaw. All the crowd down there at the wreck, saving things from the sea, if you mind to.'

Barny began laughing, imagining the scene on the night following the wreck. 'What did they take?'

'Wudn much left, by all accounts. They said it was what Joe would have wanted. Sweeting says they took the yacht's safe, with all the papers and money.'

'I heard nothing about all this.'

'What do 'ee expect, stuck down there?'

The safe wasn't very big, but it was too heavy to carry very far. It took all the strength of Zeke and a couple of the other mad-brains from the pub to get it to his cottage in the night, and it took him three days to open it. He gave the mad-brains a few quid and there was a large, anonymous donation in the lifeboat collection box the following day. Zeke was more interested in the papers.

He knocked on Barny's door, one evening when Louise was working late, and said, 'I got something to show 'ee.'

'Come in, boy. What've 'ee invented now?'

Zeke paused on the threshold, about to turn away. He was carrying a black plastic bin bag, folded flat over something under his arm. A decision was made, and he entered. He saw the inscription on the beam.

An Lavar coth, yu lavar gwyr –
Byth dorn re ver dhe'n tavas re hyr
Mes den hep tavas a-gollas y dyr.

'I like that,' he said.

'The old speech is the true speech.
To be long in the tongue, is to be short in the hand.
But the tongueless man has lost his land.'

'Tha's near enough,' Barny said. 'I didn't know you could speak the language.'

'You're like a lot of others. You think I'm daft, don't 'ee?'

And, while Barny was fumbling for words, Zeke went on, 'A lot thought Joe was daft because he couldn't read English and the same ones d' think you're daft to learn a language tha's nearly dead. They think I'm daft because I d' knaw things they've never dreamt of. 'ess well... . Tha's enough of that. Have a look at this,' he said as he removed a thick bundle of papers from the plastic bag and spread them on the table.

Barny looked them over, saying nothing.

'And this one,' Zeke insisted. 'Look here, one from the Marine Insurance Company. She wudn insured cuz the premiums hadn't been paid.'

'Have you shown these to anyone else?'

'No. Not a soul. They're worth a fortune.'

'What 'ee mean? All this correspondence from his financiers can only mean one thing. He's bankrupt!'

'All this other stuff,' Zeke said. 'He wudn want that to come out. And he waint be bankrupt. People like he don't go bust, only his companies. Never spent a ha'pmy of his own money in his life, more'n to buy nicey and fags.'

'So?'

'Newspapers.'

'You wouldn't do that.'

'I would for Boy Steve.'

Barny considered that: Zeke's darting eyes, his earnest expression. 'I would for Boy Steve'.

Yes. And so would Barny, for Old Joe.
'We can do it nonimus,' Zeke said, and they laughed.
'Yes, we'll do it "nonimus".'
'*Hep hynwyn.*'
'Where's my pen?' Barny said.

For weeks after the wreck, Barny seemed like one in a daze to his acquaintances. He had lost his father and one of his oldest friends in a single stormy night, and he sensed that Louise was drifting away from him too, to be lost in tempests of her own invocation. He assumed it was to protect herself from the pain of involvement and forgave her, for he was aware that in some ways he was behaving in exactly the same manner towards his own friends because, despite telling Louise otherwise, he kept away from them, unable to cope with more than his personal grief. He saw Anne, now and then, aware that she too was distant, unwilling to adopt the role that should now be Louise's. She looked at him with pity when his eyes were averted.

Steve had little to say. Old Baragwaneth had done very well. We caint be first and last too, and that was that. As for Joe, as for the wreck, and as for the whole folly of men, well, what can 'ee say? He saved my life, the damn fool.

But life, as they d' say, must go on. Barny found that Beth was his primary source of encouragement, and this by example rather than by precept. She spoke of preparing the ground for next year's crops, the mild weather, the cuttings she had struck and only once, when they were alone in her house, did she refer directly to Louise and her resumed preoccupation with her job. 'She's afraid,' Beth said, looking directly into his eyes, 'to swim in deep water.'

Barny smiled at her analogy. 'True,' he responded ruefully. 'She doesn't seem to realise, even now, that most drownings occur in the shallows.'

That there was some new trepidation troubling Louise, he had no doubt. She seemed to exploit every minor difference of opinion between them with the intention of precipitating a major quarrel. Of his friends, of his way of life, toward which she had previously expressed admiration, she now spoke with deprecation, pointing out the limitations of their narrow, parochial lives.

'Look at Steve's son,' she said. 'An intelligent young man like that could have gone far in life.'

'He's where he wants to be.'

'But what will he ever do to expand his mind, to develop as an individual? His life here is so insular.'

This was absurd, Barny thought. She must be seeking confrontation on any pretext, looking for a substitute upon which she could lay reason for decisions already taken, or a narrow rift to be prised apart. He assumed she was smarting from some imagined slight, about which she was too sensitive to speak. It was time she learned to be honest with him and he denied her his retaliation, merely smiling as he said, 'If you say so.'

'You must agree with me,' she said, and he could see that she was hoping otherwise. She was trying to provoke a quarrel, as an excuse for distancing herself or denying him her body. But that, he reasoned, she would do regardless of his response, if it was her intention.

'Despite what happened to his father's friend, he's prepared to go on pursuing a dangerous occupation for little return. Why doesn't he get some qualifications and take up something more rewarding? He could even get a grant.'

Ah, Barny thought, it's time to tell her a few things. 'Boy Steve,' he sighed, 'is a Bachelor of Science. He has a first-class honours degree in biology from Newcastle University.' Barny was loosing his patience with her. 'Which makes him, I believe, more highly qualified than you with your two-two in a subject you have abandoned. And yes, his job is dangerous, but I suspect there might be proportionally more deaths in fast cars driven by those trendy executives you so wish to emulate.'

She could not answer him. 'Be careful, Loopy,' he said, taking pity on her, 'of making rash judgements on people you don't know. Boy Steve is living the life he chose. Apart from fishing, he's involved in research for the Ministry, tagging lobsters and fish for migration studies, taking sea temperatures and water samples for analysis. He's a happy man.'

'Well,' she said, defensively, 'How was I to know? You never told me anything about him. And in any case, what you have just said merely corroborates my opinion. Qualifications lead to fulfilment in life.'

'Depends what you mean by qualifications,' he said, conceding a point, 'and fulfilment too. I'm happy enough, and I have no formal qualifications. I had no formal education at all, really, apart from learning to read and write. We left school at fourteen, as our parents had only their fair share of the world's riches and couldn't afford to buy us an education. Knowledge was like a commodity in this country, only available to those who could afford to pay.'

'It makes me angry,' she said, 'to think that people who are working pay taxes to support people like you.'

How often people change their religion or politics according to the viewpoint from which they survey them, he thought. Here was one who was destitute a few months ago, glad to claim every penny from the state, even housing benefit to which she was not strictly entitled as she was sleeping with her landlord, now accusing him of some heinous crime because he did not want, or need, a job. Everything he owned, which included his time as well as his possessions, was paid for with the fruits of his own labour. Even his knowledge was self-acquired. He owed nothing to anyone. Her accusation, far from angering him, amused him, although he felt entitled to point out her changing attitude.

'You were glad of the State when you first came down here.'

'With the amount of tax I'm paying, they'll soon get it back.'

'How,' he said sadly, 'are the fallen mighty!'

She looked at him with a sullen glare and he gave in to her. 'Why are we quarrelling, Loopy?'

'I don't know. It makes me so unhappy. I do love you so.'

After the fine days following the storm, there was a period of dull overcast weather which lasted well into November. During the dark evenings they sat beside the fire, reading or listening to music. She seemed tranquil and content, yet he could not get close to her and, by the fact that she rarely mentioned her job, he assumed she now had sufficient confidence to cope without his continual support. At times, that expression of fragile insecurity clouded her eyes and she turned to him with a gesture of affection, as if she needed the confirmation of his love, and his heart stirred with concern for her. Yet at night a chill came over her which was evidently a warning to keep his distance, and he slept beside her in trepidation. The evenings were now dark when he picked her up from work, the mornings grey in the dawn light, and she saw little of the countryside: only the damp road and the moors on either side, swirling with mists as the pale sun rose across the bay. There came a fine weekend, however, one of those cloudless days when the long shadows intensify the colours, and he persuaded her to go down to the cliffs and walk with him for a while, get some fresh air in her lungs. The wind was light, hardly enough to stir the white grasses in the bogs, with the horizon a clear demarcation between gentian and powder blue.

'But education is available to everyone, you know that. My parents were not well off, the state paid.'

'Yeah, well, for a few years in the post-war recovery the state needed an educated population, so the state provided. Things are changing, back to where they were before. We have computers to do the thinking now, so why waste a high percentage of Gross National Product on education that nobody needs... .'

'God, you have become such a cynic. What's happened to your optimism?'

'It's still there. With a bit of luck the catastrophe will come early, while the planet still had the resilience to recuperate, and people will learn to live again.'

'Some people believe that earning enough money to own a nice house and drive an expensive car is living.'

'I doubt it. Most of them are far more concerned about convincing other people that they're living. The last reason for owning an expensive car is for driving somewhere.'

'You're being silly, or trying to wind me up again. Our system of living at least enables you to live the way you wish, with all your needs provided for. Why do you insist on being so scathing about it?'

He should have stopped then, Barny was to remember in his painful recollections of these days in times to come. He should have let his opinions and scepticism lie, kept quiet, said it in his poetry, but he did not do so.

'Nobody provided me with anything,' he said, 'except myself. You've fallen for one of the great myths of our time, which is that governments provide. They don't, and never have. There's not a single state where prosperity is the result of government policies. From the beginning of civilisation governments have merely been systems of exploiting the enterprise of others. They can't provide anything, because nothing is theirs to dispense.'

'Oh!' Louise said. 'You do exasperate me. I did study economics as part of my degree course. You're talking nonsense.'

'It's the result of having no education. My mind is undisciplined, thank God.'

'And you an atheist.'

Barny shoved his peaked cap to the back of his head. 'I've never said I am an atheist. I know too little about gods to deny them.'

He could see that she was getting angry with him for not taking life, as she saw it, seriously, and he grinned at her knowingly.

They walked in silence for some time, with Barny desperate for some common thread of conversation. She was deep in her own thoughts and he could find none. They stopped at a stile, where the footpath crossed a stone wall, with the sea below them, the high moor rising inland. A few flowers of gorse and some late campion glowed in the shelter of the boulders beside their feet. In the distance stood the lighthouse, with the crumpled folds of the coastal contours sloping to the black rocks fringing the sea.

'It's lovely,' Barny said, 'even at this time of year.'

'Yes.'

'Look!' he said. '*Ottoma Rialobran hag y Myghternes*. Here come Royal Raven and his Queen, come to survey their kingdom. What splendid things.'

They watched the big black birds, with the sun glinting on their glossy plumage, circle and climb high into the blue before flying off inland towards the carn. Barny looked at the colour all around them and laughed aloud. 'How could we live anywhere else?'

'I have to go to a new store,' Louise said. 'I have to stay up there.'

Only for a little while, she said. They had more or less forced her into it, for to refuse would be construed as not having the best interests of the company in mind and she would be overlooked, regarding promotion, for ever in the future.

So what? was Barny's reaction She's happy where she is, at last, and they won't sack her, so why let herself be pushed around? This was obviously what had been bothering her for weeks.

'I did tell you,' she said.

'Did you? I don't remember.'

'You never listen to what I say.'

'Well, I'm listening now. Where will you stay?'

If I try to dissuade her, she'll accuse me of trying to restrict her life.

'I'll have to get a flat or something.'

She might have been discussing the groceries... . I'll have to get some salt. As if it were not really important.

'A flat? You mean move up there? But why?'

'It's too far to commute everyday and the trains are unsuitable. You would hardly see me during the week anyway. I'll be home every weekend.'

As the time grew nearer for her to move to her new job, she let it be known, in casually telling him of the arrangements she was making, that she intended taking all her things.

'Not your books,' he said. 'You won't need to take your books.'

'I'll need them in the evenings when I'm all alone.'

All of them? When she had not looked at them for two years? Home, he thought, is where the books are, that's what she'd said, Where the books are. His face was openly crestfallen when at last she looked at him.

'It's only for a little while,' she said. 'And it will make you appreciate me.'

'I do that now. How can you doubt it?'

And there it was once more, that fear for her which tingled the hair on his nape, that relict sixth sense of his ancestors, that irrational foreboding, come again to bedevil him.

'But I still think you're making a mistake,' he said.

An angry flash sparked briefly into her eyes. 'You're trying to dissuade me from furthering my career.' She faced him with defiance in her eyes. 'What do you want me to do? Spend the rest of my life around here making you cups of tea?'

They stared at each other for what seemed an interminable silence. Barny endured a physical pain, stabbing at his heart, and was unable to believe what he had heard, unable to speak.

Louise eventually relented. 'I'm sorry. That was cruel.'

'Yes,' Barny whispered, 'it was.'

One of the men from work, she said, had offered to take her belongings up in his van, and Barny contrived to be out of the house on the day he came, for he would have no part in expediting her departure. There remained only a few clothes and personal odds and ends and, when he returned, the house was naked.

She was quite affectionate towards him for the next few days, even cuddling up to him at night, but his desire for her was inhibited by the suspicion that her overtures were insincere, merely a ploy for avoiding an emotional scene.

On the morning of the day of her departure, when she was to take the afternoon train, Barny woke early after a fitful night. In her sleep, she had put her arms around him and he had lain looking at her face, their heads close together on the pillow, unwilling to disentangle himself from her embrace. Her expression was utterly serene, with her eyes lightly closed, and her full lips relaxed, a child in her oblivion.

The dreads came over him as he looked at her, thinking, what will become of us, Loopy? Like a black fog the terrifying thoughts came out from behind the curtain of subconscious mist and coalesced into the vision of his fate. He fought them off. Not now, damn you. Not now! And he clung to his beloved woman, saying, 'Oh, my darling. Hold me. Hold me tight. Don't leave me.'

She drew him close to her warmth. 'I'm not leaving you,' she murmured, sleepily. And she soothed the terrors away with caresses and terms of endearment. 'I'll never love anyone the way I've loved you.' Still drowsy from her deep, untroubled slumber.

When Barny's fears subsided, they fell back into sleep, entwined and content, until the dawn. As they stirred into consciousness, Barny found himself realising how much alike they were, in that they loved each other most in the moments of the other's weakness, no longer seeing their strength as a threat. This had not occurred to him before.

The proximity of her body was exciting him, so he drew away that she might not feel it against her thigh. He would let her sleep, content in his arms, where she belonged.

'Don't you want me?' he heard her mumble in a drowsy voice, her eyes still closed.

He could live with her for a thousand years and still not understand her capricious moods. What had induced a desire for him now? He moved his hand from under her shoulder blade, to her ribs, her hips and around into her *gwylfos du*, where he found a flooded pool awaiting him. Is it, he thought, my weaknesses that quicken her? Is this the essence of her feminism, that she should dominate me, both mentally and physically? Would she then despise him for his subservience, and not know why?

'Of course I want 'ee.' he said. 'I shall always want 'ee.'

After his abstinence from her for so long, during the recent weeks of her impassivity, Barny became enormously excited by her unexpected incitement and he desired her as never before. He threw off the bedclothes and held her close to him, saying, already breathless, 'Oh. How I love you. How you excite me. I thought I'd lost you for ever.' Kissing her temple, mouth, neck, breasts, adoring every little morsel of her as she responded with a touch of her hand upon him. 'My black bran. My wild raven.'

'Do you really want me?' she said. 'Tell me. Tell me how much you need me, what you would like to do to me.' Burying her wet mouth against his neck, with her teeth holding a fold of his skin as she anticipated the chronicle of her lusts... . 'I'd like to tie you down... to get you so roused you would not care how I had you... . I want you by the ass.'

And there came over him an urge to submit her to these abominations with which she had induced him to stimulate her only to withdraw in fear at the merest suspicion that he might perform them. Now, he found himself with a wish to dominate her, subdue her, force her to submit to her own desires and take her into involuntary ecstasy by the sheer fervour of his passion, to grapple with her for supremacy of body and mind.

'Me on top,' she said as he rolled over onto her. 'I want to go on top.'

He resisted her. Holding her down by the weight of his body. Now, she could submit to her other demands, the demons of her carnal flesh as opposed to her fastidious mind. Now, he would fuck her.

He prised her legs apart with his knee, struggling hard against her resistance with words of obscene chastisement flowing unspoken through his mind. Open your legs, you slut. Why have you tortured me? As he slowly forced his way up inside her thighs before she collapsed in exhaustion. Lift your fucking knees up. Fight me. Retaliate, you selfish bitch.

'You're hurting me,' she said. And he rolled off, appalled at his own lechery, and recovered his breath.

'Come on then,' he said, resignedly. 'You on top. If that's what you want.'

So, once more it was all for her. He gave himself to Louise again and she took him, hardly aware, it seemed to Barny, what man she had beneath her as she screamed to a climax and fell upon him, sobbing with relief.

He held her, encouraging her tears, as full of desire for her as ever, until she lay quietly beside him. 'I still want you,' he said. He could not let her go away leaving him swollen with desire.

'I'm too sore,' she said. 'I've rubbed myself raw.'

Barny could not, would not, constrain himself. He did it with his hand, kneeling beside her, and felt it rising within him as he tried to get into her, nearly demented with frustration. He wanted to be inside her, to feel himself surrounded by her as he burst forth with the gush of passion, but she closed her legs.

'In my mouth,' she insisted. 'In my mouth.'

She had a bath as Barny lay in bed, physically satisfied, bodily exhausted, yet emotionally disturbed, angry with himself for not having insisted on entering her, wishing he had raped her.

She has, he thought, sucked me dry.

On the following Friday, when he was due to pick her up from the station, she phoned from a call box, for there was no telephone in her flat, she said.

'I can't come down for the weekend. I have to work. Sorry.'.

CHAPTER SIXTEEN

An Pen wyth. The very end.

'...and you never saw him again...?'

'I must have been mad to leave him. I'm mad aren't I? You think I'm mad, don't you..?'

After the wreck I thought that I could never fit into Barny's community. The tragedy drew them together but they could not see my predicament, my isolation. I felt like an alien. Barny thought I was disparaging the whole community as parochial and insular and withdrew from me, not sharing his grief. They seemed to give me no recognition as an individual, I was seen only as the company representative. I felt rejected, glad to get away from it all. There seems to be nowhere where I belong... .

The pressures on me were too much. My ambition to succeed, our deteriorating relationship, my family, my past, were all too much. All the unresolved stuff that Barny had brought out about my groundless guilt. All the memories of failure. I could stand no more. It drove me mad, didn't it?'

There was to be no local superstore, so I went straight to head office and cracked up, and they brought me here. They destroyed me. There was no mercy. I'd said I could do it, they said, so bloody well get on with it. Stop wingeing. I couldn't cope all by myself, with no one to love me... .

And I couldn't go back to Barny. I assumed he hated me for what I had done to him and would never have me back. I thought it best for both of us, the sudden departure. He would get over it, I thought. He always said he was a tough old bugger. I loved him. I really did. I tried writing a few times, but I lost my nerve and tore up the letters. It was too much of a humiliation. I didn't mean to destroy him. I'd failed in everything, everywhere, when all I wanted was to be loved and respected.... . I can't think straight any more. Am I? Mad?

'No, you're not mad. Perhaps you should phone him... .'

Boy Steve paused in his work and watched Katie Stevens coming down along the wharf. So like her mother, he thought, and me so like my father, it d' make 'ee wonder if we can have any identity of our own, here in this small town. Are we destined to perpetuate the feuds and passions of our forbears down the generations forever? Look at her! The shape of her, the very eyes of her are Sarah Stevens's. I do adore her and because of the animosity between our mothers I ab'm so much as kissed her. She'll finish up like Sarah too, alone in her old age with nobody to take care of her and love her. Can't Sarah see that? How don't she like me?

Katie passed behind the lodge, where the smoke from the iron chimney-pipe poking through the roof rose straight into the grey sky before levelling off and drifting east across the bay. She was wearing a white, knitted bobble-hat, jeans and a loose sweater, white trainers, but no clothing could conceal the carriage of the head, the walk that was, if only people had seen it, the replica of Joe's, with its swinging stride. She was carrying a small green rucksack, slung over one shoulder, and waved to Boy Steve as she came to the slipway. He quickly shoved his tools in the wheelhouse and went to meet her. Now was as good a time as any to open the hatches, show her what he was, tell her what he thought.

'Barny phoned,' Katie said. 'He wants to see us, together. He wouldn't say what for.'

'The police have had me in again. They still believe I killed Langley.'

'I know.'

'You do? How?'

'Everybody knows. The whole town is talking about it. They say it's only a matter of time before you're formally charged.'

'And what about you? What do you think?'

'Let's walk down the quay,' Katie said.

They reached the top of the quay in virtual silence, he waiting for her answer, she reluctant to speak.

'Up this way,' he said. 'There's too many down there.' And he led her through the narrow streets, bereft of life, with all the houses empty for the winter, past the old Seamen's Mission and out to the headland, where they could look back over the bay and the grey slate roofs of down'long and see the houses sprawling up'long towards the last green fields in sight. They leaned over the wall where the bird-watchers lined up during westerly gales and he said, 'They all think I'm a bit of a mad-brain, don't they? That I could have killed that bastard Langley.'

'Do they?'

'The police do. Sarah do. And so do you.'

'Do I? Don't you think you are making assumptions without reason?'

'No. And neither are you. You're right, you and your mother,' he said, sullenly, 'I'm a murderer.'

Katie watched a line of gannets follow the contours of the waves, swinging low, in line ahead, their white plumage brilliant against the dull sea. 'Are you?' she said.

''es. At least by nature, because if I had a been there that day I would have strangled him with my bare hands.'

Katie believed it.

'But I wasn't there,' he cried. 'I wasn't bleddy-well there. Why won't you believe me?'

'If it wasn't you, it must have been Zeke.'

'Zeke!' he exploded. 'Of course it wasn't Zeke. But it could have been you.'

'Me? '

'Yes, you! There's no less reason to suspect you than me.You're the only one who was there without a doubt.You could have hit'n in self-defence, just as you said, and then chucked him down the shaft. You never seemed very upset about his death. I don't know why the police ab'm taken you in for questioning.'

'Why should I be upset about the death of a man who was about to assault me? And the police did question me. They said that I wasn't strong enough.'

'Tha's nonsense.' He saw the flash of anger in her eyes. 'You're very strong for your size. You could easily have dragged him to the edge and thrown him over. I wouldn't blame you if you did.'

'I wish I'd never gone near the place,' she said. 'And I wish you hadn't followed me there.'

So she did think so.... 'Oh, Katie...' he said. 'I no more killed him than you did. I believe he fell in the dark, when recovering from the blow you gave him with the stone. It was an accident, and that's what the police are saying too. '

'What ?'

'Yeah. They told me this mornin', after that inspector questioned me for two hours again, just to frighten me a bit more. He, personally, still thinks I did it, but it seems that Simon Sweeting, like everybody else, has come to believe it was an accident too, though they didn't say so. They said I have been eliminated from their enquiries.'

'But it was not an accident, Steve. Oh, I don't know. Perhaps it was. Perhaps he fell in the dark. I want to forget it.'

'And me too !'

'Come in,' Barny said, and they thought how the death of his father had aged him. The sparkle had gone from his eye, his voice was tired, as if he had said too much and wished for solitude. 'Nice to see you both. *Fattel a genoughwhy?*'

'*Pyr dha, mir ras,*' Boy Steve said. '*Fattel os ta?*'

'*Dha lowr,*' Barny said. 'I'm fair enough.'

Not, they noticed, his usual cheerful self, on top of the world and full of enthusiasm for life, and there was no trace of his woman about the place, no object which was not obviously his, no feminine touch to brighten the academic severity of the room, no flowers in a vase. There was the smell of cooking emanating from the kitchen, however, a rich smell of slowly simmering casserole.

They settled themselves side by side on the old settee, while Barny sat in his chair. It was evident to them that he was irresolute, procrastinating, doubting their reaction to whatever it was that he had to tell them. He asked about their parents and was subject to evasive answers, no mention of the animosity that was certainly between them. This was what he had hoped for, to be told in no uncertain, yet polite, manner, that these things were for the families to sort out among themselves. These two could not, however, resolve their differences without his help.

'I am about to break a confidence,' he said suddenly, 'in the belief that you will not do likewise. I am going to play a tape on this contraption, just once, and then I'm going to chuck it on the fire. There are no copies.'

He waited for their response, watching them as they looked at each other, despising himself for his inadequacy, the abdication from responsibility, placing his burden upon these young shoulders. It was, he decided for the hundredth time, for their own good, that they should not spend the remainder of their days in mutual suspicion.

The tape was already in the machine, there was but one button to press. He poured whisky into three glasses, silently placed one before each of them and pressed it.

Play.

'Hullaw, Barny,' Joe's voice said again, 'Don't s'pose you expected to hear from me again. Hee hee. '

To the sound of clinking glass, Barny sipped his whisky, Boy Steve did likewise, while Sarah - t' hell! Katie, I mean - looked unblinkingly at Barny, who avoided her eyes.

'Now... Turn the thing off if there's anybody with 'ee. What I got to say, is private... .'

He had allowed time for Barny to shut the thing off if there had been anyone with him on the occasion of the first of many times in which he had since listened to this voice from the dead.

'...It's about that fella Langley.'

The acrid smell of the burning plastic briefly tainted the air in the room. Speechlessly, they watched the grotesque distortions of the writhing shape disintegrating in the flames and in the slight hiss and crackle they heard the echoes, the dripping water, the scream, and the swallowing of rubble down the dark, insatiable throat of the shaft.

'He paid for...' Boy Steve said as he reached for Katie's hand.

Barny raised his own hand. 'I don't want to hear anything about it. There's no need to mention it to anybody. We only have to decide what to do about the gold.'

'Gold?' Boy Steve asked. 'What gold?'

They told him about the nuggets. 'There could be a rich vein in there, just beyond the workings. What do we do?'

Boy Steve looked for a sign on Katie's face, some indication of what she might want. There was nothing. He looked at Barny, who gazed into the flames where the last bit of plastic glowed with a green haze among the embers. There was a shift of coals and it was gone.

Gold in the mine? It might save Sweeting's skin. It might bring death. It might bring exploitation of the land and the people. Or it might bring a desperately needed period of prosperity to the town, if only while the mine was surveyed and exploratory shafts sunk into the deep granite underground. The gold could be just the excuse for deep diggings which might house nuclear waste.

'Where are the nuggets?' Boy Steve asked.

'Here.'

Barny took them from the drawer. Boy Steve weighed them in his hand, asking, 'How much are they worth?'

'I'm not sure,' Barny said. 'They weigh two pounds in total. Say there's a pound of gold in them. I asked the jeweller in town how much a pound of gold is worth. He said, depending on the bullion market, about three thousand pounds. He thought I was talking like a tuss.'

Boy Steve whistled. 'Good God! Who knows about them?' he asked.

'Only us.'

'Three thousand pounds would come in very handy right now,' Steve said.

He passed the two pieces of ore back to Barny. Barny put them on the low table between them and reached for a log which he placed on the fire. The November evening was darkening the room, and the window framed a picture of mist, gathering about the carn.

Katie looked at Steve with a blank expression on her face, waiting for him to say more.

'We could throw them down the shaft,' Boy Steve said, 'back where they came from.'

Barny pushed the nuggets toward Steve and Katie. 'They would be found. Keep them. Or chuck them in the sea. I leave it to you.'

Katie reached for Steve's hand.

They ate the casserole and, while Barny was pouring the second glass of wine, Katie said, 'Where's Louise? I haven't seen her for weeks.'

'Gone away,' he said. 'Gone away for a while.'

At first, he expected her to return, hoping that all her previous declarations of love and devotion would prevail and that she would indeed be unable to survive without him, as she had so often proclaimed. He could not accept that her precipitate departure had been inevitable, that he himself had predicted it from their first days of tempestuous passion. All his instincts had warned him that she was dangerous, to fend her off, but he had become hopelessly enslaved by her, believing that he was in control of his emotions until it was too late, and she had devoured him. And, despite her betrayal, he still wanted her, hoping that she needed him now as she had in those fearful nights of depression. Every knock on the door, every rattle of the letterbox raised hopes of her return or a letter of love. He listened to every passing car, praying that it might be a taxi from town, dropping her with her few belongings, her clothes and beloved books, at his gate. He learned to recognise the sound of every vehicle in the district as he sat brooding over what he had done to alienate her. There was nothing, no sign, no letter, no tearful figure at the door. She was departed as in death, and he suffered agonies of bereavement for the third time in that year of drought.

The winter was terrible: endless days of dull, mild weather, with little rain and no frosts or storms, during which he brooded over the loss of her, unable to stir himself from the lethargy which had overcome him with the realisation that she went from him for ever on that morning when he might have raped her.

The silence of his cottage, which previously had been so conducive to writing, as unobtrusive as breath, became so tangible that it filled the rooms with the intensity of tortured screams. There were nights when he lay awake, listening to the voices in his head, unable to sleep or think of anything except what she might be doing at that moment, remembering how she had looked as she lay beside him, with that slight smile of contentment on her lips. At times the silence of the house became so unbearable that he was forced to go out and, whenever he did, he left the door unlocked as always, but now, during his absences, he lived in the hope that upon his return he would find her in his bed, with her long hair strewn over the pillow and her arms reaching to embrace him as they did in his dreams.

He could no longer bother to cook for himself and ate from tins. Even the empty chair, opposite him at the wooden table in the kitchen, invoked memories of her long fingers buttering bread or holding a glass of wine. The very music he had loved, his beloved Mozart and Orff, he could no longer bear to hear, for every cadence and phrase had now acquired some connotation, or memory, of times when they had listened to it together, entwined in each other's arms. Her presence about the place was like a melancholy ghost, haunting his every action, every minute of the day. There was no escape from her. Even when he walked the moors or the coast, she was with him as he remembered the hours they had spent together, when he had shown her the seals or the hissing, copulating adders. On some despairing nights he exhausted himself with frantic, desperate masturbation, forcing himself into two, or three, agonised ejaculations with a sweating determination to purge himself of all desire for her, without lust or sensuality.

It was absurd, he told himself. Of all the women he had ever known, she was the most difficult and exasperating of the lot. She was selfish and demanding and he was well rid of her. The time would come when he would regard her departure as a lucky escape. He tried to hate her, to convince himself that she had used him as an emotional catalyst, destroying his equilibrium in the process of her own conversion, but he came only to hate himself. With all his experience of life, he should never have allowed himself to become so vulnerable. How could a life so contented and complete, as his had been, be so utterly destroyed? He had lost Joe, his father and Anne: everyone who had been so dear to him, except for Beth, but she could never be his, although he was hers, which merely aggravated his despondency.

He stayed up late at night for fear of waking early in the morning and having to face another long, empty day. At times he read through all the letters she had sent him, promising himself that he would destroy them, tomorrow. He lined up her photographs and fought back tears of grief as he looked at her captured moods. He would not cry for her.

In the new year, after spending Christmas with Sam and Beth and the children, he went down to his father's house. Everything was gathering dust. He spent two days cleaning the place up and covered things with sheets. The model he took home, just to look at for a while, for he would not keep her. He saw everybody, from time to time, and they kept him informed of what was going on. Everything at Penavon was at a standstill and likely to remain so until the slump was over. Yachts, like houses, were for sale and falling into disrepair everywhere. There was no hope of a marina, and just as well, he thought, or there would be more drownings. He swore to himself. Why am I so bloody miserable? Why can I not get over her?

'Because,' he told himself, 'You're still, and forever, in love with her.'

Just once, he swallowed his pride and went to see Anne, to alleviate the loneliness, and they took a stroll down'long on a February night, with the lights reflected in the still water of the harbour, and there was nothing he could tell her that was not obvious, that he was in despair at losing Louise, as there was nothing she could tell him that was not also obvious. 'What do you want from me? I don't see what I can do for 'ee.' Her compassion not concealing the admonition in her voice, for she had warned him time enough. And he suffered the more when she added, with a note of sadness in her voice, 'I'm not going to be anybody's second best.'

Then, all the fearful dreads, which had plagued his life, came sidling into the images of his dreams, terrifying him into staring alertness, with cold sweat on his brow. These horrors, which he had previously resisted, took on a fascinating logicality. Perhaps they had been a premonition of his ultimate destiny, as he had seen it in others, that he should live out the nightmare, and kill himself.

As the dreads became more frequent, he discovered that he could induce them at will, or follow them through to their end in morbid fascination, and not be terrified at the prospect. The fear became a welcome emotion after the long, empty days. There was nothing to live for, for without Louise life was futile. There was no reason why he should not end the pain. It would be self-administered euthanasia.

He decided to do it after the gale that blew the winter away in a devastating tumult of shattered trees and flying slates. The wind had strengthened to a dull threatening roar, like pounding surf, which reverberated around his cottage for three days without abating. His new roof withstood the fury and his precious camellia lost no buds in the shelter of the escallonia hedge around the garden. Barny went out in it, went down to the headland where the white lighthouse stood and the furled halyards on the flag-pole whistled to the sirens in the splintering waves. He went to the headland on his hands and knees, cursing the wind but determined to be subjected to its fury rather than shelter at home, waiting for, yet uninvolved with, its passing. He defied the elements about him, exhilarated as he crawled to the edge of the cliff. He defied her Goddess, the Mother of Men, Daughter of Men, Manipulator of Men, to do her damnedest to him, to destroy his body as her acolyte had destroyed his mind. He challenged her to pluck him from the thrift and fling him to the sea.

It would have been easy then, to stand upright and let the wind take him, to do what it would with him, take him to the sea to be smashed to pieces in the white anger swelling over the rocks at the bottom of the cliff. That was not the way, for she had done enough to him and he would not offer himself as a sacrifice, neither would he willingly follow so many of his forbears to that purple gloom in the depths. The wind would not take him, for it was was but a puff compared with the storm which had taken Uncle Joe.

There, in the gale, at the edge of the sea, where so many of his most creative thoughts and inspiration had arisen, he made up his mind at last, after months of prevarication, and the doubts and procrastination fell behind him like a shroud of doubt. He resolved to have done with it, to put himself going.

He decided to 'put his affairs in order' and could even smile to himself at such method in his life. The bills were paid, papers sorted, rubbish thrown away. He went to a solicitor and made a will: something for Beth, the rest for Katie and Boy Steve. A sensible precaution, he was told; saves a lot of trouble for your beneficiaries. You can always change your mind, you are still young.

The images of the dreads, in the dark nights or the flickering flames of the fire, recalled the way to tie a noose. He practised tying it on a piece of string, one turn for each of the jury, as he used to tie them when he was a boy. They showed him places to hang it from, the beam by the stairs, a certain tree in the woods. There was a way of tying one's hands behind the back, of kicking away the stool. He turned his face to the pillow, or to the arm of the tattered sofa where she had lain her head, and said, 'Louise, Louise. Come back to me.'

Beth came to comfort him. He made her weak tea and they sat side by side, talking about it. Talking about Louise. 'Have you heard from her, Beth?'

'Not a thing.'

Once, he fell to his knees, and buried his face in her lap.

'I want her back.'

'She would go sometime. It's best now.'

'What has she done to me?'

He always felt calmer after talking to Beth. Her serenity was mellowing and he became briefly whole again, seeing hope for the future and his torment as transient. For one so much younger than himself, her maturity amazed him. She was in such contrast to Louise that he wondered how he could love them both, concluding that each and all his women satisfied some isolated need in him, for whereas Louise had invoked his paternity, vitalising his benevolence and devotion, Beth was his emotional refuge, a haven of tranquillity, to whom he could unashamedly reveal his weaknesses, for which Louise, and Anne too, would have derided him. He was closer to Beth, in many respects, than to Louise or Anne and he saw that he could become dependent upon her, which would not do, for that would compromise her marriage and he could not risk that. The loneliness would persist. There was no way out. The prospect of the looming years was unbearable and there was no reason for enduring it. He had attained all his ambitions and the rest was merely a wait for death, whenever it might come. There was no further reason for living.

On a fine morning, he went for a long walk, up over the moors and right into town, seeing everything for the last time. He went into the fishermen's co-op and bought a length of smooth nylon rope, slippery stuff, which would slide easily in a noose. He felt outside of himself, as if he were a spectator of his own life. The man in the shop coiled the rope expertly, slipped it into a carrier bag, saying, 'You don't want to walk around town like a man looking for a lamp post to hang himself on.' Barny smiled, as if appreciating the joke.

The sun was still shining as he walked back home. The granite carns on the hills were outlined crisply against the blue spring sky. Celandines - he would never see them without pain - were opening along the ditch. He cried. At last, the tears rolled down his cheeks and he shook his head, saying, 'Louise Louise.' again and again as he trudged down to the beam beside the stairs. He thought of going to Sam and Beth, for the last time, to tell them how much he loved them. To what end? To be cheered up and have the futility of his life temporarily palliated, only to be endured again in the lonely nights. There was nothing to be gained by postponing the thing.

After midnight, he decided. This last day he could endure to the end, but another, with the aches and remorse eating him away, would be a repetition of torture already suffered. He looked at his garden as he passed through the gate, the shrubs he had planted, the young trees leaning away to the hills as they cowered from the westerlies. There was the camellia, with the plump flower buds swelling with promises of blooms on the first warm day.

Inside the cottage, he prepared a meal, cooled some wine and drank it as he read through his poems, with the rope thrown over the back of the chair, from whence it looped to the floor, coiling like a sleeping serpent on the carpet.

This will endure, he thought. And with it the ethos of the last of his tribe. None who followed would experience the final throes of his people's extinction as he had done. He had been of the era. This stuff would live on after him. It was vibrant with nostalgia, yet unsentimental, expressing the resignation of accepting inevitable annihilation. There had been so much more he had wanted to say. His mind had been bursting with ideas, so many interpretations, sentiments, that two lifetimes would have been insufficient to express them. And now, it was gone. There was only the void left by the departure of Louise, an emotional vacuum which nothing, and no one could fill. As he read the poems the thought occurred to him, or rather, he found the revelation slowly crystallising in his mind, that he had never written a poem to, or about Louise. He dropped the papers on the table, frowning at himself in perplexity.

Why? Why no love poems? Despite the passion he had for her, despite the total commitment he felt to her.

He took up his pen and a pad of note paper. Under the poised nib, the clear space waited and mocked him.

There was nothing there. He tried to recall his intense love, the tenderness he had felt for her, to write a poem which would fill her with remorse for what she had done to him. A poem to invoke all the pain, the passion and laughter they had experienced together. There was nothing. He was finished. Dried up. Sucked dry. He had lost her to a shop, to be employed in the selling of catmeat and beans. A fucking shop! And she had taken his strength and creativity along with her, stolen them, leaving him hollow and sere.

'Oh Louise.' he said. 'Louise, Louise. What have you done to me?'

Whatever had he seen in her? He had forseen disaster the first time he set eyes on her. He did not know, but he adored her. God damn her! he thought. She must be forced to see what her callous use of people could do them. She had murdered him, and he would punish her. He would torture her with remorse if there was a grain of humanity in her being. He would take her with him, destroy her by his death, as she had destroyed him in her rebirth. She was his, he had made her, and he could do what he damned well liked with her. He wrote words on the paper, meaningless phrases, gibberish, obscene, dirty expressions of hate. He tore them up.

'Oh Louise. My love. My life.'

She had driven him mad. He had thought himself into lunacy and had the mind of an imbecile. He fell to the floor on his knees with a great choking sob, unaware of the reason for this intensified despondency. He was only aware that it was unendurable, and must end. There was still time, before the sun rose at the start of a new day. He rose dejectedly from the floor and sat at the table. After a few minutes, he reached for his pen and paper and stared into times gone by. *termyn ys passyas.*

He heard a cock crowing from Beth's chicken house. The pen was still in his hand, the page before him. He rose in alarm, trying to find himself, for he thought that he might have already done it, that he was seeing himself in death, but the snake was still coiled on the floor, the chair under the table. Hours had passed, hours in which his mind had no longer functioned. There was a faint light in the eastern sky, he felt as if his head was filled with cotton wool or compressed volatile gas, about to explode, for he could not formulate a single cohesive thought. He stared through the window, unaware of objects within his vision, listening to the discordant voices in his head, murmurings, shouts, the screams of a thousand unbearable tortures, all contorted into silent, unexpressed confusion.

317

The scribbles on the paper before him seemed to have materialised from nowhere, for he could not remember writing them. They were like words written by someone else, or spatters of ink blown by wind... *You have killed me*, he read. They were meaningless to him. He was losing time, losing his last hours in amnesia, and he struggled to recollect some thought, some manifestation of his existence since picking up the pen. He had not slept. He had not moved. He had become anaesthetised by the anodyne of the mind, protecting him from pain, for his thoughts could only have been of her. It worried him. Being of sound mind, he thought. He would not do it in madness. Suicide while of unbalanced mind! None of that. It must be a positive, logical step, a final step, from a life that had already ceased.

His hand found the rope. The smooth coils slipped through his fingers. He made a double loop in his palm, just as he had done in his terrifying dreams, made the required number of turns around the loops. He counted them... one, two, up to twelve, and passed the end through the loop. It must be the easiest knot to tie. There was no fear, no trembling hand. The terrors of the dreams were fled in the face of reality. This was his desire.

He felt strangely refreshed, as if the lost hours had been expended in the most deep and refreshing sleep. The clouds in his mind dispersed as he sat dangling the rope and remembered her. How she had come into his life a terrified kitten and grown into a spitting she-cat of selfishness. The loving, the tenderness, all his strength, lapped up like milk in a saucer to nourish her feline ambition.

He read the fragment before him:

...You have killed me. By destroying my confidence and creativity, you have deprived me of my life. That which I am about to do is merely the hastening of the inevitable. Only the carcass remains of me. This empty cadaver of withering flesh, discarded like a spider sucked hollow by its mate, hangs suspended in your abandoned web, trussed in the threads of silken lies. Your endearing phrases, and declarations of love, bound me with such strands of tenderness, that I mistook their spinning for caresses...

...the scrawl went on and on.

The noose fell to the floor, and with his elbows on the table he held his head in his hands as his tears smeared the words on the paper.

'Louise,' he groaned. 'What have you done to me? What have you done to all of us? You and your kind?'

As his eyes cleared, he read the words again... *You have killed me.* They filled him with a fierce anger and he crumpled the paper and hurled it into the dead grate. God damn her!

He felt the anger against Louise and his failure to understand her burning into him, a clear, honest rage which gradually scorched all the other emotions from his head, and he snatched another piece of paper from the box.

He paused, and took his time, and wrote at the top, in clear, legible script:

HORN OF STRANGERS
A Novel

by Barnabas Baragwaneth

Yn termyn ys passyas...